SALUTE
THE DARK

ALSO BY
ADRIAN TCHAIKOVSKY

SHADOWS OF THE APT 1
EMPIRE IN BLACK AND GOLD

SHADOWS OF THE APT 2
DRAGONFLY FALLING

SHADOWS OF THE APT 3
BLOOD OF THE MANTIS

SALUTE THE DARK

SHADOWS OF THE APT

ADRIAN TCHAIKOVSKY

an imprint of **Prometheus Books**
Amherst, NY

Published 2010 by Pyr®, an imprint of Prometheus Books

Inquiries should be addressed to
Pyr
59 John Glenn Drive
Amherst, New York 14228–2119
VOICE: 716–691–0133
FAX: 716–691–0137
WWW.PYRSF.COM

14 13 12 11 10 · 5 4 3 2 1

Library of Congress Cataloging-in-Publication Data

Tchaikovsky, Adrian, 1972–
    Salute the dark / by Adrian Tchaikovsky.
        p. cm. — (Shadows of the Apt ; bk. 4)
    Originally published: London : Tor, an imprint of Pan Macmillan Ltd., 2010.
    ISBN 978–1–61614–239–1 (pbk.)
    1. Insects—Fiction. 2. Imaginary wars and battles—Fiction. I. Title.

PR6120.C53S25 2010
823'.92—dc22

                                                                2010020631

Printed in the United States of America

To my parents,
who are wondering how they lost out on book 3 to a dead Frenchman

ACKNOWLEDGMENTS

I cannot thank enough: Simon, my agent, for his constant inspiration and encouragement; Peter Lavery, the mastercraftsman of editors; Annie, my wife, for her help; and Alex, my son, for not playing up too much when deadlines were looming.

Beyond this: thanks to Hellfire and Horrors (Oxford), Storm Wolves (Reading), Wayne, Shane, and Martin, and everyone else who has been there to support me.

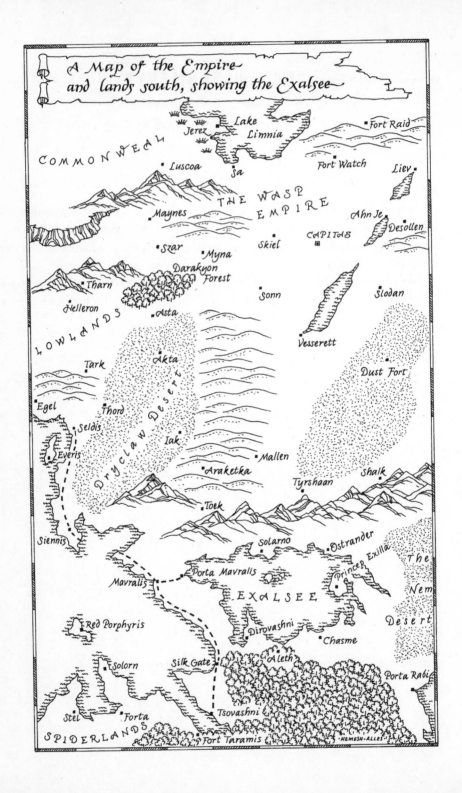

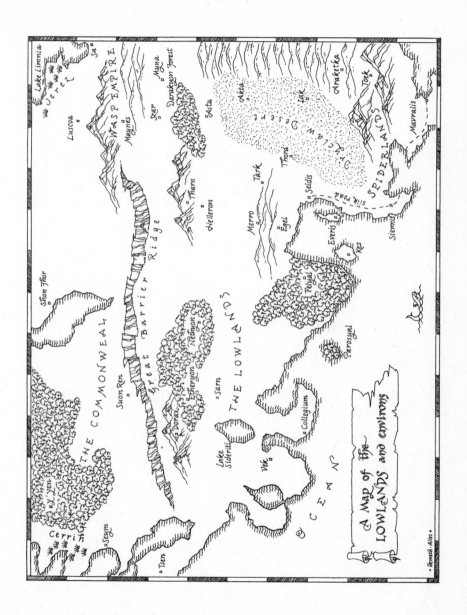

A Map of the LOWLANDS and environs

GLOSSARY

PEOPLE

STENWOLD MAKER—Beetle-kinden spymaster and statesman
CHEERWELL "CHE" MAKER—his niece
TISAMON—Mantis-kinden Weaponsmaster
TYNISA—his half-breed daughter, Stenwold's ward
ACHAEOS—Moth-kinden magician, Che's lover
ATRYSSA—Tynisa's mother and Tisamon's former lover, deceased
THALRIC—renegade Wasp-kinden, former Rekef major
NERO—Fly-kinden artist, old friend of Stenwold
FELISE MIENN—Dragonfly-kinden duellist
TAKI—Solarnese Fly-kinden aviatrix

LINEO THADSPAR—Beetle-kinden Speaker for the Collegium Assembly
BALKUS—renegade Sarnesh Ant-kinden, Stenwold's agent
SPERRA—Fly-kinden, Stenwold's agent
DESTRACHIS—Spider-kinden doctor, companion of Felise Mienn
PAROPS—Tarkesh Ant-kinden, leader of the free Tarkesh
JONS ALLANBRIDGE—Beetle-kinden aviator
PLIUS—foreign Ant-kinden in Sarn, Stenwold's agent

PRINCE MINOR SALME "SALMA" DIEN—Dragonfly nobleman, leader of the Landsarmy
PRIZED OF DRAGONS—Butterfly-kinden, Salma's lover
PHALMES—Mynan Soldier Beetle-kinden, former brigand, Salma's lieutenant

TEORNIS OF THE ALDANRAEL—Spider-kinden Aristos and Lord-Martial
ODYSSA—Teornis' chief agent in Solarno
CESTA—Assassin Bug-kinden killer in Solarno
SCOBRAAN—Soldier Beetle-kinden aviator in Solarno

LAETRIMAE—Mantis-kinden ghost from the Shadow Box

XARAEA—Moth-kinden intelligencer in Tharn
TEGREC—Wasp-kinden major and magician, governor of occupied Tharn
RAEKA—Wasp-kinden, Tegrec's body-slave

KYMENE—Mynan Soldier Beetle-kinden, leader of the Mynan resistance
CHYSES—Mynan Soldier Beetle-kinden, Kymene's lieutenant
HOKIAK—Scorpion-kinden black-marketeer in Myna
GRYLLIS—Spider-kinden, Hokiak's business partner

ALVDAN II—Emperor of the Wasps
SEDA—his sister
MAXIN—Wasp-kinden general, Rekef
REINER—Wasp-kinden general, Rekef
BRUGAN—Wasp-kinden general, Rekef
MALKAN—Wasp-kinden general, Seventh Army
LATVOC—Wasp-kinden colonel, Rekef, Reiner's aide
GAN—Wasp-kinden colonel, governor of Szar
ULTHER—Wasp-kinden colonel, former governor of Myna, deceased
AXRAD—Wasp-kinden lieutenant and aviator
UCTEBRI THE SARCAD—Mosquito-kinden slave and magician
GJEGEVEY—Woodlouse-kinden slave and advisor

DARIANDREPHOS ("DREPHOS")—half-breed auxillian-colonel and master artificer
TOTHO—half-breed artificer in Drephos' cadre
KASZAAT—Bee-kinden artificer, in Drephos' cadre
BIG GREYV—Mole Cricket-kinden artificer, in Drephos' cadre

PLACES

CAPITAS—the capital of the Empire
ASTA—Wasp staging post for the Lowlands Campaign
COLLEGIUM—Beetle-kinden city, home of the Great College
THE COMMONWEAL—Dragonfly-kinden state north of the Lowlands, partly occupied by the Empire
THE DARAKYON—forest, formerly a Mantis stronghold, now haunted
HELLERON—Beetle-kinden factory city, occupied
MYNA—Soldier Beetle city conquered by the Wasps
SARN—Ant-kinden city-state allied to Collegium
SOLARNO—Spider-ruled city on the Exalsee, occupied

SPIDERLANDS—Spider-kinden cities south of the Lowlands, believed rich and endless

SZAR—Bee-kinden city, conquered by the Wasps

TARK—Ant-kinden city-state, occupied

THARN—Moth-kinden hold, occupied

VEK—Ant-kinden city-state, recently at war with Collegium

ORGANIZATIONS AND THINGS

THE ANCIENT LEAGUE—a Moth–Mantis alliance of Dorax, Nethyon and Etheryon

ASSEMBLY—the elected ruling body of Collegium, meeting in the Amphiophos

BUOYANT MAIDEN—Jons Allanbridge's airship

CRYSTAL STANDARD, PATH OF JADE, SATIN TRAIL—Solarnese political parties

ESCA VOLENTI—Taki's orthopter

GREAT COLLEGE in Collegium, the cultural heart of the Lowlands

LANDSARMY—force of refugees and irregulars led by Salma

MERCERS—Dragonfly-kinden order of knights errant

PROWESS FORUM—duelling venue in Collegium

REKEF—the Wasp Empire's secret service

SHADOW BOX—an artefact holding the heart of the Darakyon

SKRYRES—the magician-leaders of the Moth-kinden

STARNEST—great Wasp airship used in the conquest of Solarno

WINGED FURIES—name for the Wasp Seventh Army

*F*ollowing his victory over the Sarnesh field army, General Malkan prepares to lead his army toward Sarn itself to destroy the military capability of the Lowlands. The alliance of powers that Stenwold brokered at Sarn is still gathering its strength, so it falls to Salma's Landsarmy to hinder the Wasp advance while the Lowlanders prepare.

Over the winter the Wasps have added the Spider city of Solarno to their Empire, and also the Moth hold of Tharn. However, careful manipulation by the Moth Skryres and their agent Xaraea has ensured that Tegrec, the new governor of Tharn, is secretly sympathetic to their case, being a magician who has hidden his true nature from his kin.

Meanwhile the maverick artificer Drephos has been ordered to take his secret weapons to the city of Szar, whose Bee-kinden people are in open revolt after the death of their queen, whom the Empire was holding as hostage for their continued servitude. However, amongst Drephos' cadre is Kaszaat, a former citizen of Szar, and the lover of Stenwold's former student Totho.

The mission to recover the Shadow Box has failed after Tynisa, under the control of the Mosquito-kinden Uctebri, stabbed Achaeos, leaving him severely wounded. The box, meanwhile, has fallen into Uctebri's hands, and he has promised the Wasp Emperor that he will use the artefact to make Alvdan immortal. However, at the same time, Uctebri plots with the Emperor's sister to dethrone her brother and make her into an undying Empress.

hy do these things always come to plague us?

A fatuous thought for a man about to fight a war, but the war had not even begun and already Stenwold had seen too many people hurt—and hurt on his business too. The knot of horror he had felt when they had brought Sperra out had not gone away. And now this.

Achaeos this time. O poor Che, my poor Che, to have come home to this.

And not just Che.

"I am so very sorry," Stenwold said softly. He tried to put a hand on Tynisa's shoulder, but she flinched away from it and would not let him.

"It isn't me you should be sorry for," she said. He had never seen his ward like this—Tynisa had gone through life without fear, the face and grace of her Spider mother, the lethal skill of her Mantis father and a Collegium citizen's implacable self-confidence. Now she was standing at the door of the College infirmary, afraid to go in, yet unwilling to leave. The beds were not short of patients still recovering from injuries sustained in the Vekken siege. On one bed lay Achaeos, his eyes closed, grey skin gone so pale it was almost white. He had yet to wake up, yet to speak. The College physicians would not commit themselves on whether he ever would.

By his bed sat Che, holding the ailing Moth-kinden's hand. The sight of her clearly tore into Tynisa with a raw pain, yet she could not take her eyes away. Her sword had put Achaeos where he was, though Stenwold had not needed her father's protestations of magic to know that she could not have meant the man any harm. That itself was a tragedy, but Stenwold knew that it was the injury to Tynisa's foster sister that cut deepest: the grief inflicted on Che, that marvel of innocence and foolishness, who would never again be quite the same.

Tynisa shuddered, and Stenwold as much as saw her think, *I have now severed her from me for always.*

"This war is not finished with its casualties," Stenwold murmured. He was thinking about Sperra again, his thoughts returning and returning to the moment when the Sarnesh soldiers had brought out the little Fly-kinden's tortured form. Sperra, who was walking now, even flying a little, but who would never forget what had been done to her. *And by her allies! We do not even need the Wasps to maim us when we can harm ourselves.*

"Tynisa . . ." he began.

"No," she said, "I don't care what you want, Sten. I can't go out there again. I'm not safe now. I don't want to do it anymore."

"Tisamon has explained to me what happened—"

"My father has simply invented something to make himself feel better." She glared round at him. "Don't tell me you believe it?"

"I believe that he truly believes it, and he knows more about such things than I." Stenwold shrugged. "Tynisa, you've been to the shrine on Parosyal."

"That was different. They drugged me, and I saw . . . visions, hallucinations."

He stared down at his hands. "I used to think the way you do, but I've now seen so much. . . . There is more to life than just the things we can see. Achaeos would say the same, of course."

"Much good it did him."

"Tynisa . . . will you come with me to the council?"

"No," she said. "I'm sorry, Sten, but I can't. I can't trust myself anymore. You'll have to find someone else."

He nodded slowly. *I can't force her, for all that I need her.* Perhaps Tisamon would have more luck in persuading her. He spared one more look for his niece, Che, and then turned to go.

So the ranks diminish, he reflected sadly, yet the Lowlands was readying itself for battle. Sarn and Collegium and the Ancient League were summoning their allies. Stenwold needed every agent he could get, and he was still short, but he could not make the numbers add up. Sperra was now lost to him, as was Achaeos, who could have proved so useful amongst his own people. Tynisa would not fight, and he had not even asked Che to help him. His resources were growing fewer even as the Wasp armies massed.

He arrived at the council chamber early. Today was another war council and people were still calling him War Master since the siege. He was expecting to see old Lineo Thadspar turn up, and a score or so of other Assemblers, each with their own schemes and advice. There would be Tisamon as well, standing at the back and saying nothing, with a look of disdain on his face . . . and probably the Spider, Teornis . . .

Even as he thought the name the man himself came striding into the chamber, rubbing his hands briskly. He had chosen to wear a bone and leather cuirass over a red silk robe, while a cap of chitin, adorned with the feathery fronds of moth antennae, made him look like some ancient warrior-mystic. Behind him came the diminutive form of the Fly-kinden pilot known as Taki, who had brought Che home from her birthplace of Solarno, fleeing in the face of yet another Wasp conquest.

"Master Maker," the Spider said, "times move faster than we do, I'm afraid."

"In what way?"

"I've had news that calls me home, as swiftly as I can make the journey. I've arranged for an airship to take me and my retinue to Seldis."

"The Wasps?"

"Camped outside our borders again, but this time it doesn't look as though the Mantis-kinden will do our dirty work for us."

"You'll fight, then? The Spider-kinden will fight?"

"Impossible to say." Teornis smiled. "However, retinues and mercenaries are mustering at Seldis and Everis, and once they're gathered there I can make use of them. What's the use of my being a Lord-Martial if I can't lord it? Meanwhile, there's more business afoot at Mavralis on the Exalsee, which is why I'm taking Taki here with me. I fancy the Wasps could do with being jabbed in the rear."

Stenwold nodded. "My reports seem to suggest that, with their occupation of Solarno, the Empire is becoming overextended."

Behind Teornis' smile, something slipped aside to reveal for a moment the genuine tension within him. "My friend, we had better *hope* so, because if they aren't, then there'll soon be a great deal of black and yellow all the way down the southern coast. It may all come down to the abilities of some Wasp clerk filing supply requisitions in Asta, Master Maker. As you know, wars are fought by soldiers but won by logistics."

"And you're happy to go with Teornis?" Stenwold asked Taki.

"Sieur Maker, remember I've served Spider-kinden all my life. I want to free my city, and the Spiders want my city free."

"There is another travelling companion that I shall be taking from your side, Master Maker. I trust you will have no objections," Teornis said.

Stenwold looked at him blankly. For some reason he thought, *Tynisa?*— perhaps because the girl so clearly wanted to go somewhere and find some purpose to take her away from her guilt.

Teornis' smile twitched. "I believe Master Nero wishes a return to Solarno. I had not realized that the city had so exercised its . . . charms on him."

With that, Stenwold could not help glancing down at Taki and thinking, at first, *The old lecher*, and then, *I am in no position to judge!*

"What use he'll be, I don't know," Taki remarked. "I just hope he can keep up with me, is all. But, anyway, we've got him, so we'll just have to make some use of him."

The other members of the war council now were filing in and taking their places, so Stenwold clasped hands with Teornis and then with the Fly girl.

"Good fortune to you," he said.

"Good fortune to all of us," Taki corrected him.

His stance was perfect for his blade: crouched a little, knees bent and balanced to move him forward or back at the speed of his reflexes, not of this thoughts. His arm was not straight like the arrow of a rapier duellist's stance, but crooked in so that the claw blade ran almost down the line of his forearm, looking deceptively passive but ready to lash out and draw back just like the killing arms of his people's insect namesake. His off-hand was held out, pointing forward, spines flexing all down his arm to the elbow, ready to beat aside an attack and thus create a gap into which his claw would strike.

He looked down the crooked line of his arm and claw. He looked at her.

Her stance was different in almost every particular, yet identical in its perfect poise, in its patience. She stood with one leg forward and almost fully extended, the other bent beneath her; her back straight. The sword, with its long hilt gripped in both hands, she held low and almost vertical: her entire being and energy focused on its leading edge, its diamond point.

They had not moved, either of them, for what must have been ten minutes, barely even a blink.

He wore his arming jacket of course, dark green padded cloth with his gold brooch, the Weaponmaster pin, on the left breast. She had eschewed her armour, instead wearing the closest she could find to Dragonfly garb: loose clothes of Spider silk pulled in tight at the waist, the forearms, the calves. She wore shimmering turquoise and gold, with a black sash for a belt.

Tisamon and Felise Mienn watched each other narrowly and waited for the other's move.

His soul was focused on the razor edge of her sword. They could only spar with real blades. To propose otherwise would be an insult to their skill.

Somewhere in the back of his mind was a memory of when they had fought each other on the streets of Collegium. She had thought him a Wasp agent, and for the first time in many years Tisamon had been truly fighting for his life in single combat. For ten years previously he had made a name for himself in Helleron, hiring his blade to whoever could meet his fees. The money was nothing; the fights were all. He had thought that he was taking pride in his skills, displayed in all those brawls and formal duels, but now he discovered that he had been waiting to meet the one who could properly challenge him. In Collegium she had found him.

After they had fought, after she had stepped out of the fight so abruptly, she had left him so inflamed, so fiercely *alive*, that he had even spared Stenwold's Spider traitress. In that moment it had not mattered, because only *she* signified— only this woman who had walked in and out of his world in those brief minutes, to scar it forever.

Somewhere deep inside, he was now out of balance, as though he had been struck, back then, and was still reeling. Seventeen years of penance he had endured, in Helleron and other places: penance for betraying his race by consorting with the Spider Atryssa; penance for trusting in her false heart; and, at the last, penance for mistrusting her, who had died while being true to him. *And I loved her, and she did not betray me after all.* It was the most jagged wound of them all that it had been he who abandoned her, in the end. *How she would have hated me, had she lived.*

His eyes were now fixed on Felise's—her eyes that were almond shaped, and shifted from blue to green even as he watched and waited for her to move.

It has been so long. His kind bore some of their scars forever, but it had been so long. *And I have broken the rules before.* Felise's face remained impassive. He could read nothing in it. He sensed no tension there, could foretell no gathering strike.

He had been dead, he realized, those seventeen years. Only Stenwold's return and the discovery of Tynisa had awoken him to some kind of half-life, but beneath it all some part of him had slumbered on. *Until Felise.* He had not known who she was, what her purpose, or her allegiance. He had not needed to, and would not have cared if she had served a Spider lady or been a slave of the Arcanum, or even worn the black and gold. Skill spoke a language all its own and, when he had fought her, even as her blade drove for his heart, he had thrilled to it. If she had killed him, as well she might, then he would have cried out in joy as her sword ran him through.

And he knew she understood that. She was no Mantis, but her kind understood such perfection, such dedication.

She moved, stepping in suddenly with a thrust. He caught it with his claw, parrying it aside, his off-hand lashing in to beat her blade aside.

They stopped, that single move and countermove frozen in time, standing now within each other's reach, face to face. She would seem beautiful to others, if made up as the Spider-kinden painted their faces, yet to him she was beautiful in every line of her body. Something within him was screaming, as he moved his hand to within an inch of her face, the spines flexing on his forearm.

There was a heavy tread, heralding a Beetle-kinden approaching the silence of the Prowess Forum. It was dark outside, and had been before they began his poised vigil. Tisamon broke away first, still gazing into her face.

It was Stenwold who entered, looking more haggard than ever. He nodded at the two of them but saw nothing of what had existed between them.

"You weren't at the war meeting," he said.

"I'm a soldier, not a tactician," Tisamon reminded him.

Stenwold considered that. "True, I suppose. I missed you, though. I like to be able to look over at you and remind myself of the reality of warfare. How so many people became experts on fighting wars without ever picking up a sword I'll never know."

He frowned suddenly, becoming aware in some small way of the tension here. "Is . . . everything all right?"

"Just sparring," Tisamon replied briefly. Then: "Tell me, you and your . . . Spider girl, you are happy together, yes?"

Stenwold grinned a little sheepishly. "More than I deserve, with Arianna, yes. But you were right in what you said. After all, the war's on us now, and who knows where I'll be when it's done—or where she'll be . . ." He pressed his lips together then, no doubt imagining some harm coming to her, or to himself. "Anyway, I'll leave you now to your practice. Four hours of talk is enough for any man."

Tisamon barely noticed as the Beetle shuffled off. He himself had said that, had he not? He had said that Stenwold should take happiness where he could, and when he could. The future was looking uncertain—less certain by the day. A hundred thousand Wasps and more were on the march beneath their black and gold banner. There was a score of battlefields ahead waiting to be filled with the fallen.

Tisamon settled into a new stance, holding his claw high and back now, his pose more aggressive, more reckless. Felise countered with a low stance, one leg straight to one side, the other bent beneath her, sword held at waist level and pointing directly at his heart.

There was something in her eyes that pierced him. He dared not name it, but he saw it. He felt the wound.

TWO

The squad of Wasp scouts touched down around the farmhouse, half a dozen descending at the front of it whilst two came down behind and one perched on the roof.

Their leader looked about the farmyard. It had clearly been abandoned for some while, the occupants having fled before the Wasp advance. Most likely it had already been picked clean, but there was still the possibility that something of value had been left inside. He nodded to one of his men, and the soldier kicked in the door, its dry wood splintering on the second impact.

They paused, listening carefully. There was no sound from inside. There was always the chance that this place had been chosen by the brigands to hide out in. "Brigands" was what the officers were calling them, but the sergeant had never known such country for bandits. The Lowlands was said to be a violent and divided place, but there seemed to be hundreds of armed men just waiting for imperial scouts to come their way. In the sergeant's view that was the organized behaviour of an army, not a rabble of bandits, but he would not dream of stating such an opinion before his superiors.

However obvious it seemed.

Yet, if it was an army, it was an army that would not fight—that would not even be found. Scouts went out regularly and found dead trails, cold ash where fires had been. Or sometimes they went out and did not come back. This loss of scouting squads had become so draining that at first the officers had started sending their scouts out in larger and larger forces, but even squads of fifty or seventy men had seemed able to disappear without trace in the barren, rocky land between the Seventh Army's camp and the Ant city of Sarn, vanishing amongst the stands of forest and the creek-cut gullies.

Later, they had tried sending no scouts at all beyond clear view of the main army, and thus the force had crawled on and found bridges smashed, terrain spiked with caltrops, wells poisoned. The army's progress, mere days from the camp, had slowed to a crawl. So they had started sending out scouts again.

This did not inspire confidence, and everyone knew General Malkan was spitting fire about it. Two days before they had captured a couple of men believed to be part of the bandit army, whereupon Malkan had personally overseen their questioning, racking them pitilessly until they divulged the location of a camp.

They found nothing there, of course. There was nothing that even suggested there had ever been a camp there.

The prisoners, before they died, had also said that there was a bandit king. He was a great magician, one of them had claimed. He knew everything, and could not be beaten in a fight. He could walk through walls and read minds.

Malkan had let it be known that there would be a reward of four hundred gold Imperials for the man's capture, or half that sum for his death. Nobody had been over-keen to claim it, though, save that perhaps the scouts who disappeared had let the bounty tempt them a step too far.

Whenever the bandits were seen, by men who survived to report back, they often wore repainted imperial armour, carrying Wasp swords and spears. Each squad that vanished was making the enemy a little stronger. Malkan had tried using Auxillians as scouts, reasoning that the Seventh could stand to lose some of its conscripted slave-soldiers more than its regular Wasp-kinden. When the Auxillians disappeared, it was rumoured that they were seen alive later amongst the bandits' ranks. So that put a stop to that.

The sergeant pushed his way into the farmhouse, not wanting to be the first inside but not wanting to be far behind in case anything valuable had been left there. It was an unspoken rule that sergeants got the best of the loot. The officers were too proud to look and the common soldiers had to wait their turn for plunder.

"You round the back!" he called out. "I hope you're keeping your eyes open."

He used his dagger to lever open the drawers of a table, finding a few loose coins there. He took them without hesitation, pride being no issue in this job. One of his men was meanwhile clumping up the stairs.

As the army advanced on Sarn there would, of course, be richer pickings, places not already abandoned, extra prizes for the diligent sergeant. Women perhaps? The Sixth Army was bringing in a detachment of the Slaver Corps, and they would pay a finder's fee, and not enquire too hard as to the captives' condition.

In the next room there was a chest tucked in under the bed. The sergeant went over to it and found it locked. He knelt down beside it, something nagging at him. There was just room between case and lid to get the thick blade of his dagger in, and he began levering, trying to either snap the bar of the lock or pry the lock from the wood.

He grunted with the effort, and the thought came to him that the men out back had not acknowledged his earlier order. Bad discipline, that was. "Hey, out back!" he called again.

Still silence.

He kept up the pressure on the chest, but something was beginning to worm its way into him.

"On the roof!" he called out, at the top of his voice. "Anything there?"

Silence.

He stared at the wall, continuing to lever, feeling something finally give within the chest. His heart was quickening, still hearing nothing from the floor above.

"Soldier, report!" he shouted out, not caring which of them should answer him.

None of them answered him.

The lid of the chest came free suddenly, and he lurched forward. He saw at once that he had, at last, struck lucky. The chest was full of plate, both gilded and silver, obviously too heavy for the hoarding farmer to take with him.

He saw himself reflected in the top plate, a hunched figure against its tarnished silver. There was a man behind him.

He reached down for his sword hilt, moving his hand very slowly. His other hand opened, ready to sting. Without making any sudden move, or anything else to trigger an attack, he very carefully stood up and turned around.

The man before him was not much beyond a boy: a gold-skinned Dragonfly-kinden from the northern Commonweal, wearing a banded leather cuirass, bracers and greaves, and Spider silks beneath them. He had a simple Beetle-kinden helm, open faced but for a three-bar visor, and he held a sword of Ant-manufacture loosely in one hand.

Beyond him, the sergeant saw the bodies of three of his own men. He had heard nothing of it. *How could they . . . ?*

It did not matter, he realized. Kill this boy, dash outside and take to the sky. *Back to the army, and bring a hundred of the light airborne back here as quick as you can.*

"Looks like it's you and me then, son," he said, making a show of readying his sword whilst bringing his off-hand up to loose a sting shot.

"No," said the Dragonfly simply, and just then the sergeant felt something slam into his back, punching him forward so that the boy had to step back quickly to avoid his pitching body.

Salma looked down at the dead soldier, seeing the tiny nub of steel where the bolt had gone into his back. Outside the window, a Fly-kinden woman raised an open palm for him, the Wasp sign of defiance that had since become their adopted salute. There was a snapbow in her hand: such a useful weapon, for all that he did not understand it, especially since the more inventive of his people had found that, if they "undercranked" it, whatever that was, it was as quiet as a crossbow. Still, most of their work was still down to knives and wires and short swords.

I have gone from bandit to assassin, he reflected, but he could not afford moral scruples now. Too many people were depending on him.

Outside, he gathered his people, a mere dozen of them but most of them skilled stalkers and wilderness runners. The one exception, and their one non-combatant, came up to him now and embraced him, as she did after every mission like this. She was Prized of Dragons, his love, his soul, the Butterfly-kinden with lambent, glowing skin who had brought him back from the gates of death. He knew that she hated bloodshed but she knew that he only did what he had to. They had established an equilibrium, and she would not let herself be left behind. They had been apart too long.

"We should go and see how far the army's got," he said. The Wasp advance would be moving into more broken territory, a land riddled with gullies and canyons that were thick with undergrowth and forest. He could no longer afford to just hit isolated bands of scouts, and must soon commence attacks against the leading edge of the army itself. After all, he had made a bargain with the Sarnesh, and he only hoped that they were keeping their part of it.

It was a long haul back to his own camp, but they were used to that, running and flying over terrain that was becoming as familiar as home to most of them. When they were close enough, Fly-kinden messengers began dropping down toward them, keeping pace with Salma and rattling off reports.

"Have the Wasps found us here?" he cut through them.

"We've killed a patrol. Fifteen men," one of the Flies replied. "We're packing up. We'll be gone before they even miss them."

Always the same, always on the move, dodging the blade of the enemy, and impossible to predict. His people were split up, linked only by the diligence of the Fly-kinden who ran the gauntlet in all weathers to keep each leader informed of the others. They left almost no trace: when they had broken their camp, their own woodsmen muddled and obliterated their tracks. The Wasps' advance was blind. *And now time to take advantage of that.*

As he arrived, they were still training. He stopped to watch the prodigy of it, though feeling his heart sink. Neither men nor beasts were much taking to the idea of discipline.

He had sent to Sarn, to his man Sfayot there: *Give me all the horses they can spare, all the riding beetles, every beast broken for riding and not too weary to gallop.* He had been obliged to send twice, because the Sarnesh had not taken him seriously the first time. Then the animals had started to arrive, trains of five, ten—twenty even. Two-thirds were horses, which he preferred for riding, being better for stamina and speed than most insects. Beyond that, they had been gifted as motley a nest of creatures as he had ever seen: a racing beetle long past its prime; a dozen plodding draught animals with high, rounded shells; a brace of nimble coach-horse beetles, fiery of temperament, their tails arching like scorpion stings. There were even a couple of exotic creatures that might have come from a menagerie: a black-and-white-striped riding spider that had the alarming tendency to jump ten feet when it became unsettled, and a low-slung, scuttling cricket that could give a horse a decent race over any short distance. The animals' overall quality was variable, their temperament uncertain, since cavalry had little place in the Lowlander or imperial view of war. A combination of airborne troops, accurate crossbows and the Ant-kinden's reluctance to rely on any minds not linked to their own had seen no development here of the noble art of horsemanship. Riding, after all, was for scouts and messengers, not real soldiers, so when Salma had told them what he planned, they had looked at him as though he were mad.

Except, that is, for men like Phalmes, who had served in the Twelve-Year War against Salma's own people. They had seen how the Commonwealers fought.

Of course, the Commonwealers had better mounts, and longer to train. Still, the circling mounted rabble that Salma was now watching was at least managing to remain in the saddle. Phalmes, in the lead, kicked his mount on to a gallop, and most of the rest followed, the horses changing pace from a canter with rather more will than he had witnessed before, the insects scuttling after them, their legs speeding into a frantic blur.

Phalmes spotted him and slowed his mount, letting the column of riders behind disintegrate into a rabble. The Mynan rode over, looking as though he had been playing teacher to them far longer than he was happy with.

"How goes your cavalry?" Salma asked him.

Phalmes spat. "Three more broken legs since you went off," he said. "Still, the Sarnesh finally made good on those new saddles you designed for them, and riders are staying on more often than not, now we've got them. I haven't yet explained why we need them, because I didn't think they'd like it."

Of course the Commonwealers had better saddles, too, and Salma had sketched his recollection of them, and sent the resulting drawing to Sarn for their leather-workers to puzzle over. It seemed that something had actually come of that, although he had not been hopeful. The high front and rear were not to keep the rider seated so much as to prevent a charging lancer from being flung from the saddle on impact.

But Phalmes was right: it was not the time to explain about that.

"Are they ready, then?" he asked.

"Not by a long ways," Phalmes told him. "Keep training them, they'll get there eventually, but if you've got something happening soon, we can't rely on them."

Salma bared his teeth, but nodded. "I trust your judgment," he said, "but we need to make a stand sooner rather than later. Malkan's reinforcements are with him already: the Sixth is joining the Seventh, and that means they'll stop dragging their feet and start marching properly at last. If we're to make good our promises to Sarn, then the time is upon us."

General Malkan had ordered an automotive driven out to oversee the arrival himself, standing on its roof with some guards and his intelligence officer, eyes narrowed as he watched 15,000 soldiers marching toward his temporary camp.

"Tell me about the Sixth, then," he directed, having observed they were in good order. Despite the long march, the troops on the ground were keeping ranks, forming columns between the snub-nosed wood and metal of the war automotives embellished with their turret-mounted artillery, and amid the huge plated transporters that plodded along patiently like enormous beetles. The scouts that had flown ahead and those on the flanks of the army were pulling in now as they neared the Seventh's fortifications, filtering down to land ahead of the column in order to make their reports.

"Well," the intelligence officer said, "you must have heard that the Sixth took the brunt of several engagements against the Commonwealers in the Twelve-Year War."

"Battle of Masaki, wasn't it?" Malkan asked.

"Well . . . 'battle' is probably overstating the case, General," the intelligence officer confessed. "Their then commander made the mistake of pushing too far into Dragonfly lands, ahead of the rest of the advance. My guess is that he mistook a lack of technical sophistication for mere weakness. In any event, the bulk of the Sixth was ambushed near Masaki by a Dragonfly army that outnumbered them at least ten to one. It was perhaps the largest single force the Commonweal ever put together."

"You sound impressed, Captain," Malkan noted.

"Organization on that scale for an Inapt kinden is indeed impressive, General," the man said blandly. "Certainly it must have represented the high point of Commonweal strength, because the balance of the war was just a staggered holding action."

"So what about the Sixth? I thought it was a great triumph."

"Oh, well," the officer said, "a small detachment of Auxillian engineers had been split off to fortify a nearby camp, and thus escaped the massacre. Then they came under attack themselves from what should have been an overwhelming Commonwealer force. However they managed to hold out for seven days from behind their fortifications, and killed so many of the enemy that the relieving force was able to put the Dragonflies to flight and save the honour of the Empire."

"And those Auxillians were Bee-kinden?"

"Yes, sir. And so the new Sixth, when it re-formed, became known as the Hive."

Malkan watched as the gates to his camp opened, and the newcomers began to file in. At the very head of the army, the vanguard itself was composed of a rigid block of heavily armoured soldiers, too short and stocky to be Wasp-kinden, and dressed in black and gold uniforms halved down the front, rather than sporting the usual horizontal stripes. It seemed the Bee-kinden at Masaki had won themselves some privileges in their mindless defence of another race's Empire.

"So tell me about General Praeter," he said. "He wasn't the original general, of course."

"No, sir. General Haken died at Masaki, which most think was the best thing that could have happened to him. Praeter was merely a lieutenant at the time, but he had already been given command of the engineers. Rumour suggests that he was not popular with his superiors, and it was a punishment duty."

"Engineers and glory seldom go hand in hand," Malkan admitted. Praeter had been the man the Empire chose to make a hero, though. He had been the only Wasp-kinden officer available for the post, hence the man's sudden rise through the ranks.

"They say he is a little . . . too comfortable with the Auxillians," the intelligence officer said carefully, "and he likes things done his way. Traditional ways."

"We shall have to see about that," Malkan decided. "Send a message to him. Give him two hours to settle his men, and then I request his presence."

Praeter was older than Malkan had expected, and his short-cut hair was liberally dusted with grey. He must have been quite an old lieutenant, at Masaki. He was relatively slight of build, neither tall nor broad of shoulder. The two Bee-kinden soldiers who clanked in alongside him were barely shorter, and much more heavily set. He wore a simple black cowled cloak over his armour.

"General Praeter," Malkan acknowledged.

"General Malkan."

Malkan had expected resentment from the older man forced to serve under the younger's guidance, yet Praeter's manner was anything but, which triggered a current of unease.

"Alone, General," he suggested. "I think we should speak alone." His pointed glance took in the two Bees, without deigning to acknowledge his own intelligence officer.

Praeter frowned, glancing back at his men.

"I did not ask you here to have you murdered, General," declared Malkan, with hollow good humour.

The older man nodded to the two Bees, who ducked back out of the square-framed tent that Malkan commanded from. Nevertheless the sound of the two of them taking up stations outside the door was pointedly clear.

"They're obviously fond of you," Malkan noted.

"We've been through a lot," Praeter agreed, expressionless.

"How many of them? Bee-kinden Auxillians, I mean?"

"Two thousand, one hundred and eight."

Malkan glanced at his intelligence officer, his smile brittle. "General, are you quite mad? Surely you've heard the news from Szar. What happens when your Bee-kinden troops hear it too?"

"They have already."

"Have they?"

"Unrest in Szar," Praeter said. "Their queen dead. They know it all."

"And you're not worried?"

"No." Without ceremony, Praeter drew off his cloak. The armour beneath was not the banded mail of the Empire but a simple breastplate, half black and half gold. "That's why they've sent us out here, to keep us away from Szar, though there's no need."

"Is there not?" Malkan asked.

"With respect, no. My men are loyal."

"They're Auxillians nevertheless, General. You surely can't say that they're as loyal as the Imperial Army."

"They are *more* loyal," Praeter said simply. "Nobody understands the Bee-kinden—not even after we conquered their city. The inhabitants of Szar were loyal to their queen. It was a commitment that they never even thought to break. When we had the queen, we had them too. Now the queen is dead, they have no reason to obey us. That is the root of Szar."

"But *your* men are different?" *Something's wrong here*, Malkan was thinking. Praeter was like a man with a sheathed sword, just waiting for the moment to present it. All this talk of Auxillians was just a prologue.

"They have sworn an oath to me," Praeter said, "and they will not break it. An oath from Masaki, which binds them and their families, their fighting sons, to me."

"And if you die, General?"

"You had better keep me alive, General Malkan."

Malkan nodded. *Here we go.* "I must admit, General, that I had expected a frostier man to stand before me. After all, it's a rare senior officer content to serve beneath someone twenty years his junior." That "twenty years" was a deliberate exaggeration, but not a flicker of annoyance crossed Praeter's face.

"Why, General Malkan, you mistake me," he said blandly. "I have no intention of doing so."

Malkan carefully raised a single eyebrow.

Praeter smiled shallowly. "Perhaps this will explain." He reached for a belt pouch and retrieved a folded and sealed document, which Malkan took cautiously.

Men have encountered their death warrants like this, he was aware, but he opened it without hesitation, seeing on the wax the sigil of the palace.

In a scribe's neat hand, there were a few brief lines written there: *This commission hereby grants to General Praeter of the Imperial Sixth, known as the Hive, on account of his seniority and notable war record, joint command over the Sixth and Seventh armies, for the duration of the campaign against the Sarnesh.*

Malkan peered at the signature. "General Reiner," he said slowly.

"Of the Rekef Inlander. He is most kind," Praeter said flatly. Malkan felt the situation now balanced on a fulcrum. The Sixth were settling themselves in, the Seventh were already established. A single word from him and things could get bloody. *Bloody and potentially treasonous.* The mention of the Rekef, the Empire's secret service, had charged the air in the tent as though a storm was about to break.

"You are aware that I was installed in this position by the grace of General Maxin," Malkan said. "*Also* of the Rekef Inlander."

"Do you have his sealed orders to confirm that?" Praeter asked him expressionlessly.

Well, no, of course not, because since when did Rekef generals actually put their own cursed names on such things? Since when was that the drill? But the answer to that was *since now*, he supposed, because here was Reiner's own name, clear as day. Malkan had been distantly aware of the Rekef's internal squabbling, but he had never thought it would come to bludgeon him out here on the front. *Don't they know there's a war on?*

"Well, General," he said, with brittle brightness. "Do you have any orders for me, or shall I have my intelligence staff brief you on our present situation?"

THREE

Balkus shuffled, shrugging his shoulders about and looking uncomfortable. "Remind me again why I'm doing this?"

Stenwold looked the big Ant-kinden soldier up and down. "Because you're desperate for a reconciliation with your own people."

Balkus spat. "Not likely. They'd lynch me." He shifted his broad shoulders, trying to settle the new armour more comfortably.

"They won't. You're not turning up at their gates as some kind of renegade," Stenwold pointed out. "You're arriving there as the field officer of a Collegiate relief force, Commander Balkus."

"*Commander* Balkus," the Ant mused. "Hate to say it, but a man could get to like the sound of that."

Stenwold shrugged. "You wanted it, I recall."

Balkus scowled. "You get tired of being on your own. It's in the blood," he muttered. "Never thought I'd end up going home, though." He bit his lip.

Stenwold reflected that all the renegade Ants he had ever known who had turned their backs on their home and people, they were each of them still chained to their heritage. Growing up with a mind full of the thoughts of others left a big, empty gap when they set out on their own. How many of them were drawn back, eventually, for all that it would usually mean their deaths?

Balkus was obviously thinking on similar lines. "And they're fine about it, are they? My . . . the Sarnesh?"

"They know all about you. I've sent word to them, saying who I've put in charge."

"That isn't the same!" Balkus objected. "Look, I don't want to go up that rail-line only to find they've just been sharpening the knives."

"We're at war now, and the Sarnesh understand that they have to put aside their preferences," Stenwold replied. "And you have more experience than anyone else in the army here."

"Well, you've got that right," Balkus grunted.

"Shall we inspect the troops, now?" Stenwold asked. The Ant nodded gloomily and led the way out of the hall of the Amphiophos, Collegium's seat of government. While Stenwold had been in Sarn, arguing diplomacy, Balkus had been training troops here at home. Collegium had never possessed a standing army and, although the recent siege by the Ants of Vek had created hundreds of veterans, it was short of full-time soldiers. Balkus would not normally have been considered officer material in anyone's book, but he had a loud voice, and he was an Ant, meaning warfare in his very veins. What he had so far made out of the recruits they had given him was nothing to compare to a properly regimented Ant-kinden force, but it was something entirely new to Collegium.

There were already a dozen other officers waiting on the steps of the Amphiophos, leaders of the merchant companies watching as their troops assembled in the square below. They were Beetle-kinden men and women for the most part, broad and solid of build, wearing breastplates over quilted hauberks padded out with twists of rag and fibre that, in theory, would slow or even stop a crossbow or snapbow bolt. They also wore caps armoured with curved metal plates designed to deflect shot. As armour went, it was very new and mostly untested. The breastplates had all been stencilled with the arms of the Prowess Forum, namely a sword over an open book sketched in silver lines across the dark metal, but many of the officers and their gathering charges had overlaid these with sashes and surcoats carrying the various company badges they had chosen to display.

There had been no time for complex planning, or for establishing elaborate networks of supply or support. On the other hand, since Collegium had begun building its army from scratch, it had created something uniquely Beetle and previously unseen. The term the war council had coined was "bow and pike." A third of the soldiers were equipped with glaive-headed polearms, the stock-in-trade of watchmen everywhere, to hold off an enemy either on the ground or in the air. The rest were armed to fight at a greater distance. The Wasps were not an enemy to stand solidly together like Ant-kinden and hack at close quarters. Instead they moved swiftly, struck from range or attacked from above. The square before the Amphiophos was currently filled with repeating crossbows, nailbows and the new snapbows, the Beetle-kinden having taken to the weapon so readily that its designer might have specially intended it for them.

Could it be that the Wasps themselves have given us the tool we needed to defeat them?

There were some from other kinden too, for Collegium was not too proud to turn away any who wished to help. The army would include Fly-kinden spotters and archers, and some of the pikemen were Mantis-kinden or Spiders. There were Ants of four or five different cities amongst the ranks, all former renegades like Balkus who had given their tireless loyalty to Collegium.

The city was now sending just under a thousand soldiers to reinforce Sarn—because if Sarn fell, then Collegium might as well surrender. It was the one point that the war council had not bickered about. Several times that number of battle-ready troops would remain to guard the walls of the city against a surprise attack by the Wasps, or even by the Vekken. Meanwhile volunteers kept arriving in droves for the new regiments.

My city will be changed irrevocably by this, Stenwold reflected. *Not for the better, either—we could have lived happily without this war.*

The sound of precisely marching feet came to his ears and the final part of the relief force came into view with a discipline that shamed the locals. Commander Parops had arrived, with seven hundred pale-skinned Tarkesh Ants to his name. This was the bulk of the Free Army of Tark, as Parops himself had named it, comprising the military strength of his currently occupied city. They were the best-armed Ant-kinden in the world, just now: every second man of them carried a snapbow as well as a sword and shield, and many sported nailbows and crossbows as well. Their linked minds meant that this entire force could go from weapon to weapon, in whole or in part, as the battle demanded. They would form the core of the Collegiate force, from whom the locals would take their strength and their example.

Parops halted his men and strode up the steps toward Stenwold.

"All ready to go, War Master," he said, and smiled because he knew Stenwold could not abide that title.

"The troop trains are waiting at the station," Stenwold confirmed. "Already loaded with supplies, canvas, even some light artillery, I'm told." He clapped the Tarkesh on the shoulder. "I know what's at stake for you, Commander."

Parops nodded soberly. "The Sarnesh are bound to be cursed ungrateful hosts as well, but we're short of choices right now and my soldiers want to fight. With your permission, I'll begin getting them stowed on board."

Stenwold nodded silently and the Ant marched back to his men and began to move them out. Stenwold turned to Balkus to find him now a little distance away, kneeling down by a small figure that was hugging him tightly. Sperra, Stenwold saw, was looking better in health than she had been before, though clearly upset that the Ant was leaving. She and Balkus had been close since their time as agents working for Stenwold's cause in Helleron.

"You look after yourself, you oaf," Sperra was ordering him. "Don't you dare let anything happen to you."

"What could happen to me?" Balkus replied, trying hard to smile. "And if those Sarnesh give me any grief, I'll give them double in return."

"You do that," she hissed fiercely, and clung to him one last time, before letting go and giving place to Stenwold.

"Suppose this is it." Balkus grimaced.

"You've said your other goodbyes?" Stenwold asked.

Balkus grinned. "To those that have time for it. Everyone seems to have something urgent on their minds right now."

"That's true enough." Between Achaeos' injuries and whatever emotional gauntlet Tisamon seemed to be putting himself through, it had been a lonely time for Stenwold recently. "Good luck, Commander. I hope you won't need it, but good luck all the same."

"A man always needs luck," Balkus murmured, and went down into the square to order his troops. All around the Amphiophos square men and women were bidding goodbye to their loved ones: wives, husbands, parents, children. Beetles in unfamiliar armour bent for a last embrace from a lover, friends clasped hands, business partners thrust forward knapsacks of choice tidbits from the stock to lighten the journey. Eyes took one last look over the roofs of Collegium, the Amphiophos and the College, and there cannot have been many who did not wonder whether they would see any of it again—or what flag would be flying over it if they did.

Tisamon had spent the day deliberately seeing no one. He had found a high tower of the College, the stairs leading to it thick with dust, and some abandoned study given over by its occupant in exchange for somewhere less exerting. It gave him a fine view of the city, if he had wanted it, but instead he looked up at the sky. Even the clouds that scudded there, ragged nomads in that vast blue, weighed upon him. He felt as though he was dying.

He should be with Tynisa now, he knew. She was suffering, and he should go to her. It was good Mantis suffering, though, and that was what she did not understand yet. They had brought her up amongst soft Beetle-kinden, who did everything in their power to stave off pain, and so she had never learned the catharsis of hurt.

It was a Mantis thing: to have slain or injured a fellow by tragic mistake, in the madness of battle—the songs were legion that told this same story. She should bear up to the deed, take it inside herself rather than hiding from it. He himself should be teaching her all this.

Except that he was no role model—at least not now.

The storm had come, at last. He had felt the winds rising before he had left for Jerez. He had given Felise into Stenwold's care, but not for her sake, never for her sake. He had felt the storm winds in his soul, and he had gone off with Achaeos to shelter from their blast.

The storm had inevitably come.

She had been practising, he heard, while he had been away. She had been dancing through all the infinite moves of her skill in readiness for his return. They had sparred; they had matched their skills. It had been his doorway back into a world that he had long been barred from. It had been the world of his people, and hers, the perfect expression of the duel, but all the histories of his race were cursing him for how he felt now.

The air was chill up here, but he hauled off his arming jacket, tore apart his shirt, bared his chest, tried to freeze the malady from himself. Yet the cold could not touch sufficiently deep in him: there was not mortification enough in all the world of men to do that.

He hurt with a pain he had not felt in a long time. Even when the Wasp intelligencer Thalric had seared him with his sting in Helleron it had not hurt like this. When Stenwold had suddenly thrust an unknown half-breed daughter on him, it had not hurt like this. He was impaled: writhe as he might, he could not escape. He could now not even seek sanctuary in his skill, because of the gaping absence he felt when he trained and danced alone.

This is wrong. Betrayal on betrayal, he who had already sold so much of his heritage to indulge his personal lusts. All the ancient traditions of his people were in pieces at his feet, and now he would trample them one more time. And he would grind a heel into *her* memory as well, for good measure: the Spider-kinden woman he had made his sacrifice for so long ago, who had been everything to him—and was she just one more thing to cast off, when he felt the urge to? And if so, if that was all she had been, why had he cast aside so very much, just to be with her?

So turn away! Run away! He should leave Collegium. He should seek the Empire out, and then kill Wasps until they brought him down. He should flee so far that none who saw him would know him. He should open his own throat here and now rather than contemplate this sin.

Mantis-kinden pair once, and are faithful beyond death. Everyone knows this.

But his mind came back and back to her perfect grace, her eyes, the line of her blade and the flash of her wings, and he *hurt* with the sheer bitter longing of seventeen bleak years.

Ancestors, save me.

The sky grew dark as he sat up in his tower, and when the night came he had made his choice. He padded down the dusty stairs that were marked only by the tread of his own ascent, and he felt like a man falling. Something had infected him, had gnawed him to the heart. He let it take him away from the College, padding past over-late students and home-bound Masters, unseen by any of them.

It was a short enough step from the gates of the College to those of the Amphiophos. Here there were guards, but he passed them unseen for all their vigilance. His disease had made him skilled.

He could not stop himself now. He had fought that battle up in the tower, and he had lost. It was the hurt, that razoring hurt, that drove him on: a burning he could not quench save in this one way. He crept, quiet and half clad, through the corridors of the hostels behind the Amphiophos, through the diplomats' chambers and the rooms for the foreign guests of the Assembly. He knew he was ill.

Ill and incurable, Tisamon thought. *I should not be here.*

There were more guards here, of course, in case of Wasp assassins. Some were Beetles in their clanking mail; others were Fly-kinden, more subtle and able to see better in the dark. Tisamon evaded them easily, for he had spent a portion of his earlier career in the factory city of Helleron, moving unseen through buildings like this. Everyone knew that his race was full of pride and honour, and so few realized how neither of those qualities was in any way compromised in being a skilled assassin. What was their Mantis totem, after all, but a stealthy killer of insects and men.

It was a mark of his illness that, even as he crept past the guards, he did not think *I must tell Stenwold to bolster the security here*, but was simply grateful that the gaps in their watchfulness were sufficient for a Mantis to slip through. If they had seen him, well, they would recognize him, greet him, think no more of it, but he did not want to be seen. He wanted no other eyes to witness this failure of his. He was ashamed.

He was nearing his destination now, and his heart, which would keep a steady pace through duel or skirmish, was beginning to speed. He was sweating: he felt physically ill now, feverish, but he suppressed it. No magician had ever inspired this dread in him, nor had any threat of death or pain.

The doorway was straight ahead, down this little hall, and in his absorption he almost missed the figure lounging in the alcove next to it, very nearly passed the man by without seeing him, but then his instincts struck home. A moment later he was in his killing stance, with his claw blade at the throat of . . . it took him a moment to see that the man's face was familiar. It was the Spider physician, Destrachis, *her* constant shadow.

He saw how his metal claw was shaking, a slight but noticeable tremor.

"Interesting," Destrachis whispered, holding himself very still. "And here was I thinking you unarmed."

"People see what they wish," Tisamon said. "What are you doing here?"

"Waiting for you."

Tisamon's eyes narrowed. "Do you think it would pain me to kill you, Spider?" He would do it, too, not from will but because of the fever that clenched him in its jaws. He could not control himself. He had let slip the reins and perhaps he would never hold them again.

"I think you would rather enjoy it," replied Destrachis carefully. "However, here I am."

"Speak your piece."

"Turn back."

Tisamon stared at him, hearing his own ragged breathing in his ears, almost like sobbing.

"I know what you are about," Destrachis said. "I know also that she is waiting for you." His lips pressed together for a moment in thought. "I know of you,

Mantis. There are people in this city who remember you from years back. Both of you are bringing chains to this meeting. That is unwise."

"I know," Tisamon said flatly.

"Then turn back."

"Not at your word—not the word of a Spider-kinden. No games from you, no twists. If I think that you meddle in my life, Spider, I will kill you." *I will kill you. I will kill you anyway. I cannot stop myself.* And yet the Spider remained breathing, with that blade wavering at his throat.

"Your life can end up on a stake or deep in the sea for all I care," Destrachis said. "I care about her."

"Do you?"

"She is my patient, and I have sheltered her from the worst of the world as best I could." He sighed. "But I cannot shelter her from this. I can only ask—"

"You have feelings, Spider? You have feelings for *her*?"

"I . . . am her doctor," Destrachis said. It was not clear whether the catch in his voice came from the sudden twitch in Tisamon's blade or had some other cause.

"If I came to believe you coveted her . . ." Tisamon murmured. The threat went unsaid, nor did it need to be spoken.

Destrachis made to speak, and then again, but no words came.

Tisamon removed the blade from the Spider's throat. "Go now. Do not presume to tell me this is wrong." A spasm of pain crossed his face, making Destrachis flinch back. "I know it is wrong. I am not master of myself. I am not . . . well. So go. This is no place for you any longer. I will kill you, if you do not go. I will *kill* you."

Destrachis nodded tiredly, seeming for a moment so haggard that he must have looked close to his natural age. His eyes flicked once toward her door, but then he shook his head and walked away, padding off as quietly as Tisamon had arrived.

He is right. Tisamon clenched his fists. Perhaps he could yet salvage himself. He could step away now, force himself to go.

That perfect poise, the delicate balance of her blade. Not since her . . . Seventeen years was a long time to go without something that had once been his life and very breath. *I hurt!* He still had his clawed gauntlet buckled on, and the urge came upon him to drive it into his own flesh, to excise the hurt from himself like a surgeon.

And then her door opened, with Felise Mienn standing in shadow beyond, clad in her shift, staring out at him.

"Tisamon." His name on her lips, in that softly accented voice. He lurched a step backward, claw gone, staring. Unwillingly, as if tugged by wires, he approached her.

She reached out, but stopped just before her hand touched his chest. She, too, was shaking very slightly. "Tisamon," she said again, her voice unsteady.

She looked up into his face, and he wondered what she saw in his sharp features, his grey-flecked hair. He, who found his own face in the mirror both severe and haunted in turns, looked upon Felise and felt such fierce fire that he could barely keep his hands from her.

She is not so young, not so young as she looks. She was widow, after all, as he himself was widower. They neither of them had the fresh gloss of youth still on them. Yet the Dragonflies were a beautiful people, and none was more beautiful than Felise Mienn seen through the eyes of the Mantis Tisamon.

"Please," he whispered, "send me away. One word from you and I will go. I cannot be here. I . . . betray . . ."

She was biting her lip, her hand still hovering an inch from his torn shirt.

"I could not keep myself from this place, because I had not the will," he confessed. "But you can banish me. Send me away. Your word is strong, where I have failed. Please."

"For so many years I have woken up screaming." She spoke at last, so very quietly that he instinctively leant in to hear—and then closer still, to scent her dark hair. "Not out loud, but in my head," she continued. "What the Wasps did to me, I carried it like a picture to look at every day. Now the picture is gone and the scream is just an echo. But it was not having Thalric at my blade's mercy that did this, for all I thought it might."

"I have no such powers," he said softly. "Do not make me into such a healer."

"What do you want here?" she asked him. "Are you here to fight me? Then I shall take up my sword. Is that what you want?"

"No. It is not." He swallowed. *I want to feel your golden skin, to taste the sweat on it, to bury myself in your grace and poise.* No matter how he tried, the thoughts would not stay away from him.

Abruptly his arms had swept her into his grasp and, with the same instinct that guided his blade faster than thought could take it, he had kissed her. For a moment she was stiff with shock, but then her arms gripped him, nails digging into his back, across pale skin sparsely signed with old scars and newer burns. Her thumb claws inscribed fresh writing on him in shallow blood.

He pushed her into the room, the door swinging shut behind them. He lifted her shift over her head, and his breath ran ragged with the sight of the lithe economy of her body.

◊ ◊ ◊

A hand abruptly closed on Che's, startling her out of half-sleep. For a moment she could not work out what had happened, and then she looked at him—and Achaeos' eyes were slightly open, a line of white showing beneath each lid.

Her heart shook, for joy, for worry. Was he even conscious? Could he speak?

"Achaeos?" she whispered. Around her, the other casualties slept on, turned restlessly, some murmured to themselves.

She saw his lips move, moved her head closer to hear him, but there was no sound.

"Achaeos, can you hear me?"

"Che . . ." Little more than a breath, but it was her name he spoke, her name on his breath. He still looked pale and hollow cheeked, as though he should be dead. His featureless eyes might be focusing on her or staring into the abyss. He had said her name, though, and that was all that now mattered.

"I'll go and get a doctor . . ." she started but his hand twitched on hers.

"Che, wait," he breathed again. The interval before his next laboured words was agonizing. "I need . . . healers. No doctors. No physicians . . . I cannot stay here. I cannot heal here . . . this Apt city is killing me . . . this is not medicine." That much effort exhausted him and she clung to his hand as though he was drowning, being dragged into the dark water, and she was his only hope of rescue.

"I don't understand," she said, and then, "This is . . . your medicine is different. But that is because we are Apt here, and we do things differently. I remember . . ." She recalled his own medicines of herbs and poultices at their first meeting, while she stitched his wound. How was it that he had such a habit of getting injured?

"Che . . . the box . . . is it . . . ?"

She did not want to tell him. She did not know if he could stand the news. Still, if she lied now then she would always have lied to him, whatever her reasons for it. Besides, he would inevitably read it in her eyes. She shook her head. "I'm sorry."

He shuddered. *All that for nothing*, he must surely be thinking. "Che," he said again, "help me."

"I love you, Achaeos. I'll do anything for you. Just say it."

A fragile smile touched his lips, and she bent closer to hear him speak.

Ten minutes later Cheerwell Maker paused on the man's threshold, seeing a strip of lamplight beneath the door. A late night for him, then, and what would Major Thalric be doing up past midnight?

She knew she should knock straight away, but, standing here, she ran her mind through the road the pair of them had travelled together. Herself as his prisoner, under threat of rape, under threat of torture; a pawn in his political games. She owed him no courtesy, she decided.

She was about to throw open the door but changed her mind. She was here to beg, for all that it sickened her. She could not see any other way this could be done.

Che raised her hand to knock, and his voice came from within: "Whoever is out there, what do you want?"

She stood, frozen, feeling guilty and already hating him.

"Open the door, clumsy assassin," suggested Thalric's voice, and helplessly she did, pushing the heavy wooden door open and letting the lamplight stream out to narrow her eyes. Some had wanted him locked up still, but Stenwold had ruled against it. *Perhaps,* Che thought, *my uncle hopes that he will overplay his hand, somehow, and reveal himself as a traitor.* As a traitor yet again, she supposed, since he had already betrayed his own people.

Thalric was sitting at a desk as if interrupted in the act of writing. He had an open palm raised toward the door. After a thoughtful pause, he lowered it and sat regarding her without expression.

"Mistress Maker," he said. "Not a visitor I'd expected."

In the absence of either dismissal or invitation, she stepped into the room, closing the door behind her.

"What are you writing so late?" she asked him.

"Reports on Jerez," he said, and on seeing her look he added, "Who for, you ask? I don't know, but old habits die hard. I fear nobody will believe them anyway." He put the pen down. Che saw that it was a good-quality Collegium-made reservoir pen. He had obviously not been slow in taking advantage of his hosts.

"So," he said, "are you here to warn me that the Dragonfly woman wants to kill me again, or is it simply that I'm to be arrested and tried at last?"

"Would I come here alone for that?"

"Perhaps you'd enjoy delivering such a message in person."

She stared at him, loathing him, yet knowing that she now needed him. "Don't think that we're like the people of your Empire here. We don't all take joy in other people's suffering."

"Perhaps not," he said. "Yet your Mantis would kill me without a thought."

"But he wouldn't torture you. He'd make it quick."

"What a consolation," he observed. "If a quick death was attractive to me, I'd have let my own people do it. This situation is ironic, is it not?"

"What?"

"You now have the say of life or death over me. It's not so long since our places were reversed."

"I remember you were intending to torture me."

"I remember that I never did."

She felt her anger flare up. "Because I was rescued! Not through any grace of yours!"

For a second it seemed he would argue the point, to her astonishment, but then he just shrugged and turned back to his papers. From nowhere she could identify, she felt a sudden stab of utterly unwelcome sympathy, at seeing the failed spy still clinging to his ritual, for want of anything else.

"Thalric . . ."

"Mistress Maker." He did not look up at her.

"I need your help."

He snorted with laughter, pen abruptly scratching on the parchment: not laughing at her so much as the sheer absurdity of that statement, after her words to him before. "What could I be qualified to do for you, Mistress Maker? Does the Assembly want some prisoners racking, whilst keeping their own hands clean?"

She approached quietly, was at his desk even before he had finished speaking, her hands gripping the edge. He looked up at her at last, his gaze measuring, considering.

"What, then?" he asked, realizing that she was serious, and desperate. "What is it?"

"I need your help," she said again, slowly. "I need to get into a city that your people have occupied, and I don't know how to do it."

She waited for some reaction, but there was none. He was an intelligencer by trade, and whatever he thought of her request was played out inside, and hidden from her.

"Tharn," she said. "I have to go to Tharn."

FOUR

The rap on his door was insistent, though if Stenwold had already got as far as his bed he would have ignored it. He heard Arianna stir at the sound. She had fallen asleep waiting for him, expecting him to join her hours earlier. But he could not sleep; he was too caught up with his worries: the defence of Sarn, and Balkus' relief force; Salma's mad Landsarmy; Tynisa's guilt and Che's grief; the litany of the wounded; the gallery of those faces who he would never see again, yet wished so dearly to take counsel with.

Stenwold went to answer the door, if only because it gave him at least a brief respite. He discovered Destrachis standing there, the lean Spider with his long, greying hair. Stenwold blinked at him.

"Are we under attack?"

"We are not, Master Maker. Not yet." Destrachis made no sign that he wanted to come in, just hovered beyond the doorway, clearly ill at ease.

"What time is it?"

"Four bells beyond midnight. Still one or two before dawn."

Stenwold goggled at him. "So late?" *I must go to bed. I will even drug myself to sleep if I have to.* "What . . . why are you here?"

"It would have been earlier, Master Maker . . . but I have not known how to say this to you. I have no claim on you, and yet I need your help. I have spent hours hunting for answers in my mind. I need you to do something."

"At this hour?"

"I need you merely to commit now. Act on it in the morning, but I need your word now, Master Maker."

"You're mad," Stenwold told him, "and so am I for not being already in bed. How can it be almost dawn, for the world's sake?"

"Master Maker, *please*," Destrachis implored, his composure slipping for a moment. Stenwold heard soft footsteps from behind him. Arianna, wrapped in a bedsheet, was coming to investigate.

"Back to bed, please," he told her. "I don't know what this is about but—"

"Stenwold, why are you still dressed? Why are you even answering the door?" she asked.

"I . . ." He decided to avoid the first half of that inquisition. "I'm answering the door because this man has decided it is a civilized time to call. Destrachis, what do you want? What is it, this thing you want from me?"

"Find a suitable use for Felise," the Spider replied flatly. "If you do not, then I do not know what she might do come the morning. Surely your great plans can take account of her?"

"I . . ." Stenwold shook his head. "I'd supposed she would fight if ever the Wasps get this far, but . . ."

"Master Maker, there is no time," Destrachis said urgently, and Stenwold was surprised by the glint of tears in his eyes, whether of frustration or emotion, he could not tell. "Master Maker, I have a plan for you."

"More plans. My head is already full of them. No more plans, please, at this hour."

"In the morning, then. Promise me, Master Maker, that you will hear me as soon as first light dawns."

An hour till then, two at the most. "All right," Stenwold said, "I promise. Now just . . . go, please." He cast a look at Arianna. She was eyeing Destrachis distrustfully.

"I'll go," Destrachis said, "but you must believe that I am right in this. It means life or death, Master Maker."

"Life or death in the *morning*," Stenwold said firmly, but before he could even close the door on Destrachis there was someone else running up, shouldering the Spider aside.

"Sten!"

It was Tynisa this time. Stenwold stared at her helplessly, feeling his grasp of the situation slip further from him. He was wrong-footed by the impression that, whatever Tynisa was here about, Destrachis must already know of it.

"What now?" he asked, more harshly than he meant. He saw then that her face was blotched, her eyes red. *Has the matter over Achaeos finally become too much for her?* A sudden horror caught him. *Is Achaeos dead?* His voice now unsteady, he asked, "What is it?"

"It's Tisamon," she told him simply. "He's gone."

"Gone? Gone where?" He held on to the doorframe, unable to keep up with events.

"I don't know but . . ." She held her hand out to him, something glinting in her palm. "He's really gone. Something's happened to him. He's left us. This was pinned to my door."

In her hand was the sword and circle broach of a Weaponsmaster, which Stenwold had never seen Tisamon without.

They searched, of course, he and Tynisa together. First the Amphiophos, then Tisamon's other haunts in the city, from the Prowess Forum outward. In the last hour before dawn they ransacked the city for him, sensing they were already too late. He had pointedly left behind the symbol of his office. It was no mere errand he had departed on.

Then they came back, and found the long-faced Spider-kinden doctor again waiting for them, looking old and ill-used. In the sallow, early light they allowed him to finally explain to them what had happened between Tisamon and Felise Mienn, and the thing that Tisamon had done that had driven him away. Destrachis' sad, tired voice related the story in measured tones, as though it was some medical curiosity, and yet it barely scratched the surface of the Mantis-kinden nightmare that Tisamon had become lost in.

"Poor Tisamon," was Stenwold's comment at last. "Oh, poor Tisamon."

"Poor *Tisamon?*" Destrachis exclaimed. "Perhaps I have not explained things clearly enough."

"No, no," Stenwold stopped him. "I understand. So he went to her at last." He looked at his own hands, broad and scarred, resting on the table. "I should have seen it in him, but I have been so taxed with other matters of late."

"There was no sign in Jerez," Tynisa said softly. "But then he kept himself occupied, always."

The conference was just the three of them: the Beetle War Master, his adopted daughter and the Spider doctor who had never looked so old as now. In the harsh light of morning Stenwold saw now that his hair was not just greying but grey, almost white at the roots, in need of further dyeing. Spiders aged gracefully, and so Destrachis must be old—older than Stenwold by ten years and more.

"He went to her, then. He slept with her." Stenwold's hands clenched into fists, almost of their own accord. "And, in the aftermath, he thought of . . . of *her.*"

"Atryssa," Tynisa agreed, although her thoughts surely ran, *my mother.* Stenwold wondered if Tisamon had thought of his daughter as well, seen a second betrayal there, where Tynisa would surely have been happy for him. *After all, she's not one to be easily shocked.* But of course Tisamon would not have seen it like that.

"Mantis pride," said Stenwold. "Anyone else . . . *anyone* else, given that chance, would have held on to their luck and not asked any questions. Anyone else would have been *happy.* Anyone but a Mantis, of course. So he's been putting himself on the rack about what he'll see as a betrayal. A *final* betrayal. He betrayed his own kind, and then he betrayed her, after Myna, and now . . . mantids pair for life, I know. They never do what he has done—or so they tell each other. And Tisamon believed it, too. Poor Tisamon."

"And Felise is abandoned by him now," Destrachis said. "And who wouldn't, in her place, take the blame on themselves, or at least part of it? I know she has."

"How is she?" Stenwold asked him.

"After I left you, I went and sat with her until dawn." From the Spider's haggard looks Stenwold could well believe it. "She will kill herself."

Stenwold and Tynisa stared at him, while his face took on an expression of excruciating patience.

"She lost all her family, you'll recall. She lost everything to the Wasps. To survive that loss she tracked the man, Thalric, across the whole of the Lowlands. That kept her going. Then she met Tisamon, who gave her another purpose, gave her—curse the man!—even a normal chance at life. And now he has gone, and she has nothing."

"And so you want her put into my plans, somehow. You think I can find her a purpose. You have a scheme?" Stenwold said. "Destrachis, I do not mean to insult you . . ."

The doctor watched him with a faint smile, waiting.

Stenwold sighed, and continued. "My people say that Spiders always look in at least two directions at once. I confess I have been an intelligencer for twenty years, but I cannot read you. We Beetles are infants at these games compared to you. So what precisely do you want?"

Destrachis waited a long time before answering, still with that slight smile. "Ah Master Maker," he said at last. "I would tell you that I am a man of medicine and have a duty to my patient. Or insist that even Spiders know some little of honour and duty. I would tell you that I genuinely care that Felise Mienn, having suffered so much, should be happy, and does not destroy herself. I would tell you all of this, and you'd not believe a word of it, so therefore what can I tell you?"

"Tell me your plan."

"I am no tactician," the Spider said, "however I understand this: the Wasps have more soldiers than you have—than you and the Sarnesh and all the little cities put together. The Empire is very large, the Wasps and their warriors are very many."

"We have the Spiderlands," Stenwold pointed out.

"You do not trust me, and yet you suggest relying on the Spiderlands," Destrachis said disdainfully.

Stenwold nodded, conceding the point. "Then you are essentially correct, yes."

"So you make enemies for the Wasps—as with Solarno, for I have heard about this from your niece. Now the Wasps have another city to keep under control, another battle to fight."

"The Wasps took Solarno of their own will," Stenwold argued.

Destrachis shrugged. "Still, there are a few thousand Wasps there now who won't be at the gates of Sarn. Well, then, the Wasps have other enemies."

Stenwold opened his mouth, then shut it again. Destrachis waited for the moment of comprehension, for the moment when Stenwold said, "You mean Felise's own people? You're talking about the Commonweal."

Destrachis nodded evenly.

"But there's been no contact, no diplomatic relations at all—and besides, they must know—"

"What do they know?" Destrachis interrupted him. "What do most of your people know about the Twelve-Year War? The Commonweal is very old, and it has been collapsing in stages since long before the Empire ever arose from the dust. To the Dragonfly-kinden, everyone living outside their borders is a barbarian. There are only a few who have any interest in the Lowlands—such as your man who now fights with Sarn."

Destrachis has been busy listening, I see. In fact Stenwold could hardly blame him.

"If the Empire is attacking the Lowlands," the Spider continued, "then the land lost by the Dragonflies in the Twelve-Year War is open to being reclaimed, but the Commonweal must be made to understand that. They must be invited to join us, for they are a formal people. Felise can be your safe passage. Whatever she has done, she is still one of them."

"And you would come along as well?" Stenwold asked him.

"I would, but if this plan is to be of any assistance we must leave now, and by air. Otherwise your cities will have fallen by the time we even make our request."

"And if the Dragonflies should attack the Empire . . . well, the Wasps have a lot of soldiers but they cannot be everywhere at once. Especially if Teornis can persuade the Spiderlands to rise up also . . ."

"For you and for Felise, Master Maker," Destrachis said. "I do not ask this for any profit to myself."

Stenwold stared at his hands once more. "It could work. And you're right, we must attempt it. We cannot ignore any source of aid, or means of dividing the Empire's attention." He nodded, his decision made. "I myself shall go. Collegium should not need me now, not until Sarn is decided one way or the other. So I shall go and . . . Tynisa, will you?" *You also need something to occupy your mind.*

But Tynisa replied, "No."

"Tynisa, surely . . . ?"

"Because there is something else I must do."

"Ah, no." Stenwold held up a hand, as though he could forbid her.

"Yes, I must follow Tisamon and bring him back."

"He will not thank you for it."

"I do not want his thanks. I want merely to tell him that I do not care what he has done—and that he should not either. I want to speak to him for myself, and my mother. I want to pull his guilt out of him, before the wound festers."

◊ ◊ ◊

The train rattled and jolted its way along the rails, each carriage packed with soldiers sleeping fitfully, or awake and sharing quiet words, games of chance, perhaps a communal bottle. The Collegium relief force was on its way to Sarn.

Balkus passed down the train from carriage to carriage, stepping over carelessly stowed kitbags and the outstretched legs of sleepers, checking on the welfare of his men. Enough of the waking had a nod or a smile for him that he felt this inspection was doing some good. They belonged to all walks of life, he knew, and many were men for whom Collegium had never found much use before. Those were strong-armers, dock brawlers, bruisers and wastrels, but the Vekken siege had overwritten their many years of bad living with the lesson that even they could be heroes, even they could become the admired talk of their city. Others had signed up simply for the money, to escape creditors or enemies. More were simply those who wanted to do their bit as good citizens: he had here his share of shopkeepers, tradesmen, runaway apprentices and College graduates. There had probably never been an army in history with so many men and women who could strip down an engine or discourse on grammar. He even had a couple of College Masters, whom he had promoted to officers.

What a rabble, though. Most had fought the Vekken Ant-kinden, but the frantic defence of a walled city against one's neighbours was not a field battle against a mighty Empire. He was amazed that there were so many ordinary citizens signed up, and still signing. The people of Collegium were not like Ant-kinden to be so slavishly selfless, nor were they fools either. They were stepping straight into the fires with their eyes open, in full knowledge of what they would face.

The very thought brought a lump into his throat. It brought back moments of the fight against the Vekken, especially after they had breached the walls. He was no Collegiate man himself, but he felt a stubborn knot of pride in the way these shopkeepers and artisans had proved they would *fight*. Their military skills were suspect, their equipment untested, but their hearts were the hearts of heroes, one and all.

He eventually found himself back at his own carriage, where Parops opened one eye on hearing his approach.

"Everyone tucked in?" the Tarkesh asked.

"Going to have to kick them all awake soon enough," Balkus replied. "We can't be far from the city, now."

"I could tell that from your enthusiasm," said Parops drily.

Balkus nodded again, heavy of heart. He sat down wearily, staring out of the window. Not being a man much accustomed to examining his feelings he could not have said whether this sudden despondency was due to the imminent return to his long-abandoned home city or the prospect of leading so many untried soldiers into battle.

I should have stayed simple, he reflected. Ambition was the root of this. He might not even be on this troop train if he had not pushed his way to the front when they were calling for officers. *I'm not commander material. I know it.* But the men of Collegium had instantly seized upon him in the sure knowledge that Ants like him all knew their business when it came to war.

And here he was in the small hours, the train pulling closer toward Sarn, with both a responsibility and a reconciliation that he never wanted.

The feel of the engine, thrumming through the wooden floor beneath his feet, changed noticeably: the train was slowing. Throughout the carriages, soldiers would be rousing on feeling this change of pace, or their officers would be shouting them awake.

"Will you look at that," Parops exclaimed, from the seat opposite in what was nominally the officers' carriage. "It looks like the place is already under siege."

Balkus leant out of the window, seeing hundreds of fires and, beyond them, the dark heights of the walls of Sarn. "What in the wastes . . . ?" he murmured. The train was swiftly passing them now, all those little campfires, and the tents and makeshift shacks that sprouted around them. "This lot wasn't here when you and Sten came?"

"All new to me," Parops confirmed.

Balkus tried to get a clearer impression of the people huddled about those fires, aided by the train's slowing pace. They were a ragged lot—he saw the pattern quickly because he had expected it: lots of children, old people, few men or women of any fit age to bear a sword.

"Refugees," he decided.

"From where?" Parops asked him.

Balkus looked out again, recognizing Beetle-kinden, Flies, many others. "Everywhere that lies east of here, I'd guess," the big Ant decided, the thought of such displacement settling on him heavily. "Where are they supposed to go when the Wasps get here?"

The train rolled on, seemingly heedless, passing inside the city walls and coasting to a slow halt at the Sarnesh rail depot. Balkus stood up, feeling a hollowness inside, a gap into which the idle thoughts of his kin everywhere around were already leaking. It all looked so painfully familiar to him: the gas lamps glowing throughout the squat, square buildings of Sarn proper, whilst on the other side of the train gleamed the disparate lights and lanterns and torches of the Foreigners' Quarter. There were soldiers everywhere: he saw them up on the walls, installing new artillery, or waiting by the train to load and unload, or just marching and drilling, making ready.

"The last time I saw so many Ant-kinden under arms," he said, "they were trying to kill me."

"You realize everyone expects you to do the talking, I hope," Parops said.

"Why me?" Balkus stared at him. "No, anyone but me."

"Your fellow commanders are all Beetle-kinden," the Tarkesh pointed out, "which in their eyes makes you the logical choice, because you at least can over-hear what the Sarnesh are saying to one another."

"It's been a long time," Balkus replied slowly. He could indeed feel the hum and buzz of Ant-kinden conversation from outside the train. He had been actively fighting to blot it out. It had been such a very long time. *But we now need to know if my former countrymen will deal honestly with us.*

"Pox," he spat, "you're right."

"Don't worry," Parops reassured him. "As the leader of Free Tark, I'll be right there beside you. They'll love that."

◁▷ ◁▷ ◁▷

It should have been a bleak and blustery day suitable for their departure, but the mocking sun was bright in a cloudless sky, beating down on the Collegium airfield as if a summer day had been imported early.

Stenwold had spent the last two days arguing bitterly with—it seemed—almost everyone. Lineo Thadspar had done everything in his power to persuade Stenwold not to go at all. Stenwold had done everything he could to persuade Tynisa to go with him, instead of just casting herself into the void by going in search of her father.

"Tisamon can look after himself," he had insisted.

"Tisamon will go looking for a fight," she had told him. "And if that one doesn't kill him, he'll go looking for another, just like he did after Myna. Oh, he's good at it—I have never seen anyone fight as well as Tisamon—but that doesn't mean he's immortal. I need to find him before he goes into one fight too far."

And she had been right, of course, and Tisamon himself was not so young any more. *We none of us are.*

Amidst a scatter of larger airships, the *Buoyant Maiden* seemed makeshift and dowdy. Jons Allanbridge had been more than happy to renew his contract with Stenwold and, based on Tynisa's recommendation, Stenwold had been more than happy to offer it. Destrachis had been right, they would need to travel by air, and Allanbridge seemed to be a good man for slipping something as large as an airship into places with a minimum of fuss.

The Spider himself was already at the rail of the gondola, gazing back at Collegium without expression. The Lowlands were full of odd homeless types, hiring out their skills wherever the road took them. *Tisamon has rejoined that brotherhood now.* Destrachis, too, was on that path, but Stenwold wondered whether he secretly hoped the Commonweal would take him back.

Standing at the Spider's shoulder was the cloaked form of Felise Mienn. She had said nothing yet to Stenwold, who did not know what to say to her. The bulk of her shrouded form showed that she wore her armour again. He guessed it provided a protection that was more than the mere physical. She would be a difficult travelling companion, he thought.

"Are we ready for the off?" Arianna asked, at his elbow.

He gave her a weak smile. "Not you," he said.

She stared at him. "Sten—"

"I have done my thinking. I would have argued it out with you before, save that everyone else has claimed my time in other arguments. Not you this time, Arianna."

Her look was pure hurt. "After all we've done, you don't trust me?"

"No! Hammer and tongs, no! Of course I trust you, Arianna, and I love you. You have brought to me . . . such joy as no man in my place deserves." He gripped her by the arms. "And it could have been you, you must have known, that the cursed Sarnesh had stretched out on their rack. You instead of poor Sperra. No, Arianna, you stay here."

"Oh, Che's already told me how much you like to keep people safe—"

"Well, this time I'm bloody well going to succeed at it," he said.

"And it could have been you on that rack, too," she pointed out. "And then what would *I* have done? Sten, you can't—"

"This is *my* war," he said simply. "I was fighting this war when you were—hah, when you were still a child."

"But you *need* me."

"Yes, yes I do." The utter sincerity in his voice finally got through to her. "Yes, I need you. And because of that you must stay here. You'll not be idle, either. You'll be running my agents while I'm away, taking in the intelligence of the Wasp advance, liaising with the Assembly—and I'm sure you'll charm those old men and women far better than I ever could. But this is a mad journey, and a long one, and I . . ." He found he was trembling. "I realized at Sarn that if anything happened to you, it would break me, it would destroy me. I do not know the Commonweal. No Lowlander does. This voyage is a necessary madness and I do not want to draw you into it."

There were tears in her eyes, tears beyond any Spider pretence. "This isn't fair."

"No," he agreed. "But it's the only way I can do this. I'm sorry."

He held her for a long time, aware and careless of Allanbridge and the others watching and waiting for him.

But even after Arianna had fled the airfield they would wait longer, for here was Tynisa now with her pack slung over her shoulder. No airship for her, though: she would be making her own way, tracking any news of a lone Mantis duellist whose passage, like enough, would be written in bodies.

Stenwold started over toward her, and she regarded him cautiously, as though she thought he might suddenly order her to be placed under lock and key just to keep her here. He had ceded that battlefield to her, though. He merely held out his hand, offered like the hand of a soldier, and they clasped as comrades.

"Good luck," he said softly. "The world around us is about to fall apart at the seams, and I suppose a father is a better reason than many for casting yourself out into the storm." In his heart, he had no belief she would ever find Tisamon—or that the Mantis would welcome her if ever she did.

"And good luck to you," Tynisa responded. "Do you have even a clue what the Commonweal is going to be like?"

"No, but I know who does. If I'm lucky I'll encounter Salma in time for a rec-ommendation on the way."

"Give him my love," she said, her voice sounding oddly flat. Stenwold knew that she had been fond of the Dragonfly prince once, and that the intervention of Grief in Chains—or whatever the Butterfly-kinden was now calling herself—had thrown her badly. She had been used, at the College, to having her own way in such relationships. *And let us hope it is just that, and that she will not take after her father in matters of the heart.*

"Maker, we have the wind! Let's *move!*" called the impatient Allanbridge from the rail of the *Buoyant Maiden.* Stenwold spared Tynisa one last nod, then he was hurrying for the rope ladder, clambering hand-over-hand up into the air even as Allanbridge cast off. Tynisa watched the nimble airship rise and tack, its engines directing it north, toward the distant Barrier Ridge that marked the Lowlands border with the mysterious Commonweal beyond.

"Well, he's gone," she then called. "You can come out now."

Che made her way warily on to the airfield, looking up at the diminishing globe of the *Maiden's* airbag. "I couldn't face him," she said, almost in a whisper. "He'd have forbidden it."

"Che, if I had any say, *I'd* forbid it, too," Tynisa remarked bleakly. She watched as a pair of white-robed College men carried the stretcher toward the clumsy-looking flier that Che had piloted back from Solarno. "My offer is still open."

"You have your own path to follow," Che told her firmly. She now looked so very serious, all of her awkward youth burnt off her.

"But this is all my fault . . ."

Che shook her head. "You just find Tisamon and talk some sense into him. Achaeos needs me. But he needs his people too, so they and I will have to get along as best we can. And, anyway, I won't be alone."

Tynisa made a disgusted noise and, right on cue, the fair-haired, square-jawed Wasp-kinden came to join them, wearing now his own imperial armour, just as if he had never turned his coat.

"Thalric," Tynisa acknowledged his arrival coldly.

The Wasp looked at her, his smile devoid of love or humour. "How good of you to see me off." He held up a hand to forestall her. "Can we take all your oaths of vengeance as already said: if I betray you, if I harm Che, so on and so forth, I'm sure all the venom and vengeance of Spider and Mantis will descend on my head."

Tynisa stared at him levelly. "Remember those words when we next meet, Thalric," but her voice rang hollow, because if he now chose to make Che the latest in his history of betrayals, there would be nothing she could do about it.

It was a grim flight from Collegium for those on the *Buoyant Maiden*. Felise was bitter as ice, locked entirely in her own pain. She had nothing to spare for Stenwold and he was grateful for that. He had no way to intrude on her, or to help her, so he left her to herself. Destrachis hung about near her like a shabby ghost, bringing her meals but never venturing to speak. It was plain to Stenwold that the Spider had found the limits of his own expertise and was simply hoping that she would reach out to him.

Is that what he seeks there in the Commonweal: no more than a familiar landscape to console her? But Stenwold suspected the Commonweal would bring no fond memories for Felise Mienn.

Stenwold himself spent his time with Jons Allanbridge, occupying his mind with whatever small mechanical tasks the aviator found him fit for. It was almost like being a student again, serving anew as an apprentice. It was oddly comforting to leave their journey in Allanbridge's hands, and to shoulder none of the responsibility.

At last they came down beside Sarn. Stenwold had earlier sent a messenger ahead by rail, with no certainty that word would reach Salma in time, or at all. As it turned out, though, there was a blue-grey-skinned Mynan Beetle-kinden waiting for them, riding with two others, and a string of horses and riding insects. They had been in Sarn when the message arrived, and so had waited the extra day for Stenwold's appearance. The Mynan left his mounts in the care of a subordinate, and joined them in the *Maiden*, directing Allanbridge east away from Sarn. *Toward the Wasp army*, Stenwold thought. Salma would face his own ordeal, there, and soon.

They were guided to a camp, and then to another camp, widely spaced, and Stenwold guessed that Salma must be living a mobile life. In the third they finally found him, sitting in a tent and making plans. Whilst the others waited outside, Stenwold himself was allowed in to speak to him.

Amid the gloom of the tent the Dragonfly prince stood marking notes and arrows on a map he had tacked to a board held in his off-hand. It was impossible to know how much attention he was paying to his visitor. "It's been a while, Sten," he remarked.

"How is your position?"

"Fluid. So tell me about Che," Salma said. "How is she?"

Stenwold watched him. With no more reaction to go on than he could glean from the Dragonfly's back, he explained Achaeos' circumstances, described Che sitting distraught at his sickbed.

Salma nodded. "I recently dreamt of her passing into darkness. Of course, to the Moths that would be a dream of good omen." Outside the tent there were hundreds of armed men and women busying about. They had none of the uniformity of soldiers, but they were clearly fighters, composed of a dozen kinden and all now engaged in packing up their camp and preparing to move. The *Buoyant Maiden* had tied up in the midst of this chaos of dissolution.

"And Tynisa?" Salma asked. He handed the map to a Fly-kinden woman and turned round. As Stenwold recounted Tynisa's burden and present mission, he re-evaluated the Dragonfly before him.

Salma looked every part the brigand chief. The armour had changed since Stenwold last saw him, presumably the pick of whatever equipment they had liberated from the Wasps. Now it was a cuirass of layered leather with bronze studs over a suit of silk, all of it meticulous Spider work. The sword at his belt was slender and long hilted, not true Commonweal but of no manufacture Stenwold could identify. About his forehead he wore a gold-inlaid leather band, complete with cheek guards.

"You have arrived at a difficult time, Sten," Salma said at last, "and apparently travelling to see my people, no less."

"You think they won't help?"

"I cannot say, save that they will do whatever they do for their own reasons only." Salma tacked another blank sheet to his writing board and began to scribe on it. "Don't assume they'll sit like Beetles and listen to hours of argument. Just ask and then accept whatever answer they give."

"I'll remember that." Stenwold flinched as something dragged at the side of the tent. A moment later daylight cut in, as the heavy fabric was rolled up around them, a gang of huge men taking the tent apart with care, without effort, even as he and Salma were still inside. He started back from them, for they towered over him, pitch-skinned giants, either with shaved heads or else mops of white hair.

"Mole Crickets," he identified them.

"Two score of them," Salma agreed. "Together with half a hundred Grasshopper-kinden from Sho El, which I understand is somewhere as far east as you can go without leaving the Empire. They are Auxillian deserters."

"I didn't think the Imperial Army was that easy to desert from."

"Normally there are reprisals against their families, back home. Here, though, we make a practice of not leaving any enemy bodies if we can help it. Whole scouting parties have vanished completely, and the Auxillians along with them. The Wasps cannot then know who has died and who has deserted. And of course some Auxillians themselves realize the potential of this practice—and that here, of all places, there is someone who will take them in. Morleyr and his people came to me of their own will."

One of the great Mole Cricket-kinden turned and nodded at that, regarding Stenwold suspiciously.

"Go to Suon Ren," Salma said, as he unpinned the paper and passed it to Stenwold. "Prince Felipe Shah may yet be holding his winter court there. He will remember me still, I hope, so this shall serve as your introduction."

"Suon Ren," Stenwold repeated. In his head he conjured up what he had gleaned of the Commonweal, pinpointing the name as belonging somewhere north of the Moth hold of Dorax, toward the Commonweal's southern border.

"You should go right now, though," Salma informed him. The Mynan warrior had just run up to him, handing over what looked like a scribbled land plan, with arrows and blocks sketched in. "The Wasp Sixth is advancing on our position," Salma explained. "We're already blinding their approach, vanishing their scouts, but they've put a couple of flying machines in the air just now, and that could cause some problems with your departure."

"I'll go now," Stenwold confirmed.

Salma held one hand up. "There is one name from the old times that we haven't yet mentioned, Sten."

"I know."

"He is . . . ?"

"Totho is with the Wasps still, insofar as I know. He will most likely be with the army now marching on you."

"Ah." Salma looked down for a moment, then reached forward to clasp Stenwold's arm, wrist to wrist. "Good luck, Sten—and fair winds."

"Good luck to you too," Stenwold said, already beginning to back toward the *Buoyant Maiden*, straining where the wind tugged at it. His last sight of Salma was as the single still point in a camp that was disintegrating into nothing all around him.

FIVE

"**I**t can't really be just because of the girl, can it?" Teornis asked. The Spider Aristos did not look at Nero as he asked the question, but purely because the artist was intent on a profile sketch of him just then. "After all, you didn't exactly spend much time with her, before she set off on her own."

"She didn't exactly spend much time on board ship," Nero pointed out.

Teornis spent a further moment in composition, the chitin-shard pen poised deftly between his fingers, then he scratched a few additional notes to a report he was sending on. He had already played host to two Fly-kinden couriers bringing document packets, and a third was anticipated soon. Their airship was passing over the isle of Kes even now, with the Ants' metal-gleaming navies mustering below in preparation for war.

"I had thought Fly courtship to be a fairly straightforward affair," the Spider said idly.

"I've got no idea how they do things in Solarno—probably slap each other with fish or something. All mad in that city. Sure, in the hollows it's simple enough," Nero remarked, meaning Egel and Merro. "That's because it's mostly arranged. Everything's run by family there. That's why I got out, and that's why you find so many of my people away from home. Easier for us to live anywhere but directly under the noses of our own kind. Why, how's it work with your people?"

"I've no idea how they do things down in the gutter," Teornis said, with a dry imitation of the artist's tone in his voice. "Amongst the Aristoi, however, it is a very delicate and intricate business. If a woman wishes a man's companionship, he is allowed to discover it from some third party, but most often the woman merely waits for suitors, no mere man being considered important enough to attract her attention. Once his affections are engaged, the man is expected to approach the woman carefully, respectfully. There is a chain of social observances that he must perform: questions to be asked of her servants and friends, discreet giving of gifts through intermediaries, the scribing of poetry or the commissioning—as you must know—of artistic works for her."

Nero nodded, making connections. "I didn't realize I'd become part of some Spider fellow's love games."

"A minor and preliminary part," Teornis said. "Then there comes the meeting with her closer court, perhaps a duel, a challenge made by some unimportant member of her cadre—the skill of that challenger varying, of course, in inverse proportion to her favour of the admirer's suit. Then they will meet by her arrangement, on an occasion unknown in advance to him. She will evaluate him. If he has displayed sufficient wit, beauty, charm, whatever virtues she seeks in him, then he may gain further access to her household, to her chambers, finally to her body. If not, well, if he is lucky he will escape with his life and reputation, but that is not always the case. Wooing a Spider-kinden Arista is a perilous business for the unprepared."

"And if she's made it known to him that she wants him, but he doesn't want her?" Nero asked, fascinated.

Teornis chuckled quietly. "Little man, *his* interests are of no importance in this ritual, save to explain why so many of the men of *my* people are also to be found living in the cities of others." In that revealing moment of frank humour, Nero almost liked him.

There was a respectful knock at the cabin door and, on Teornis' invitation, one of the crew let a Fly-kinden messenger in. The woman was obviously used to serving Spiders, finding nothing unusual in seeing her target sitting for a portrait, and simply presented him with another wallet of documents. If she had flown herself ragged in meeting up with the airship her manner certainly did not show it.

"Find her some victuals," Teornis ordered the crewman who had escorted her in. "I shall have returns for her to take away shortly."

He unsealed the wallet carefully and stripped out the topmost scroll, reading down what Nero guessed was a summary of the most important points of the enclosed documents. Nothing in his face betrayed any reaction but, when he finally spoke, he announced, "It would seem that the diplomatic channels are closing."

Nero said nothing, waiting for further exposition.

"We sent ambassadors to the Wasp forces massing at Tark, and to Solarno as well. Now we have the response."

Again, Nero waited. Teornis' smile had become a hard line.

"We have been told that all land north of Seldis is officially the Empire," Teornis said, "and that, if we interfere, then Seldis itself shall be invested in siege. My own efforts, it seems, have stalled them as far as they are willing to be stalled, and now they set about the business as Wasp-kinden are wont to do: with simple force. The Wasp Second Army has marched from Tark against Merro and Egel, and the Eighth sits in the Ant city still, waiting to strike if we venture outside our walls. Well, we are at war now, so we must expect such treatment." He paused a moment, perhaps evaluating how much Nero actually needed to know. "Our ambassadors to Solarno were killed, I see. They were seized as spies and executed.

I am afraid that you are flying into a tempest, Master Nero. Therefore I hope you and your friend are strong enough to battle your way through."

After Nero had gone, Teornis returned to the reports his agents had brought him. They were penned in elegant hands, a collection of polite nothings, niceties, social calendars and fashions. It took a true Spider-kinden Manipulus to pierce through the nothings and decode to the steel core of information within. *It is all coming together*, which meant that it was all falling apart. Teornis read and read.

I have to assume, he thought, *that there will come a time when the coming-together and the falling-apart converge.*

Distant news informed him that two Wasp armies were marching on Sarn and its allies, but he was barely interested in that. The Ants now had their chance: they would grasp it or fail. If the worst came, then the northern half of the Lowlands was expendable. That it would complicate the defence of Collegium was the only way in which it mattered to him. Collegium he wished to keep free. Its value as a grateful tool of the Spiderlands was too high to neglect. He had not gone so far to lift the siege the previous year, just to have the Wasps taking the place now.

Even if it lost eventually, Sarn would occupy its Wasp tormentors for many tendays before *they* occupied *it*, and after Sarn the mopping up of the so-called Ancient League would take even longer. Teornis was meanwhile more concerned about local conditions.

The Wasp army that had left Tark so recently had set course directly for the Fly warrens of Merro and Egel. True to form the Fly-kinden had surrendered without even drawing a blade, swearing fealty to the Empire from a distance of many miles, just as they would happily swear to the Spiderlands or the Tarkesh or whoever else came against them. Such fealty would, of course, last only as long as there was sufficient strength to enforce it, but the Wasp possession of the two interconnected Fly warrens was a fact he had to live with.

From Egel and Merro the going got tougher for the Empire as their supply lines became increasingly stretched, by then conveniently close to the Spiderlands border and wanting but a knife to cut them. Beyond the Fly-kinden territories was the island city-state of Kes, a formidable investment for any besieger, especially with the new weapons that the Kessen had taken away from Sarn. Down the coast from Kes was the Felyal, whose Mantis-kinden were still bloody-handed from their destruction of the Imperial Fourth.

The imperial strategists must surely have a plan for Kes and for the Mantids, but as yet Teornis' agents had not uncovered it. He suspected that the general of this latest army was keeping it mostly within his head, where it could not be easily spied upon.

There was also the problem of the fortified garrison that the Wasps had left north of Seldis, and the Eighth Army waiting in nearby Tark. The Spiders still controlled the sea, as the landlocked imperials did not seem to recognize how useful it might be as a means of attack down the coast, but if Teornis wanted to move soldiers north by land to support the Lowlands, then he would have to fight them for every inch of ground.

Well, it may come to that, he decided. His family, the Aldanrael, was already gathering its allies and forces in Seldis and Everis. House guards from a dozen of the noble Aristoi families were jostling shoulders in the streets and challenging each other to duels, whilst mercenary and Satrapy companies were either shipped in or marched up the Silk Road past Siennis. More than half of the contributions had been made by Spider families that would have marked the Aldanrael down as their bitter foes not long ago. The imperial capture of Solarno had damaged Spider pride, and Teornis was making good use of the backlash.

Solarno, of course: another angle to consider. Solarno, the renegade city that declined to be part of the Spiderlands, instead enmeshing itself into the provincial politics around the watery expanse of the Exalsee. Easy to see why the Wasps had thought they could take it, although, as in so many things, they failed to understand. Solarno was a renegade, yes, but it was the Spider-kindens' own pet renegade. It was the little political backwater where a Spider Aristos could go and paddle about, and not worry too much about who they upset or fret over any repercussions. It was the manipulus' seaside resort. A great many influential families had a fondness for Solarno.

Not so the Aldanrael, but the family had seen just how useful a banner the invasion of Solarno would provide. Teornis thought about the Fly girl, Taki, how dreadfully serious and earnest she was. *Well, good luck to her.* Whether she liberated the city or if not, either outcome would serve.

He turned to the next report, from an agent within Kes, and tried to measure how long it would be before the Wasps were, one way or another, at the gates of Collegium.

Subterfuge and distraction. That was the Solarnese game, of course: the very board on which he had just placed his ignorant agents. Nero seemed a capable, if uninspired, choice and Teornis always preferred Fly-kinden tools where Spiders could not be risked. The aviatrix, though, was an unknown quantity. *She could be dangerous. She could also be invaluable. I hope she's as good as she thinks she is.* His mind focused on Taki, already far ahead of his airship in her refurbished flier. *Save your city if you can, girl,* he thought, *but, above all, give the Wasps something still more to think of. If you can manage that, then let Solarno burn to the ground for all I care.*

Taki made the flight from Seldis to Porta Mavralis by coasting on the updraughts above the Silk Road that skirted the edge of the Dryclaw. From there her last chute wound the engine enough to bring her into the Mavralis airfield.

Nero would be following by whatever means he could. He had even exacted from her two-thirds of a promise to stay there until he joined her.

"Just wait for me," he had requested her. "I won't be long. You don't want to go off half ready, so why not taste the air, scout about, but wait for me."

She had folded her arms. "If I learn that someone needs me back home, then I'm going. If Solarno needs me, or my friends need me." Seeing his pained expression, she had then relented a little. "But other than that, I'll wait—so long as you don't take too long catching me up." She regarded him dubiously. "I'm going to have to ask, though, why do you even care? It isn't your fight, so why are you even here?"

And his smile had gone from brash to self-mocking to brash again. "Because I like you, girl, why else?" A bald, knuckle-faced man twice her age, and not even of her profession.

She was still trying to work out what she thought of that. Still, he might be useful back in Solarno, if she could judge from how swiftly he had won over Domina Genissa, her previous employer.

The shock of the imperial invasion was still resounding through Porta Mavralis. Trade all about the Exalsee had been thrown into chaos, with the Wasps still trying to clench their fist on the city. They were turning most ships away from Solarno docks, impounding some, allowing a few others to trade freely, all decided apparently at random. Listening to this news, Taki formed the opinion that the Wasps themselves were divided, different officers ordering different strategies, and she further understood that the Crystal Standard party was still trying to assert itself as the new master of Solarno against the resistance of all the rival factions. There would be a reckoning for that pack of traitors, she knew, when they found out what kind of venomous creatures they had given their city over to.

Teornis had not sent her off with no help at all. He had given her a sealed introduction to his chief agent in Mavralis, and Taki met with her on the second day after her arrival: a lean, sly-looking Spider woman named Odyssa.

"Refugees are still fleeing Solarno," the spy explained. "There's almost a quarter of the Path of Jade's members of the Corta Lucidi set up here in Mavralis, claiming to be a government in exile. Others have dispersed further around the Exalsee, to Princep Exilla, Ostrander, Diroveshni and Chasme. The Wasps are still fighting to lock down the streets and gain total control of the city. Their colonel has not even been able to proclaim himself governor and four or five of the top Crystal Standard collaborators are dead."

"By whose hand?"

"Nobody knows," the Spider replied. Odyssa's smile said that she had her own thoughts. "There's enough general mistrust, though, that Wasp assassins are not so far from people's thoughts."

"Good." *Let them continue to fight amongst themselves, especially before their prize is secure.* "I need to find out where certain individuals have gone, if you can help me."

"My Lord-Martial does not prohibit it, so give me a list of them and I will see what I can uncover." Odyssa slid a blank scroll over to her, with an inkpot and chitin quill balanced on it.

They may be all dead, Taki thought. *Some of them will surely be dead.* She was thinking of her fellows, her peers, the fighting pilots of Solarno and the Exalsee. *My brothers and sisters of the air, my glorious enemies and closest friends.* "What else are you allowed to give me," she asked, "or is it just information?"

"By no means, for my Lord-Martial is not so parsimonious," Odyssa replied. "I myself am staying at the Cartel-House of the Craesandral family. Do you want to know who my fellow guests are there?"

Taki ground her teeth. "Forgive me, Bella Odyssa, but I am a pilot, not a game player. My city is under the yoke, so please just say what you mean."

Odyssa's responding glance was pitying but Taki could live with that. "I have twenty Craesandral house guards as company, and two hundred mercenaries from Iak."

Taki blinked. "You will . . . ?"

"Make your plans, little one, and I shall help you as I may. When the time comes for blood-letting on the streets of Solarno, we shall be with you."

Two hundred and twenty. Odyssa looked very pleased with herself but Taki was already seeing in her mind the mighty imperial airship *Starnest* and the hundreds of Wasp soldiers descending from it. *And how many friends are left in Solarno that will fight?* She needed her friends, her fellow pilots, and she needed a plan.

And she needed someone she could trust to go into Solarno on her behalf, and that someone was not Odyssa.

It would have to be Nero.

SIX

There were certain businesses that did not stop even for the war. In fact there were some businesses that took on extra staff.

"Small package work," the Fly-kinden smuggler had explained to Tisamon. "Messages in. Messages out. Weapons. People sometimes. Can fit a couple back there, at a pinch."

The smuggling was accomplished via a single stripped-down automotive, with six high, narrow-rimmed wheels powered by an over-wound clockwork engine that ran almost silently, so that the vessel seemed to skate over the ground, and to fly when it vaulted a rise. The Fly-kinden drove it, and fixed it, and did his best to outrun any trouble, but now he kept a couple of guards on the payroll at all times, because he earned his high profit margins through danger and secrecy. The danger was attested by the vacancy that Tisamon had now filled.

It was as easy as that to get to occupied Helleron. Just short of two tendays, hanging from the scaffolding that was all the Fly had left of the automotive's original shell, and they were then able to merge with the stream of travellers coming into Helleron from Tark and Asta, heading up the Silk Road from the south.

"And from here on, we're legal," the Fly-kinden had explained. "The Wasps might think they run the city, but it's still a market and not a military camp. The Beetles know better than to turn people away, and there isn't a magnate in the city who doesn't make some coin for himself through the Black Guild. From what I hear, most of Wasp customs are on the take now, too. They learn fast, that lot."

Helleron, a city devoted to the eternal cycle of building and decay, where today's grinding wheel erased the tracks of yesterday: a city of machines that took in and spat out a hundred men and women a day who had come there to make their fortunes, feeding them to its furnaces. This was where he had come before, after Atryssa's betrayal of him, after his own betrayal of her. This was Helleron, where he had been able to forget, in the unqualified shedding of blood, what had first driven him there. In a twisted, bitter sense he had fond memories of Helleron.

It had been only a short space of absolution, between his leaving this place and his return to it. Stenwold's call had summoned him out of his exile, away from his meaningless round of street fighting and the settling of quarrels. It was Stenwold who had given him the chance to redeem himself, to make himself the man he should be. For a brief span—fighting the Wasps here and in Myna, training his daughter, questing in Jerez—it had seemed that he would succeed in rediscovering himself.

Weak at heart. He should have stayed in the Felyal, remained true to his kinden, but he had betrayed them for a Spider woman, and thus had begun the road of failures which had led him here. Looking about him at the grimy bustle of Helleron, he smiled thinly. What better tomb for one such as he than this filthy warren of blackened metal.

The building he sought had not changed, the door's plaque almost unreadable beneath the dirt of a year: "Rowen Palasso: Factor." Once inside Tisamon gave his name and had no more than a minute's wait before being shown to the third-storey office of the proprietor herself.

Rowen Palasso was a Beetle-kinden woman of middle years, probably not far from Tisamon's own age. Her hair had been dyed red not too recently, and her face was baggy and lined. She was one of the middle-merchants of Helleron, who had worked at her trade all her life and never quite made the fortune and the success of it that she had planned, a type the city was full of. Her trade was a liaison for men and women of undoubted but clandestine skills: housebreakers and thieves, thugs and strong-armers, duellists and killers. In defiance of the darkened-corner conventions of her associates, her office was as domestic a place as Tisamon had ever seen, with cushions on the chairs and little embroidered pictures on the walls with homely mottos. In fact, it was calculated to put her patrons and her clients off their stride with its cosy banality.

"Tisamon of Felyal, as I live and breathe," Rowen exclaimed. "And here was I thinking you'd given us the slip. They always come back to Helleron, though."

"It seems that way," he said quietly.

"And here you are, looking for a little work to tide you over?"

"I want to fight," he told her.

"Of course you do. It's what you're good at. Carpenters want to make things out of wood, and artificers want to tinker with machines, and you want to kill people. Why not? Go with your talents, that's what I say."

It was indeed what she said. He had heard it a dozen times before, at least. "What do you have for me?" he asked.

"It isn't as easy as that, dear blade, not at all," she told him. "City's under new management now."

"I refuse to believe the Wasps have put your trade out of business."

She gave him a bleak smile. "Not quite, Tisamon, not quite. Your old stamping grounds have mostly gone, though. It's like the end of an era. All that gang fighting, street fighting, where you made your name: gone now, the lot of it. The Empire has been rooting out any fiefs that won't bow the knee. The only work

I could get you in that direction would be signing up for your own suicide with those few still holding out."

Tisamon nodded, thinking.

"On the other hand, if you were interested in something a little different . . ." Her bright smiles were less convincing than her bleak ones.

"Tell me."

"The Wasps have brought in a new kind of entertainment. They're very keen on it, and so all the locals who want in with them are keen on it too, though it's a little . . . gauche."

"Prize fighting," Tisamon filled in.

"It's not like the skill matches the Ants have," Rowen warned. "Bloodsports—men against animals, or a duellist against a pack of unarmed slaves or prisoners. Nothing *honourable*, Tisamon. Not your line, I'd have thought." She watched him keenly. "But if you were interested, I could make the arrangements. It's very new, and anyone can put up a fighter. Slaves get entered, mostly, but there's no law about it . . ."

And so you have found your new place in the order, Tisamon considered, and did not know if he meant the woman or himself.

"Arrange it," he told her.

◊ ◊ ◊

Seda had never before seen the Mosquito in anything other than robes of black, or the imperial colours her brother sometimes dressed him in, but now she had discovered him, sitting cross-legged on the floor of the mirror room, surrounded by a glitter of candles. He was swathed in pale clothing that was as tight on his limbs as bandages, secured by ribbons of red tied at his elbows, wrists and knees. His otherwise uncovered head had a band of dark cloth circling his brow, making the white flesh of his skull look more corpselike than ever.

"What are you dressed as, sorcerer?" Seda asked acidly, once the guard had left. That she was now allowed to be alone and unwatched with Uctebri was a recent occurrence, and she did not know whether it was down to her brother the Emperor's preoccupations elsewhere, or to Uctebri's subtle influence.

When he lifted his head to look at her, she took an automatic step back, because there was something in that skull face that she had never seen before.

Satisfaction, she realized: naked, gloating satisfaction. His bloody eyes, that raw, shifting mark half covered by his headband, pulsed scarlet and wild. His lips pulled back into a grin that showed her every pointed, fish-like tooth in his head.

He lifted his hands toward her, and within them was clasped a gnarled wooden box, its surface carved and carved over again.

"Through hardship and travail . . ." he hissed. "Through blood and fire, treachery and theft, it is here. The Rekef have prevailed at last. *And the box is mine.*"

She made herself regard him coldly. "And was it worth it?"

"A thousandfold," he said. He rose smoothly, all pretence of age and infirmity now gone, and she wondered whose blood he was replete with, to have given him his youth back. "I have just been performing certain introductions. This garb of mine, these ribbons, there is nothing magical in them. They are, however, symbols that have significance to certain things from a certain time. I have thus identified myself to them, so they will not turn their influence onto me."

"Where will this influence fall, then?" she asked him.

"Where I will it, or where it will, so long as it does not meddle with my plans," Uctebri replied. His robe had been discarded by one wall, and he retrieved it with one spindly arm and shrugged it on, still holding tightly to the box with the other hand. She had the odd idea that he had seen himself through her eyes for a moment, and found himself feeling self-conscious.

"This box," she said. "Is it something for your amusement, or does it bear on what we must do?"

"How goes your work?" he asked, drawing his cowl up. She thought that he sounded disappointed, almost. Had he wished her to seem more impressed?

"I have some colonels on my side, Brugan among them. I flatter old Governor Thanred, for what little influence he has left. A major of engineers, a major of the Slave Corps, two factors of the Consortium, all with me now. Disappointed and passed-over men, the ambitious and the vengeful. I am spinning my webs as if I was born a Spider."

"Good," Uctebri said. "Then, in answer to your question, the Shadow Box does not merely *bear* on our plans; it *is* the plan. Life and death, my princess, both reside within this box, and are there for me to draw upon. Life, for you, and death . . ."

She raised a hand before he could say it, even though she knew they could not be overheard. *I cannot trust you, can I?* She knew he must be planning to control her as a puppet ruler of his Empire. *Still, he gives me more chance than my brother.* "It seems very small," she said, archly disdainful. "I do wonder whether you do not throw this object in my way simply to amaze and mystify me."

His grin broke out again now, within the confines of his hood. "My dear doubting princess, do you believe in ghosts?"

She made to say that of course she did not, but he was so plainly waiting for this response that she just gave him an uninterested shrug.

"I cannot hope to make you understand how the world is truly made," he told her. "Metaphor, then: the world is a weave, like threads woven into cloth." His hand came out of his sleeve with a strip of his red ribbon.

"If you say so."

"Everything, stone, trees, beasts, the sky, the waters, all are a weave of fabric," he said patiently. "But when you *think*, it is different. Your thinking snarls the fabric, knots it. If you were a magician, you could use the knot of your mind to pull on other threads. That is magic, and now you see how very simple it is. I wonder everyone does not become an enchanter." With a swift intertangling of his fingers, there was now a lumpy knot in the centre of the ribbon.

She managed to shrug again. "I cannot deny that you have a power, Mosquito. I cannot think to ever understand it—and I think it is better I do not."

"Perhaps." He grinned at her. "What happens, though, after you die? What happens to the knot?" He pulled at the tape's ends sharply, and the knot had vanished, as though it had never been. "Alas, unravelled in an instant, my princess." His grin was conspiratorial. "But what if it were not?"

"I . . . do not understand."

"The body gone—dead, rotten, decay and then dust—but the *knot* of mind still there, trapped within the weave, impossible to undo." Now he was moving about the room, pinching out candle flames between his fingertips, bringing on a gloom that she felt must match the evening outside.

"I do not see how that can be."

"But then you do not understand any of what I say, for you merely see the convenient images I speak of," he said. "Laetrimae, would you come forth? Drama now requires it."

Seda frowned at him. "What are you talking about."

"Drama indeed," said Uctebri. "Perhaps more than is required, but the Mantis-kinden were always a race prone to the grand gesture."

It was chilly in the room, and the dark seemed to have grown more swiftly than the dying candles could account for but, most disturbing of all, Uctebri was looking behind her, past her shoulder at something *else*.

She turned, and screamed at what she saw there, falling backward on to the floor of the mirror room and scrabbling to put more distance between herself and the apparition that had manifested between herself and the door.

It was a woman, tall and lean and pale, and clad in piecemeal plates that might have been armour or chitin, and her body pierced through and through with briars that twisted and arched and grew and impaled her over and over, and yet, despite it all, her face was calm and beatific and quite, quite insane.

"Behold the greatest mistake of the Moth-kinden," hissed Uctebri, "the greatest knot in the weave of history, and a knot that will continue on and on and never be undone. She, however, is only their spokeswoman, my princess. There are a thousand others of them, snarled together like the vines that pierce her, and they are Mantis and Moth both, tangled and matted and interwoven. The creation of the single greatest act of magic ever known, and here I hold it in my hands."

The tortured woman's face had adopted a new expression, and Seda saw that it was loathing, and that it was directed entirely at Uctebri. She found that she sympathized with that emotion wholeheartedly.

◁▷ ◁▷ ◁▷

Tisamon returned to his rented rooms feeling shaken and sick at heart.

It was not from the fighting, which had been the only part of it to make sense. After all, the complicity that existed between people trying to kill one another bred a brotherhood he had long been a part of.

They had converted a marketplace into an arena, the Wasps ordering the locals to tear down their stalls and put up ranks of tiered seating instead. It looked not so different from the Prowess Forum, of fond and distant memory. That was what he had expected, too: duels of skill, followed by polite applause. To a Mantis-kinden there was nothing inherently wrong in a duel of expertise that ended in death. It was the logical final expression of the art form, that was all.

What he had just been through was different, and soiled him in a way he could not have guessed at.

He had entered into the arena with a dozen other fighters. Each had been introduced, lifting a weapon high for the crowd's approval. They had been a motley band: Beetles, rogue Ants, half-breeds, even a Scorpion-kinden with a sword standing as tall as he was. There had been no alliances between them, no rules. When the official Wasp overseer had cast down his gilded wooden baton, the fighters had simply gone at each other. At that moment Tisamon had felt the calm trance of his profession come upon him, and he had cocked his claw back and met the nearest opponent joyfully: a Beetle-kinden armoured with overlapping plates as far as his knees and elbows, who had swung at him with a double-headed spear.

Tisamon had caught the spear in the crook of his claw, slammed the spines of his other arm down into the gap between the man's neck and shoulder, and then slashed him across the throat as he staggered backward.

Next had been an Ant-kinden with a tall shield and a short sword, and no armour save for a metal helm. Tisamon had killed him, too, and then two more, and by that time the remaining fighters had taken notice and turned on him. There had been six of them, determined to take him down all together before resuming their separate quarrels.

It had been a demanding contest, for they had none of them been poor fighters, but they were not Weaponsmasters, either, nor trained to fight alongside each other. He eventually finished them all, killing four outright and cutting two so badly that they could not fight on.

Only then did he hear the uproar of the crowd. Whilst fighting, he had been oblivious to it. He had not been fighting for *them*, but for himself.

They had gone mad: cheering and shouting and shrieking. He had stood in the arena's heart with the blood of eight men on his blade, and the sheer force and power of their acclaim almost drove him to his knees.

They were not done with him, though. They had then wanted him to kill the two opponents he had let live.

It was *unclean*.

He realized then, looking up at the faces of Wasp soldiers and administrators, at the faces of the Beetle-kinden wealthy and their servants and guests, that they did not actually *care* about the skill. It did not matter to them that he was a Weaponsmaster, that he had perfected a style of fighting that was a thousand years old and that he was *good*. They were there only for the blood, and if he had come in and butchered two dozen pitifully armed slaves they would have called out just the same.

But now they loved him. He was their champion of the moment, because he had shed more blood for them than his defeated opponents had.

The next match was indeed two dozen slaves: convicts from the cells, men and women from the Spider-kinden markets, or simply those who had somehow displeased Helleron's new masters. He had not wanted to fight them, but they had been promised their freedom if they killed him, and so they desperately tried. He waited for them, gave them every chance. As they neared him, he had discovered that his hatred for slave owners was very readily turning into contempt for those who had let themselves become enslaved.

And the crowd had applauded him, as though it was all some kind of *show.* Looking about him, he saw how the Beetle-kinden of Helleron were learning very swiftly from their new masters. Their shouting was the loudest and longest.

When it was over he had told them to send his fee to Rowen Palasso, and then he was gone.

Never again. There were other ways, honest ways, for a man to make a living by the blade. He now sat on his bed in the dingy little top-storey room he had rented, and thought hard. He found that his hands were shaking: it was not the blood of others that could do this to him, but their approbation.

Differing kinden had differing traditions, in the duel. The Ants loved their sword games, but they loved the skill and precision most, and seldom took matters beyond drawing the first blood. In Collegium it remained a polite sport of wooden swords suitable for College masters and youngsters to watch. The Mantis-kinden killed one another sometimes, but only by mutual agreement, and never for the amusement of an audience.

He knew that the Spider-kinden had their slaves fight one another, sometimes, simply for the sport. He had not thought to find the same decadent tastes magnified in the Wasps.

Tisamon rose and went to the door. He would find some other way of surviving, or some other city. This life was not for him.

He was not alone in the room.

He turned instantly, the claw appearing over his hand, its gauntlet about his arm, slashing out at where he *knew* someone stood.

His shock, when it clanged off the swift parry of an identical blade, held him motionless, easy victim to a riposte. He could feel the steel there, but saw nothing.

She formed out of the air as a faint shadow, writhing and twisting with vines and thorns.

Tisamon, she named him. *Weaponsmaster.*

He stared, feeling fear creep over him. Magic was something he had no defence against.

Tisamon, she said again. He could just make out Mantis features there, amidst the blur of leaves and the glitter of compound eyes.

"What do you want with me?" he asked.

I am here to judge you, she said. *Are you not seeking judgment?*

He realized that he had already fallen to his knees. "Judgment . . . for what?"

Her eyes, insubstantial as they were, held him tight. *You know your own crimes. Are you not seeking atonement even now, in this spiritless city?*

"There can be no atonement," he choked out.

And so you must atone forever? That is a familiar concept of our kinden. We have so many laws and rules, and therefore we cannot avoid breaking them. We are always imperfect by the impossible standards that we set ourselves. Do we not therefore live our lives in an agony of thwarted desires, our laws pressing against our skin like sharp thorns?

"Who are you?" He stared at her. "*What* are you?"

I am a monument to Mantis pride and failure, Tisamon. They called me Laetrimae, before my fall. Five hundred years I have wept and atoned, and yet I still have not escaped the consequences of my actions. Nor shall you.

He had no words, no thoughts save that surely this must be the thing he had gone looking for when he fled Collegium. Surely this was the judgment he deserved.

What shall I judge you for, Tisamon? she asked him. *You were false to your people in the lover you took. You were false to yourself, in the guilt you felt for it. You were false to your lover in your abandonment of her, and of your daughter as well. You have been false to your past lover in your new love, and now false to your new love in your turning away from her. Is there anything of worth you have not cast aside, Tisamon?*

"No."

But there is. You may have thrown aside the badge, but you are a Weaponsmaster still. Are you not aware of the duties that role carries? You are yet the defender of your people, all your people—even those such as I who have fallen so far that your own disgrace now seems but a stumble.

"What could you need defending from?"

Evil and rapacious men who would steal that which belongs to our kind—our legacy, our history.

"I am unworthy—"

It is because you are unworthy that I reach out to you, she continued urgently. *You have suffered, but there is a suffering and disgrace that no one of our kind should bear. Who else but a vessel already broken can be asked to withstand the strain?*

"What do you want of me?" he demanded.

There are, even now, men coming to take you prisoner, Tisamon. You have attracted their notice. They wish to take you and enslave you. You have been sold by your own factor. She leads them to you even now.

He was on his feet on the instant, the blade of his claw opening. "Rowen has betrayed me?"

The betrayer betrayed. Her words silenced him. *If you would truly seek atonement for your pride, Tisamon, you must let them take you. You must submit to the worst before you might hope for any redemption.*

"Take me? You mean . . . ?"

Or have you pride, yet, that fears to be broken?

He was at the door now, pointing his blade at her. "You cannot ask me to become a slave. No Mantis has ever fallen so far."

The shadow that was Laetrimae drifted closer, passing right through the cramped bed. *I am a slave, Tisamon. I am a slave to the Shadow Box that you let slip. Now, as a result, I am a slave of our enemies. Believe me, I am all that is Mantis: all fragile pride and fear of failure. I do not ask this of you lightly.* She was standing before him, still transparent, a mere smudge on the air. *In this way you may erase the stain that you see on your soul.*

"Is it so bad?" he said hoarsely.

No, she said simply, *save in your own mind. But that is one judge that you can never escape from, nor hope to deceive.*

A great weight settled on him, even as he heard the clump of feet at the foot of the stairs. That would be Rowen and whoever she had sold him to. Wasps, most likely.

He let the claw slip away, banishing it, and went to sit on the bed to await their arrival.

SEVEN

T halric straightened his armour, which felt strange on him now after even so short a time without it. *Perhaps it's because I no longer have a right to wear it*, he thought wryly.

"Right," he said. The curving-sided hold of the *Cleaver* was crowded with fuel barrels, save for a space near the pilot's chair that had been fenced off for Achaeos' sickbed. The Moth had propped himself up on his elbows, still ghastly pale, but watching Thalric with something that might, in a healthier man, be considered humour.

"So, how is this going to work, Major?" he asked, just loud enough to be heard over the engines.

Is it Major, or is it Captain? Thalric asked himself. Do I now go in as army or Rekef? Rekef would make more sense, but a Rekef major of his description might strike an unwelcome chord in the wrong quarters. It would be his wretched luck to encounter another man who both recognized him and had heard of his disgrace.

"I can see the city now," Che called out to them from her seat, peering through a viewing slit past which driving rain was lashing. Fortunately the *Cleaver* was a solid, workmanlike flier, and Thalric wondered if a flimsier vessel could even have made it here through the foul weather of the last day or so. It was the last gasp of winter, he guessed, stomping up and down the east of the Lowlands and making its presence known.

He discovered himself as nervous as an actor about to go on stage. *This is absurd. This is my profession.* Or at least it had been, not so long ago.

"Where do I bring us in?" Che asked.

"How am I supposed to know?" Thalric snapped at her. "I don't imagine the builders included an airfield, unless they were more prophetic even than legend gives them credit for."

"No, I see it now," Che said. "They've set aside some fields, I think, just some fields and some huts. There are some heliopters there, and a collapsed airship. I'll bring us in beside it. Thalric, you're ready with your speech, right?"

Thalric nodded, then realized that she could not see it, and said, "Yes, right," in a voice that, to him, lacked all conviction. Now came the testing moment.

The *Cleaver* jostled with the wind, was buffeted in return, and then the lurch in his stomach informed him that they were dropping in fast. He heard Achaeos groan at the change—for an airborne race such as the Moths it was remarkable how much mechanical flight distressed them. Then Che had touched the *Cleaver* down harder than was wise, and Thalric was bounced off his feet, sitting down hard up against the curving wall, hearing Achaeos' pained gasp. They were instantly slewing sideways, and Thalric had a moment to think of their altitude, the narrow mountain platforms, a makeshift airstrip that was no more than a mud-slicked field. He clutched at the lashed-down barrels, wondering if he could get the hatch open before . . .

The *Cleaver* struck something solid and skidded back a few feet before coming, blessedly, to a stop.

"There are some soldiers coming over here, in a hurry," Che said helpfully. Thalric straightened up and went across to the hatch, slipping back the catches that held it shut. As he pushed it open, the rain drove down hard, but he flashed his wings and pushed himself up on to the barrel-like hull of the *Cleaver.* There were indeed soldiers coming, a full dozen of them, some on the ground and some in the air, all brandishing spears. He waited patiently for them, feeling the rain soak into his hair, into the arming tunic beneath his mail. As soon as they saw that a Wasp had emerged from the unknown flier their headlong approach slowed a little, and then a sergeant alighted before him, with a salute.

"Excuse me, sir, we weren't notified—"

"You wouldn't have been," Thalric cut him off. "I require lodgings for three, an engineer to repair this vehicle, and a meeting as soon as possible with your duty officer. Oh, and round up some doctors. Local ones would be best."

The sergeant blinked at him. "I'll first have to ask who you are, sir, and what's your authority."

And here goes the dice. "Captain Manus, sergeant, on my way to Capitas. Rest assured the duty officer will get all the details he needs."

The sergeant was still not convinced, but in Thalric's experience they seldom were. Nevertheless the man sent some of his men off to relay Thalric's requests, which was perhaps as much as could be expected.

"Good," Thalric commented. "Now get two of your men inside the flier. I have a casualty that needs to get under cover without delay."

He dropped back inside ahead of them, confident that the sergeant would follow to keep him in sight, and that he would get his chance to win the man over then and there.

The sergeant and his man came next and stopped short, staring suspiciously at Achaeos and at Che.

"Is there something wrong, Sergeant?" Thalric asked sharply.

"Sir, these are—"

"Servants of the Empire, Sergeant," Thalric said firmly. "There is a war on, you may have heard. Some places are no longer safe for *servants* of the Empire." He placed just the right stress on the words because, of course, an officer of the imperial secret service, the dreaded Rekef, would never say it, not straight out, but there were always times when it paid to be recognized for what they really were.

The sergeant was clearly not a stupid man and it was fairly well known how the Rekef Outlander employed agents of all races. Now his hurried salute and his issuing orders to his men provided all the reassurance Thalric needed.

Shortly thereafter, Thalric had Achaeos safely stowed in an infirmary, with some of his Moth-kinden kinsmen staring nervously at him from around the door, and Che sitting at the man's bedside. By that time Thalric himself was standing before the local Rekef Outlander officer.

The man was another sergeant, and Thalric could not believe his luck. He guessed that Tharn merited the barest minimum of Rekef presence, probably making do with this one man alone. Nobody cared about such backward little places. As far as the Empire was concerned, the garrison here was merely to keep the Moths from bothering Helleron, so the Tharen governor was only a major and the Rekef had better things to do. He would feel ashamed, later, of the way in which he now browbeat the wretched Rekef sergeant, but maybe that aggression was something he had been needing to get out of his system for a long time.

And news travelled fast. After that, when he strode the corridors of Tharn, now lit with hastily cobbled-together gas lanterns, the locals and the conquerors alike gave him a wide berth, pointing him out to each other as *the Rekef's man*. In the shock of relief, he almost forgot that it was not true, and that Che and Achaeos were even there. Instead he went to the suite of rooms he had commandeered, with good-sized windows cut into the outer wall of the mountain, and waited there for the information he had requested. For what else would the Rekef's man do, after arriving, but receive reports and pick the local intelligencer's brains?

Che had wanted to stay with Achaeos throughout, but the Moths refused to tend him in her presence, finding that a Beetle-kinden in their halls was more of an insult than any number of Wasps. Only after she had reluctantly withdrawn did his people begin their business with him. The doctors arrived before the inquisitors: administering salves and poultices, chants and charms, two full days of careful ritual and healing skill. By the time the questions started Achaeos was fit enough to raise himself up on one elbow. He was able, at least, to look his questioner in the eye.

She was a Moth of middle-young years with a severe face, and two others came in behind her. One of them was a young scribe with a scroll, and the other a woman bearing a staff, which identified her to Achaeos as a guard, although the Wasps present would not have guessed it. He supposed that the Wasps must have banned the carrying of weapons inside Tharn, but a staff was beneath their notice.

"I understand you to be a Rekef agent," began their leader, with enough questioning in her tone for him to know that he had not been condemned out of hand. The presence of the doctors should already have told him that, but he was taking nothing for granted. Even now he did not know whether it was simply his imagined link to the conquering Empire that protected him from his own people's wrath.

"Is that all you understand?" he asked her. His voice was weak, and he kept it soft, making her strain to hear his words. At this point, words were all he had to fight with.

"You are Achaeos," she noted, "you didn't leave here in glory. In fact you nearly did not leave here at all. During this last year you have progressed from uninspired student to positive maverick—and now here you are."

He kept his feelings from his face. "Is a man not allowed to come home? I may have dallied with exile, but I do not believe a sentence of exile was ever passed."

She glanced backward, but not at her companions, so he knew that they were being overheard by another—one of the Skryres he guessed—who might be anywhere in Tharn.

"There are no Wasps guarding the door," she said, "so we speak only before our own people. Or at least *my* own people. Do you really still claim the Moths of Tharn as yours?"

"I do."

"Then you are no Rekef, or Wasp agent."

"Well deduced."

If she felt he was baiting her, she gave no sign of it. They faced each other without expression. "Our situation here is currently delicate. We do not wish some agitator appearing in the halls of Tharn, spreading confusion."

"You would rather remain slaves?"

"It takes more than a single glance to truly tell the master from the slave."

That made him pause. Again she was unreadable but there had been something in her tone, in that simple platitude, to suggest that there was more going on here than he had thought.

He narrowed his eyes as she glanced over her shoulder again. It was a bad habit of hers and there was no need for it. It suggested someone who had spent a long time away from her own people. *But where?* And the answer was quick to suggest itself. *She has been in the Empire, surely. What is going on here?*

It was not that she was simply being observed, either. She must be receiving instructions from a Skryre and they did not sit well with her. Her expression was beginning to tell him things.

"I am Xaraea," she announced suddenly.

He held on to that for a moment, feeling his heart leap, for his people did not give up their names easily. It was a sign of status: to know a name gave you power. To be given a name made you at least an equal. That could only mean he had been let into something.

"What is happening here?" he asked her.

"You know much of what passes in the Lowlands?"

"I know some of it."

She considered him. "You are not strong enough yet to leave your bed."

"I am stronger than I was, but no."

"But later you will be, and there is someone you must meet."

He stared at her suspiciously. "And who would that be?"

At last her mouth twisted into a slight smile. "Who else but our new master, the governor of Tharn?"

Che paused at the doorway of Thalric's room, suddenly doubting herself. Surely there must be some other option, but they had shooed her out of Achaeos' sickroom with venomous looks and mutterings about their *Hated Enemy*.

The corridors of Tharn had never been friendly, save when Achaeos had been beside her. Even with her Art-given sight, which could pierce the darkness the Moths habitually lived in, it was a world of hostile gazes, pointedly turned backs, and lantern-bearing Wasp soldiers who stared suspiciously at her. It was enough to make her wish she could *not* see it all.

She had spent some time at an exterior window, watching the rain lash down over the landing strip where the *Cleaver* was almost lost amongst a dozen imperial flying machines. The rain had made her unhappy. She had found herself yearning to fly, as she had done for the first time, when last she was here.

And so here she was, hand poised to knock on . . . what? The Moths had few doors, only arches and more arches, so that every room was part of a labyrinth of chambers that went back and back further into the mountain, all of them as chill as the weather outside. What doors they had were hidden screens and secret panels in the stone, which no stranger would guess were there. The Moths never seemed to notice the cold either, these strange people who otherwise seemed so frail. She had seen imperial soldiers well wrapped up in scarves and greatcoats, their breath steaming as they complained to each other, whilst Moth servants padded past them in light tunics and sandals.

She heard a shuffling noise from inside, a shadow cast over the shifting light that spilled out of the room, and there he was in the doorway: Thalric, in his banded armour still, a Wasp amongst his own people once more.

This was a mistake, she decided. The strange thing was that he seemed to think so, too. His expression, on finding her there, was bitter, almost resigned.

"What?" she asked him instinctively.

"Forgive me, it is you who appear to have sought me out," he said, stepping back. She could feel the warmth inside, a fire lit to complement no fewer than four lanterns: a little corner of the Empire staked out against this foreign darkness.

"I . . . wanted to talk to someone, anyone," she said. "And the Moths don't like me, and I can't be beside Achaeos, and I don't care for Wasps."

He raised an eyebrow at that, and she scowled at him. "You know what I mean."

"I do." He returned to his desk, where he had been sifting through papers, dozens of them, some rolled up and bound, some held open with polished stones. "Should I be flattered by that?"

"I can go, if you prefer," she said, and he was on his feet again, a strange expression on his face.

Is he lonely? But it was not that. Instead it was the expression of a man with news, who needed to tell someone. Anyone. *We are well met, it appears.*

"What is it?" she asked, sweeping some papers off a bench and taking a seat. It seemed strange to be taking the initiative with him, strange to find him appearing so shaken, here amongst his own people.

"What made you come here, now?" he asked, but it was a rhetorical question. "Cheerwell Maker, how is it that you have not yet got yourself killed? You have absolutely no sense of place or time. You just go blundering in wherever you please like . . . like a Beetle. I caught you that way in Helleron, and General Malkan caught you after the Battle of the Rails. You only narrowly escaped Solarno, from what I hear, so why are you still amongst the living?"

She could not decide whether he was truly angry, and it seemed neither could he. His words made her think, though, and made her feel sad.

"I'm not short of injured friends," she admitted. "Perhaps I'm just bad luck for others."

"A carrier of it, then, that never feels the ill effects," he said. "Cheerwell?"

"Call me Che."

He blinked at her.

"If you're going to call me anything more familiar than 'Mistress Maker,' call me Che. Because you cannot imagine the burden of going through life with a name like Cheerwell."

For a long moment he just stared at her, then, uncontrollably, the corner of his mouth quirked upward. "I suppose I can't," he conceded.

"Thalric . . ." she started, then stopped and considered. "Thalric. I see you've found a niche here. If Achaeos gets healed, and he and I leave Tharn . . . there's nothing to stop you staying behind."

The smile was gone, the tentative anger along with it. "Nothing except my own people." At last he sat down again, one hand idly knocking a few scrolls from the desk. "I have a death sentence, Cheer . . . Che. Che, then. Eventually, quite soon even, I'm bound to meet someone who knows me. Someone from the Rekef, someone from the army, just . . . someone. I have tried, I won't deny it, to find my way back to them." His new smile was composed only of bitterness. "I tried that in Jerez. I tried to sell the Mantis and the others. I tried to be loyal to the Empire. But the Empire didn't want my loyalty. The man I approached recognized me and tried to kill me. That could have happened here. It still might with every new arrival, or perhaps somewhere in the garrison here is a hidden Rekef Inlander agent who, any day now, will look on 'Major Manus' and think the name *Thalric*. Do you know what I really am, Che?"

She shook her head wordlessly.

"I am a spymaster, a major in the Rekef Outlander. An imperial intelligencer, that is what I've spent my life being. Only now they won't let me. And I was good, very good, at my job. I've been sorting through all these reports, and thinking: 'I must tell them this,' or 'the next step should be that,' and realizing that I can't. I cannot tell them anything and, even if I could, they would not thank me. Instead they would have me on crossed pikes. I cannot use my skills on behalf of my Empire anymore, so I've been sitting here torturing myself with my pretending."

"I'm sorry."

She expected him to sneer at that, but he nodded soberly. "You probably are, at that. However did you get yourself mixed up in all of this?"

"I am Stenwold's niece."

He looked back at the desk, the papers, and she knew better than to interrupt him. Some train of thought was now running its course in his mind, some weighty decision that had been weighed up delicately before she came in.

"Szar is in revolt," he said at last.

"I don't—"

"The city of Szar is in open revolt against the Empire," he told her. "Thousands of soldiers are therefore being diverted to put down the Bee-kinden with extreme force. Many of them are soldiers that would otherwise be heading west even now."

She nodded slowly. Her mind's map was hazy on precisely where Szar was, but she appreciated the point he made.

Thalric took a deep breath. "The city of Myna, of fond memory, is on the point of insurrection as well."

"Myna? That's Kymene—"

"Yes, it is. Myna teeters. The garrison has been weakened, with troops heading northwest for Szar. Still, the Empire has an iron hold on the city. So, do the Mynans risk everything with another upheaval?"

"What are you saying?" she asked, because it was obvious that something else lay hidden behind his words.

"I am saying," he said slowly, the words forcing themselves out of him, "that if some agents of the Lowlands were to find their way to Myna, and there tell the Mynans that they are not alone, that the Lowlands struggled too, and Szar, and Solarno, that the imperial forces were stretching themselves thinner every day, then they would surely rise up where otherwise they might not dare."

She stood up slowly. "You're suggesting that . . . what? I? We? *We?* Achaeos can't possibly travel."

"Achaeos is at least safe here amongst his own people," Thalric said. "But yes, *we* could fly to Myna in that ridiculous barrel of yours and stir up the pot. Because, if there's nothing else on this world I can still do, I can play conspiracy with the best of them, and whilst the Mynans won't ever trust me, they might trust you."

"I don't want to leave Achaeos . . ." But already the idea was growing on her. "I'll have to speak with him," she ended lamely.

"Of course," said Thalric. "But soon, as we must be swift. If the Mynans delay until after Szar is put down, it will all be for nothing."

"I will speak to him. Yes, I'll speak to him *now,*" she said, already reaching the doorway of the room. She looked back at him once, and he wondered what she saw there: someone almost an ally, or just a burnt-out Wasp spymaster?

But I still possess the craft. Indeed I cannot keep it from working. He was betraying the Empire every moment, with every breath, and yet he could look in the mirror and betray Stenwold Maker just as easily. *I have now found my vocation. I have more faces than shape-changer Scyla ever had.*

EIGHT

There had been a day and a night of sheer panic, as the fragile form of the *Buoyant Maiden* was hurled back and forth by storm winds the likes of which Stenwold had never known. He had now been given a full chance to get acquainted, though. As the only Apt passenger, it had fallen to him to remain on deck with Jons Allanbridge, tying off lines, strengthening stays, doing what little could be done to stop the little airship from simply flying apart, or the gondola parting company with the balloon and the machine ceasing to be anything but a collection of airborne detritus.

"Wouldn't we be safer going down?" he had shouted at Allanbridge.

The other Beetle, still winching doggedly, had yelled back, "What do you think I'm trying to do? I've let the gas go as far as I dare, but the wind's still keeping us up!"

Stenwold had wondered whether, if the storm succeeded in tearing them from the canopy, the gondola would have just gone sailing on, unsupported, as if tossing on an invisible sea.

Later on, Jons had been actively trying for all the height he could inject into his *Maiden*, generating new gas as swiftly as he could, because there had been a dark wall blotting out the horizon, and it had been the Barrier Ridge, the colossal cliff-scarp that delineated the Commonweal's southern edge.

Then, some time toward dawn, the winds had eased and Allanbridge had sent him below. He had collapsed beneath the hatch, bone-weary and aching in every joint, his hands raw, knuckles scraped, and with a massive flowering bruise across his forehead where he had been thrown into the side rail which, thankfully, had been sturdy enough to restrain him.

Now he woke, to find the wind was gone, or gone enough that he could no longer hear it. The gondola was moving badly, however: not coasting on the air as it had done, but instead rocking and swaying from side to side.

It seems we are not in the air anymore. He forced himself to go back up the ladder, pushing the hatch open. The sunlight that greeted him was bright, with a blue sky beaming through a lattice of branches.

The balloon of the *Maiden* was up there too, he saw. Punctured by a few of the boughs, it had been pushed all the way over to one side on the straining ropes, but it still seemed to be holding its shape. Stenwold hauled himself further up onto the deck, which was swinging gently from its cradle of branches.

"Where in the wastes are we?" he muttered, staring about him. The landscape was steeply hilly, but clearly something strange had happened to it in the past, because a great many of the hills had been truncated, and their tops flattened, the sides stepping in tiers down toward the valleys. *Agriculture?* he wondered, though only grass and bushes grew there now, the latter suggesting that a good many years had gone by since this land was ever farmed.

We were going north, he recalled. *We had passed Dorax and Mount Hain, and I saw . . . I'm sure I saw the Barrier Ridge. What else could it have been? So are we in the Commonweal now, or were we blown aside?* He turned about, clambering up the sloping deck to see if any familiar landmarks were still in view, but the storm must have carried them further than he thought. Their tree was one of about a dozen bare-limbed giants, lofty enough to have the *Maiden*'s gondola dangling from its lowest branches, and yet still a good ten feet in the air. There was the dense line of a forest on one horizon, but he could not tell if it was composed of the same monsters or of lesser trees.

What he did see, though, was . . .

He was familiar with the concept of them, of course, but they were simply not found in any of the lands he knew. The Lowlands had its fortified city-states, walled villages or military outposts, palisades and armed camps. What it did not have were castles, though. The Ant-kinden model of fortification, which informed all of Lowlands military design, was calculated to protect the whole community, not just provide a defensible centre surrounded by an open settlement. Nor was there ever an isolated bastion rising out of the wilderness. But here was a castle, soaring six storeys high, constructed of white, featureless stone, with a jaggedly asymmetrical crown of turrets that closed in on the centre, so that those within could not only see clearly over all the surrounding landscape, but could protect themselves against airborne attack.

The structure stood about half a mile away, Stenwold guessed, but it was hard to tell, for the scale of it troubled him. He had no idea how big such edifices were supposed to be.

Of course the Commonweal was huge, and all subject to a single monarch. Such an absolute ruler would perhaps need castles to control those broad holdings.

"All right, Maker?"

He jumped at Allanbridge's voice. The aviator was descending the ropes from the balloon.

"How bad is it?"

"A day or two to patch her, add another one for the three days it'll take to generate the gas to refill her."

"I'm sorry about the *Maiden*," Stenwold started, but Allanbridge shrugged it off.

"We've had worse, she and me." He looked bag-eyed and tired and Stenwold realized he had not slept at all since the storm started. "I never did the Commonweal run before, and I should have listened more to them that had. They told me that, around the Barrier Ridge, the weather got choppy."

"Choppy," Stenwold echoed—and then: "We're in the Commonweal, are we?"

"We are indeed," came Destrachis' voice. Stenwold turned to see the Spider climbing up through the hatch. He had a bandage about his head, showing that even those below had not come through the storm unscathed. Felise was already on deck ahead of him, standing at the rail but disdaining to hold to it, and looking out over the landscape.

"I don't suppose you know where we are, exactly?" the Spider doctor asked. "The Commonweal's rather a big place."

"None of this looks familiar to you?" Stenwold asked him.

"The Commonweal's at least half as big again as all the Lowlands put together, Master Maker. I can't claim to know more than a fraction of it by sight. All I can say is that we can't be too far north, because there's no snow on the ground still— but that's hardly helpful news."

"You've got time enough stranded here to ask the locals," Allanbridge pointed out. "After that, if you could bring some of them back here to help us out of the tree, it would make my life a lot easier."

Stenwold nodded, looking over at the castle, wondering who it had been defended from and whether its inhabitants had even heard of the Lowlands. More to the point, whether the inhabitants had spotted the pale balloon of the airship caught, like an errant moon, in the tree, and what they might think if they had.

"We'll go down," he confirmed. "We need to know how much further to Suon Ren, and whether we're even still on course. Jons, I'll leave you alone to make your repairs. Destrachis and Felise, it's now time to earn your keep."

"They don't make their terrain easy to walk over, in the Commonweal," commented Stenwold, after he had hauled himself up yet another series of weed-infested steps. The Commonweal plants growing here amidst the unruly grass all bristled with little hairs that brought him out in a rash, so that he had to wear his heavy artificer's gloves to pull himself up the tiered slope.

They seemed no nearer to the castle than before. As seen through his spyglass, of course, it had not seemed so far.

Now they stood on top of another hill, because winding their way along the lower ground looked to be a recipe for continually going astray. The land around looked so alien to him, cut as it was into descending terraces. "Why can't they just leave their hills alone?"

Destrachis gave him an odd look. "This is farmland, Master Maker."

Stenwold gave him a doubtful glance. "Well, it's a lovely crop of weeds they've got left over from last year, is all I can say."

"Well, it was once farmland," Destrachis admitted. "Not tended in the last five years, surely. I wonder where precisely we are."

"Quite." Stenwold set off down the next hillside, treading in a series of bone-jarring thumps. He had heard of step agriculture, of course. Che had explained that the Moth-kinden practised it, through lack of space. He had expected the great and unindustrialized Commonweal to be more . . . natural, though. Here every part of the landscape had been modified by man's hand before being left, it seemed, to grow wild once more. He even thought that he had spotted, from one hilltop, a waterway cutting straight as a die through the undulating landscape. *Canals?* They possessed no automotives, no rails, so canals he could understand, but to chop up what must be several square miles of hill country in this way seemed absolutely insane. "They've got plenty of space here, it seems to me. Why can't they just put up with the odd slope?"

Destrachis shrugged, his longer legs managing the constant drops in level more easily. In fact Stenwold was the only one of them having any significant trouble.

"Efficiency," remarked Felise Mienn, which surprised Stenwold enough that he stopped in his tracks. It was, he realized, the first word she had said since they set off. No, it was the first word he had heard her say since he returned from Sarn.

"Where there are many people to feed it is more efficient," she continued, in the tone of a schoolteacher. "These steps were first cut many centuries ago, each generation of the peasantry repairing and restoring the work of their fathers and mothers."

"Many people?" Stenwold glanced at Destrachis, who was peering around about the landscape, looking uneasy.

Felise stared at him, and Stenwold had no idea whether she even understood his words.

"I don't like it either," agreed the Spider. "You had a good look at the castle, though, and it seems the only landmark hereabouts. I hope we've not ended up crossing over into the Wasp-occupied provinces or something. That would be amusing, don't you think?"

"We are being watched," Felise commented, without emotion.

"Where?" Instantly Stenwold's hand had fallen to the toy he had brought along from Collegium, and that was now slung, barrels facing upward, on his back.

"Left and left of ahead," the Dragonfly replied.

Stenwold took a moment to work that out and risked a covert look. "I don't see anyone."

"They are there."

"Probably just some people from the castle, come to see the newcomers." Stenwold descended another step awkwardly. "Or guilt-ridden peasants come to continue the work of their fathers and mothers."

"The castle is deserted," announced Felise with absolute certainty.

"How . . . do you know this place?" Stenwold asked her.

"Master Maker," Destrachis said, with a strange tone to his voice, "when you were eyeing the castle through that magnifying machine, you did at least notice whether it is actually inhabited, yes?"

"It's still standing."

"Castles do that, Master Maker." The Spider pursed his lips. "They do that even when they've not been lived in for fifty years—or not been lived in by those that they were made for."

Stenwold unshipped the piercer from his back, checking that the four long quarrels were still loaded in place. Half a dozen figures had sprung up on to the top of the nearest hill overlooking them. They were Dragonfly-kinden, for certain, five men and a woman wearing cloth armour that was bulked out with sewn-in metal plates. Some had spears and others had short-bladed punch swords. Two carried tall bows.

Stenwold swallowed anxiously, because they did not look friendly. "Good morning," he called. "We are only travellers looking for—"

The arrow cut straight at him. Not a warning shot or a slip, but a casual attempt at murder even before he had finished speaking. All he could do was fall backward, the head of it snagging the leather of his shoulder. In that same instant, four of the Commonwealers had leapt into the air, wings sparking to life, and now dropped toward them.

They stooped faster than Stenwold could watch, but what rose to meet them was not the ground but Felise. Without any transition she went from stillness to a blur, sword clear and cloak thrown back, passing through the attackers in the air, to land beyond them, close to the archers who had remained behind. Of the four who had leapt, two were dead before any of them reached the ground.

The archers instantly loosed at her and one arrow glanced off her armour, while the other sprayed in splinters from her sword blade, and then she was at work, killing both of them before they could even drop their bows and take up blades. Seeing that, the two survivors were in the air again, darting off and away. Stenwold assumed that Felise would follow them, for her wings hummed and danced across her back, but she simply stood there, on the hill's crest between the two dead archers, her sword ready in her hand.

Slowly she raised it, and Stenwold heard Destrachis curse. He struggled on up the hill, and before he was halfway he observed that another dozen men and women had darted up into the air and begun dropping toward them or nocking shafts.

Felise sprang up too, her sword nipping arrows from her path. Stenwold raised the piercer and pulled the trigger, igniting the firepowder in all four chambers at once.

The actual damage that it did was so small—most of the bolts went wide and only one of the oncoming attackers was punched from the air, a three-foot bolt through his groin. The sound, though—the instant he loosed they scattered across the sky in all directions, without plan or pattern, till a moment later they had regrouped two hundred yards away in a cluster circling another hilltop.

They have never heard such a noise, he realized. He crouched and set to reloading, pulling bolts out of his pack and slotting them into place.

The Spider joined them on the hill's crest. "That got their attention," Destrachis remarked, for the dozen were already being joined by more, their number swiftly doubling. Stenwold grimly went on reloading, because at this point he felt he might as well, for all the difference it would make. "Why did they attack us like that?" he demanded. "I thought the Commonweal was supposed to be . . . civilized."

"They are renegades, brigands," Felise declared implacably, watching the swirling storm of her fellow Dragonflies. "This is an abandoned province."

"Now you tell us."

"You were the one who got a good look at the castle," Destrachis reminded him. "You couldn't tell us that it was a ruin?"

"I don't know what a Commonweal castle is supposed to look like," Stenwold snapped back at him, standing ready with the loaded piercer in his hands.

"More of them off to our right," Destrachis noted, and Stenwold turned wearily to look.

It appeared that the real problem had now arrived, summoned conveniently by the roar of his piercer. Seven or eight Dragonfly-kinden on horseback were galloping the winding path between the hills, fully armoured in sparkling plate.

"Right, now," he began carefully, "how we're going to play this is . . ."

He got no further. Felise thrust her sword into the air and cried out something, a shriek almost without words at first, as savage and unexpected as the piercer's voice a moment before. When she called out again, though, at the top of her voice, he heard words that meant nothing to him:

"Mercre Monachis!" she cried. "Mercers to me!"

◊ ◊ ◊

Stenwold had never seen such horses. In the Lowlands horses were draught animals, or else bred for hides and meat, and far and few were the animals worth riding. The Dragonfly cavalry possessed such animals as he had never imagined: sleek and long legged, dark coated, long necked. Their eyes seemed to glow with more intelligence than any mere beast should have, and they had fought boldly alongside their masters, dancing about the aerial mêlée and dashing in to kick and stamp on any of the enemy who dropped momentarily from the sky.

Their riders wore armour much like Felise's, though none quite as complete: most had sections of leather or cloth showing between the iridescent metal plates. They had the same style of sword as she did, too, in addition to their spears and bows.

She called them Mercers, and the name rang a faint bell in Stenwold's memory.

"They're the arm of the Monarch and they go back centuries," Destrachis explained to him quietly, walking along behind him with these riders all around them. "Mercre was their founder, and was a high prince—the second son of the Monarch of the time. These days they trek all over the Commonweal putting right whatever goes wrong. If you ask me, they're the only thing holding most of the place together. Only they can't be everywhere at once, or even most places, so we're lucky they happened to be nearby."

The Mercers had made short work of the brigands, killing many and driving others off to find refuge in the ruined castle. Felise Mienn, for one moment stripped of her madnesses by this return to her own past, had requested their further aid and they had agreed to escort the Lowlanders to Suon Ren.

Jons Allanbridge was somewhere above them, floating the *Maiden* awkwardly as it limped through the sky. He would soon have been prey for bandits had they left him there—as he had demanded—to repair his ship. The Mercers had stared up at the airship in wide-eyed silence. It was obvious that they had never seen anything of the type before and clearly they did not much like it.

The Lowlanders had been blown off course further than they had thought, Stenwold discovered, for Suon Ren was now actually south for them. It seemed they had crossed the border into an entirely different province, one that had lain largely vacant for many years. The lead Mercer informed him that the ruling family had died during the war, but Stenwold could read between the lines well enough to understand that the "family" had probably been no more than one or two even before then. This land had been failing inexorably and the war had only added a final full stop to its history.

Felise was now riding silently ahead of them, her moment of glory spent. Her mount belonged to a Mercer who had been killed in the fight, and whose body, slung over another woman's horse, indicated the only loss they had taken in routing the bandits. Destrachis kept a worried eye on Felise, who seemed to have sunk back totally into herself.

"Are you now wishing you'd not come?" Stenwold asked him.

"I had to do something," he said. "I still cannot know if it was the right thing."

They travelled on for days. At one point, Stenwold had suggested that the Lowlanders should all go in the airship, to keep pace with the fleeter riders, but the Mercers had balked at that. They did not yet know what to make of their visitors, these people from places they had never heard of, and they were not keen to see them vanish off into the sky. Stenwold wondered if this was because nobody in Suon Ren would later believe their story, without he and his companions presenting the proof.

On reaching Suon Ren, Stenwold had expected another castle, but what he found there was the sheer antithesis of so much stone. Seeing it, he wondered if the Commonweallers even built those massive edifices anymore. It seemed as though it might have been a phase that this great sprawling state had gone through in its more energetic youth, before settling down to an existence of quiet contemplation.

Contemplation was very much the sense he gained of Suon Ren: contemplation and wary watchfulness. Coming in from high ground, Stenwold had plenty of time to puzzle over it. The town itself was surrounded by a series of small, round platforms set atop high poles, and several of these had figures perched on them to gaze out across the carefully stepped farmlands. Many of these watchers were children, insofar as Stenwold could judge their scale, yet the platforms had no rungs or steps to reach them. They were clearly a flier's vantage point without the effort of hovering in the air. A subtle distance from the outlying buildings of the town ran two canals, with wooden slipways that were currently untenanted. Stenwold had no sense of whether boats visited here every day, or every tenday, or only twice a year, or never. Suon Ren seemed shorn of any concept of time or its passage.

Stenwold had expected some central palace or hall as a focal point. Instead, what must have been the local lord's dwelling was set a little apart from the town, on a hill overlooking it. It was built to four storeys, and seemed like the empty ghost of the castle they had seen earlier—half of the lower two floors seeming solid, but the rest, and all the upper floors, just isolated panels and scaffolding, as though the place was still being constructed. The very highest floor, elegantly supported and buttressed, seemed to be some manner of garden, with vines and garlands of flowers spilling over the edge to dangle in a fringe around it.

Beyond the watch platforms, the town was mostly empty space. The centre of it, a large proportion of the ground area of Suon Ren, was a simple open circle that might have been marketplace, assembly point or fighting ring—or all or none of them. The houses stood far apart, and there was no attempt at streets. Light and space dominated everywhere, the houses themselves built as open as possible. All were overshadowed by roofs made from flat wood and sloping in the same direction, so that there was always a higher end and a lower. Beneath the high end the walls lay open more than halfway to the ground, leaving a gap between wall top and eaves that flitting Dragonflies could easily enter and leave by. Destrachis explained that inside there would be an outer room, in a ring shape, left open to the air save when it was shuttered against the worst of weathers. Yes, the door was that slot up there, beneath the roof, but the walls could all be moved and rearranged, for ground-walking visitors. Stenwold had difficulty understanding it all for, while Collegium was a city of the earth, Suon Ren owed more to the sky.

Encircled by the outer room, Destrachis continued, there would be the inner space where the family slept, protected from cold and weather. It all looked very fragile to Stenwold, as though the storm that had caught them overhead should have blown the entire town away.

At the far end of Suon Ren, its southern edge, there was a surprise waiting. There were three buildings that seemed to lurk self-consciously on the town's periphery—all of them heavy and ugly and closed in. They were typical Beetle-style structures that might have been lifted straight from Collegium or Helleron.

"What are those?" he turned to ask the lead Mercer.

The woman looked down on him with surprise, as though he should know the answer already. "Your embassy, foreign master."

There they met a man, a Beetle-kinden named Gramo Galltree, an old man with wispy white hair, dressed in the Dragonfly manner of a simple knee-length tunic and sleeveless robe. He received them standing barefoot in his small garden, and had not seemed surprised to encounter his countrymen so far from home. Instead he ushered the two other Beetles inside the largest of the three squat buildings standing nearby.

"The little one over there is a Messenger's Guild stopover," he explained. "Only a handful of them to be found in the whole Commonweal, but those Flies get everywhere. That's how I ended up here—by following them. A whole other world, the Commonweal, and who'd have believed it?"

"And that other building?" Stenwold enquired.

"Ah, well . . ." Gramo stopped in the doorway, gazing at the medium-sized edifice that abutted the embassy. "I haven't been inside there for a good while, but it used to be . . . well, it used to be my workshop. I had this idea, when I came here . . . you know, to introduce a little sophistication, Collegium know-how . . . but I just sort of, well, lost interest—don't think I've got the knack anymore."

Felise Mienn had not gone off with the Mercers, nor would she enter the embassy either. Instead she remained outside as though standing on guard, her hands resting on her sword hilt. Destrachis sat outside with her, and it seemed to Stenwold that none of the tension had gone out of the doctor. He was still waiting for something dramatic from his patient.

"When did you first arrive here?" Stenwold asked their host. The interior of the embassy revealed the entire history of the man since he had arrived: the style and tastes of a cluttered Collegium house picked apart into the sparse and well-spaced preferences of a Commonwealer. The room he took his visitors over to had a heavy wooden desk and chair clogging one wall, but Gramo himself just sat down in the centre without thinking. Like the Fly-kinden, it seemed Commonwealers preferred using the floor, and to keep their rooms as free of furniture as possible.

The old man was counting to himself, his lips moving silently. "That must have been . . . oh, a good twenty years ago. At least twenty years."

"And who appointed you ambassador for the whole Lowlands?" Jons Allanbridge demanded. He was in an irritable mood, concerned for the integrity of his ship, and he was suffering this delay in his repairs with ill grace.

"Well," Gramo said, apologetically, "I thought it might be useful in case . . . just in case. And they have been very good to me, the Commonwealers. I did send letters back to the College, to say that I was here, you know, if they ever needed me." He looked from one face to the other, hopefully. Stenwold could imagine what reaction such missives would have received in the more conservative halls of the College.

"So tell me," Gramo said, "what has brought you so far, then?"

It seemed he had not heard of the war, although he had heard of the Empire.

"I don't really know what to say," he admitted, when Stenwold had run through an accelerated history of the last year in Collegium. "It all seems to have happened so suddenly."

"It occurs to me," Stenwold told him, "that you now have a chance to make good your position here, Master Galltree. We need to speak urgently to the local Dragonfly lord, Felipe Shah."

Gramo nodded. "Well, I knew that. I knew that even before I saw you. They told me, you see."

His visitors exchanged glances.

"Told you what? That we were coming?" Stenwold asked. "But they couldn't have known."

Gramo's smile was that of either a gleeful child or a senile old man. "Course they couldn't, course they couldn't, yet they do. They know so many things here. Didn't believe it myself, at first, but you live with people long enough, you realize that most of it comes true whether you believe it or you don't. They told me to prepare for guests almost a tenday ago, they did. Why, the Prince himself will send for you shortly."

"We won't bother getting settled then," Allanbridge growled.

"But I have already prepared beds. Several beds, since they didn't say how many." Gramo made vague gestures to suggest the other rooms of his embassy. Seeing their uncertain expressions he explained, "When I say shortly . . . perhaps that is not as short here as I remember it being in Collegium."

True to the old man's words, no summons had come for them by nightfall. Allanbridge had elected to return to his precious *Buoyant Maiden* as the sky grew dark, but Stenwold felt that he had to humour Gramo, at least. The old man had been patiently waiting here for this kind of responsibility since before Stenwold had first locked horns with the Empire in his youth.

He spent an awkward night trying to cope with Commonweal sleeping arrangements, and soon came to the conclusion that the Dragonflies must until recently have slept in trees, and only just discovered the ground. As a result, a Commonweal bed was a kind of string net slung between two supporting beams of the house, like a sailor's hammock, and throughout the night he had pitched and swung in it, and fell out of it, until he decided to sleep on the floor and to the wastes with protocol. When morning came, the searing sunrise washed into the house by every unshuttered window, as though Gramo had deliberately tried to make the place as airy as the homes of his hosts. Dawn brought Stenwold awake as readily as if it had slapped him. With every part of him aching, he sat up abruptly, cursing all the Commonweal and all ambassadors-gone-native.

He was not alone, he discovered. Kneeling in a corner, his back resting against the wall, was Destachis.

"What is it about Spider-kinden," Stenwold muttered to himself, "that they just don't respect privacy?"

"She's gone," said Destrachis.

Stenwold looked at him blearily.

"Gone," Destrachis repeated. "Gone without a word." The extent of his hurt was evident in his dishevelled clothes, his uncombed hair—a Spider without his customary armour against the world.

"Felise?" Stenwold asked.

"Of course Felise. Who else?"

"Gone where? To do what?"

"Just gone," Destrachis said. "Master Maker, I have to go after her."

"Destrachis, she's with her own people now," Stenwold said. "That means she can come and go as she pleases, surely—"

"Last night she was uneasy, unhappy. Perhaps too many memories were coming back at once." Destrachis bit at his lip. "But to go—just go without a word. Something must have happened."

"You don't think . . ." Stenwold let the sentence trail off, unwilling to voice it, but no one else would. "You think she's killed someone," he said.

Destrachis stared at him, the truth of that suggestion written on his face for even Stenwold to see. "I had thought . . . that her own people might bring her stability. When she was with the Mercers, it was as though she had never been hurt. But I saw it in her yesterday . . . it was all coming back, eating away at her."

"What will they do if she *has* killed someone? What do you know of Dragonfly justice?"

"Dragonfly justice is swift and as fair as the prince that makes it," said Destrachis. "Also, that's irrelevant. Felise Mienn is not sane, so they will not punish her. Madness is . . . special to them. They will try to contain her, but . . ." His face creased. "They are strange, when it comes to madness. They revere it."

"First things first," said Stenwold. "Let's go and see if anything has actually happened, then we can worry about the repercussions."

They found Gramo Galltree, self-styled ambassador, tending the small herb garden at the back of his embassy. He bobbed and smiled a greeting at them as they approached. Their host had still been awake when Stenwold retired, so it was unclear whether he had slept at all.

"The Mercer noblewoman?" he said, when they asked him. "They came for her late last night."

"Came? Who came?" Destrachis demanded.

"A messenger from the Prince himself," Gramo said. "Apparently someone wished to speak with her."

"Then maybe she's still there," Stenwold reasoned. Destrachis merely shook his head but said nothing.

"You are also sent for," the Beetle ambassador said. "At your convenience."

"Prince Shah?" Stenwold enquired.

Gramo chuckled indulgently. "Prince *Felipe*, you mean, but no, not him. Another at the castle requests your presence, perhaps even the same as sent for your friend. In your own time, though. When you are ready."

"We're ready now," Destrachis decided.

NINE

"So, we trust Thalric now, do we?" Achaeos asked. He was looking better, genuinely better, since his own people's doctors had started tending him. The long haul to Tharn had been worth the trouble, though now it had seemingly brought more trouble in its wake.

"I . . . I think I do," Che said.

"You think you do?" He grimaced. "That doesn't show much faith, Che."

He reached his hand out and she took it, marvelling as always at how delicate his fingers were.

"You remember Myna, Achaeos," she said. "You remember Kymene and the occupation."

"I do, yes."

"They need what I can bring them," she said simply. "Trust him or not, Thalric's logic is sound."

"Only if his information is. Assuming he isn't simply leading you into a trap."

"How can I know." She shrugged. "But if Thalric wanted to capture us, he's already had his chance. He could easily hand us over to the Wasps here. He could have forced me to fly off into the Empire—Helleron's imperial now, and only a step away. Or there's the camp at Asta, that must be seething with them. I think he's . . . lost. He's used to having a whole Empire driving him on, and now he's on his own, and he's not used to that."

"Poor little Thalric," commented the Moth acidly.

"But you see what I mean? If Myna rebels, then there will be fewer Wasp soldiers to throw at the Lowlands. If Myna and this other place rebel—and with Sten in the Commonweal trying to roust them up—we could see the whole western Empire reeling. And there must be other places who will try to throw off the yoke if they know the Empire simply doesn't have the soldiers to spare for them."

Achaeos closed his eyes, thinking. "The Ants of Maynes," he murmured, "and Sa. Great Delve. Yes, there are others." He opened those curious eyes again, without iris or pupil so that she could not tell whether he was looking at her or not. "I understand, Che, I really do. I remember Myna. Perhaps we owe them something, after all. I'm just . . . I don't trust Thalric and I doubt I ever will. And I worry about you."

"And I worry about you too," she told him. "I'm leaving you here in *their* hands, after all. And, last I heard, your own people weren't likely to step in and help you if the Wasps decided that you were a prisoner and not a guest."

He smiled slightly. "It might be that things are changing a little there. It might be that the Tharen are realizing that they're part of a greater world after all, and that someone who has at least put his nose outside once in a while is, if not much trusted, still useful."

"Really?" Her eyes widened.

"I've been meeting people," he explained. "They do not like me, Che. I have broken too many unwritten laws for them to like me. They need me, however. And things here are not quite what they seem, regarding the occupation. You forget that we are a cunning people, in our way."

She pressed her lips together. "Well, if you trust *them*, then maybe I can trust Thalric."

"Che, that isn't the same thing at all."

"I know, but . . ."

His smile became sharp edged. "I know. It's what Stenwold would do, in your place. And I know what Myna means to Stenwold. For him, it was the door that opened onto the Empire. I know." His grip on her hand increased. "And you want to be able to tell him how you liberated Myna. You want him to be proud of you."

He had cut too deep with that. "I want to be proud of myself," she protested. "I seem to spend my whole time walking from one person's cell to another. I haven't *done* anything yet. Now I want to do my bit."

She had brought the peoples of the Ancient League to stand alongisde Sarn, Achaeos reflected. She had retrieved the plans for the snapbow. She had found allies in Solarno and Tharn for her people. He knew that she would not be satisfied with that, though, for she was still in the shadow of her uncle and her foster sister, Tynisa.

The thought of Tynisa sent a twinge running through him, even though he never saw her wield the sword against him. That led him on to thoughts of the other player in this drama: the Mosquito-kinden whose servant had, through Tynisa's stolen arm, vicariously inflicted this wound he suffered. It was a matter he would have to discuss with the Skryres. Even if he could have travelled, he needed most of all to be here.

"Go, then," he told her. "You're right, you must go. Please, though, do not let Thalric guide your hand too much. Do not give him a chance to betray you. When you are in Myna, trust only Kymene and her people, even trust that old Scorpion more than you would trust Thalric. If the Empire should ever hold its hand out to him again, he is theirs."

"I know," she said.

He hunched forward, and she hugged him gently but still felt him twitch in pain.

"And don't you trust your people more than you have to," she warned him. "If they genuinely liked you, that might last, but if they only *need* you then they'll drop you as soon as that need is gone."

"Oh, I know it," he agreed. "Don't think that I don't."

And yet, when she paused in the infirmary doorway before going, he was stabbed by the sudden thought, *I will never see her again*, and did not know if this was fear or prophecy.

After Che had gone, he sensed movement nearby, and it was not long before Xaraea stepped suspiciously into the room with narrowed eyes.

"All overheard of course," said Achaeos tiredly. "I would have more privacy if I were an Ant."

"Aside from your perversions," she said, "you come close to betraying us."

"Only if you believe *she* would betray me."

"If she is to go now into the Empire, she is not safe bearing any knowledge that could harm us."

Achaeos stared at her for a long time, until she broke and asked him, "What? What is it?"

"I see why you need my differing viewpoint," he told her. "You have an imperial garrison. You have an imperial governor. What part of the Empire are we not inside?"

She scowled at him but had no answer to that, just saying, "Speaking of the governor, it is time for you to meet him. As it is not fit for him to come to your bedside, that means you will have to walk."

In the end they had to help him along. He was not even capable of the length of journey that a few turned corners and passages would have made. He was healing fast, but the wound had been an inch off mortal. The chamber they took him to was one designed for meditation. *Perhaps they hope to make the Empire think like them?*

There was a Skryre, an old woman, seated there. Her glance toward Achaeos was bleak but not hostile. Achaeos thought he saw a touch of fear there, too, in the very depths of her white eyes. She nodded to his escorts and they took him over and lowered him until he sat beside her. A Mantis-kinden in robes knelt down beside and slightly behind him, ready to assist him if he needed it.

"Say nothing," the Skryre instructed him. "Watch only."

Xaraea had now taken up station beside the door, beyond which Achaeos could already hear the marching feet: the military approach of destiny.

Their visitor wore the uniform of a Wasp officer off duty: not armour but tunic and cloak in black and gold, fastened richly with jewelled pins. He entered with a female Wasp slave-girl and with half a dozen guards as his escort, as haughty and arrogant as any Wasp governor might wish to appear.

The old woman stood up as he entered, and even Achaeos was helped to his feet.

"My Lord Governor Tegrec," greeted Xaraea, who had been waiting at the door with every appearance of calm. Achaeos knew his own people, though: she was the centre point, the knot that was holding this fragile arrangement together, and she knew it. The weight of all her people was on her, and he could detect the minute signs of strain. Achaeos had found in himself a growing coldness for his people, for their isolationism, their hostility to the world and particularly to Che's kin. In contrast he admired Xaraea. She had delivered herself into the very hands of the Empire in order to save the Moths.

Tegrec, this new governor, was not impressive for a Wasp: short and stout and garishly dressed, Still he put on a show, looking over the conquered people with the proper disdain before waving to his escort. "You may leave us." It was not reck-lessness in the face of danger that he displayed, but the confidence of a man who knows in his heart that the enemy is beaten.

The soldiers retreated, and Tegrec waited, as if listening while their footsteps receded, the light of their lanterns dimming and dying away. That left only the two torches the Mantis servant had lit to flare and gutter and cast shadows about the little room.

Tegrec smirked. That was the only word for the expression that crossed his face. He cast a look back in the direction of his retreating soldiers and *smirked*. A tension, perhaps an entirely manufactured tension, then left the room. His Mantis carer lowered Achaeos back to the floor, where he sat cross-legged and watched the Wasp governor of Tharn don a black robe and go native. Tegrec held onto the last rags of his sombre mood until his girl had finished tugging the garment into shape, and then smiled at them, and perhaps at himself.

"My Lord Governor," the Skryre said, standing almost hidden in the folds of her robe, a coiled staff in one hand. Like all Skryres, and like most Moth-kinden of station, she had not revealed her name.

Tegrec looked from her to Achaeos, and then himself sat down. In the robe, he could have been a somewhat bulky Moth student ready to learn from his teachers. *That is what he is*—Achaeos had not quite believed it, when they had told him— *a Wasp seer, and mostly self-taught, but here he is learning from the masters.*

Xaraea seated herself as well, as did the slave-girl. The aged Skryre took a few halting steps.

"This is Achaeos," she declared. "He comes to us from the Lowlands, where your people make war."

Tegrec nodded.

"We are approaching a time of crisis, Tegrec," said the Skryre. By naming him, while herself remaining nameless, she shaped her authority over him. "You, especially, face such a time too. Do you understand me?"

"I believe I do." The Wasp still smiled.

"Our bargain holds, does it not?"

"I have no complaints." He glanced at the girl beside him, and Achaeos saw that, with the guards now gone, the distance between master and slave had relaxed as well.

"You have been an able student," the Skryre admitted. "You have achieved more than we might have expected, from your kind."

Tegrec looked directly at Achaeos, as though trying to read him. In returning the favour Achaeos discerned a man out of his depth, and yet who was still swimming further away from shore.

What must it have been like, to grow up in a different world to all those around you? The division between the Apt and the Inapt was the defining line between the burning new and the fading old. There were so few that could even get close enough to see into the other side. He thought of Che, then, who had been willing to join him on that border, close enough for them to touch hands. He found himself respecting this Tegrec for what he must have achieved. Taking on the Empire with a handful of magical tricks, and then carving out his own place in it, must have been difficult for him. It probably still was.

"You are asking me to make an exchange," Tegrec said at last. He glanced at his girl once again. "You want to change our arrangement?"

"We have tried to hold back change for many centuries," the Skryre remarked drily. "We discover that it cannot be done, so, yes, there will be change."

"I understand what you are asking of me," Tegrec said, "but perhaps you do not understand what you are asking me to give up."

The Skryre's lips twitched. "This Achaeos you see here, *he* knows, for he is here only as a brief gap in his exile. He has chosen life with our enemies, rather than with his own. Still, he is here, which shows that loyalty to the great mysteries overcomes all else. Can you yourself look upon your Empire, your rank, your years of time serving, and say, 'This is a thing I cannot let go of'?"

"I must think on this," Tegrec insisted.

"Do not think overlong," the Skryre warned him.

After doffing the robe, Tegrec stepped from the room and rejoined his Wasp escort, but he said nothing to them. He was still deep in thought.

I have always walked a line.

He was Major Tegrec, governor of the little-regarded city of Tharn, a chill and mountainous backwater taken by the Empire only because it was *there*, on the edge of their expanding frontier. The Moth-kinden, isolated and backward, had nothing to offer the Empire: poor warriors, poor labourers, a nation of recluses and hermits. Tegrec himself had already confirmed this to his superiors, reporting in just the right tones of resentful suffering.

Walking the line indeed, but he was a fiercely ambitious man, always pushing, always manipulating. He could not name any other major who was a governor, even of such an insignificant place as this. At the same time he was a cripple— enduring a carefully hidden mental deformity, an inability to conceive of what others found so natural. It leaked out, it showed, and he was not liked even by those who made use of him. They knew there was something unsound in him, and they had failed to root it out only because the barrier to understanding worked both ways. They could not imagine the world he lived in.

Since coming to Tharn, he had found another line to walk. He spit-shone his public face daily: the grim imperial governor of Tharn administrating this lonely, ancient eyesore, dealing with the complaints of his staff and soldiers, who were treating their assignment here as a punishment detail. Behind that face, however, he was a changed man. Before arriving here he had learnt his magic hand to mouth, from old books, or through ailing slaves from distant lands. He had come to Tharn with a piecemeal, patchwork knowledge that had eased his way within the Empire only because he used it like a con man would: they heard his words, saw his hands move the cups, and none of them could see why the ball was not where they had guessed. He had lived his whole life in fear that he would be uncovered, not as a fake but as the real thing. He had never named himself as a Seer.

The Moths, however, had named him as just that. The Moths were arrogant, exclusive, elitist, but what they looked for was not race or birth but talent. His scraps of understanding had been patched and stitched into whole cloth during his time here. His talent was unquestioned: they had never known a Wasp magician before. Perhaps there had never been one since the Days of Lore.

I do not belong here. But nor did he belong anywhere. He had burrowed his way through the Empire like a parasite, but here in Tharn he did not have to hide what he was. He would not be the first traitor the Empire had known, nor even the first traitor governor. He consoled himself with the thought that they would never understand, back in Capitas, why he had acted as he had.

He had made his choice.

TEN

Maintaining a force of cavalry was not part of the Wasp army's mandate but General Praeter had seen enough of it during the Twelve-Year War to learn its uses. Regular horses were too fragile for a Wasp-kinden war, and so he now observed his men from the high-fronted saddle of an armoured beetle, extending ten feet from its mandibles to its tail. Around him the heavy war machines of the Sixth Army were grinding forward with a mechanical determination that he knew was illusory. Machines regularly stopped working in the middle of battles, and he had never known a combat without some automotive simply falling silent at the worst possible time. He had therefore learnt not to rely on them.

The automotives nevertheless formed the central push of his advance, screened from attack by a curtain of the light airborne winging ahead. His infantry—and the Sixth was more infantry reliant than most—was contained in great curved wings to either flank. Praeter himself kept pace with the slowest of the machines in the centre, a score of his personal bodyguard mounted alongside him and the rest keeping good time behind despite their heavy armour.

His thought, on sending his soldiers forward, was that this was all a lot of fuss over nothing, for General Malkan's scouts had indicated a force of no more than two thousand men, possibly fewer, and not even Sarnesh soldiers, either, but mere vagrants and brigands. Even so, Praeter had taken upon himself the task of disposing of them. It would not do to let Malkan win too much honour in this campaign, and the young general must be constantly reminded who was in charge.

This would not be like Masaki, though. He remembered the glitter of the Dragonfly soldiers as they had swarmed forth, clouding the air, till the ground below seethed with their shadows. He often thought of those colours, the reds and golds, iridescent greens and blues. He remembered them in their glorious, furious charges, and also when they lay dead, like blossom and leaves after a storm, carpeting the battlefield before the withering volleys of his ballistae and his crossbows.

The land here was not good for an open conflict: hilly and broken, undercut by streams and rivers that his automotives would make heavy work of. The hillsides themselves were scrubby and piebald with patches of woodland, and dotted with the huts of goat farmers or aphid herders. The lay of the land had put Praeter's left wing up on a hillside and hilltop, slowed down and pushing its way through spiny bushes, whilst his right wing was almost in a valley, just creeping up the hill on the far side, with a screen of scouts to their own right, looking out for enemy skirmishers. The automotives themselves were pressing down the centre of the valley itself, progressing either side of the stream that over the ages had somehow worn this crease in the map. Somewhere else, General Malkan would be taking the Seventh in a long, curving path north of him, intending to encircle what enemy survived, to make sure not a man of them escaped. *Mopping up is all that man is fit for . . .*

The enemy were not in his sight yet, but he saw a signal from the advance airborne and, from that, knew that the foe must have been spotted. The enemy had strung wooden fences and barricades across the valley, which would be of no protection against the airborne and merely be ground beneath the wheels and tracks of the automotives. Praeter wondered why they were even bothering to make a stand.

He frowned, holding tighter to the boss of his saddle as his beetle negotiated a rocky patch. There was the matter of the scouts, though. Whoever these enemy were, they had been remarkably good at killing General Malkan's scouts, and yet this time the scouts had seen this little holdout. They had been *allowed* to see it.

He had worried away at that thought for a long time, but come up with no solution save to spread out his forces to enclose as wide an area as possible while keeping aerial screens to either side in case of ambush. *But who could aim to ambush an entire army?*

One of the automotives lurched awkwardly and he assumed it had gone into the stream bed, but it was well clear of that: struggling for no reason at all in the dusty ground with its wheels spinning, and then sinking to its axles, throwing up a vast curtain of dust so that Praeter was blinded, covering his eyes against the grit. His ears told him that the stricken automotive was not alone. Another to his left was abruptly in difficulty, too. He brought his crop down on the beetle, driving it toward the labouring machine, and the insect stumbled, the ground giving way beneath it, its claws scrabbling for purchase before it dragged itself out. Pits, everywhere: the valley floor had been undercut. There had been no sign of it until now, and the men on foot had been too light, but all around him now he could hear the wheeled and tracked automotives grinding helplessly, choking on the earth, whilst those that walked on metal legs must be striding too far ahead.

"Send to the lead automotives, tell them to reduce to half speed!" he ordered, and immediately one of his men spurred his animal into motion, guiding it between the beached metal hulks. "Call some engineers here to free the automotives," Praeter added, and another man rode off.

"General!" A soldier dropped beside him, choking through the dust. "General, the left flank is under attack."

"From where?"

"Enemy concealed in the woodlands ahead, sir."

"Then charge them and drive them out."

"We're taking heavy losses, sir."

"How?" Praeter leant down toward the man. "How many enemy?"

"Unknown, sir. But they're armed with snapbows, sir. We're closing on them now, but they're picking off our fliers."

Praeter opened his mouth to reply to that, but even as he did so something exploded ahead, both to the left and to the right, showering stones and dust down on them.

I need to see what's going on. "With me!" he shouted, and turned his beast to grapple its way up the hillside, knowing that his bodyguard would follow close. The air was solid dust, and he guessed that the charges detonated ahead had not been intended to injure but to throw up as much cover as the enemy could manage, in order to conceal whatever it was they were actually doing.

Something else then flashed within the dust cloud behind him, thundering dully. The sound was familiar enough to him: he had not worked with engineers all those years to fail to recognize a grenade now. He could even tell from the sound that it was one with a hatched casing, rather than a simple smooth one, so that the metal shards would fly outward in an even rain of shrapnel.

Before he was clear of the cloud, there were another five retorts behind him. He found it maddening, to be thus blinded to what was going on, not knowing if his entire force was being wiped out or whether this was just a gnat's sting. There was now a chaos of men flying around him as Wasp soldiers took to the air to escape the dust. He could hear the crackle of sting shot, and the solid thump of one of the motorized leadshotters that he had brought for artillery support. Then finally he was cresting the hill, the dust falling away behind him.

◁▷ ◁▷ ◁▷

"They'll be fighting now," Parops remarked.

"Who? Oh, you mean Stenwold's friend, whatever his name is." Balkus frowned. Up on the walls of Sarn, he had a good view of the great town of refugees that the Sarnesh were slowly letting into their city, in groups of ten or fifteen at a time. The Ants of Sarn were caught on a two-pronged fork of dilemma. On the one hand, the last thing they wanted in time of war was a vast crowd of clamouring, hungry and suspect foreigners within their walls. On the other hand, as Parops said, that Dragonfly boy would be fighting for them even now, trying to slow the Wasp advance so that the Sarnesh could perfect their defences. The Sarnesh were pragmatic, as Ant-kinden always were, but because of that they understood an obligation and, if they cast out Salma's people now, the remembrance of that betrayal would taint all Sarnesh dealings with foreigners for decades to come.

"They call him the Captain of the Landsarmy, Lord of the Wastes," Parops observed.

"The *Prince* of the Wastes," agreed Balkus, savouring the foreign word. "Boy's done good. Let's hope he lives through it."

Parops turned to watch a new siege engine being slowly winched up to the wall top. It was a giant repeating ballista with two sets of alternating arms and a shield before and above, slotted for vision. It was far more effective than the big catapult that had graced his own tower back in lost Tark.

If we had been better artificers, then . . . ? But the fall of Tark had been so decisive that he was not sure anything could have saved them. Then, of course, there was the history: centuries of isolation, and more dealings with the Spiderlands and the Scorpions of the Dryclaw than with the rest of the Lowlands. Sarn had the edge with weaponry because it was arm in arm with the Beetle-kinden, abandoning some of its Ant-kinden heritage to take up the Beetles on their strange ideas. More foreigners on the streets, more foreign ideas in the city mind. No slaves, either. *No slaves!* Parops, though he had personally had little use for them, could still barely imagine that. *How did things get done?*

As well as Salma's refugees, there were the new arrivals from the north. Many of them had yet to even request entrance to the city, and if they decided they wanted in, the chances were they would just fly over the walls and put the new Sarnesh anti-airborne defences to the test. It had taken a long time for the so-called Ancient League to gather its forces, and even longer, so the story went, for them to decide how many to send. Balkus had joked that he half expected to see a single Mantis warrior turn up at the gates of Sarn one morning, claiming to be the army of Nethyon.

Mantis-kinden were a notoriously standoffish race and, although the men and women of Etheryon often hired themselves out to Sarn, the hold of Nethyon was perhaps the most isolated and insular state in the Lowlands. Still, they had come in the end, and they were still coming. They had arrived with their customary arrogant disdain, singly and in twos and threes, and then in dozens, and twenties, until there was a loose camp of many hundreds of them, always shifting and moving around, impossible to count. They were still arriving and nobody knew, perhaps not even the old women who led them, how many there would eventually be.

The Moth-kinden had come with them: fewer, but still a few hundred grey-skinned, blank-eyed men and women. Not just crabbed quacks or scholars, either: the people of Dorax came attired for war in armour of layered leather and cloth, with their bows and knives, but above all with their wings, with their dark-piercing eyes. The possibilities had the royal court of Sarn almost frothing with new thought.

"Commander Balkus!" someone was calling from halfway up a stairway running up the inside of the wall. They leant over to see a corpulent Ant-kinden with bluish-white skin, wearing wealthy Beetle-styled clothing. Two Sarnesh soldiers had stopped him there, and he stood looking up at them with a baggy hat in his hands. "Commander Balkus! I need to speak with you urgently!"

"And who are you supposed to be?" Balkus demanded, stomping over to the stair top.

"My name is Plius. I am known to your master, Stenwold Maker."

Oh yes, you are, Balkus thought. *And he suspected you were up to something.* He went down the stairs toward the small group, knowing that Parops was backing him up almost as certainly as if he could feel the man's mind.

"What do you want?" he asked. The new arrival was smiling too much, plainly someone desperate to inspire ill-placed trust. Balkus felt his hand drift toward his sword.

"I want to speak to a tactician of Sarn at the very least. The King would be better, but one of his court otherwise."

"Why?" Balkus demanded, and even as he said it, he felt the stir, a sudden rustle in the mind of Sarn. His erstwhile people kept him out, but their thoughts leaked in nonetheless, and something was happening now. He became aware of soldiers suddenly spurred into action, armoured men and women running.

"I think we are about to see why," Plius explained helpfully.

Ten minutes later saw the three Ants, from three different cities, standing up on the west wall with a grey-haired Sarnesh woman, a genuine tactician of the Royal Court. They were watching the approach of more soldiers. The distance was too great to see in any detail, but there were already Fly-kinden being sent out as scouts to assess their strength and nature. One thing was clear, at any distance: by their regimented order they were Ant-kinden.

"Six hundred soldiers," Plius explained. "Soldiers of Tsen."

"Where or what is Tsen?" Parops asked.

"A city on the western coast of the Lowlands, beyond even Vek," the tactician said slowly. "Explain yourself," she instructed Plius.

"Easily. I am not, or not only, an agent of Master Maker of Collegium, but also an agent of the Queen of Tsen. Since I came to Sarn, that role has not encumbered me with any actual duties save for my reports, but a month back I received new orders. Specifically, I am appointed their ambassador, if you will have me."

"And what does the spy-turned-ambassador have to say to us?" the tactician demanded sharply. What Plius said to her, he would be saying to the King—and to the whole city if that was deemed wise.

The fat Ant-kinden shrugged. "Tsen is a long way off," he said. "Tsen is small and friendless. If the Wasps destroy your city, then eventually they will come against us, and we will not be able to defend ourselves. There, that's a frank admission of our position that your own sources can surely confirm."

The tactician nodded.

"Well, then, Tsen now sends you these soldiers to assist in the defence of your city. We can spare no more, and we know this gesture will not sway the battle, but we need to do *something*. We have not been part of your counsels, nor would we make ourselves part of the Lowlands, because we are happy in our distance from the stormy centre. However, we recognize the need." He crushed and tugged at the hat in his hands, and it was only this that told them of his nervousness. "The need," he confirmed, "is great."

◁▷ ◁▷ ◁▷

Praeter took quick stock of the situation. Here was his left wing, with solid formations of his heavy infantry making slow progress across the thorny, uncertain terrain, their shields raised. The light airborne were above them, making sallies forward, but then recoiling back. There was no sign of the enemy, just a patch of woodland that extended back along the ridge of the hill and down, but already there was a litter of Wasp bodies between his advancing infantry and the trees.

Damn Malkan for letting them get the new weapon. He tried to estimate how many soldiers could be hidden in those woods, and guessed that if they were crammed full it could even be a full thousand.

The leadshotter spoke from nearby, arcing a solid ball of stone over the infantry to crash into the trees. *I need more of those here.* But there was no chance that the right-flank artillery could get over here in time and, besides, they might need it themselves. He cropped his beetle, sending it skittering behind the slowly advancing infantry. *Too slow.* He saw them ducking behind their shields. At this range the snapbow bolts were dancing off them, but his soldiers obviously knew that would not continue to be the case if they got much closer.

"Signal me the officers of the airborne," Praeter ordered, and one of his bodyguard unfurled a red flag and began waving it in great sweeps. "And get me some of our own snapmen up here." That now proved to have been his first true tactical mistake. He had not sufficiently trusted the new weapon, and so the snapbowmen were bringing up the rear.

The leaders of the airborne were dropping down around him, and he twisted round in his saddle to regard them. He saw Wasp soldiers in armour light enough for flight, equipped with swords, spears and the fire that their Art gave them. These were the mainstay of the Wasp army, but they died, he knew. They died in their hundreds to give the infantry a chance to close. It was their purpose in his plan of attack, however, so he could spare them scant sympathy.

"It's time, men!" he shouted to them. "I need the heavies into those trees and rooting out the enemy, but if our fight with the Sarnesh told us anything, it's that snapbows can cut down an armoured line without pausing for breath. You know where that leaves you, so I want you to rush the woods, all the way along its extent, and get as many of you as possible into the trees where they won't be able to get clear aim at you." Even as he spoke, there were more explosions down the hillside. His head jerked that way automatically, which was bad. He should be able to ignore it and thus show them his strength in doing so. "You understand your duty," he admonished the airborne. "Now go to it."

He saw more than one hollow gaze amongst them as they cast their wings out again and launched up to rejoin their men. Praeter wheeled his steed and sent it scuttling back along the rear of the line, calling out, "The airborne is going to buy you the time to move! Don't waste that time! As soon as they dive in, I want to see every man of you *running*!"

He looked into the sky, seeing the airborne mass there. As he had known they would, the enemy had predicted the move and, even before that great dive had started, dozens of Wasp soldiers were dropping, spinning helplessly out of the sky. Praeter watched them because it was his duty, in return, to observe the carnage that his orders had created.

Then they dived, a great cloud of them, hundreds of soldiers sweeping in for the trees, packing closer and closer as they came, until the snapbow shot of the defenders was mauling whole clumps of men out of the air at once. Praeter was only peripherally aware of the clatter as the heavy infantry began to rush forward as best it could, spears held high to clear the brush.

"General!"

He turned to see a messenger alighting beside him, so coated with dust it was impossible to make him out clearly.

"What is going on down there?"

"Fly-kinden, General," the messenger reported. "They're passing over us, dropping bombs on us. They're targeting the automotives."

The only thing they could make out, in this dust. "Press forward," Praeter instructed. "Press forward with infantry and engage their fortified positions from ground and air. Have the airborne keep the skies clear. That's the only way to counter grenadiers."

"Yes sir." The messenger leapt into the air again, but began falling instantly, twisting desperately with a bolt clear through him.

"General!"

But Praeter was already turning to see where the missile had come from.

A hammer blow of shock hit him. There was a new airborne coming in now, but it was not imperial. Instead it was a ragged assortment of men and women: Flies, Moths, Mantids, even Beetles and half-breeds. With the most immediate

Wasp airborne of this flank already engaged in the trees, they had the sky to themselves for just enough time to drop onto the advancing heavy infantry and take them in the flank, scattering across them, shooting crossbows and shortbows or simply throwing things. This was no disciplined attack, nothing an imperial officer would suffer from his men, but there was nevertheless a core of unity there. This ragged pack of brigands had obviously trained together.

The infantry was responding with sting shot, the air above them crackling with it, but the enemy fliers were already fleeing, leaving behind them a formation that was stationary and broken up.

Praeter grimaced. "Get me a unit of the heavies back here!" he shouted at one of his men. "Make that two."

"General—?"

"Do it!"

He turned his animal, because he had the plan now. At last, when it was almost too late, he had an understanding. Where would the earth now erupt with them? Why, from behind—or from the far slope of the hill he was watching from. The enemy had been given ample time to work the land, to sap and mine it with remarkable skill. The advance scouts had seen none of these flanking forces.

Those earthworks and palisades ahead would be deserted: he would stake his rank on it. But then he had known it was a trap from the start, and at last he had seen the way the jaws of it hinged.

The infantry was clattering back around him now, and he called for them to form ranks before him.

"Sir, the airborne . . ." one of their officers began.

Praeter spared one glance for the light airborne, who were still battling at the forest verge. He had thought that the enemy there might flee once their bait was taken, but that did not seem to be so. The enemy general was a cursed mix of evasion and bravado, which in a Wasp would have been admirable, but in an enemy was something to be crushed as quickly as possible.

Behind him, amidst the ranks of the infantry, the hill suddenly exploded. His beetle lurched forward, then reared back on to four legs, antennae flicking madly. He clung to the tall saddle with his thighs, looking up for the grenadiers, but there were none.

He heard the hollow knock of a leadshotter, but not close. A spume of smoke rose from a neighbouring hilltop also swathed in greenery.

Artillery? His own leadshotters were tilting toward the smoke, his engineers frantically taking measurements, calculating angles.

It was then that the enemy appeared, swarming along the ridge of his own hill with a motley of fliers above them. Praeter found his throat instantly drier even than the dust could make it. They were coming at a run, all shapes and sizes of them: armoured Ant-kinden soldiers, Mantis archers and swordsmen, Spiders, Beetles, Scorpions, Mynan Soldier Beetles, lumbering Mole Crickets. These were the dredgings of the Lowlands and the Empire both, a great froth of angry men and women now rushing the Wasp position.

His eye counted, even while his mind reeled. Two thousand, perhaps three— and how many of them wearing pillaged Wasp armour or using imperial weapons? *Have we come this far just to arm every ruffian in the Lowlands?*

"Set your spears!" he shouted, leading his cavalry between the infantry blocks. "Someone call some airborne from the other flank. We need them here! This must be the main attack!" *Send word to Malkan.* But he bit down on that last unspoken command. He would not do so, not for all the soldiers who might die here. He would not bend his pride so far as to ask for Malkan's aid.

Taking his entire force into account, he outnumbered this enemy ten to one, but *here*, right here and now, he unfortunately did not.

She, the one who had been Grief in Chains and was now Prized of Dragons, watched as the flying soldiers of Salma's army dived in again, plunging down into the dust. Her blank white eyes followed their course, and she wondered how many they would lose. She hated fighting. She hated all war.

She loved Salma, who had come after her, even into the teeth of the Wasp army. For that she called herself Prized of Dragons now, who had been Grief in Chains, and then briefly Aagen's Joy. One of the things that she loved most about Salma was that he, too, had no love of war. Perhaps he did not hate it as she did, but he took no joy in it. He was doing this, mounting this savage assault on the Wasp advance, because in his heart was his love for her and a prince's love of his subjects. He had thousands of people in Sarn who needed his protection, and this battle was the price—as would be all the battles still to come.

Salma touched down lightly near to her, glancing about. She ran to him, her robes flapping. His smile, when he saw her, was like the sun to her.

"Surely you must flee now, Salma," she said to him. "Their army, all their other soldiers, will be coming."

"That's precisely what I need to know."

There were warriors of Salma's ragtag army passing back and forth all the time—busy hurrying the injured away or rushing in from other engagements. Salma peered through them until he saw a squad of horse cavalry galloping in.

"Phalmes!" he cried, and the Soldier Beetle reined his horse in, skidding slightly on the loose sand and stones.

"General!" the Mynan acknowledged. It was a title that Salma did not want, a Wasp title, but to his men he had become a general, and there was nothing he could do about that.

"Where is their main force now?" he asked.

"The harriers have done what they could," Phalmes reported. Prized of Dragons noticed how his horse panted. Phalmes must have ridden miles back and forth today.

"We've pulled out?"

"Broken, almost. We're gone, though." The harriers had been squads of men designed to make the far flank of the Wasp army assume that it was the main point of attack. They had been instructed to sow as much confusion as possible, while the real assault would come at the opposite corner of the advance.

"We need to finish here. How do we stand?" Salma asked.

"You need to see for yourself," Phalmes said. "There's only one group standing here, but they won't budge."

"Show me."

Phalmes wheeled his horse, and his men—mostly his original bandit followers from before he met Salma—rode after him. Salma's wings flared and he coasted over Phalmes' head, and Prized of Dragons let her own bloom into the air in a rainbow splendour of dancing light to follow him.

Phalmes' words were instantly clear. The Wasps had been thrown off this side of the valley, killed and scattered or simply retreating in good order. Smoke from burning automotives still thickened the dusty air. Only one band of black and gold remained, a few hundred men surrounded by a loose cordon of Salma's people. Prized noticed that only a few of them were Wasps.

"Auxillians, Salma," she observed. "They are Bee-kinden."

"I see them."

"We have little time, General," Phalmes reminded him.

Salma nodded, walking forward. He saw a few crossbows lift, but trusted to his reactions and the obvious threat of retribution to safeguard him.

"Who commands here?" he demanded.

There was a stir amongst the soldiers, and then an old Wasp-kinden walked forth. Salma, who had been hoping that these would be unattended Auxillians ripe for desertion, grimaced.

"You must be the Lord of the Wastes," the Wasp said, his clear voice cutting across the distance. "I am General Praeter of the Sixth Army."

There was a stir through Salma's troops at that news. *A general? A real Wasp general!*

"General," Salma said, aware that, all the time, the rest of the Wasp army would be moving. "I have one chance to offer you and your men. Surrender now, throw down your arms, and I will spare you."

"I must congratulate you on your conduct of this war, Commonwealer," General Praeter said, with all the time in the world. "I see now how little of resources you had, and how far you have marched on it."

"Will you surrender?" Salma demanded of him.

"You know I will not."

Salma ground his teeth. "Then I call upon your Auxillian troops gathered here. You have no reason to stand and die for your oppressors. You may join us, or simply go back to your homes or wherever you choose, but you must drop your arms, and do it *now*. I have not the time to give any of you a second chance. Why die for the Empire when you can live for your own people?"

Silence then, with the Bee-kinden staring at him. Not a one of them moved, and Salma read quite clearly the pride, the almost tearful pride, on General Praeter's face.

"You have your answer," said the Wasp. "You must come and take us." He walked back into the ranks of his men, who closed their shields protectively after him.

"Salma, their army will have regrouped by now. We have no time."

I cannot let them live, Salma thought coldly. *Not with a general. Ah, the things we must do in war.*

"Bring up the snapbowmen," he said quietly, and Phalmes galloped off without hesitation, crying out the order.

"I am sorry, General," Salma said, stepping back. "For what it is worth, I salute you."

"Come away," Prized of Dragons advised him, one hand on his shoulder. "You do not wish to see this."

"No, I do not," Salma agreed. "That is why I must."

◈ ◈ ◈

The new king did not meet with him, which Salma took at first for a bad sign. He had come to Sarn as fast as he could, wearing a horse out to make the distance, and with two of Phalmes' ex-bandits acting as escort. He had left Phalmes himself to hold the Landsarmy together until he came back.

Out there, the Wasp army was stalking forward, making good time despite the constant attacks of Salma's people. The death of General Praeter had halted them for two days, while General Malkan made the necessary reorganization, but now they were ploughing forward again.

He had met with the Roach-kinden, Sfayot, after entering Sarn, hearing the old man's account of how the refugees had been treated. Phalmes might order his army, but here was his nation: three times as many noncombatants led by an elderly Roach.

The meeting in Sarn was barely a council of war, more of a military briefing. The time for idle talk, rather than orders, was almost done. The room was small, with a single table hosting a mere dozen of them. These were not the statesmen or the leaders on whose words war was unleashed or reined in, but rather the commanders who would enact the war itself. Here was Salma of the Landsarmy himself; Balkus, Parops and Plius the foreign Ant-kinden; Cydrae, a lean, hard-faced Mantis woman commanding the Ancient League warriors, along with a silent Moth-kinden in layered armour who did not give her name; a fat Beetle-kinden man representing something called the Sarnesh militia that was a force of irregulars put together of their own volition by the inhabitants of Sarn's Foreigners' Quarter. To these were added a single Sarnesh woman, a tactician from the Royal Court, with grey-speckled hair. Salma had been hoping for the King himself.

But of course the King will be listening. That would have to be enough. Salma nodded a greeting to Parops, whom he had not seen since the ravaged streets of Tark.

"Commanders," the Sarnesh said, addressing them all equally. "They are upon us. The fight is, by our estimates, a tenday away at most."

"Probably less," Salma interrupted. "By my reckoning."

The Sarnesh woman regarded him without expression. *Am I expendable now? Have I outlived my usefulness?* In the face of that blankness, concealing all the thoughts of the city of Sarn, he felt himself shrinking: from a prince and a military leader to a mere brigand and retainer of the greater Ant city-state.

Then she said, "You are more soundly placed to know, tactician."

He almost missed it, although the other Ants at the table went quite still on hearing the word. What was in a word, though?

"My people say that you have cared for them well," he said. "I was not sure, after the death of the Queen, how we might stand."

She was expressionless, still, but surely he was used to that from Ants: expressions or visible mannerisms did not come naturally to them. He had no other clues.

"The movement of the crown is not succession, but continuity," the tactician said. "The King was party to the agreement made with you and your forces, and he considers himself bound by it. We understand that you have been doing good work in the east. You received our Lorn detachment, we believe?"

A hundred Sarnesh soldiers, that was all that they could spare him. They had clearly expected him to meet the Wasps nose to nose, and for all to die in a glorious waste of time. He hoped he had not disappointed them by surviving and by not losing a man of their Sarnesh suicide force.

"They were invaluable," he said.

"But they did not fight," the tactician noted.

"I had other uses for them," Salma replied. He had spread the Sarnesh throughout his troops, and used their ability to speak mind to mind, to coordinate the various wings of his disparate force. Without them it was certain that some part of his attack would have been too late, too early, caught out or overextended.

He had thus made the Lorn detachment his strategic eyes and ears, giving orders and receiving reports to dozens of scattered detachments.

"Sarn requires your services once again," the tactician informed him. The other commanders were watching closely. This was not a council of war, but the officers of the Sarnesh main army gathered to meet with *him*.

"We have our agreement," he replied, with an easiness he did not feel.

"We wish to meet them on the field," she then told him. "The Royal Court has determined that a field battle represents our best chance of victory."

"Despite the Battle of the Rails?" Salma asked, seeing the same question in other faces around the table.

"We are better prepared now that we have snapbows of our own," the tactician said. "Even so, we recognize the risk. A field battle will at least allow us to retreat to the city walls if all goes badly. However . . ."

Salma waited for her words, already putting together in his mind what would come next.

"However," the Sarnesh woman continued, "we will be leaving our city poorly defended, if we commit the full force that this venture requires. If matters do not fall out according to plan," she explained, and perhaps there was the tiniest tremor in her voice that translated, *if we all die on the field*, "our people—and yours—will have no protection save the walls and defences of Sarn itself. We have heard from our ally of Tark," she picked out Parops. "Wasp-kinden are no strangers to breaking sieges. In order to risk a proper confrontation with the Empire, we require an assurance that our walls can stand, at least until a relieving force can be brought home."

Salma nodded slowly. He might not understand the mechanics of the machines involved, but he knew what a siege entailed. He had seen that already at Tark. "And so, before you meet them, you want their . . . what, their . . . ?"

"Artillery," Parops intervened in a clipped tone. "A strike against their siege engines."

"Indeed," the tactician confirmed. "We can provide material and artificers to assist, but your own force has the greatest chance of achieving this end."

Salma looked around the table, from face to face: Parops was grimacing, not liking the odds; the two Ants beside him exchanged uneasy glances; Cydrae the Mantis gave him a single, respectful nod.

Oh, Stenwold, if you could see me now.

"I must trust that your artificers will know what to destroy and how to do it," Salma replied finally. "I confess that I know nothing of that skill. I can get them in, though, with a swift, sudden strike. That I can do."

"We understand what it is we are asking of you."

"So long as you understand what *I* have asked of *you*."

The tactician, and by extension the city-state of Sarn, nodded. "What you ask shall be accomplished in every particular, so long as Sarn survives to undertake it."

◊ ◊ ◊

He began calculating, on the hard ride back, his mind working through days and numbers. *Are we ready for this? If we are not ready for this, what then?* His special project, this meant, which had drained Sarn and its surrounding countryside of riding beasts. His people had been training since the spring, or at least every one of them with any aptitude for the saddle.

I am trying to fight a Commonweal war with Lowlands soldiers. That was not quite true, for the war he was fighting had never been fought before in anyone's histories.

Phalmes greeted him as he rode into camp. The Mynan looked as though he had not slept much since Salma had seen him last, for the Wasp advance was forcing Salma's irregulars to fall back before them, still harassing scouts, setting traps and deadfalls for their automotives, and never letting the Wasps forget about them or think themselves safe.

There must have been something in Salma's face, because Phalmes bared his teeth unhappily as soon as he saw his leader.

"That bad, is it?" he asked. "They've cut us loose?"

"Not quite," Salma said. "Sarn is on its way. They intend a field battle."

"Cursed Ants never learn," spat Phalmes. "Another field battle."

Salma shrugged. "I'm not going to try to teach warfare to the Ant-kinden. They and we both need Sarn to remain safe, whilst the city's army is abroad."

"I don't like this."

"I don't think anyone does," Salma told him. "I can see the logic, though."

"That means we're where the metal meets, aren't we?"

"We have been that way for some time," Salma sighed. "You've scouted the army, yes? Its disposition, how it's broken up?"

Phalmes nodded. "You want me to get the lads together for this?"

"It might be best."

"The lads" were Salma's officers, such as they were: as ragged a band as his army itself was, without uniform or discipline, and yet they were devoted to him. More, they were devoted to what he was trying to achieve. Phalmes and the Fly-kinden woman Chefre had been with him from the start, as had a Maynesh Ant-kinden who had been one of Phalmes' bandits. There was a laconic Mantis-kinden hunter, hooded always, who was incomparable with his bow, which was six and a half feet from point to point. Morleyr, the hulking Mole Cricket, was an Auxillian deserter, just as Phalmes himself was, and had been crucial to their land-engineering, his people carving out trenches and pits underground with their Art and their bare hands. There was an elderly Fly-kinden who was a skilled artificer, and a Beetle-Ant half-breed from Helleron who was a solid infantry officer. To this jumbled rag-bag Salma had added the Sarnesh officer in charge of the Lorn detachment, and now the leader of the artificers that the King of Sarn had sent them.

He explained it all to them as concisely as possible. In fact there was not much to say. *We must destroy their machines of war.* He listened to them talk, one speaking over the other, ideas being hammered out, picked over, discarded. This was his governance: the melting pot of thought that he could skim from. He ladled out the best of it: the diversion, the reserve, the sudden strike, the aerial attack.

"Their general will expect something like this," Chefre warned. "He's no fool."

"That's only because it is the strategy that we must accomplish," Salma told her. "And we shall."

ELEVEN

I'm getting too old for this.

The old Scorpion-kinden known as Hokiak paused a moment, leaning on his stick, his other hand, with the thumb claw broken off, resting on the handle of the door to his back room. He could just turn away, he knew. This was not a matter of profit. He had been in the game long enough to profit from anyone and everyone, and no man had ever accused him of being partisan.

Business had not been good recently. The Wasps knew that there was constant trouble on the streets, even if Kymene's resistance groups kept eluding them. The response of the new governor was to employ an iron hand. Where old man Ulther would have set traps to lure them in, the new man's response was almost panicky, and made more enemies than it intimidated.

The new man in question was Colonel Latvoc, who Hokiak knew for a fact was Rekef Inlander. Latvoc was not a man with any interest in Myna, and he made that clear in his every move. He did not hold audiences, he did not consult with Consortium merchants, but instead remained holed up in the palace like a man waiting for a siege. That was something that Hokiak expected Kymene's people would eventually oblige him in.

For the last tenday it had been hard to do business in Myna, even for Hokiak. The garrison force had been out on the streets in force, meting out justice and injustice in equal measures, as Latvoc tried to scare the city into behaving itself. Hokiak knew of a dozen tavernas that had been officially closed down as meeting points for the resistance, and he also knew that some establishments had been just that, and others had been entirely innocent of it. People who had nothing whatsoever to do with the resistance had been dragged from their beds and thrown into the interrogation rooms, where, under threat of torture, a welter of unverifiable misinformation emerged to obscure whatever the genuine revolutionaries they captured might have revealed.

Then there were the internal purges. At the same time as all of that public activity, Latvoc was going through his own officers. Several men had already been made to disappear, and it all seemed the actions of a man who was either blindly committed to some ideal or else absolutely terrified.

Yes, business was difficult and yet business was booming. The resistance had never been stronger and Hokiak was happy to sell them whatever they wanted, so long as they met the high prices he charged. At the same time he had smuggled Wasp officers out of the city, or falsified papers to help others escape the continuing cull. The one thing he always made sure of was that his clients did not get to meet each other. He was not inclined to sell information these days, for each side was too prone to exact singular vengeance if betrayed.

Which brought his thoughts round neatly to the new arrivals waiting in his back room, the people who had been asking to speak with him.

A man tries to keep his books straight. He had known, surely, that the day would come when someone would ask him to take sides: Kymene herself had already thrown enough hints his way by declaring that she considered him a true citizen of Myna. The Wasps, too, would surely realize soon enough that a man of his activities must know more than he ever revealed. The day would surely come.

It had come.

"What if I ain't playin'?" he asked, scratching the creased and baggy skin under his jaw with one claw. "I don't have to go in."

"Then don't." His business partner shrugged. He was an old, dishevelled Spider-kinden, skeletally gaunt and with long grey hair, going by the name of Gryllis. "Let them just kick their heels."

It was an apposite image, signifying both waiting and being hanged, because Hokiak thought he had guessed the truth about his visitors' real allegiances, but he didn't *know*.

"We ain't goin' to win out of this business either way," he complained.

"We've always managed so far, old claw," Gryllis remarked, but there was a lack of certainty in his deep-set eyes. "Or do you think it's time for us to move house?"

"I been workin' on this place a long time. Ain't lookin' to let it go to rack and rot just yet." Hokiak filled his pipe one-handed, by dint of long practice, and then lit it, taking comfort from the smoke. "You jus' make sure you get the boys watchin', in case things go wrong. I want the bodies out of there and into the river 'fore anyone can blink."

"Right you are."

Hokiak pushed open the door and surveyed the little back room where his select clients came. He knew most of them gathered there by sight. The two Maynesh Ants were mercenary bodyguards, closer than sisters and waiting for their next patron. The young Mynan woman in the corner was a pawnbroker of rare articles, who paid Hokiak a percentage to keep shop on part of his premises. The rowdy card game between the Fly-kinden knife thrower and the three local bruisers was just a cover for Hokiak's own men, who were waiting for his word. The half-breed facing the main door, marked with Mynan and Wasp features, must be the new smuggler in town who was reputedly trawling for business. Hokiak would speak to him later. This current business came first.

They were seated, the two of them, at a table near one of the corners. He recognized the girl instantly, because he might be old, but his memory for faces was still young. There she was, but what was she now, the one who had been Stenwold Maker's niece?

Che rose from the table as the old Scorpion hobbled over. Beside her Thalric sat merely as a cloaked, cowled and brooding presence.

"Hokiak," she greeted him. "Thank you for seeing us."

He squinted at her through yellowed eyes. "Ain't usually expecting to find any Lowlanders round here." His eyes flicked to Thalric briefly.

"Do you remember me?" Che asked him. "I'm Cheerwell Maker, Stenwold's niece." She kept her voice deliberately lower than the murmur of the other patrons. A young Fly-kinden boy stopped at their table with three shallow bowls of beer. Hokiak nodded to him absently and then made a great show of lowering himself, creaking joints and all, into an empty chair.

"You I do remember," he said. "So tell me, what's his nibs's kin now doing round old Hokiak's place? Ain't a good time, this, for social calls. You're delivering messages? Perhaps a gift for the old man?"

"I . . . I have some money," Che said, and immediately bit her lip. "I'm sorry, I'm not really . . . Stenwold doesn't know I'm here, Hokiak. He thinks I'm in Tharn, the Moth city. But I heard of how things were in Myna."

"And you jumped on a flier and decided to pay old Hokiak a visit." The Scorpion began relighting his pipe. "Good of you to think of me."

"Hokiak, you're the only person I know in Myna that I could easily find," Che replied. "I need your help."

"Seems just about everyone does." He settled back in the chair. "But don't get to reckoning that, just 'cos I know your uncle, you can get credit, girl."

"I know how you've helped the resistance—" Che started.

"I ain't never helped no one. I just sold to 'em, because I ain't choosy that way. The Red Flag pay like everyone else." He was obviously waiting for something that she had not given him yet.

Is it the money? She persevered regardless. "Hokiak, you've got to . . . I need your help to get in touch with them."

He smiled, the pale skin creasing about the stumps of his tusks. "Now then," he said slowly, "how come I already knew that, eh?"

"I don't have much, but I can pay—"

Again he stopped her, his clawed hand raised. "I do remember you, girl."

"Good, then—"

"You was the one the Wasps got—the one that Stenwold's lot came over here to spring."

"Me and Salma, yes."

"I heard they put you to the question."

She could not avoid glancing at Thalric, who, after all, had been the man who put her on the rack, for all he had not, in the end, actually tortured her. "I . . . in a way."

Hokiak sighed heavily. "And now you want in to the resistance."

Che heard Thalric shift in his chair, tense all of a sudden. A moment later she, too, was aware that the sound of the room had changed. The boisterous pack of gamblers had fallen quiet. She heard chairs scraping back, and glanced at Thalric again.

"Someone must have cheated at cards," she said weakly, trying to work out what was wrong.

The gamblers were heading over. Che stood up hurriedly as she saw knives drawn. Only when they surrounded the table did she realize, so very late, that they were Hokiak's men. She found herself with her hand only halfway to her sword hilt, feeling foolish and off balance, and completely blind to what was going on. Thalric was still seated, leaning back in his chair, but she knew him enough to see that he was coiled ready to move, whether to kick the table back in Hokiak's face or to blast the nearest man with his Art.

"What's going on, Hokiak?" she asked. "You . . ." She felt her world shift beneath her. "You've gone over to the Wasps?"

Hokiak laughed out loud at that, genuinely if not pleasantly. "I have, have I? You sit down again, girl. You listen to old Hokiak for a moment."

"Sit," hissed Thalric, and she did so without quite deciding to.

"Well, now," said Hokiak wearily, "Sten's little niece is all growed up, is she? She's in town again and wants to keep up with her old friends in the resistance. She don't even care that the Wasps are here, ready to slam her back in the machine room? No, she don't." He chewed on his pipe stem for a moment. "So what a feller gets to wonderin' is just what the girl is doin' here with a Wasp-kinden handler. Bit obvious, maybe? Not very subtle, but these ain't subtle times. You I remember, him I don't. More, you won't be the first to come out of the machine room with a change of heart. I hear they can be right persuasive in there."

Che stared at him. "What are you saying?"

"He's saying he thinks you've been turned," said Thalric, with a certain satisfaction. "He's saying he doesn't trust you."

"What? But I'm Stenwold's niece—"

"And old Sten himself would know that doesn't carry much weight with me . . . Oh, I forgot, he don't know you're here."

Che looked from the Scorpion to his men. "But . . . what can I do to make you believe me?"

Hokiak shrugged. "Don't have to make me believe you. I ain't no more than a simple pedlar. All that happens now is who you get peddled to."

"So we're your stock-in-trade now, are we?" Thalric asked him.

Hokiak leered at him. "Man's got to make a livin'."

Che sensed the Wasp about to move, and she said hurriedly, "So sell us to the resistance. That's fine. Kymene will know me. Just let me speak to her."

"Che—" Thalric started, but she shook her head and went on.

"I'll go unarmed. I don't care. Look, I'm not working for the Wasps, and Thalric here isn't either. He's gone renegade."

Hokiak's eyes narrowed. "Thalric? Ain't the first time I heard *that* name."

Thalric cursed and kicked over the table.

It was so without warning that he caught them, and Che, by surprise. The round surface of the table sprang up, toppling Hokiak backward, still on his chair, slamming into two of the bravos and sending them stumbling. Thalric's hand flared and the man closest to him was punched from his feet, to land heavily, his chest now a smoking ruin. The Wasp vaulted the tipped-over table with his wings coursing from his shoulders. Hokiak's Fly-kinden flung a blade at him, but Thalric loosed his sting at the same time. The Fly ducked back, his aim going awry so that the hiltless blade skimmed Thalric's scalp rather than taking him through the eye. Another man tried to get in the Wasp's way and caught Thalric's elbow in his face. The single leap had taken the Wasp halfway across the room.

Che went for her sword, feeling horribly slow and clumsy. The Mynan closest to her got his blade out of the scabbard first and tried making a stab at her, but too close to make a good job of it. The tip scored into her leather artificer's coat and she fell back, reaching and grabbing his baldric as she did so, pulling the man on top of her. His sword thudded into the floorboards instead and the blade snapped.

Thalric did not wait for her, powering his way toward the door that would take him into the cluttered trading front of Hokiak's Exchange. It opened before he reached it and he saw an old Spider there with a knife just clearing his belt. Thalric, with no time to scorch him, simply collided with him shoulder first, bowling him backward with all the momentum his wings could give him. A moment later he was in the Exchange, and a moment after that he had vanished into the street.

"Alive!" Hokiak was shouting. "Take her alive, curse it!"

Che threw off the half-stunned man atop her, but before she could try to escape he had grabbed her ankle, bringing her down again. She scrambled to her hands and knees, and at that moment Hokiak's cane gave her a ringing smack across the side of the head. She cried out, falling sideways, and then Hokiak's man was forcing her face into the floorboards, dragging her sword from its sheath and casting it away.

"You traitor!" she yelled, fighting furiously, but utterly ineffectually, to get free. The point of Hokiak's cane came back down into her range of vision.

"One of my men's dead," she heard the Scorpion say. "A moment ago I had me a choice to make, whether to do what you wanted, or to sell you. Now I ain't choosing. Your friend there's just gone and forced my hand."

"He's a renegade!" Che shouted helplessly at his feet and the ferrule of his cane. "He thought you were going to turn him in."

"Sure, I bet," sneered Hokiak. "I know, girl, I *know* that Thalric is Rekef. I know that name well enough. More fool you for spillin' it, but then I reckon you ain't been in the trade long enough to get things right."

"What are you talking about? I only wanted to see Kymene."

"And you're goin' to," he assured her. "Gryllis, how are you feeling?"

"I've seen better nights." The Spider clawed at the doorframe to pick himself up, one hand pressed to the back of his head.

"Send a message to the Flag," Hokiak said. "Tell 'em we got a Wasp turncoat all packaged for them. Girl, you're now goin' to find there are worse things than an Empire machine room, believe you me."

◁▷ ◁▷ ◁▷

There had been the one event that Tynisa could not explain, and which had brought her to this point.

At first news of her father Tisamon had remained scarce. He had not been hiding his trail so much as travelling so swiftly and surely as to leave none. At last, and after twice drawing blood in order to preserve herself, she had fallen in with some black marketeers. In a taverna on the Collegium riverside she had encounted an old half-breed, Beetle and Ant-kinden mixed. Had he seen a Mantis-kinden man of just this description? As it happened he had, and in that very taproom, agreeing to take service with a package shipper bound for Helleron.

Helleron? It had made perfect sense, of course. Where had Tisamon gone previously, to forget his past? Nowhere but Helleron, where people seldom asked about such trivial comings and goings. She should have thought of that sooner.

It just remained to get herself there and she decided to follow Tisamon's own strategy. Despite the war, or because of it, there was a regular and shady trade between the occupied Beetle city and its free sibling. Tynisa then remembered the city of Myna, and Hokiak, and how the old Scorpion had claimed that the Wasps themselves liked to keep a little of the black market going.

She had therefore taken up with a Beetle-kinden smuggler by the name of Artelly Broadways, who ran a little airship catering for small and easily portable goods. He had himself and a Fly crewman on board, but he needed a couple of guards too, and Tynisa fought off two other hopefuls for the job without much effort.

The problem came when they were still two days from Helleron, blown east by inclement weather and with the balloon and gondola seeming equally rickety. Tynisa had realized by then that Broadways was a man whose confidence and optimism outstripped his ability, and that he was not nearly as experienced in the trade as he constantly assured her he was.

Shortly after that the Wasps caught them. It was sudden enough. A fixed-wing had come from out of the sun and danced contemptuously past their bows, throwing Broadways into utter confusion. A moment later there had been Wasp soldiers in the air all around them, darting past the stays to land, crouching with swords drawn, on the deck. Broadways' one piece of wisdom had been to offer no resistance at all.

They had forced him to bring the airship down, to find more Wasps waiting there. In total there were barely a dozen of them, patrolling the Silk Road from Tark to Helleron with their flying machine in the air and a big docile spider, laden with packs and water bottles, on the ground. Tynisa had instantly started considering her options. She could probably not manage to kill them all, but she could eliminate enough to get away, but then they could still fly after her and shoot at her, and there was also the fixed-wing somewhere nearby to take into her equations.

Broadways had no convincing explanation for them, but the leader of the patrol looked sufficiently venal to Tynisa's eyes. She virtually had to kick the Beetle-kinden before he took the hint and led the man aside, offering to make a contribution to the Emperor's war chest. Thankfully, the goods he was carrying included machine-cut gems from Collegium's workshops, which served to smooth the way well enough.

It was then that the inexplicable happened, for, looking at the leader of the Wasp patrol, she heard words inside her head. The voice that spoke them was not a voice as she recognized it. It was composed of whispering and rustling and the darkness between trees, all forced through the gaps of human words, and it said to her, *Go with him.*

She started so suddenly that the Wasp officer stared at her, perhaps thinking she was about to try something violent.

"What?" he asked of her. "She's your crew is she, or a passenger?"

"Crew. Guard," explained Broadways.

"Excuse me, Sergeant," Tynisa said. "I was just wondering . . ."

"Wondering what?" He looked her up and down, but the expected smile did not come. He had a broad-jawed, solid face that did not show his feelings much.

"What's work like in the Empire?"

The sergeant looked from her to Broadways. "Fed up with this fellow's company are you? Can't say I blame you."

"I'm sick of working for clowns," she said. "You people always seem to have it worked out." She ignored Broadways' squawk of protest. "Is there anyone I could speak to, back where you're based, or is it a closed shop?"

At that he did smile, if only slightly. "You ever heard of the Auxillians? They come in all shapes and kinden." She could not tell his thoughts but guessed that he was considering the war with the Lowlands, the possibility of a useful spy or agent. *So let him think that.* "I can take you to the camp at Asta, if you want," he continued. "I'll fit you up with someone, I'm sure, if they reckon you're useful."

"That," she said, "would be very acceptable."

She did not bid farewell to the scandalized Broadways, only watched his patchwork airship sail on toward Helleron. Helleron, where she too was supposed to be going—so why was she not? Because of a voice, just a voice in her *head*, which had said, "*Go with him.*"

She wondered if Felise Mienn heard voices in her head, or whether the Dragonfly woman's madness was of a different sort.

Still, Tynisa was committed now. The Wasp patrol trekked north and east with their patient spider pack-beast, with the fixed-wing circling sometimes overhead. She tried to recall her memories of Asta: a midnight reconnaissance with Tisamon while in search of Che. It was little enough. She was alone now, living on her wits and on three words spoken to her by a voice she did not know.

She gave them two days before she broached the subject. In that time the Wasps had got used to her. They did not include her, their talk and occasional laughter being about people and rituals she did not recognize, but she proved that she could keep pace with them, and that went a little way toward being accepted.

"Sergeant," she finally said, those two days in, "I don't suppose you see much in the way of Mantis-kinden this far east."

The look he gave her sent a thrill through her because, however flat his features, *something* moved there. Voice or no voice, she was not just casting herself into the void.

"Strange question, that," he said.

"There's a particular man," she explained. "I've been tracking him for a while. Just asking out of interest, you understand."

"I understand your kinden and theirs don't get on," he remarked. "Odd thing is, yes, we've got one at Asta right now."

At Asta? What is he doing at Asta? But of course it need not be Tisamon. There was no reason at all for it to be Tisamon. *No reason except the voice . . .*

"Maybe I'll take a look at him when I'm there."

"You're likely to enjoy it," he said, although he did not clarify.

Asta was larger than she remembered it, at least twice the size now. There were more and more of the same hastily constructed barracks and storehouses, and a field of tents bivouacked beyond. Tynisa's party arrived around noon, and it seemed to her that not one of the Wasp-kinden she could see kept still. There were troops of soldiers marching or flying in, unpacking their kit, setting up tents or taking them down, packing up, moving out north or west or south. There were flying machines, automotives, pack animals. There were Auxillians of half a dozen kinden amidst the Wasps. Entire armies were on the move.

The patrol she was with did not slow for any of it, and so she was plunged into the hurly-burly of the Imperial Army like a stone thrown into unruly waters. For a moment they were shoulder to shoulder with other Wasps and their slaves, thronging back and forth, and she felt that she was drowning in the sheer scale of the Empire, of which this was just an outlying camp, just a small drop in their ocean.

The sergeant turned to her. "You stay here while I report. I'll come out soon enough, or someone else will." The look he gave her was calculating, narrow eyed, still weighing up her usefulness.

He left her then, pushing his way through the throng, and his men quickly dispersed, seeking food, drink, dice games and whores. With no option left to her, she waited. After a while of being jostled, she found a nearby automotive wagon and climbed up the side of it, gaining purchase on the smooth wood and metal by her Art, until she could sit aloft, gaining some illusion of being apart from it all. Even then, soldiers were constantly buzzing overhead, close enough for her to reach out and grab. The air was full of Wasps and Flies, and other kinden in the Empire's colours.

It was more than an hour before someone came for her, and then it was not the same sergeant but a narrow-faced Wasp, middle-aged and with rank bars that she identified as a major's, alighting atop the wagon and looking down on her. He put her in mind of the first Wasp she had spoken to, and deceived: Captain Halrad aboard the *Sky Without*, whom Totho had killed for her.

"You want to make yourself useful, do you?" he asked flatly. "What are you? Spiderlands spy, perhaps?"

She made herself smile at him easily. "Would I tell you if I was? Besides, since when was the Empire at war with the Spiderlands?"

"I expect news of that hourly," he said, regarding her doubtfully. "So, what are you, precisely?"

"A mercenary," she replied.

"An honest one, then?"

"Just so." She leant back. "So, Major, can you think of any use for me?"

"Don't play games," he told her, but she could see a glint there, which showed she had reached some vanity within him. "I could have you arrested."

"Yes, but what would you gain?"

"You tell me. What's your name, first off?"

"Atryssa." She had not meant it, but the name came out without a thought: her mother's name. Surely it would not have been begrudged, if permission could have been asked for. "Your sergeant told me you have a Mantis here."

"And he told me you're looking for one. Some kind of vengeance, is it?"

She read his tone carefully. "Not that can't be put off. Just a dangerous man I'd rather keep track of."

"Or he was hunting you, was he?" he smiled then. "You don't think much of us Wasp-kinden, I'll wager. You Spiders, you look down on all sorts. When did you last catch a Mantis alive, though, in your webs?"

"You have him prisoner?" Her own anxiety bled through, even though she reminded herself, *It need not be Tisamon*, once again. He read her question as simple surprise, though.

"More than that. Nicely broken in, and playing for the crowd."

Despite herself, she made herself sound impressed. "I should like to see that." *Can it be this easy?* she thought, and then, *It cannot be him, not the man this Wasp describes.*

She was all wide-eyed for him, and she was young, and he was a man who liked to impress. He hopped down from the wagon in a brief flurry of wings, holding his hand out. "Come and see what the Empire can accomplish," he told her, and she jumped down after him, knowing in her heart that it could not be *him*, just some other Mantis pressed into servitude here.

He led her across Asta, shouting at any soldiers that got in his way, and that told her a lot about him, more than did their conversation. They wove their path through the tents and the press of bodies and the machines, around the buildings that were already showing the wear and tear of their impromptu nature, until she came to an arena.

It was as temporary as the rest of the place, crates and boards nailed together, thrown up to enclose a circle no more than thirty feet across. Wasps stood at the railing or hovered above. Officers got to sit on stacked boxes and crates that formed the crudest kind of raked seating overlooking the fighting pit. She noticed a lot of soldiers in the enclosed helms of the Slave Corps.

The major was leading her straight to the stacked-up seating, saying, "I don't suppose they even have this pastime where you come from."

In Collegium? No. But she said, "Do you think we don't know good sport in the Spiderlands, Major? I happen to have a fondness for it. Fancy a wager?"

That made him grin properly, as she had hoped. "A patron of the games, are you? Good. I don't know what use you might be to the Empire, but it was the sergeant mentioning our Mantis that caught my attention. I don't want anyone tampering with my prize."

"*Your* prize?" she asked him, as he evicted a lower-ranking officer to make a space for her. She sat down uncomfortably close to him, and in the pit below she saw two Beetle-kinden, bare-chested and armed with swords, face a Wasp contestant with a spear. She could tell that neither of the Beetles was a warrior, as they stumbled about and waved their blades frantically. Only after a moment did she notice that they were bound together, wrist to wrist.

The Wasp constantly played with them, vaulting backward and forth, wings a blur, until he put his spear through the chest of one, leaving it there and taking up the victim's dropped sword. The surviving Beetle tried to back away, dragging at his companion's fallen body as the Wasp stalked him, every slow move for the entertainment of the crowd. Tynisa made herself seem to enjoy it, cheering and shouting whenever the major did. Inside, as she watched the second Beetle eventually dispatched, she thought, *Is this really how they like their victories? As simple and predetermined as this? How pathetic of them.*

The major called down some question that she missed amidst the noise of the crowd, and one of the slavers called back to him.

"You're in luck," the major informed her. "He's next."

Tynisa steeled herself, but she did not feel she had it in her not to react, if it was *him.*

The audience of soldiers had now fallen silent, almost respectfully. She caught sight of fair hair as the new fighter was led in, and then *he* stepped into the rough ring. He was not wearing his arming jacket but was bare to the waist, like the Beetles had been, all his fighting history traced on his hide in burns and scratches. His claw gauntlet was on his arm—Tisamon the warrior, the Weaponsmaster.

"It's him, isn't it," the major enquired. She could hardly deny it.

"I'm amazed you caught him," she heard herself say. "He's been a great deal of trouble for everyone."

"There's little the Empire can't do, when it sets its mind to it," he bragged.

From the far side of the ring to where Tisamon had taken his stand there came a sudden rattling and a scraping. They had a corral built there, and now they hauled up a slatted gate, and out came one of the desert scorpions, its tail and claws raised in mindless threat. A creature longer than he was tall, Tisamon watched it without moving as it explored its environment, first trying to climb up the wall and being prodded back by the spears of the slavers, all the while becoming more and more enraged.

At last it either saw or scented him. The creature's pincers gaped wider, and she heard a shrill hiss emerge from it. Tisamon slowly, very slowly, fell back into a defensive stance. The soldiers grew murmurous with speculation, and by that she gathered quickly that he had fought for them many times before.

"You're lucky to have arrived when you did," the major said, his eyes fixed on the beast. "A couple of days and he's leaving us, if he lives that long."

"For where?" she asked.

"Oh, he's a commodity now," he said. "He's too good for the provinces. If he's going to get cut apart, let it happen before a more discerning audience."

Lunging forward, the scorpion struck, but Tisamon was already gone, and when it turned on him again it was missing a claw. It backed off a little until its tail touched the wall of the arena, and then rattled forward again, and he lopped the stinger from its tail, but still did not kill it.

It is almost as bad as the last fight, Tynisa thought. *How can he allow himself to become a part of this?*

But now he drove in to finish the beast off, cutting half the remaining claw away, stepping within its impotent reach and then driving the claw blade straight down into its eyes, not once but three times, until the wretched creature twitched its last and finally lay still.

And how they cheered him! He did not acknowledge it, merely stared down at the dead beast, and it seemed to Tynisa that he were wishing their positions were reversed.

"He's a valuable commodity," the major repeated to her, "so if you try to harm him, we'll make a slave of you, too, no matter how useful you might otherwise be. He'll cause you no more trouble, though. You can see that. He's ours now."

She forced herself to smile at him, though it proved her hardest deception. "I see that he has been punished more than I could ever hope for," she said, feeling her heart break at her own words.

She had assumed that the major would deal further with her, take her along with him. Instead the man was gone the next night, and his prized fighter too, and without a word to her. *He feared I wanted to kill Tisamon.* The man must have read something in her, the ferocity of her emotion. He had not wanted to risk her harming his prize.

She had made an attempt to follow them, a pack on her back, a lone Spider-kinden heading off into the depths of the Empire. Something of her foster father Stenwold had rubbed off, though, to make her reconsider the idea. *Alone in the Empire, they will make a slave of me, or I will shed enough blood resisting it that they will have to kill me.*

Tisamon was being hauled off in chains, further and further away each moment, and yet she must now play a delicate game. She was in the Empire, where every pair of eyes belonged to a spy that could denounce her. She did not have the craft for this, nor was her kinden such that she could walk through them unnoticed. She had a bitter moment of longing for the skills of the face-changing Scyla, who could have gone anywhere and done anything, but who had squandered her gifts so meanly.

Tynisa had to wait two days before the right man came along. Until that time she slipped through the ordered commotion of Asta like a slim-bladed knife. She gave herself airs, behaving as though she was the agent of someone of status. She remembered the little she had gleaned from Thalric about the shadowy Rekef, so she let people believe by looks and omissions that she might be Outlander. To the officers she was a worrying enigma, because they did not really know if they wanted her. Nor did they know if they were allowed to be rid of her. She walked a tenuous line, staying out of the way of the highest ranks and bewildering the sergeants and lieutenants.

To the common soldiers serving below them she made herself something different. She could never be one of them, being the wrong kinden and the wrong gender, but still, she made herself their companion. She sat at their games of chance, joined their conversations, though it was hard for her: far harder than simply cloaking mystery about herself for the benefit of their superiors. She learnt a lot about the people she had been fighting and killing for the last year. She learnt about the intense rivalries between armies, between companies and squads within those armies. She learnt that they envied the engineers their pay and privilege, yet looked down on them for never getting their hands dirty. She learnt that they loathed the Slave Corps but joked about the Rekef in a way that their officers would never have dared. She learnt that many of them were here in the army just as much against their wishes as were the Auxillians they fought alongside. The sense she got of the Empire was frightening: that it fought because it could not do anything else. If the Empire ran out of enemies, it would tear itself apart.

Thus, between the officers and their men, she held an uneasy place: an intruder, a parasite, in their hive of dedicated activity. There was only one strange encounter, when a junior lieutenant caught up with her and talked in circles around her for the best part of an hour, strangely hesitant, oddly delicate, as though he was reaching his hand into a trap in order to draw some valuable thing out. Only later did she wonder if he had been a Rekef agent, and been trying to determine whether she was genuinely Rekef also. The encounter had left her with no answers, but something to ponder. *So, the Rekef is not as unified as all that. Well, didn't Thalric say that it was his own sneaks that tried to kill him?*

After those two days, she at last found her mark. His name was Otran and he was almost universally loathed by officers and men alike. He was a major in the Consortium but, more than that, he was a tax-gatherer, a bureaucrat. He arrived in Asta, a small, angry Wasp-kinden man with an automotive and a squad of armoured sentinels as his guards, and then he took the Emperor's cut of everything that had been gathered in from the Lowlands campaign so far. He was, she could see, keenly aware of the hatred with which he was regarded. After a little observation she could tell that he was highly upset by it too. He considered himself a serious military officer, given an unpleasant task, rather than the belligerent little moneyman that everyone saw him to be. In short, he was perfect for her.

She courted him. It was not difficult, either. Major Otran was a man who craved recognition, and he was snubbed at every turn by his own people. The presence of an attractive Spider-kinden was nectar to him. She even suspected that her swift association with the man only confirmed, in the eyes of others, that she was indeed Rekef.

Otran was going on to Capitas, that was the important thing. Capitas was where they had taken Tisamon, apparently, for there was an ever-hungry market there for fighting slaves. It was an important form of Wasp entertainment and that explained Tisamon's value to them. The Mantis seemed to be willingly cooperating with their estimation of him, and she could not understand that. She could only hope that he had some plan, but that man she had seen bloody-bladed in the makeshift Asta arena had given no sign of it. He had been more a dead-eyed machine ready to cut apart whatever was set against him. Seeing him like that, she had no doubt that, if she had stepped into that ring, he would have killed her, too.

Otran's machine pressed eastward, and she went with it. His guards were suspicious of her, never letting her alone with the tax money, though they cared not at all if she was left alone with Otran.

In her mind she was trying to imagine what she could say to that bleak-faced killer from the arena that would recall her father to her. Mantis pride! It was something she had not inherited and it was something she could not understand.

At night, when not closeted with Otran, she took out Tisamon's brooch—the sword and the circle—and tried to find in it some clue to his present state of mind.

TWELVE

He went by the name of Wen, and he called himself Jemeyn: both Solarnese of the Path of Jade faction and currently in hiding, but not so well that Nero had not been able to track them down.

Jemeyn fancied himself as a duellist. He was all for action, so long as it was the Satin Trail's people he was leading into battle. The Path of Jade had suffered badly under the Wasp administration, ever since some of their members had set up a Corta-in-exile out of Porta Mavralis. A dozen of the Path's high-rankers had since been arrested, and those arrested by the Wasps were usually never seen again. Popular rumour, which Nero guessed was well founded, said that such prisoners were sent north, past Toek, and into slavery.

Wen, on the other hand, was a long-term thinker. At first Nero had been worried that her "long-term" would see them all dead of natural causes before the time seemed right to her to act. He then saw that she was exaggerating her stance simply to keep Jemeyn in check, and quite soon Nero and Wen were doing business. She was short for a Solarnese and darker than most, looking more like a Lowlander Beetle-kinden. When he explained that there was a move afoot, abroad, to liberate Solarno, and that she should start stockpiling arms and recruiting people to use them, she seemed confident enough that she could do it.

They had met in the back room of a singularly low dive in the alleys around the murkier end of the Solarno docks. After Wen and Jemeyn had left, Nero sat with his harsh wine half drunk and thought about his next move. He had made his contacts with Taki's old employer Genissa and some others of the Satin Trail, who were at least paying lip service to the Wasps and their Crystal Standard allies, and had avoided the worst of the persecution. Now he had the Jade under his belt, but Taki had given him more names to look out for: duelling circles, trade guilds, a half dozen little unofficial collaborations that could be of use.

There was a clearing of someone's throat and Nero jumped up sharply, ending with his feet on the table, ready to bolt. He saw a lean, russet-haired man leaning nonchalantly in the doorway, a baldric of throwing daggers slung across his belt. He was not of any particular kinden that Nero could name by sight, but Nero knew him nonetheless from one brief glimpse in the Venodor, and from Che's detailed description.

He found that his hand had dropped to his knife hilt. The man in the doorway smiled slightly, still lounging in his unconcerned way.

"Do you think that you could?" he asked.

"I think that I'd try." Nero swallowed. "I know you. You're Cesta the assassin."

"Full marks. Top of the class."

"You're doing the Wasps' work now, are you?" Nero tensed, ready to put his Fly-kinden reflexes to the test against the flash of a thrown blade.

"No, I am not," said Cesta. "You, however, should be more careful. You've been ringing bells all over the city, Sieur Nero."

"Is that right?" Nero ostentatiously took his hand from his hilt, and dropped himself down to the floor. "And why should you care, Master Cesta? Che told me all she knew about you, and it makes no sense to me."

He made to leave, and Cesta stood graciously aside for him, falling into step as they crossed the darkened taproom beyond.

"I don't like the Wasps, Sieur Nero," Cesta said. "I don't ask much out of life, less than most in fact. I don't ask for a happy home or a family, even a people to belong to, those things that most take for granted. All I ask is a certain freedom."

Nero paused at the door. "Freedom to ply your trade," he suggested pointedly.

"Yes, but also just freedom. Freedom to live, to go where I want, to live how I want. The Wasps would stop that, for the Wasps mean control and laws. I could be a killer for the Wasps, Sieur Nero, but I would be their man if I did so. Bella Cheerwell was right about that. I am nobody's man. I am *free*."

Nero pushed open the door and stopped sharp, his heart plunging. After a moment he swore.

There were three dead Solarnese there, all wearing the blue sashes of the Crystal Standard. Beyond them there lay half a dozen Wasp soldiers, just as dead. Nero glanced back at Cesta, who remained expressionless.

"As I said, you should be more careful," the assassin told him. "Now, having presented my credentials, what else can I do for you and your allies?"

"My allies . . ." Nero scowled at him. "My allies don't like you, assassin."

"Ah, yes." Cesta's smile was sad and genuine. "And where is the delectable te Schola Taki-Amre?" At Nero's stubborn silence, his smile grew. "You don't need to answer, Sieur Nero. I can guess it."

Chasme was like a dark boil on the south coast of the Exalsee. It was a perpetual blight on the Solarnese, who often spoke of taking a fleet and putting an end to it. Spider merchants from Porta Mavralis said the same, yet nobody did anything about it. The truth was there were plenty of Spider-kinden and Solarnese who had interests in the place. Chasme was all about money.

It was not quite a city. For that it was too small. It was a stopping point for those heading around the Exalsee: a cluster of heavy, humpbacked buildings, some built on sunken pilings on the land itself, and others on pontoons out to sea. Some of the buildings belonged to merchants and others to labourers, but Chasme was known primarily as a town of foundries. They churned out weapons and armour, and machines most of all. Chasme was the engine that provided flying machines and pilots to the Inapt Dragonflies of Princep Exilla, and to pirates and air brigands all over the Exalsee. Chasme was the gateway for the wealth of the unexplored south, which arrived as slaves and carapaces and precious metals. Chasme was a rogue city, without law or morals, ruled by a handful of fantastically wealthy renegades.

Chasme was also beyond Wasp reach, for now at least, and that was why Taki had chosen it. Chasme, despite so many decades of antipathy, suddenly found itself in common cause with Solarno. Nobody wanted to see the Empire rooted on the Exalsee.

The people of Chasme were a baffling mongrel mixture. More than half of the citizens were half-breeds drawn from a welter of Fly, Spider, Soldier Beetle, Dragonfly, Bee and a dozen other kinden. Amidst all that confusion, in a bar dug underneath one of the automotive factories, Taki's little assembly blended in perfectly.

Here were her pilots, her friends and her adversaries: all that she might consider her peers. She sat them around three tables hauled in close together, and waited until they all had received drinks and had finished jockeying with each other for position and status.

Here then were the Solarnese: Niamedh, her expression made more stern by her shorn hair and eyepatch, also the bulky Scobraan in his gold-winged breast-plate, together with a handful of other free aviators. Here was te Frenna, the only other Fly-kinden present, her face still bandaged from the glancing heat of a Wasp sting. Here were the local Chasme mercenary pilots, all of them tough and ruthless men and women: among them the taciturn half-breed known as the Creev and the infamous pirate Hawkmoth, an exiled Bee-kinden whose orthopter, *Bleakness*, was known across the whole Exalsee. Here were a dozen beast riders out of Princep, with the arrogant and painted Drevane Sae at their head, a gathering of barbaric splendour in wooden armour, beads and tattoos.

"It's no secret why we're here," Taki announced, as soon as they were finally settled.

"Solarno needs bailing out," said the man called Hawkmoth. He was a vicious-looking specimen, almost as small as a Fly-kinden, bald and leathery with a fierce forked beard. "But what do most of us owe Solarno?"

Taki grinned at him, matching fierce for fierce. "Oh, if you really thought that, Sieur Hawkmoth, you'd not be here. You and I know each other: we have crossed paths before. Still, if you cannot see there is now an enemy greater than all of us, then there's no point in me staying longer."

Some of the Dragonflies scoffed at that, and Scobraan stood up angrily, his big hands rocking the table. Taki had to shout at all of them to shut their mouths and just *listen* to her.

"All right, you want me to shame you with the facts? I will then," she told them. "All right, Sieur Hawkmoth, let's look at the freebooters of the Exalsee, shall we? Why are you still free and living, Sieur?"

"I'm a better pilot that any man or woman here, is why," Hawkmoth growled.

"And you never sleep? And your flier never needs to land? No, you're free because the Exalsee is so big, and those who would hunt you down can never quite net you in. Do you think the Wasps would seriously want for men and flying machines, Sieur? Attack one of their ships or fliers and they'd search every island in the Exalsee until they had rooted you out of every possible hiding place—and once they're established there will *be* no ship or flier that is not flying their flag! And you know it, and that's why you're here."

Hawkmoth glowered at her for a moment, and then nodded slowly.

"And you warriors of Princep Exilla," Taki went on, "you must see that your sovereignty's days are numbered. What do you think the Wasps will do, on finding a city of Dragonfly-kinden on their southern doorstep? The Lowlander Cheerwell Maker once told me something, she told me about the Twelve-Year War—a conflict between the Wasps and your kinden."

"Those we left centuries ago," Drevane Sae said dismissively. "Those in the north. They are not our people any more."

"*The Wasps won't care*," Taki insisted. "You are still their enemies. In fact, we're *all* their enemies. And as for Chasme itself? You tell me, Creev."

The Creev inclined his head. "They will either take us over or wipe us out."

"So what are you suggesting?" Drevane Sae asked harshly.

"Drive the Wasps from Solarno," Niamedh replied instantly, standing up.

"So easily said? If it is so easy, then they are not a threat!" Hawkmoth snapped. "If they are as you claim, it is like trying to hold back a tide. It cannot be done."

"Listen to me!" Taki said again. "I have travelled a long way west—further than anyone present here, believe me. I have flown pàst Porta Mavralis to lands that half of you haven't even heard of, but where they are *also* fighting the Wasps. I have come back in the company of a Spiderlands lord who, too, is looking to fight the Wasps. I even have a few hundred Spiderlands mercenaries stashed ready for my signal. The problem is that none of you, not one of you, has any sense of the world beyond the Exalsee. You don't understand that the world—the whole wasting world—has been pulled into this war."

She realized that, for the first time, they were absolutely, genuinely silent.

"The Wasp invasion of Solarno is nothing, in the eyes of their Empire," she continued softly. "They reacted like a greedy child reaching out for something bright, for no other reason than because it is there. North and west of here, there are Wasp armies tens of thousands strong currently marching on other lands. The Wasps aim to conquer the whole world, a city at a time, so they are always fighting. And right now they are fighting a greater, stronger enemy than they have faced before, so their men, their machines and resources, are more and more being committed to this larger fight. If Solarno sits still under her shackles, then she shall remain a slave forever, and the Exalsee with her, but if she rises *now*, if we come to her aid *now*, then perhaps we shall throw the enemy off—because the Wasps have their swords primarily directed elsewhere. Otherwise we lose our chance, and the Exalsee shall become an imperial province, city by city, and every one of us will be lost even to the histories."

"I commit myself to nothing," said Drevane Sae, and then, "but what do you ask?"

"I ask for every flier that can be spared," Taki said. "Even now I have insurrection being stirred up in Solarno, and I have Spiderlands troops ready to march. But I need orthopters, heliopters, fixed-wings, whatever you can give—all of you. From the Principality to the free corsairs of the Exalsee, I need you. I need you, every one."

She realized that she was standing upright to her full minuscule height, and that they were all listening to her as though this was something entirely reasonable and necessary she was asking from them, and the responsibility of it scared her half to death.

It was raining in Solarno, a light, lukewarm drizzle coming in off the Exalsee and clouding the streets with mist. Late in the evening, the setting sun was striking rainbows far off over the water, and Nero was hurrying. The Wasp-kinden had imposed a curfew now, and for the next tenday. They were turning the screws of their power, constantly raising the pressure in the city as if to see what steam might escape.

We'll show them steam. But Nero himself was not a fighter by choice, and this entire plan was looking more and more like a wild gamble.

He ducked past an imperial patrol, making himself just one more Fly-kinden in a city full of them, worse dressed than most and nothing remarkable. His path took him down an alley, and then he went straight up, flying along the vertical wall, into a second-storey window carelessly left unshuttered.

Jemeyn and Wen, the resistance fighters, were already there. Wen studied him, eyes hooded, from her seat in the corner. Jemeyn had been pacing the floor.

"Where is everyone else?" Nero demanded. "What's gone wrong?"

"Mostly downstairs," Wen explained briefly, and added, "Nothing is wrong."

"*You* might say say nothing," Jemeyn snapped at her, "but three of my men were arrested only today. Clearly we've been compromised—"

"They were arrested while agitating against the Wasps, what else do you expect?" Wen shot back angrily.

"Can they lead the Wasps to you if interrogated?" Nero asked nervously.

"I don't think so. The only place they know, I'm not there any more," Jemeyn said, and would have said more had there not been footsteps coming up the stone stairs. Nero shifted closer to the window just in case, but relaxed when he saw Taki enter. She spared a glance for the two resistance fighters, and then looked at Nero.

"Not dead yet?"

He gave her a smile and it was returned. "If you want me to stop saving your city, you can ask any time."

A Spider-kinden had slipped in with Taki, and Nero recognized her as Odyssa, Teornis' agent. Alongside her was a heavily built half-breed who presumably must be one of the free pilots of the Exalsee.

"We're all here?" Taki enquired.

"Not quite," Nero said. "I was expecting someone from the reds at least."

"They're lying low, trying to get the Wasps to like them," Jemeyn said disgustedly.

"We can't do this without them," Nero pointed out. "We just haven't got the numbers."

"If it kicks off," Wen decided, "they'll join in. They just won't help us start it."

"That's a shaky place to stand," he said, looking to Taki for support.

"For what it's worth, I'll get a message to Domina Genissa. I think the Satin Trail will rise," she said.

"We're all on the wire if they don't," Nero insisted.

Taki nodded, shrugged. He was right but what could they do?

"In four days' time the Wasps will stamp their image on this city," Wen explained. "They're doing it in proper Solarnese style: a full ceremony right out in front of everyone. They're testing our boundaries. If they can perform their inauguration without trouble and get their governor installed, they'll know we'll stay beaten."

"So we strike later?" Nero said. There was a silence; he looked from face to face. "What, now?"

"You're not Solarnese," Taki said.

He gave her an aggrieved look. "I've been risking my skin for Solarno, though."

"That's not what I mean."

"Solarnese pride," said the big half-breed. "That's what she means. The Wasps know their business. Wait until it's done, and no one will follow your flag."

"So . . ." Nero took stock. "You're saying now that the Wasps will be expecting trouble at the inauguration, and we should give it to them."

It was indeed what they were saying. He shared a glance with Odyssa, and saw that she was as unhappy about this as he was.

"There will be soldiers there, most of the garrison and—" he started.

"Precisely," interrupted Wen. "Which means that, if we can strike hard enough, we'll finish them then and there."

"If," Nero echoed. "*If.* We're going to need something pretty special to deal with that kind of opposition."

"I have pilots and machines," Taki said. "We have Spider troops and mercenaries ready to land at the docks. We have the resistance inside the city."

"Most of whom you *hope* will join you," Nero pointed out.

"We can cut and cut at the Wasps forever, and that means they'll just tighten their grip," Taki said, annoyed with him now. "The more time we give them, the deeper they'll dig in. Your Lowlands is fighting them *now*, but for how long? If Solarno is to free itself, we have to break the chains before they can add any new ones."

They were all in agreement. Nero ground his teeth. "If that's the way you want to play it," he said, reluctantly. "We'll need a signal . . ." Before he could be pelted with their ideas on the subject, he raised a hand. "I'll arrange the signal. Leave it to me."

"What will it be?" Wen asked him.

"Well, if I can't arrange anything else, it'll be me baring my buttocks and mooning the new governor. But let me work on it," he told them.

It got a smile out of Taki, and it was almost worthwhile, just for that.

When they had gone, he sat himself on the floor, as Fly-kinden from his part of the world were used to, and thought. After a while he said loudly, "You might as well come in now. I'm sure you heard it all."

Cesta came into the room, head first through the window. He must have been crouching outside in the shadow of the eaves. With a lazy grace he dropped to the floor.

"They're right, you know," he said, "about the timing. I know this city. Let the Wasps have their ceremony, and any resistance will drain away. They're all about fierce action and regret in this city."

Nero gazed at him for a long time. Eventually he said, "I have no right to ask anything of you."

Cesta nodded. "That's true. So don't." He wore a small smile. "What will you do if you win, Nero? What if the Empire is beaten back on all sides, and Solarno is saved? Back to the Lowlands with you, then?"

"I'm a traveller," Nero said. "There's a whole world out there. I'll find somewhere."

Cesta shrugged. "Perhaps the Lowlands has need of another assassin." His smile twisted. "You'll have your signal, Nero, so don't you worry. It will be unmistakable."

THIRTEEN

I t was a long road to Szar, travelling only at the dragging pace of the machine wagons. Drephos' mobile workshops, his mechanisms and tools, pieces and parts, furnaces and refineries, had all been carefully packed into a convoy of a dozen great hauling automotives. The master artificer himself spent the time cursing the lack of rails, and fitfully designing a rail-laying automotive that would allow him to go anywhere, with his entire surroundings, as fast as he pleased.

His staff received less preferential treatment than his working materials. A single automotive was assigned to carry them, and the huge Mole Cricket, Big Greyv, took up most of that. The others perched on top, or moved between the wagons, or dropped back and conversed with the soldiers who were escorting them.

Kaszaat had no talk, however. If not for Totho's presence she would have passed the entire journey without one single word. For Kaszaat was going home.

At nights, Totho led her away from the others, to the camp's fringes sometimes or into one of the wagons. She could not bear to be near Drephos, even to be anywhere he might turn his head and see her.

"He thinks I will betray him," she said.

"No," Totho assured her, and it was no more than the truth. Drephos did not think of her at all.

"But the others do. They know where we're going, and why. We're going now to kill my people. My own people."

Totho regarded her carefully. Tonight they were in one of the machine wagons, nestled amongst the canvas-wrapped crates and boxes.

"How did you come to leave your home?" he asked, hoping that there was some bad blood to uncover, some injustice she could cling to.

"I was conscripted, sold into the army, what did you think?" she snapped at him. "I had training, so they put me with engineers. I was passed hand to hand. Then Drephos saw me, took me. Now they will kill me."

Though curled up in his arms, she was tense as a drawn bow. By "they" he did not know whether she meant the Empire or her own people. Neither did he have any simple answers. *What will she do, when we face her family?* He did not want to find out, but each morning, as the lumbering caravan set off again, it took them closer to that inexorable confrontation.

It was Totho's first experience of travelling officially through the Empire, rather than as on that hurried and furtive expedition to Myna to rescue Che and Salma. He was not sure that he preferred the change. The Empire was not so dissimilar to the Lowlands. Once they were past the Darakyon and the northern fringe of the Dryclaw, they passed into hilly farming country, with fields being ploughed by hand or with the help of draught-beetles, and with little goat- or sheep-herding villages huddled between the rises. The difference was in their reaction to the convoy. As soon as it was sighted, the locals, be they Soldier Beetles or Bee-kinden or Wasps, turned themselves more diligently to their work. They would not even look on the convoy or its escort, but Totho could read the sense of fear in them. The Empire was a harsh master.

And I am now a part of the Empire. Not a new thought either. If he let himself recall the despite he had suffered for his heritage, he could wash his guilt away easily. It was a constant effort to stave the idea off.

For the first tenday of the journey, Drephos had kept to himself in icy anger, not speaking to anyone, glowering at the crew of the automotives or at the soldiers of the escort if they dared approach him. He hunched over his drawings, scoring them through and making better copies, still smarting from being wrenched from the mechanical wealth of Helleron. After that, he recovered something of his usual character, and then it became a daily business of conference with the Beetle twins and Big Greyv, whilst the other artificers were let loose to do whatever they wished. Aside from sitting silently beside Kaszaat atop one or other of the automotives, watching the sparse countryside pass them by, Totho worked on his elaboration of the snapbow. He thought he had a design now for a repeating model, although he doubted it would ever prove economic enough to furnish an army with it. Still, he had no other project to hand.

When they were only a tenday or so from Szar, by their best calculations, the twins disappeared. The vehicles had set off that morning, no different from the last, but then one of the other artificers had remarked on their absence. Drephos had the convoy halted at once, sending the soldiers out in all directions to search for them. He was not overly concerned, and Totho could detect no thought in him that the two Beetles might have come to harm. Instead, Drephos was inconvenienced. He merely wanted the two of them returned so that he could continue his work. All the while, Big Greyv dogged his steps solemnly, carrying cases of scrolls and books without complaint.

It took the soldiers almost half a day to find the missing artificers, and they brought them back nervously for Drephos' inspection. Both were dead, though unmarked. All thoughts instantly turned to possible enemies in the villages around them. Perhaps the Bee-kinden had sent assassins out. Kaszaat found that idea ridiculous. Drephos himself conducted the examination of the bodies, hunched over them as though they were malfunctioning machines that he could bring back to life with the right repairs.

He did not speak to Totho about his findings, but he must have told someone other than the habitually silent Big Greyv, because rumour leaked out. The twins had been poisoned. They had, by all appearances, poisoned themselves.

From there it was a matter of remaining quiet and listening. Totho was good at that. The convoy meanwhile was rife with speculation. Drephos and Big Greyv seemed the only two not talking about it. Totho had not known the two Beetle-kinden, but posthumously he discovered a great deal.

After that, one night on which the convoy had stopped close enough to Szar for Kaszaat to be staring off toward the northeasterly horizon anxiously, Totho crept about the haulage automotives and inspected the contents, looking closely at form and function and drawing his conclusions.

It was something he should have been able to work out before, had he only thought of it. It was something, he suspected, that all of the other artificers had realized but were pretending otherwise. It was Drephos' new weapon.

That night, after these conclusions, he sought out Kaszaat and guided her away from the convoy, passing between lax sentries until they were on a hilltop overlooking the circle of machines, and well out of earshot.

"They'll think we've gone the same way as the twins," she murmured, looking down at the cooking fire, the pole-mounted lanterns of the sentries.

"Kaszaat," Totho said, "the twins . . . they weren't actually machinists, were they?"

"Of course they were, we all are," she said, and then, "but not just that. Not only."

"I've heard people talk about those two," he said. "They were alchemists as well. That was why Drephos recruited them."

"They worked the reagent that brought down the walls of Tark," Kaszaat agreed. From a certain reticence evident in her tone, Totho knew that she had already guessed at the suggestion he was about to make. Out there was her home city, currently in arms against the Empire, while here came Drephos to reforge the chains and bonds of imperial servitude.

"I'm sorry," he said, and she did not ask, *For what?* but just leant into him. She was trembling slightly.

Why doesn't she flee? he wondered. *Why doesn't she go back to her own people?* But he knew the answer to that. It was the same invisible leash that kept him here. They had all of them severed their ties to their former homes when they joined Drephos' cadre.

He was not sure what impulse had made him spare her a further revelation that most likely would reveal nothing she had not already grasped, but instead he held close to her and said nothing more.

Certainty was closer than he thought.

They arrived in Szar itself soon afterward. Smoke hung over its far side, smogging the city's low, domed buildings. The only people abroad in the streets were Wasp-kinden soldiers and a few Scorpion Auxillians with mottled, yellowish skin and long-hafted axes cocked back over their shoulders. The artificers' convoy made a snaking circle around a resting marketplace, where the rags and splinters of ruined stalls still crunched underfoot. Totho glanced at the nearby houses, expecting to see the faces of locals peering out suspiciously, but they seemed empty. The doors were mostly broken in, and some had been burnt out.

Drephos half climbed and half flew down from the lead automotive, pausing halfway to look critically about him at the city. Totho could see what must be the governor's palace, a heavy ziggurat of Wasp architecture louring over the smaller native buildings. As the convoy approached it, a delegation of Wasp soldiers issued forth in a large enough number to make Totho suspect some plot against Drephos. Their attention seemed locked toward the north, though, and the bulk of the city in that direction. There was a large Wasp of middle years nested within these soldiers, who only stepped forth when his escort had merged with that of the convoy. His face was marked with a livid, painful weal that seemed almost in the shape of a small hand.

"Colonel Drephos?" he asked uncertainly, and the hooded half-breed raised his one metal hand.

"You're Colonel Gan, I take it. The governor here?"

"I am, yes. I think—"

"Have your men unload my wagons. I want as much space as possible within your palace cleared for a workshop."

Colonel Gan bristled. "Colonel-*Auxillian* Drephos . . ."

"Listen to me, Governor," Drephos said sharply. "I did not ask to come to this wretched place. I did not ask to be the agent to relieve you from your own failures. I have work to do and a war to fight, and I want none of this provincial brawling. I will do here what I am commanded, and then I will leave."

"Now listen here—" Gan puffed himself up, acutely aware of his soldiers listening.

"Are you aware of my orders?" Drephos demanded.

"Of course—"

"Repeat them to me, if you will."

"Repeat them?"

"I wish to ensure," the master artificer said, "that you are fully aware of my brief, Governor. If you please."

"I am told, *half-breed*," Gan said pointedly, obviously wishing he could have Drephos struck dead on the spot, "that you are here to put down the rebellion in my city."

"At whatever cost," Drephos prompted.

"At whatever cost," Gan agreed. "And believe me, if you fail, they shall hear of it in Capitas."

"No doubt. Now kindly have my machinery unloaded so that I may get to work." Drephos turned his back on the purple-faced governor, and limped back over to his team. Behind him, soldiers had already begun to unbuckle the automotives' loads.

"Any comments?" he asked his cadre.

"You . . . are clearly not interested in making friends here, master," Totho said slowly. Some of the other artificers laughed a little at that.

"The Empire has dozens of heavy-minded buffoons like Colonel Gan, all men of good family and narrow views. There is only one of me, however. Do not fear his retribution, for we will not feel it."

At that moment there was a loud clang as one of the unloaders dropped some piece of equipment, and Drephos rounded on them furiously.

"Be careful, you fools!" he shouted across at them. "There is not a piece there that is not delicate."

The Szaren garrison men stared back at him sullenly. Totho guessed that, while they might not be overfond of their own commander, they resented this half-breed artificer striding into their city as though he owned it.

One of them, quite deliberately, took the keg he was holding and dropped it ten feet off the back of an automotive, staring at Drephos expressionlessly. That was when it happened: Drephos twitched as if stabbed, and then shouted a warning at them all to move back and clear the entire area. The artificers were sufficiently used to his commands to scurry away as quickly as possible. Totho could even hear the faint hiss from the keg and, looking back from a distance that Drephos seemed to think was safe, he thought he detected a faint yellow mist in the air.

By that time the garrison men nearest to the keg were either dead or dying, convulsing and arching their backs, clawing bloody lines in their own throats and faces. The rest were already running or airborne, but the slowest of them collapsed before they were clear of the circle of automotives, until there was a sprawl of dead soldiers radiating outward from the dropped keg and a dreadful silence throughout the ruined market, the survivors staring not at the corpses but at Drephos.

"Once again," the master artificer reminded them, "be careful. Am I understood?"

FOURTEEN

"**Y**ou get used to the waiting, after a while, but I'm out of practice," Destrachis explained. They were at least arguably inside the castle: arguably because they were within the boundaries of the edifice, and yet there were no doors to keep them in, and few enough walls. They were instead in some kind of open garden, surrounded by a framework of struts that could become the supports for a ceiling or walls if needed. The town of Suon Ren was spread below and clearly within their vision, and Stenwold was constantly thrown by the loss of barriers, of structural certainty. *In Collegium, I would have a score of people always close enough to touch, save for the walls between us. These Commonwealers certainly do like their space, their light and air.*

"They have a different sense of time, I suppose," Stenwold said vaguely.

"The smallest measure of time they generally admit to is the passing of the seasons," Destrachis said. "But it's their curse, I think, for they believe the world does not change, only revolves in its cycles. Their enemies—the Empire, the bandits—they try to make them seem just a passing blight that the next spring will cure."

"I hope I can convince them otherwise," Stenwold murmured. He meanwhile hoped that Allanbridge was not fretting too much. The invitation here, apparently, had been offered only to Destrachis and himself. Even Gramo had been turned away, mouth open like a fish's, from the doors.

And yet I could probably spot them down there, somewhere, seeing as there's nothing but space between us. Only etiquette kept anyone from simply walking inside the palace's notional boundaries. Was this a lesson about the Commonweal?

"Ah."

Stenwold turned to see a Dragonfly woman standing in the garden, and it was hard to say precisely where she had emerged from. She was perhaps a little younger than either of the Lowlanders, yet her hair, cut very short, was starting to grey, and there were lines of care on her face, unusual for her kind. She wore a plain quilted robe of green, edged in a metallic blue cloth that Stenwold had never seen before. She was barefoot.

"Now," she said. "The physician is which of you?"

"I am Felise Mienn's doctor," Destrachis said. The woman strolled to the garden's centre and sat down on a flat stone there, surrounded by burgeoning shoots.

"So possessive," she noted. "Well now, sit, if you will."

Destrachis chose not to. "Do you know where she is? Felise Mienn?"

"Now? No. I spoke with her before she left, though."

Unwillingly, Destrachis sat down before her. Stenwold knew he himself should back out of earshot, even leave the room. There was no room to leave, though. He had no idea of the proper distances and borders observed here. Besides, he wanted to know more.

"Now," the woman began, "you are known as Destrachis. You have been in the Commonweal almost long enough to be considered a native."

"On and off," Destrachis conceded. "Please . . ."

"One might wonder why you came here."

The Spider's hands twitched in annoyance. "That's my own business. The usual reasons, however, and all a long time ago. But—"

"Felise Mienn has left this place," the woman explained. "You did the correct thing in bringing her to me."

"I didn't bring her to *you*. Who are you, anyway? Tell me that at least," he demanded.

"I am a mystic," she said with such simple gravity that the statement, which would have sounded ludicrous in Collegium, struck Stenwold as entirely reasonable. "You may call me Inaspe Raimm, if you wish, or whatever else you will."

Destrachis visibly calmed himself. "I know the Commonweal well enough to know that the word 'mystic' represents a world of possibilities in itself. Which are you, though, and what did you say to her?"

Inaspe Raimm smiled—a sad, pleasant thing. "Felise Mienn had lost her way," she said. "She had borne loss and pain more than she could carry. She had become detached from her purpose."

"Purpose?" Destrachis asked.

"All things have a purpose, although not all fulfill them."

"And this purpose, will it . . . will she . . . ?"

Inaspe reached out and touched his face unexpectedly, making him flinch back. She looked straight into his eyes and Stenwold saw the Spider's face twitch with undefinable emotion.

"You have been a good friend to her, though never appreciated, Destrachis. You have saved her over and over. You have done all you can. If in the final cast of fate, she is not to be saved, then it is not you who have failed her. You have given of yourself all that could be given."

"I am a doctor," he said hoarsely. "I'm supposed to save people."

"Not everyone can be saved."

"You think she's going to die," he accused her. "You've sent her off to die?"

She was still touching his face, and that seemed to hold him in place. Stenwold saw one of his hands clench and unclench, as though wanting to reach for his dagger.

"I have sent her away to fulfill her purpose," Inaspe said, and then: "But that is sophistry. Ask yourself, does death represent part of Felise Mienn's purpose? Her own death or the deaths of others?"

At last Destrachis relaxed, with the faintest, bleakest of smiles appearing on his face. "Well, of course," he replied blackly.

"We are not blind, Destrachis. Our eyes see many things." Her voice had become very gentle. "You would go with her if you knew where she was bound. You would do that not because you are her healer, but because you wish only to be close to her."

Destrachis made such a strange, wordless sound that Stenwold wished he had absented himself. This was something he should not hear.

"Know this, noble doctor: we have removed her from your care not from our concern for her but because we value you yourself. Have you not foreseen that she would slay you, sooner or later, if you kept pace with her? You have given her a reprise, but you cannot save her from her purpose," Inaspe explained. "Instead, we choose to preserve *you*, in whom we have found such admirable qualities. If you seek a reward, for warding our wayward daughter, you shall have it. Prince Felipe Shah shall gladly bless you. Your part in her life is done, though, and we now save you for greater things. We welcome you as a servant of the Commonweal."

Stenwold saw Destrachis rise to shout, to protest, but her hand was still on his face and something passed between them. Stenwold could explain it no more than as if Inaspe Raimm had somehow taken her own understanding and gifted it to the Spider, shining a light into his troubled mind. He opened his mouth again, and for a moment his face was just grief, all his buried emotion drawn to the surface by the woman that faced him.

"She will die," he said.

"All things die," she told him. Such a truism, it was the trite utterance of any street-corner philosopher, but coming from Inaspe Raimm it sounded different. "All things reach the end of their journey, be they trees, insects, people or even principalities. All things die so that others may take their place. To die is no tragedy. The tragedy is dying with a purpose unfulfilled. You have fulfilled your purpose, Destrachis. Now let Felise Mienn fulfill hers."

A great sigh went through him. "Well, then," he said, and, "Well." He did not seem to have anything else to say. She took her hand away and he seemed to deflate, a ragged Spider-kinden man with greying hair. He looked so old, just then, older than any Spider that Stenwold had ever seen.

After Destrachis had left, locked up in his own thoughts, wrestling with what he had just been told, Stenwold came to sit before the self-proclaimed mystic.

"My name is Stenwold Maker of Collegium," he announced, "but probably you knew that already."

She smiled at him, almost conspiratorially. "How many ears have heard that name? How many mouths might have told me? Yes, Stenwold Maker, your name is familiar to me. It takes no magic to know it."

"And my purpose?"

"I am not Prince Felipe Shah. This is *his* land, and therefore his is the right to summon you to audience. Which he will. I, however, have advised him on many things, and my words fall sweetly on him. I would therefore examine you, Stenwold Maker. I would assess you, inspect you."

"Are you going to tell me my future, O mystic?" he asked wryly.

"No, I am going to tell *the* future," she replied, thus silencing him. Immediately he became aware of movement all around him. A dozen or so Dragonfly boys and girls, all seeming perhaps fourteen years of age, had suddenly appeared, holding . . . mirrors? No, but sections of glass, coloured glass in broad, oddly shaped panes. As Stenwold stared at them, and without their even acknowledging his existence, they began to take to the air, flitting up to the wooden framework and hanging their burdens here and there about it. The pattern they created was bewildering, without any logic and yet precise. The separate plates of glass, two and three feet across, were aligned and linked until the open garden had become a patchwork glasshouse, with walls and roof of stained green and red and blue, and open patches where the glass did not reach. The entire operation, bizarre and intricate, was completed in just ten minutes as Stenwold watched, utterly confused.

He glanced at Inaspe when it was done, and saw that she, and the garden, and he himself, were all mosaiced in slashes of coloured light. The notional room had now become one bounded by colour, the sunlight being split around them into a prism of conflicting and complementing shades.

"I have no idea what is going on," he admitted, bringing a wider smile to Inaspe's face.

"There are those in every age whose deeds echo in the world, for good or ill, and it is a great and terrible opportunity for a poor fortune-teller like myself to be faced with such a man. You have made yourself the point of destiny's arrow, and by casting your future I might see the course the whole wide world will take. Indulge me, Stenwold Maker. Felipe Shah shall smile upon you for it." She cleared the ground between them, and he saw that it was precisely where the colours met: a kaleidoscope in miniature. The entire room around them had become a lens that focused its hues right here. The artificer in him protested. Light in the Commonweal did not seem to behave in the same way as light in Collegium.

"I don't really believe that people can predict the future," he admitted.

"People predict the future every day, Stenwold Maker," she replied, studying the rainbow carefully as the glass panels shifted slightly on the creaking wooded framework. "If you drop a stone, you may predict that it shall fall. If you know a man to be dishonest, you may predict that he will cheat you. If you know one army is better trained and led, you may predict that it will win the battle."

He could not help smiling at that. "But that is different. That is using knowledge already gained about the world to guess at the most likely outcome."

"And that is also predicting the future, Stenwold Maker," she said. "The only difference is your source of knowledge. Everything that happens has a cause, which same cause has itself a cause. It is a chain stretching into the most distant past, and forged of necessity, inclination, bitter memories, the urge of duty. Nothing happens without a reason. Predicting the future does not require predestination, Stenwold Maker. It only requires a world where one thing will most likely lead to another. So it was that I could not tell Felipe Shah precisely that Stenwold Maker of Collegium would come to him and seek audience, but I could say: there will be emissaries from the south, and they shall come to speak of war, they shall come by air and—because they do not understand the air—they shall be caught in a storm."

"Guesswork after the fact," Stenwold protested.

"Guesswork *before* the fact," Inaspe replied. "Once one has learnt how to converse with more abstract sources of information, one's guesswork can become remarkably accurate."

Stenwold felt a little shiver go through him. "I have known other people who believed in this. I too have seen things I cannot explain. But still, I cannot accept it."

"I have heard of those such as yourself in whose world the future is but darkness, while to us it is second nature to trust in prediction. To us you appear blind—and yet you are able to make such things, such metal creatures, and we are just as blind to *your* craft as you are to ours. How ingenious you are." The bleakness in her tone Stenwold ascribed to memories of the Twelve-Year War.

She had scooped something into her hand from a bag, and now she cast the whole handful onto the pattern of light before her. Straws, he saw, and most of them instantly blew away in the breeze. Only a few now remained: a random scatter of pale stalks dyed in all colours by the glass. He himself could see nothing there, no patterns, no significance. When he looked from this display to Inaspe's face, though, something sank inside him. He saw there such a certainty of woe, as though a Fly-kinden messenger had rushed up to present her with it in writing. She met his eyes, and he saw how she would take it all back, her talk of prophecy, if she could.

"Speak," he said. "For what it's worth, speak."

"Perhaps you are wise not to credit prophecy," she said carefully, "for all your future is the shadow of the world's own."

Caught between doubt and dread, he forced himself on. "What have you seen?"

"Do not ask me."

His instincts were telling him that he should obey her in that, and leave his curiosity unsatisfied but, in the end, his heritage rose up within him, the practical Beetle impatient with such mummery, and he insisted, "Speak."

She sighed. "Stenwold Maker, you are destined for great loss, to both yourself and those close to you. You are caught in the jaws of history, and its mandibles tear pieces from you."

He shrugged. "It takes no prophet to foretell that."

She looked up from the pattern to assess his reaction, as though the idle fall of sticks had produced such a clear picture that he should recognize it immediately. "Autumn leaves, Stenwold Maker, that is the future shown to me. It is not too late, not quite, for you to escape the vice of winter, but the leaves are already falling."

Her hands passed over the sticks, and a slight cold breeze suddenly passed over Stenwold, and made him shiver. He heard the woman murmur. "A city by the lake sits beneath a rain of burning machines. Red hands, long dyed up to the elbows in the blood of others, plunge in one last time. The sky is on fire with the deaths of the brave. The slaves are being beaten. The hand that holds the whip is raised. I see a whole kinden on the brink of oblivion. A man with an iron fist reaches to snuff them out like pinching a candle flame. The proud one is in chains, and though he turns on his great master, he shall shed not one drop of his blood. The spinners' webs are burning. The great plotter has out-thought himself."

Her eyes were wide now, blazing with conviction. "They are fighting now, the warrior-breed, but there are flames around them. They are falling like moths in torchlight. So many, there are now so many rushing to their deaths."

"Enough—" Stenwold started, but the rush of words did not heed him.

"The machines of war are turned on your own people. Your friends are loyal to you, and they shall die for it, or be scarred through, and never to recover what they once were. Blood is born of blood, welling up between the trees, beneath the gold lightning. Ancient evils brought to light, the dead tradition of the life-drinkers remade, and armies marching under a standard of black and gold and running red. A pillaging of the past for power, so that even the worst excesses of the old times are dug up. *The worms of the earth!* I see the worms of the earth feasting on all our corpses. Autumn leaves, Stenwold Maker. So many that you shall not see again. They fall and fall, the leaves of autumn, red and green and black and gold."

"But can we win?" he demanded, forgetting that he did not believe.

"What is it to win? How much will you sacrifice for it, when victory is more costly than defeat?"

She took a deep breath. "Your future. All our futures. I am sorry."

Felipe Shah was a man of indeterminate age. His face was that of a young man, but his hair grey above the ears. His princely court was open to the sky, a courtyard within the palace-castle that overlooked Suon Ren. He was like the rest of his kind to Stenwold's eyes: slim and golden skinned, dark haired. He sat in the courtyard's centre, on a blanket spread on the ground. The four figures standing round him, whom Stenwold had initially taken for soldiers, became statues of burnished wood when he looked closer. Felipe wore a robe of shimmering red and blue, with an edging of gold discs, very much like the robe in which Salma had first arrived in Collegium, wondering why everyone found him such a spectacle.

The rest of his court, about thirty other Dragonfly-kinden, sat about him in what Stenwold assumed was a precise pattern, not just before him but on all sides. Some sat in nooks up on the walls. Some held scroll and stylus, poised to write. Others were simply sitting there, not even paying any particular attention to Felipe Shah. They wore the usual loose, flowing Dragonfly garments, and Felipe Shah himself was by no means the most ostentatious. Like Spiders they managed to carry it off without seeming overdressed. *If I had myself got up like that, I'd be vulgar*, Stenwold conceded.

Stenwold himself now sat to Felipe's left, and he had no idea whether this was a position of honour, of security, or what any of it meant. The precise patterns on which the Commonwealers so obviously organized their court were opaque to him. He wished Destrachis was still here to advise him.

Looking around, Stenwold spotted the fortune-teller, Inaspe Raimm, with three other Dragonflies seated in a shallow curve behind her. She did not glance at him, however, looking straight ahead only. There was something strange about the way she sat there, something in her positioning, that suggested things were not as he had understood them—but more than that he could not discern.

A whole life spent in the intelligence business and I'm now completely out of my depth.

There was a handful of Mercers present in their full armour, and now one stepped forward to hand something to the prince. It was Salma's letter, Stenwold saw: Prince Salme Dien's message to Prince Felipe Shah.

The prince read it in silence and the court waited. Nobody had mentioned what this document was and yet everyone seemed to already know, as though they were Ant-kinden linked by a common mind. Stenwold increasingly felt that he was skimming the surface of a vastly complicated world. *Of course the Commonweal is both vast and complicated, so I should expect this bafflement. Yet it is still hard to deal with, when matters are so pressing back home.*

There had been no news, of course. For all he knew, Sarn could have fallen by now.

Prince Felipe Shah began to weep, and Stenwold started in surprise. He had not set eyes on Salma's message, but he could not think of anything his former student might have written that would have sparked this reaction. Still the Prince wept silently, tears trickling down his face, unwiped, and falling to spot his robe. It was impossible, Stenwold realized, to tell what emotion was being displayed here, only the intensity of it. All around, the other Dragonflies were nodding silently, clearly approving whatever was going on. Stenwold ground his teeth in frustration at his inability to grasp it.

A servant stepped forward with a white cloth. Felipe Shah quickly wiped his eyes and then sat with the letter in one hand, the cloth clutched so tight in the other that his fist shook. The rest of him, in poise, manner and expression, remained utterly calm, as though he had transferred his inner feelings over to the cloth as naturally as doffing a hat.

"Master Stenwold Maker," Prince Felipe began, "your ambassador has stated that you wish an audience."

Stenwold was aware of how Gramo, sitting nearby, straightened up proudly.

"I would owe you the hospitality that I owe to all who visit my court in peace," Felipe continued slowly. "I owe you more than this, though, for you have brought me the farewell of my kin-obligate, who I shall not see again."

Stenwold, though bursting with questions, forced himself to remain silent, but something must have shown on his face.

"You do not have this custom, in your own land, I am sure," the Prince said. "Here we do not keep our children close to us, Master Stenwold Maker. We ensure, instead, that they reside in the houses of others, to thus learn their ways, their world. So they learn to judge, or to labour, or to peer into the waters. Prince Minor Salme Dien came to me, when he was young, to learn governance. He was not my son, and yet he was a son to me, while my own children were far away."

"Did . . ." Stenwold waited to see if he would be silenced, but Felipe Shah nodded for him to continue, "did you send him to the Lowlands, master—your Highness?"

Felipe inclined his head then. "It was my choice that he went."

"We have been very blessed in his addition to our people," Stenwold proclaimed, aware that he was becoming rather overflorid in attempting simply to be polite. "Could I ask why you did so? Otherwise there has been very little contact between our peoples, the ambassador excepted."

There was a pause then, and it was to Inaspe Raimm that the Prince's eyes flicked. "Two reasons suggest themselves," Felipe said at last. "But who can say which is the truth? After the war with the Empire, I thought we needed to know more about our neighbours. Also divination suggested that the Commonweal would benefit."

"I cannot comment on the second reason," said Stenwold awkwardly. "As for the first, we are fighting the Empire even now."

"We know this," Felipe Shah confirmed.

"And if the Empire defeats the Lowlands, then they will come north." Realizing what he had just said, Stenwold smiled weakly. "I'm no fortune-teller, but I can predict that, I think."

Felipe put the tear-stained cloth down and placed his hands on his knees, and from the reaction of the entire court Stenwold saw that this was a significant gesture, as though, back in Collegium, one man around a table had just stood up to speak.

"Before you came, we had long discussed this," the Prince declared. "The Commonweal has suffered greatly under the Empire's advance. Our people have died and been enslaved, in numbers so great they make us weak to consider it. Now you, the new kin-obligate of Salme Dien, have come asking us to join in a common cause."

Stenwold blinked at the new designation he had been given, but nodded anyway. "That is so," he allowed.

"We fought the Empire," the Prince said, his voice falling so low that Stenwold could barely hear it. "We resisted them with our blood and our bodies. The road their war machines travelled on was made up of the bones of our people. There are those among us who wonder what it was for, all that valour and passion. What did we accomplish, that our sons and daughters bled for?"

Stenwold opened his mouth to retort, as though this was the Collegium Assembly, but the character of the silence told him that his words were not wanted. For a long while the Dragonfly lord stared at the ground, and not a single one of his followers moved. *Autumn leaves*, came a voice in his memory. *Green and red and black and gold.*

"The place is not mine," Felipe Shah said at last. "I am but a prince amongst princes. The Monarch alone must give you our answer."

"It is then possible to secure an audience with . . . with the Monarch?" Stenwold felt as though he was walking a fragile tightrope of etiquette. The Commonweal was vast, the Monarch doubtless distant and mighty. How many such baffling audiences would he have to sit through, how much *time* before he could put his case? Could the Lowlands last that long?

Felipe Shah's melancholy did not break, precisely, but there was a curious spark in his eye, a slight creasing about his face, as though he nonetheless saw that something in his view was amusing. Looking around, Stenwold saw an identical expression on all the courtiers' faces, a polite and pointed fixedness of feature.

At last he saw that one Dragonfly face remained composed and still, and then he understood.

With the greatest possible care, Stenwold stood up and made a low bow before Inaspe Raimm—teller of the future and Monarch of the Commonweal.

"I . . . am a fool," he confessed.

"That understanding is the first step to wisdom," the Monarch replied softly. "Perhaps Prince Salme Dien has not spoken to you of the proper role of a prince of our Commonweal. It is not to be heaped with honours and raised high, but to stoop low, to bear burdens for the people that the prince must serve. So it should be for a prince, and so much more for a monarch."

"And I am fortunate to come and find you here when . . ." His voice trailed off. "Or you knew, and came here especially to meet what the Lowlands would send." He had no scepticism left. Here in this ephemeral court they had finally drained him of it.

She nodded slowly. "I have enjoyed our meeting, Stenwold Maker."

"But if I had known . . . I have requests . . ."

"I am glad for your ignorance, then. I know already what you would request."

"What I came all this way to ask . . ." he put in, feeling that he was teetering on the very edge of propriety. "Please, let me ask it."

"Even if we are bound to refuse?" she said, and he gaped at her.

"But you can't know what I intend to ask you."

Her face remained very composed, solemn with melancholy. "We already know, Stenwold Maker, but if it would help you, please speak your requests. Let there be no possibility of doubt between us."

He had by now lost track of Commonweal opinion, whether he was being honoured or just very rude. He was struck suddenly with a great sense of urgency, absurd considering the long journey here, the distance involved. "We fight the Wasps even now, as they march on our cities. We lack strength to fight them, our enemies—the enemies of all of us, the Wasp Empire." The words came spilling out from him unsorted and jumbled, but still he pressed on. "I know from Salma the injuries they did to your own people, the bitter years of war, the principalities they stole from you with their treaties and their demands. I am a fool, perhaps, but not such a fool that I cannot see common cause. The Empire's armies run thin, for they are fighting on all fronts, pushing outward. They are mad for conquest. A Commonweal force that marched or flew east now could reclaim all that you have lost, and the Wasps would have no strength to resist you. And while they recoiled from you, their strikes at us would also weaken. They would be stretched until they snapped."

He finished, slightly out of breath, waiting anxiously for her response.

It was too slow in coming. "Help us," he begged. "Help us, and help yourselves—please."

Inaspe Raimm lowered her gaze. "You do not understand. We cannot do as you ask. It is impossible."

Stenwold made sounds that he could not force into words. At last he said, "But . . . even a modest force?"

"We cannot retake the lost Principalities," she said, simply. "The reason is very clear: we have signed the Treaty of Pearl. Those lands were ceded to the Empire."

Stenwold felt his mouth fall open, staring. "But they *forced* you to sign that treaty. You cannot have signed it willingly. Twelve years of war . . ."

"*I* signed the Treaty of Pearl," she told him, and the hint of emphasis in her voice silenced him. "It is a shame that I myself shall continue to bear, and pass on to each monarch that succeeds me. True, we were dragged to it through a sea of our people's blood. True it was a device of the Empire that they themselves would not pause for a moment before breaking. But that is not material."

"I don't understand . . ." he began.

"Then I am sorry. Perhaps the Wasps did not understand either, when they bound us to the treaty, but I am the Monarch, and therefore responsible for all my people. The whole of my kinden have pledged themselves, through me. It was an oath, a promise made by the Commonweal entire. So we can never march upon those lost lands. We cannot go against our own soul. We cannot go to war with the Empire to aid you, though we would dearly wish to. Our word is final."

"Oh . . ." Stenwold said weakly, feeling as though she had just stabbed him through the gut. "Oh . . ." *All this way, through storm and bandits, and for nothing. Losing Felise, losing Destrachis, and all for nothing.*

"The Wasps will tear that paper up as soon as they are done with us," he protested hoarsely.

"It seems likely," the Monarch agreed sadly. "Until they do, we remain bound by it. I am sorry that we cannot help you, Stenwold Maker. Your need is great and you are deserving. Perhaps some escort could travel with you back to your lands, to safeguard you."

"A Lorn detachment," Stenwold said, although they would not recognize the term. All hope was leaking out from him like life's blood.

To stand so fast by a meaningless treaty. The Wasps truly cannot have known what they were winning, through that one piece of paper.

And then a thought: *the Wasps will still be ignorant of what they have gained.*

"I . . . have an idea, O Monarch," he said slowly.

"Speak, Stenwold Maker."

"Sleight of hand, Monarch. Shadows and illusions. Spider games. You are not without such resources, here in the Commonweal?"

A few knowing looks around them. "Indeed we are not," Inaspe Raimm replied.

"Then . . ." This time he ordered the words carefully before he uttered them. "If a force was to mass . . . close to the borders of the stolen principalities. An army of soldiers, beasts . . ." He had nearly added engines, war machines. "All the business of war, in fact. The treaty makes no mention of that, I am sure."

She regarded him, but he thought he saw a slight smile of comprehension there.

"A Commonweal army on the border, O Monarch," Stenwold continued. "That is surely the current nightmare of the Empire, the Dragonflies returning for their lands. They cannot know, they do not know, that you will still honour your word. It would never occur to them, who would break their own so readily. Is that possible, O Monarch?"

Inaspe Raimm looked past him to encounter the gaze of Felipe Shah. When she met Stenwold's gaze again, she was nodding. "It is possible," she said. "It might indeed be accomplished."

FIFTEEN

Hokiak had kept her in a cellar for what had felt like an age, but was probably only a couple of hours. Che had thought, *Again! Again in someone's cell.* At the time she had not believed his claims. She had assumed that he would hand her over to the Empire, or perhaps simply to the highest bidder.

She hoped Thalric had got away, at least. It was a strange thing to wish for, considering her own extremity. She had no illusions that he might come back for her.

Then she was dragged up into the old Scorpion's back room again, hauled into the lamplight and cuffed sharply when she stumbled. Hokiak was waiting there for her, leaning on his stick.

"As promised," he said. His clients were all cloaked but, on peering up at them, she found herself looking into blue-grey Mynan faces.

"Please . . ." she said. "Help me—"

Without otherwise showing any particular acrimony, one of them kicked her in the stomach, knocking the wind out of her. As she choked and gasped around the pain, the other handed a pouch to Hokiak.

"Compliments of the Red Flag," she heard.

The Scorpion nodded. "And be sure you give your chief my regards. Anything she wants, she knows where to find me."

Without another word, the two Mynans hauled Che effortlessly upright. She felt something cold pressed against her side and knew it was a dagger blade.

"Any struggle, one word from you," the man said, "and your masters'll still be picking up the pieces in a tenday's time. Understand?"

"Please," she got out, "just take me to Kymene."

The dagger pricked her and she stopped.

"One more word," said the Mynan flatly. "Any word you please, and I'll gut you right here and now."

They hurried her through the city by the backstreets. It was night and she got little sense of the place, but there was a tension in the air. A lot of the locals were out under the dark sky, standing aimlessly as though waiting to be told what to do.

Thalric was right about this place, she thought. *Shame everything else has gone so wrong.*

They reached an anonymous-looking house in one of the many districts the Wasps had left to decay, and bundled her swiftly into it: from Hokiak's cellar to the cellar of this place with the minimum of fuss. They locked her in, and left her there with her hands tied.

It will all be all right, she tried to tell herself. *Kymene will come, and she'll believe me. It will all be all right.* It served as a hollow little mantra to recite to herself.

She guessed that most of an hour had gone past before the door opened again, and a Mynan man stalked down the stone steps toward her. A second man stayed aloft with a lantern, but Che did not need its light to recognize her visitor. For a moment his name escaped her, then it was blessedly in the front of her mind.

"Chyses!"

He stared at her, motioned for the lantern to come closer. The man had changed little, save that his expression of bitter dissatisfaction had deepened. He had a knife in his hand, and she realized it was not to frighten her so much as to whet his own anticipation. *Tynisa always said she didn't like him . . .*

"Chyses, it's *me*," Che said. "Don't you recognize me?"

"Of course I recognize you," the Mynan said coldly. "That's usually the case with traitors."

"I'm no traitor," she protested.

"Hokiak thinks you are."

"Hokiak is wrong! Hokiak only thinks so because I came in with a Wasp. If I was really trying to infiltrate your people, would I do that?"

Chyses regarded her without love. "I can't think of *anyone* who would do something that stupid, so why not a traitor? It makes sense to me. Besides, I hear the Wasp ran after killing some of Hokiak's men."

"He's a renegade and the Empire wants him dead. He must have thought Hokiak was going to sell him out."

"You tell whatever story you want, right now," Chyses said. "Give me time and I'll pare the truth from you, so you just go ahead and babble."

"Will you at least let me speak to Kymene?" she asked.

Chyses gave a smile that was brief and unpleasant. "Be careful what you ask for. She's coming to see you, girl. For old times' sake, maybe."

Maybe she thinks she owes me that much, Che thought. *Or maybe she just wants to see me cut up with her own eyes.*

"I can help you, help the whole resistance," she insisted. "I came here to help."

"Of course you did, only not to help us." He crouched by her, the knife prominent. "Don't worry, we'll have a talk, you and I. We'll bare everything, every truth. Have no worries about that."

She was about to appeal to him again, but she could not. This was a man short on trust. He had lived his life in an occupied city, fighting his own private war, and to him she was just another excuse to sharpen his hatred. She guessed that he even preferred killing traitors to killing the enemy. Probably he liked to take longer over it, too.

Then Kymene herself was stepping down into the cellar. The sight of her showed just how far the revolution in Myna had progressed. She wore a robe, but it was open down the front, exposing her black breastplate adorned with the two red arrows of the resistance: *We have fallen, we shall rise again.* She was armed, and she must have walked openly through the streets like that, along with her guards and unchallenged by the Wasps. Che guessed that areas of Myna like this must be virtually off limits to the invaders now.

But Kymene herself, beyond the clothes, was the same woman Che recalled: young and fierce and proud, her hair cropped short, truly a warrior queen of Myna. In her expression there was no acknowledgement of the night that both women had been freed from the Empire's cells, no common cause.

"It is her, isn't it," she declared.

Chyses nodded, stepping back. Che tried to speak but, in the face of Kymene's piercing gaze, the words dried up.

"Cheerwell Maker," she said, "they tell me you're a Wasp agent these days."

"No," Che whispered. Kymene knelt beside her, scabbard tip grating on the stone of the cellar floor.

"I liked your uncle," the woman said. "As far as I'd trust an outsider, I'd trust him. You're not him, though, for if he was here, like this, I'd take his word."

"Please," Che said, looking into her eyes. "I'm no traitor. I came with news, to help you. The Wasps never tortured me to make me their agent! They're fighting my people even now."

"We have people in the palace—we had them there even then—and they know you were taken off to be interrogated. They heard the machines working, though sometimes all it takes is just the sight of them to break someone's spirit." Kymene said it in a tone of dreadful reasonableness.

"It . . . they didn't really do it," Che insisted, aware of how wretched that must sound. "It was just a ploy . . . the man in charge was doing something complicated, political. He, please, he needed the noise as a cover to talk to one of his own agents . . ."

"Did he. And who was this man?"

"He was . . ." *The same man who fled from me at Hokiak's.* Kymene was eyeing her expectantly, though, so silence was not an option.

"His name," Che said finally, "is Thalric. He went renegade later, for another reason. It's complicated but, please, you have to . . ."

Kymene cut her off with just a gesture. A thoughtful expression came over her face. Chyses shuffled, sensing a new turn in the conversation which he was not happy about.

"Thalric," the Mynan leader repeated.

"Yes . . ." It was obvious that Kymene knew that name, but for the life of her Che could not work out how.

"Kymene, this is nonsense," Chyses grated. "Let me work on her now. I'll have the true story in two minutes."

"Thalric," Kymene repeated. "Yes, that was his name."

"What?" Chyses demanded.

Kymene stood up abruptly, and Che wondered if it was because she did not entirely trust Chyses behind her with a knife.

"Thalric was indeed doing something *political* right then. I have cause to know it. So that much, at least, is true."

"Political? What's that supposed to mean?" Chyses snarled.

Kymene's smile was brilliant and hard. "He was killing the Bloat, Chyses. He's the one who killed our last governor for us, rid us of good old Ulther."

To his credit, Chyses made no protest, merely stared.

"Keep hold of her," Kymene ordered. "Untie her but keep her guarded. Find me this Thalric. Find me also people from Hokiak's who'll recognize him. I want to talk to him."

Thalric had found himself a low taverna by the river by the name of Flaneme's. Under the stern gaze of a woman of the same name, who was a broad-shouldered, massive-armed matron, he took a cup of wine and considered his options.

How madly optimistic he had been to think that his name would not have become common parlance in Myna! Seeing the facts inscribed on paper, uncovered during his idle investigations at Tharn, the idea had seemed clear to him. He had put himself seamlessly back into the spy game without recalling the pain that had sent him away from it.

No doubt that old rogue Hokiak had since heard all the Rekef news: who was in and who was out. He bared his teeth in frustration and glowered into the wine, seeing there a darkened glimpse of his own reflection. Hokiak had obviously pegged Che as a Rekef turncoat, this new allegiance twisted into her painfully in the torture rooms of the governor's palace. The irony of that notion was not lost on Thalric, who had in the end never quite found the proper moment to put Che to the question. Now he could spare a thought to wonder whether the Scorpion would sell her either to the resistance or the Empire—and which of them, at this stage, would be kinder. Beyond that single speculation his own fate consumed his thoughts entirely.

He was being shadowed, he knew. Whoever it was, acting for whatever side in the little brawl that was brewing in Myna, they did not yet want to broach him openly. They were waiting for him to put himself neatly where they could descend on him with the minimum of public fuss. That might mean that it was Kymene's people come to finish him off. Or it might mean that it was the Rekef, who preferred to have people disappear without even a ripple. He was definitely being watched, however. He had come into Flaneme's place because it was near-full with rivermen and labourers, men and women whose politics were probably not hot enough to set them against him. Still, he had gathered some filthy looks on entering, so the intelligence he had perused in Tharn had been right. Uprising was hanging on the air like smoke.

Why in blazes did I come back to this wretched town? His past had crossed with Myna's too many times: in the initial imperial conquest, when he had been a raw young officer under Ulther's patronage; his betrayal of that same patron all those years later, on the orders of his Rekef masters; and now a third time with this debacle. He should have left it at just twice.

He had to leave Myna immediately. He caught himself wondering how he would break this news to Stenwold. *Fool!* But it was true that abandoning Che had left a foul taste in the mouth. In a life composed of so many dark deeds this one, he realized, would stay with him.

Just one more amongst the host, though, so he would live with it.

A shadow crossing him made him look up. Flaneme stood there, burly arms folded. "Time for you to leave, Master Wasp."

He stared up at her, biting down his instinctive response. He knew this game well, for he had played it from across the table often enough.

"Right then." He put the wine bowl down, still untouched, flexing his hands in readiness. Out there his persecutors would be waiting. They had passed their message on to Flaneme, who, like any good taverna keeper, would try to keep each side of the fight happy. She was telling him that he was no longer protected here, and she would call on her other patrons to throw him out or beat him unconscious if she had to.

He stood up, throwing back his cloak to free his sword hilt. The taverna door was already open, with a cold breeze ghosting in. With a slight smile he stepped out, seeing a full dozen cloaked men waiting for him, most standing on the ground, a few hovering on rooftops. *It was the Rekef then.*

"I take the numbers as a compliment," he said, mostly to himself. The door slammed shut behind him, and he heard the bar go down into place.

They moved in on him, rushing forward directly or stooping from the roofs. He thrust his open palms toward them, summoning the Art of his people. The smile still had not left his face.

〈〉 〈〉 〈〉

In the end they had been hampered by their need to take him alive. Thalric had made no scruples of abusing that advantage. In the quick, vicious scuffle, as they descended on him from all sides, and then as they wrestled to subdue him, he had killed five of them with his sting. It was an Art he was strong in. Putting his hand to a man's chest, he could punch a fist-sized hole right through his victim. In a brawl it was better than any hidden knife.

He did not earn their love, for that. Their orders to keep him alive had not specified in what condition. By the time it was over he was bruised and bloody from the beating they inflicted.

He had awoken, not in a cell but a small billet, the kind of room where a sergeant or junior officer might live out his life. There was a guard just within the door, and as Thalric stirred the man passed the word to others waiting outside.

A prisoner now, and aching all over, Thalric found a strangely high mood on him. He realized that it was because, amidst all the pain and bruising, there was barely a stab from the deep wound that Daklan had inflicted on him outside Collegium, that had come so close to finishing him after his fall from Rekef favour. That wound, unlike the betrayal, was now consigned to the past.

So where in the wastes am I? There was a quick enough answer to that one, since the men who had jumped him had been Wasp soldiers. This spartan little room he was in could be in the barracks, or perhaps in the governor's palace. There was a high window, suggesting his cell was probably on the level just below ground. He considered flying up there to look out, but decided that it was better not letting his captors know whether he could fly or not.

Of course, I can't be sure myself. He seemed, nevertheless, to have come through the beating better than he might have done, but then he had always been a tough one to keep down. *Captain Rauth, Ulther, Tisamon and Tynisa, Arianna, Daklan, Felise Mienn*: they had all done their best, at one time or another, to put him out of this world. He wondered who would try next.

Lying on the hard bunk, with the guard eyeing him cautiously, he had to concede that his life so far seemed to have been a whole lot of effort to achieve a great deal of nothing. *I would have stayed with the Rekef if I could. I have made a lamentable revolutionary.*

But now what? He was not bound, so he could kill the guard now and make a run for it. He might get quite far, and he could certainly kill a considerable number of his captors before they were forced to reevaluate just how alive they wanted him to be. Clearly he was being sent a message by someone confident he would be able to work it out: *Wait. All is not lost.*

Had he been intercepted by rebel elements within the palace? If there were still Mynan staff and slaves here, then the resistance would have its own people nearby. Perhaps Kymene or Che had . . . but then he did not even know if Che was still alive. It seemed quite possible that, after his explosive exit, Hokiak's people might have butchered her—or that Kymene might have had her killed as a Rekef agent. *Such irony!*

And then, after a moment's consideration, *I am both betrayed and betrayer.* The Empire's rejection of him had turned a life of estimable service into one of perverse deceit, and when he had tried to go back over that path, to knit the wounds he had caused, he had only made everything worse.

He was not made to be maudlin, though. *I am alive*, he reflected. It was the first and best building block that he could work with.

Two soldiers entered the room without preamble. Their demeanour showed that they were fully aware of what their fellows—and their late fellows—had gone through to bring him here. They both loathed him and were frightened of him.

"Well?" Thalric asked them. "What now?"

"Come with us," said one. His lips twitched, as if at a foul taste, when he added, "sir." The word struck Thalric like a blow. He almost toppled back on the bed, his legs suddenly weak at the power of a mere three-letter word. He had endured a long, harsh winter since anyone had truly called him that. The word was a whole life away for him: a door onto better days.

"Sir, is it?" he managed to get out, hoping that his face showed none of his surprise.

The man merely replied, "I have been ordered to request your presence, sir. You are sent for."

And you don't like it, soldier, but you'll obey your orders. That was the underlying principle of the entire Wasp nation, who were by nature so quarrelsome and undisciplined.

"Lead on, soldier," Thalric said it as casually as he could manage.

As soon as he got out into the corridor he knew that this must be the governor's palace. He had no fond memories of it, for he had been through as much pain here as he had at any time before, and he had lost a good friend, too. The only luck thrown his way, aside from his continued survival, was that in the end it had not been his hand that had scorched out the life of Colonel Ulther, at the last. Mere chance, too, and he had no right to feel better over mere chance.

They took him up three levels and he applied his mind to drawing himself a map of the place as he recalled it. These were the quarters of important guests and higher officers, up here. He had even stayed here himself. There were public staterooms too, though he was already above the grand hall that Ulther had held court in. Wherever he was being taken, it was to be behind closed doors.

Do they imagine I know something, and wish to woo it out of me? Do I now turn informant against Stenwold and his people? And why not?

If they had wanted information, they needed only put him under the machines, for surely the ways and means had not softened so very much. *But if I myself were in charge, would I not ask nicely first? Sometimes it is more efficient.* Of all the hypotheses milling in his brain this seemed the most likely. He should not therefore get used to his current liberty. *Which means I should exploit it as soon as the chance arises. Just give me a room with a decent-sized window.*

And, obligingly, they did so. This palace, like most large Wasp-constructed buildings, was a ziggurat, and the room they brought him to even boasted a balcony, beyond which the blue sky stretched broad and inviting. He stayed put, though. He wanted to know where he stood, before he ran. There were two soldiers at the door, keenly watching over him, but they did not yet figure in his calculations. Five dead men could become seven soon enough. He had nothing to lose and it made him feel immortal.

The room itself had little of the garish style that Ulther had loved: the gaudy and overdone, the displayed loot from a dozen conquered peoples. This was Capitas-style Wasp: the long table devoid of ornament and a single frieze on the wall, in the local style but depicting the battle for occupation of the city itself, eighteen years before. Thalric wondered idly if he could pinpoint one of those images of triumphant, larger-than-life Wasp soldiers as his younger self. Perhaps one of them was Ulther, commanding the attack. He glanced from the frieze to the soldiers, young men both. *They were not there, of course.* They had probably not even fought in the Twelve-Year War against the Commonweal. It made feel him oddly lonely. He had now more in common with Stenwold Maker than with these men. In the end the burden of cultural identity did not weigh as much as the years.

They had come to attention swiftly, and he positioned himself across the table from the door, waiting. Some instinct told him that he recognized the tread, even before the man himself appeared: a grey-haired, severe-looking Wasp-kinden. A colonel and, as he saw now from the additional insignia, a governor.

Of course. The new governor had not been referred to by name in any of the documents he had seen because there was no need, but if he had really, really tried, then he could have worked out who the man was. There was no reason for him to be surprised.

"Colonel Latvoc," Thalric said. "Excuse me for the informality, but I don't feel that I'm in a position to salute."

Latvoc's stare was all ice, but Thalric had not expected anything else. In a clipped gesture, the colonel ordered the two guards out of the room. "You didn't have to kill five of my soldiers," he said.

Thalric raised an eyebrow cynically. "The last time the Empire showed an interest in me, Colonel, I barely lived to learn a lesson from it."

"Even so," Latvoc said, "you've made things . . . very difficult."

And why should you care? But Thalric could see it already. A Rekef colonel put in charge of the garrison, leaving the soldiers unhappy and mistrustful—and why not? What was there to trust?

"Sit down," Latvoc ordered him flatly. When Thalric did not move he narrowed his eyes. "I am still your superior officer."

"Am I still in the army?"

Latvoc stared at him. Looking back into his sallow face, Thalric saw a man who had slept little recently. *Local or imperial worries, I wonder? Or both at once?* Abruptly, as though he was seeing a shape suddenly appear in the outlines of a cloud, Thalric saw the sheer, naked desperation within Latvoc. The man was on a knife edge, and barely balancing even on that.

"I'm not exactly in love with the Empire, after recent treatment," Thalric said. That part of him that had been loyal was horrified at his own daring.

"In love?" Latvoc spat, each word he uttered becoming a separate fight to control his temper. "You are—were—an imperial major. You were a Rekef officer. It is not for you to criticize the Empire. It is not for you to put your *petty* personal concerns before the demands of your masters. If the Empire wanted you dead, you by rights should have *died*. If it wishes now to recall you from the grave, then you shall *return*."

And I myself have used such logic once: after Daklan stabbed me, and I would rather not have lived. But recent association with Stenwold's pack of misfits seemed to have rubbed the gloss off those arguments.

"What do you want now?" Thalric asked. "You want me dead? Well, you had your chance. So what do you want?"

"*I?* I want nothing," Latvoc said coldly. "There is another, however, who is generous enough in spirit to give a broken vessel a second chance to be of service."

Thalric studied him: the Rekef colonel who, at their first meeting, had shot him through with fear for his own future, a man on whose word so many hundreds of other lives had turned. He found himself unmoved.

"Bring on your man," he said.

"He is already here," Latvoc informed him, and the colonel's eyes strayed past Thalric toward the balcony. A man was standing there. *Standing outside, or has he just flown down?* It was a child's trick, despite the silent skill with which it had been accomplished.

The man was merely a knifelike silhouette for a moment, then he stepped forward and stared into Thalric's face, and Thalric recognized him. Despite himself, his heart lurched.

It was General Reiner, one of the three men who ruled the Rekef.

Reiner glanced at Latvoc and made a small signal, and the colonel backed out of the room with an angry glare. For a long while, Reiner and the renegade measured one another in silence. Then the general gestured to the table, and Thalric cautiously took a seat across from him.

"So, General," he said, "if this is to be an execution it's a needlessly grand one. These days a knife in a back alley would be more my level."

Reiner opened his mouth to speak, but the words were a long time coming. Thalric realized that he had never heard this man speak before, and the first sound that Reiner uttered was so low and croaking that Thalric could not make it out.

Reiner tried again. "That will be enough, *Major* Thalric." Coming from a man of such power, the voice itself seemed weak and thin, but the words were another matter. Thalric felt the mention of that rank strike him like a blow so heavy that he actually rocked back in his chair.

And is it so? And is a year of my life thus erased, the disgrace forgotten, the sins undone? Is that certainty, that righteousness that they stripped from my every action, now dropped back on me like a blanket, and just as comforting?

"Since when was that *Major* still the case?" he got out. More angrily he added, "They tried to kill me."

In the silence after that he heard a slight shifting, not coming from Reiner but from beyond the room. He filed it neatly in his mind: men concealed, false walls. Not so very trusting after all.

Reiner took a deep breath. "We are at war, Major."

"I had noticed, General."

"I do not mean the Lowlands," Reiner said dismissively. "*Real* war. Maxin is trying to take over the Rekef. Maxin is the true enemy." His eyes twitched about the room as though naming his fellow Rekef general might somehow conjure him up.

"General Maxin," Thalric said slowly.

"His orders, to kill you," said Reiner. "Not mine."

Thalric remembered his last conversation with Daklan before the man had done his level best to kill him. Yes, Daklan had named Maxin as the source of the death warrant, but he had spoken of Thalric's supposed patron as well. *You could have protected me, General Reiner,* he thought. His imperial conditioning was meanwhile subtly falling back on his shoulders, conjured up by the mere mention of his vanished rank and privilege.

"So where does that leave me now?" he said, and then added unwillingly but inexorably, "Sir?"

Reiner's eyes alone acknowledged the concession. "We need capable agents," he rasped. "You are capable. Maxin had no right. You are mine. You are my major until I say otherwise." The speech seemed to exhaust him and he sank a little into his chair.

"What do you want me to do, sir?" Thalric asked him. *What could I give to you now? The secrets of the Lowlands . . . Stenwold's plans . . . Che's plans? I could take Che back from the resistance and make her in fact what they took her for in error: an agent of the Rekef. I could single-handedly secure the future of the Lowlands campaign.*

He looked into General Reiner's dry, barren face, and thought, *But you don't care.*

"Capitas," Reiner said. "I will send you to Capitas with false papers. The usual. I have work there for a capable man."

"Of course, sir," said Thalric. *I'm back in.* It was like a triumphant shout within his mind, the last months unwritten, wiped clean. He had never been cut loose from the army, from the Empire. He had remained loyal Major Thalric all this time, and the great cloak of imperial necessity had shrouded all his deeds in impenetrable *rightness*. But the rush of relief, of release, did not come. He waited for it eagerly but he was still wound up as tense as a bowstring inside. He felt sudden frustration with himself rise up inside. *Can I not take this gift, now? Is this not what I wanted?*

"Sir, may I ask a question?"

Reiner nodded.

"My work here at Myna, before—the removal of the old governor—I assume that you were preparing the ground. He was Maxin's man?"

Reiner nodded again.

"Good," Thalric said, and the slightest smile moved across Reiner's face.

I'm back in, Thalric told himself. *I'm back in. No more associating with lesser races, or running their errands. I've got power again. I can have my revenge on that Beetle whoremaster and his Mantis executioner, and the whole bloody lot of them.*

Another voice, so recently heard, said in his mind's ear: *It is not for you to criticize the Empire. It is not for you to put your* petty *personal concerns before the demands of your masters.*

The thought was gall in his mouth. *It cuts both ways, that does.* It cut down to the lowest slave and servant, and it cut up all the way to the top. Empire over all. For the Empire, not for himself, not for a general, not for the Emperor, and not for the Rekef. *And not for some grasping general's bastard faction games!*

Something inside him wailed in despair at his conclusions, losing a second time what he could hardly bear to lose on the first occasion.

"General," he said, "when you sent me to kill my former friend Colonel Ulther I did not want to do it, but when I did so, at least it was because he was guilty of an actual *crime*."

Reiner's eyes widened and his mouth opened, but Thalric did not have time to wait for that hoarse voice to emerge. The flash of his sting shot was concealed beneath the table, but the blast of it smashed the Rekef general's chair into pieces even after it had passed through the occupant's body.

SIXTEEN

He stepped out on to the sand, the sun suddenly bright in his eyes. He put a hand up to blot it out, and could then see the walls of the place curving away from him, scarred and blackened by years of abuse.

His life had become a kind of waking dream. They took him from place to place, caged like an animal, and whenever they halted, he fought and killed. He had ceased to care what they put before him, save that, whatever it was, they had not found the thing to beat Tisamon yet.

Beyond the walls' ten-foot barrier, ranks of seats rose steeply on all sides. Mostly there were simple benches, but at one end there was something grander, a cloth-roofed pavilion furnished with wooden chairs for honoured guests. He wondered how many were watching today, the Wasp-kinden and their favoured servants and slaves. More than last time, certainly, and last time there had been hundreds.

The arena was bigger than last time, too, and stone-walled rather than roughly-hewn wood. He decided he had not been here before.

There was a constant murmur of anticipation around him, as if they had never seen a Mantis-kinden fight before. He stood halfway toward the centre, the sand around him already crusted and stained with the memory of some previous fight, and waited there for his opponent. His metal claw flexed slightly, as though of its own accord.

The gate opposite him, built of wood studded and reinforced with iron, ground upward, and he caught sight of a flicker of movement in the gap below. He instantly dropped into his fighting stance, claw drawn back across his body and folded ready along his forearm.

Out of the gate came a beetle, but of no kind he knew. It was a long, lean creature, twelve feet from head to tail and supported high off the ground on its slender legs. It moved fast, rushing out from the darkness and halting immediately across from him, the same distance from the centre as he was. Its green carapace was dappled with white and gold, and it had huge eyes and mandibles like scythe blades. The crowd picked up. They knew this beast or its type, and were in favour of it.

If only Stenwold's kind had taken their Art from this thing, rather than the plodding soil rollers, Tisamon thought wryly. The beetle was regarding him with a keen awareness that most mere animals had no right to. He was not surprised, though, for the mantids of his own homeland could think and reason, and outwit the men that came to hunt them. So why not this splendid, predatory specimen?

Abruptly it rushed him, from motionless to full charge without a break, and the crowd roared it on hugely. Tisamon leapt high, seeing the scimitar mandibles clash together beneath him, got one foot on the insect's thorax and kicked off, skidding a little on the sand behind it but knowing it would have already turned to follow him. Even before looking round he had lashed back at it, but there was no contact. The beetle had reared back onto four legs, threatening him now with its hooked foreclaws. Tisamon backed up, a slight smile appearing on his face, while the huge, glittering eyes regarded him intently as it sank back down. For a moment they paced each other, Tisamon circling, and the beetle retreating or advancing, but always facing each other head on.

It made a second charge, as swift as the first, and again he hurled himself out of the way. His blade swung back to bite into the armour of its carapace, leaving a shallow cut along its wing case. The crowd howled, so he knew that the beetle was right behind him, turning itself faster than he had thought. He could not hope to outrun it, so he threw himself up and back. The point of one mandible snagged his shirt briefly, and he drove his claw down into its thorax.

The tip of it dug in, then skittered out again across its armour, and he fell onto the creature's back and rolled off instantly, a second hasty swing cutting across one of its midlegs. It rounded on him yet again.

They understood one another. He had fought so many other men and women on his way to this place. There had never been this same connection. The mottlings of its carapace were the scars of old battles, he knew. They understood one another.

As it rushed him with jaws gaping, he let his feet skid out from under him, saw the shadow of that lethal head pass over him, claws on all sides of him scrabbling to stop its charge. Without hesitation he drove his blade up into its thorax, between the roots of its legs, drove it in right up to the wrist.

When the beast was finally dead, Tisamon knelt beside it for a moment, laid a hand on its stilled head, within the arc of those great jaws. Then he stood up again and let them take him away. The crowd were now shouting deliriously for him, just as they had been shouting for the creature he had slain.

Capitas. He came out of his waking dream just enough to recollect the destination he had reached. *I am in Capitas, the heart of the Empire—and with a drawn blade.*

They next set him against deserters, as a special treat for the crowd. Before releasing him into the the arena they had brought in eight men, and manacled them by the leg to a ring at the centre of the sand, giving them a generous length of chain to let them move. The master of the games had put up wooden barricades and walls to make a fake ruin that was low enough for the raised audience to see over, but high enough so that the deserters, or their opponent, could hide behind it. The condemned men had no idea what was coming against them. They had no armour and carried knives rather than swords, but they still had their stings. They had been promised their freedom if they survived the contest.

Tisamon came into the arena so subtly that most of the watchers did not see him. Slowly he stalked the chained men, letting only the spectators notice him, moving from cover to cover. The deserters looked about for him, aware from the reaction of the crowd that *something* was now loose in there along with them, but something they could not see.

Tisamon showed the onlookers something new: how the Mantis-kinden hunt. His first rush was without warning, accelerating from stealthy pace to a full-scale charge within an instant. He was through the centre of the arena and away again in three steps and a leap, blade dancing on all sides. Four men died. The others loosed their stings but he was gone. They scorched only the wooden stage-scenery, and came close to burning each other.

Then they began to argue. They shouted at each other. They had completely forgotten the crowd. They only knew that they were alone in a hostile place, and hunted.

One of them started trying to smash at his chain with a stone. The others kept their hands outspread, searching for their enemy. The crowd was completely rapt. They could see that Tisamon was right there with the surviving men, almost amongst them. He slowly picked up a knife in his left hand, a blade dropped by one of his victims. With a flick of the wrist he sent it flying into the throat of the one furthest from him. The others, slaves to instinct, turned to look.

And it was done.

He let himself be taken back to his cell, in the holding pens beneath the arena. A strange and nightmarish place, it was a maze of iron bars with no walls and no privacy. Its designer had made it infinitely movable, so that a small cell for a man could be opened into a larger cell for a beast, or for a group of wretches destined to spend their last hours together, and then die in one another's company. A low light was provided by bowls of burning oil hung from the ceiling. This warren of cells predated much of the Empire's technological development, and was almost the oldest section of Capitas still standing. The Wasps had maintained certain priorities.

Tisamon's eyes were better than most in such gloom. When he came out of his killing trance, in the long hours when he could not avoid thinking about what he was reduced to, he wished they were not. These chambers beneath the arena were a reeking, smoky hell. Some of the cells contained other successful gladiators, who sat and waited there to be taken for exercise or training, or simply to be fed. They were not Wasps, however. Unlike the deserters or those of lesser race, the true Wasp gladiators were heroes and lived as free men. They were adored by the people of Capitas, but Tisamon had killed several of them, so now they did not pit him against them. The bulk of Tisamon's fighting companions belonged to a dozen other subject races: Ants, half-breeds, a Mole Cricket, a Thorn Bug. They were the outstandingly skilled ones who had lived through enough fights to become a commodity—as he was.

Other cells held another kind of commodity: a disposable, consumable one. The arena was like a meat grinder, and the Capitas crowds loved to see their share of blood. If it was not quality, with men like Tisamon or the Wasp professionals meting out skilled slaughter, then it was quantity they craved. The arena had an inexhaustible hunger for slaves, foreigners and prisoners of war. These were forced to hack clumsily at each other as an amusing warm-up, or else they were roped to each other and made to fight against giant beasts. Some were pitched against terrible automotives and machines. There were forty or fifty of them within Tisamon's view at all times, but the individual prisoners varied from day to day, sometimes hour to hour. There were men and women of all kinden included amongst them, and children also.

There were beasts, too, but they were further back. Tisamon saw little of them, heard only the occasional scuttle and hiss. They were cared for better than the men, with expert handlers and trainers. In this society of the violently doomed they were a kind of aristocracy. Compound eyes glittering in the smoky light, they watched their keepers constantly, looking for a chance to escape. It seemed to Tisamon that captivity had brought them closer toward the human condition, even as it had degraded the morose and silent gladiators toward the level of the beast.

After a while, a handful of slaves passed between the cells, mostly Fly-kinden whose eyes could cut through the gloom as keenly as Tisamon's own. Behind them came an old Wasp man, almost bald with a sour and leathery face. He limped, though he disdained a stick, and at his belt were hung a studded club and a whip. His name was Ult, he had informed Tisamon. He had been Slave Corps once, before becoming a trainer of gladiators. Now he was their keeper.

He had stopped by Tisamon's cell two days before, and sat there regarding the Mantis doubtfully for a long while, neither of them saying anything. The next day he had stopped again, and again the Fly-kinden boy he kept as a slave had put down the little three-legged stool, and Ult had sat there thoughtfully. Eventually he had spoken: "You know why I'm interested in you?"

Tisamon had merely stared at him, feeling like one of the animals caged beyond, just waiting for its moment.

"I get men like you all the time: the older ones, who've had their share of fights and gotten used to it," Ult had said. "They sit and they brood. Look, you can see a dozen of them from here, men whose card's marked for death. They just don't know when and don't much care. But still they fight. At least they're not prisoners when they fight, eh? This down here, it's not real to them. Only the fighting is. You're like that, too."

No, I'm a beast, caged, Tisamon had thought, on hearing that, but failed to convince himself. Ult had smiled, which caused a scar to stand out white across his left cheekbone.

"You want out?" He had given Tisamon enough time to respond. "You don't want out," he had concluded. "But you caught my eye, you did. Not 'cos you're a Mantis. I've had your kind down here before. No, it's 'cos you're already dead inside, even before you got here. It usually takes them a few tendays at least, to get to where you are."

"I know," Tisamon had replied. It was all he had said, but they both knew it was a concession.

Now Ult came along yet again, after the slaves had doled out the evening slops. The boy put the stool down, and the old gladiator-trainer perched on it, close enough to the bars for Tisamon to grab at him. In just two days he had taken the Mantis' measure, and the Mantis had taken his.

"Mantis-man," Ult began. "I saw your fight again today. Very good. Very entertaining. I even had two colonels and a general tell me how much they enjoyed the show."

Tisamon grunted, a shrug showing how little he cared about that.

"Too good, almost. They'd rather the last man had got you instead."

"The last man?"

"Oh, yes, they want their blood, after all," Ult said. "They want the last blood to be a foreigner's, though. You cut them boys down too easily. Deserters, sure, but Wasps still."

Tisamon shrugged again.

"You don't understand," Ult observed.

"So they'd rather I was dead," Tisamon said. "What else is there to understand?"

"It's about race," Ult said. "I never been to your lands, but I been to the Commonweal, and I seen a few other places before the Emperor rounded them up. It's different here. You know any Ants, Mantis-man?"

"I've known a few."

"We're like them, really. You know how Ants reckon everyone else is off the mark, not as good as they are? We're like that, too. Me, I seen all sorts—not greatly in love with any of 'em, me. Don't care for my kin nor yours, nor anyone's. I understand the punters, though. What they want to see is *foreign* blood shed. You take me for a philosopher, Mantis?"

"No."

Ult chuckled, then coughed. "Oh, I know my trade. It makes a philosopher out of you. This isn't just a whole round of fun, see? There's a point here, when you get to it. There's meaning, Mantis."

Tisamon shuffled closer, despite himself. "Meaning? To all the slaughter?"

"Right." Ult closed his eyes, as though the whole circus of all the fights he had seen could thus be summoned up to parade about his mind. "This is all about us and you, us Wasps and everyone else. We go out to your lands, see? We catch you, we drag you back in chains. You fight for our pleasure. We bring in your beasts and make you fight them. We chain up the whole world and bring it here. That makes it ours, see? There are people out there who only see a slice of the Empire, a smaller slice still of what lies beyond, but here they see it all, and the end has to be the same. A dead foreigner—dead by our hands, or by beasts, or by each other, but dead foreigners all the way."

"What an art form you have here," Tisamon commented dryly.

"You'll understand soon enough. It's why you've become a problem, old Mantis."

"Because I don't die?"

"Right," Ult said. "I've got the big games coming up, and you deserve your spot in them, but what am I supposed to do with you to keep them happy? You'll kill beasts and you'll kill men, and about the only way I could bring you down would be to stick so many people against you that nobody'd see what was going on. And don't forget, it's all for show. If there's no show there's nothing."

"You want me to throw a fight, then?" Tisamon asked him. "Fatally?"

Ult grinned at that, revealing teeth stained yellow. "I don't reckon that's going to happen, though. I'll just have to keep you for some other day. But it's a shame, you're just too good."

"So what's happening, that's so important?"

"Coronation Day." Ult stood. "Nine years since Himself took the throne. And I mean *took*." Ult glanced about him, taking a wary step back after he saw that Tisamon was on his feet.

"In that case I want to fight there," the Mantis announced.

"I want you to, as well," said Ult. "But I just can't see how."

"I'll go in barehanded. I'll go against men, beasts, machines, whatever you—"

"Mantis, old Mantis," Ult interrupted him, "if I got nothing else from all my years, it's an eye for the fighting man. What have I got available here, now, that would give you a run? I'm sorry, really. I want to see you killed as much as you want to die." His smile was genuinely friendly. The camaraderie might have seemed absurd, but was just as real. "Let me think about it. You deserve your audience, I'll grant you that."

When the Wasp Second Army arrived within striking range of the Felyal, it began building its fortifications without delay. The engineers of the Empire lifted their premeasured wooden wall sections from their hauling automotives, and constructed themselves a camp great enough to encompass the whole army. They had a workforce of thousands, and General Tynan, who commanded the Second, had made them all practise this decidedly nonstandard procedure. He was an intelligent man, Tynan, and he had nothing but respect for the late General Alder, who had made this part of the Lowlands a graveyard for twenty thousand imperial soldiers and Auxillians. Oh, there had been mitigating circumstances, of course. Alder had been played for a fool by the Spiderlands, crippled by a lack of firm instruction from Capitas, so his men had been kept in a state of uncertainty, forever hovering in their temporary camp, forever made ready for marching orders that never came. Then they had most of them died, and the remnants had been so little fit for purpose as an army that they had been broken up, dispersed across the whole Empire. The Barbs had ceased to exist.

It was a mistake that General Tynan did not intend to repeat. By nightfall his men were already settled behind their makeshift walls, and he kept half of them awake all night, with sting and crossbow and snapbow ready for the assault. Under his eight-year command, the Second Army had gained the nickname of the Gears, because whatever they got their teeth into, they milled and crushed until it was nothing but dust. And because they stopped for nothing.

That first-night assault did not happen, the Mantis-kinden being slow to venture forth from their forest haunts. The next day Tynan had his men continue their preparations, creating a great camp of angled walls and machines, with a ring of spindly towers inside it. He knew that inevitably the hammer would fall and sooner rather than later. And sooner was better, for the Empire had a timetable for him to keep to.

From the second day onward he sent out men to the treeline with firethrower automotives, clearing the trees as they came to them. As an exercise, he thought of it as a duellist calling out his enemy. He would not have long to wait.

If he could have got a scout into the trees at twilight and out again alive, he would not have been disappointed by the news. The war host of the Felyal was indeed mustering, for the elders of the Mantids had already sent out the call to gather their people. Women and men, lean and fair, in green cloth or black-scaled armour, they came in their hundreds to the holds of their leaders. They brought their bows and spears, their rapiers and claws, and the deadly spines on their forearms. They came with their insect allies, from beasts that flew from the wrist to great armoured killers larger than a horse. The Mantids of Felyal fought constantly.

They sparred amongst themselves and ambushed the unwary in their forest, and they savaged Spider-kinden shipping off the coast. Now they were going to war, and the mechanical sounds of the enemy would be drowned in their war hymns, their oaths and battle cries.

They were silent for now, though, merely waiting in the trees. There were so many of them, too, more even than had marched against Alder's Fourth, more than had ever stood together in living memory—and they were a long-lived breed: male and female, from callow youths to grey elders, and each one a killer of excellence. They had buckled on armour that had been made before any hill chieftain had arisen to start building an Empire: cuirasses of dark scales, suits of elegant plate and delicate mail links, spine-crested helms. They had put aside their feuds and enmities, blood-hatreds generations old, to stand together now as siblings.

The elders—the Loquae of the hold of Felyal—met together, but there was little to plan. The Mantis-kinden had no use for formations, vanguards, rearguards or shieldwalls. That was their strength: individually there was not a warrior to match them in all of the Lowlands, in all the world. The Wasps and their slaves could not stand against them, with blade or bow. This was their heritage, and they believed in it with an iron-shod faith.

Parents bid their children be strong in their absence, brother and sister parted company: the older and more skilled on their way, the younger staying at home. The very oldest watched their entire families step out into the dark and head off to war.

The armed might of the Felyal arose along with the dusk, and then hurled itself against an enemy twenty times its size. They came out of the trees in a sudden rush at twilight, unnumbered and unheralded. They were savage and brave, swift and skilled: the warriors of the Felyal, Mantis-kinden fierce and free.

The first line of warriors swept on in silence, wings hurling them high into the air as they neared the makeshift walls. Their arrows took their marks, sentries falling from the ramparts or dropping where they stood. The Wasps had precious little warning before the Mantids were upon their ramparts, shooting down at the men below.

The angles of the walls were planned against just such an assault, though. They bellied to halfway up, then drew in, and slots in the upper half allowed the men below to loose their stings and weapons upward into the attackers. It took only the first sentry's death cry to set the camp in motion.

The Wasps had learnt bitter lessons from the demise of the Fourth. Their progress from Merro had been slowed by assembling their travelling fort each evening, and General Tynan himself had been surprised to reach so near to the forest before this assault came.

A full third of the Imperial Army was on night shift. As soon as the call came they were scrambling from their tents, already fully armoured and armed. All the while, the Mantids were vaulting to the wall, driving their arrows into every target in the half-light that the Wasps' eyes could not pierce. For a moment the Wasps could not form a line. Men were dropping even as they took up position, and there were Mantis warriors everywhere within the camp, their blades bloody. The balance teetered in the favour of the ancient ways of war.

All through this, engineers were at work. They did not rush forth as soldiers would, and the Mantids did not mark them, perceiving no threat in them. Even when the great engine within the ring of towers grumbled to life they were not hindered. They threw their levers and the generators whirred into motion, and abruptly there was light. The apex of each tower had burst into a blinding white flame that left the inside of the camp—and a hundred yards beyond—as bright as day. The shock of it brought the Mantis influx to a halt, the attackers reeling back, launching into the air, covering their eyes.

Wasp stings and Wasp crossbowmen now loosed at will. The new snapbows, hundreds of them shipped from Helleron and Sonn, cracked and spat their bolts, too swift and small to be cut aside or dodged. The Mantids were too widely spread for volley fire and so each of the Wasp soldiers picked a target and loosed on his own volition, and the real slaughter started.

The Mantids did not understand, and with speed and fury they kept mounting the wall and launching themselves into that steel rain of shot, and dying. They died and died. It should have been the end of them, but such was their swiftness that twice more they swept over the inside of the camp once again, lashing and stabbing indiscriminately, reaping whole blocks of Wasp soldiers with their blades. Their steel claws rent flesh and dug around armour, a spinning, lashing dance of blood that carried death to all within their reach. Their archers loosed arrows at the snapbowmen, each shot deadly, but it was like spitting into the storm. Their beasts, the terrible forest mantids, lashed out their killing arms, crushing and severing limbs or taking up whole screaming soldiers and snapping them, their knife-blade mandibles rending steel effortlessly. The Mantis war host fell on the Wasp lines with their spears, their swords and their antique armour that could not protect them.

There were too few, in the end. Against that scythe of shot, too few ever came together within the walls to break the Wasps, but they tried over and over, until the bodies of their warriors were scattered like wheat after a storm. Their armoured beasts lay still with the fletching of snapbow bolts riddling their carapaces, eyes dull and barbed limbs stilled. The Mantids shouted their defiance of the invader, each one of them honed to a degree of skill that no Wasp soldier could ever know, masters of a fighting art a thousand years old and more. The snapbows and the crossbows did not care: they found their mark, automatic as machines. And the

Mantids charged and died, and charged and died, until even their spirits failed, their proud hearts broke, and they could come no more.

The flower of the Felyal had fallen that night, and in the morning there were over 1,700 Mantis dead. Despite their technical advantages and their weapons, the imperial slain numbered 173 men more.

The next day the Felyal was burning. Mantis holds that had stood for a thousand years were going up in flames. Tens of thousands of soldiers and machines, artillery and firethrowers were working their way through the Felyal, torching everyone and everything they came across. The Mantis-kinden still fought back, and every Mantis that died within those trees had already shed the blood of many Wasps, but there were always more Wasps. The burning only stopped when the survivors at last turned and fled, leaving their homes, their lives and their history beneath the Wasp boots. They fled west—where else? They fled toward Collegium, or maybe to Sarn. They had no other choice available.

In his study in Seldis, Teornis of the Aldanrael perused the news almost dispassionately. The Mantids had served their purpose, and now they were gone. It was a small loss, at least one that no Spider would be sad about. If the war was won, then perhaps they would reestablish themselves, or perhaps not.

He had been arguing for almost a tenday now. He had been arguing with men of other families, with the women of his own. The time was right to strike and suddenly they were turning away from war. The Wasp force garrisoned north of Seldis, now comprising most of the Eighth Army, made them uneasy.

"Now is the time, only *now!*" he had urged them. His agents were ready to ignite Solarno. The Sarnesh were marching. Collegium was bristling with siege engines. The Empire was fighting on all its borders. "Now!" he had repeated.

They had not seen his "now." The matter was still being wrangled over, their endless circular arguments merely a blind for the political manoeuvres behind the scenes. Everyone wanted to be sure who would be on top, come the end of this.

Teornis looked again at the news he had received, the grievous blow to his chances and his future.

The Ants of Kes, that unassailable island city, were not sallying out to strike the Wasp supply lines, so as to do their bit for the salvation of the Lowlands, and the reason for the Imperial Second bypassing them was now clear. The Ants of Kes, after thorough consideration, had signed a mutual nonaggression pact with the Empire, and betrayed the Lowlands to the sword.

"Now!" he insisted still, but "now" was fading into the past. If he could not capitalize on all he had worked for, then he would be lost, and so, he suspected, would everything else.

Two days later and he was regretting it all. He had grasped the nettle and got stung. His kinden always placed such stock on self-control, and yet now his hands would not stop shaking. Teornis of the Aldanrael, Lord-Martial and warmonger, had been granted his wish.

On this bright morning, before the sun's heat became oppressive, the combined forces of seven of Seldis' great families had marched north from the city's walls with the aim of destroying the Wasp Empire's holding force and severing the supply lines that were all that kept the Imperial Second on track toward Collegium. In this bold stroke, the Spiderlands would secure the entire southern coast against the Wasps, and from there it would be up to Collegium and Sarn to themselves defeat General Malkan and the Seventh Army. Even this strike had taken all of Teornis' considerable powers of persuasion, all of the Aldanrael family's political influence, and a great mass of Spider-kinden self-interest to produce.

The Seldis force had been levied from a dozen different satrapies within the Spiderlands. As well as a core of Spider-kinden light infantry, drawn from the lesser families or the unfriended and the impoverished, it boasted a host of other kinden: Beetle artificers and heavy infantry with leadshotters and battle automotives; red-skinned Fire-Ant crossbowmen in copperweave chain mail marching beside hulking Scorpion mercenaries who were bare-chested and carried great swords and axes over their shoulders; flights of Dragonfly-kinden glittering and dancing constantly in the still air. There were Fly-kinden archers and scouts by the hundred, Ant-infantry from far southern cities barely contemplated by the Lowlands, desert-dwelling Grasshopper-kinden with spears and small circular shields, hairy and uncouth Tarantula-kinden that were supposedly the Spiders' primitive cousins. This was a mighty host for any Spider Aristos to command. Intelligence informed them that they outnumbered the Wasp force waiting for them by almost three to one.

While the army was settling into its blocks and ranks, Teornis had conference with his co-commanders. This was the price of war: his sovereignty was usurped. A half dozen Spider-kinden and their aides eyed each other suspiciously and made endless suggestions about how the army should dispose itself.

Teornis grew impatient. He had engineered this war and he therefore felt that it should be his to order. He himself argued for a swift attack, light infantry and cavalry on both wings sweeping forward whilst the heavy centre rumbled in to smash whatever defences the Wasps might put forth. They were cautious, and he was argued down. Their kinden was more suited to lying in wait, not charging forth. Teornis was putting his case for the third time, when a Fly messenger came hurtling into the tent.

The Wasps were on the move. The Wasps were attacking.

The Spiders could not believe their luck. Agreement suddenly flowered. Orders went out to the archery companies, the artillery, the airborne. The advancing Wasps would be destroyed by massed missile shot, then driven into the Dryclaw desert. Perhaps no foot soldier would even need to bloody his blade.

This was not my plan, was all Teornis could think now. He had wanted to attack: he could not be blamed for this. He clung to that excuse, for the scant good it could do him. Even now he was trying to rally his personal guard to retreat from the field, while retreat was still an option.

It was that cursed weapon of Stenwold Maker's. Teornis had tried to explain. He had even armed a company of his own Fire Ant-kinden with it, and they were now making a bloody accounting of themselves. The Wasps, though, possessed thousands of the things, whole airborne companies armed with them.

The battle had begun at long range, as his peers had planned. Specifically it had begun at twenty yards further than the Spiderlands bows or crossbows could reach. As the artillery of both armies had traded shot with slogging patience, the snapbow bolts, fired from shoulder to shoulder, two-deep formations of Wasp infantry, simply flayed the front ranks of the Spider army, leaving them dead in their tracks. For what must have been less than a minute, but had seemed like forever, the Spider commanders had watched the vanguard of their soldiers disintegrate, an alchemical translation of soldiers into corpses that no magician could have matched.

They were no fools, for all their division, and their orders had gone out as fast as the Fly-kinden could carry them. The Dragonfly airborne had launched into the air, either on their own wings or on the giant beasts they rode. The light archers and crossbowmen had been rushed forward into range. The spider cavalry had scuttled into action with lance and fang while the automotives had thundered forth. The artillery had perfected its elevation and begun finding the ranges on the close-ranked Wasp lines.

The Wasps were doing just the same thing, though: their own light airborne rose to meet the Dragonflies while their artillery had begun landing stones and leadshot and explosive grenades with devastating effect amidst the Seldis army. Their snapbowmen, though, had simply shot and shot again and, even when the Spiders denied them a massed target by sending their archers out in loose-knit skirmishing order, the Wasps had found their victims. Less than one in three of the Spiderlands archers even got into range before they died.

There were still some parts of Teornis' army holding, and he could not decide whether they were far more loyal than he deserved, or whether they simply did not realize how badly things were going. The Fire Ants had dug in with snapbows and repeating crossbows, and there were still some Dragonflies in the air. Meanwhile the Scorpions had actually got into close fighting, their monstrous swords and axes hacking a bloody wedge into the enemy. Despite all this, Teornis was tactician enough to see that the day was lost.

"Get me to the coast," he urged his men. No Seldis for him, because Seldis was where the Wasps would go next and, besides, his own people would hardly be glad to see him right now.

Still, where can we sail to? The reports received, in all their veiled language, had been plain enough. With the fires of the Felyal behind them, the Wasp army was tearing up the coast toward Collegium, not stopping for anything but travelling as fast as its motorized siege train would let it.

Something snapped in him, just for a moment, and Teornis whipped his rapier from its scabbard and slashed it across all the papers and reports and maps he had been living with for the last two tendays, scattering them through the air like whirling insects, like cinders. His cry of rage and frustration brought his people running, but instantly he was composed again, his face making no admission that anything had happened.

We will lose Collegium. Everything was for nothing if that Beetle city fell. The Lowlands would open to the Wasps like a virgin slave.

SEVENTEEN

The guards came rushing out at him straight away, but Thalric had caught them just as much by surprise as he had General Reiner. Thalric knew his trade and had spotted the sections of wall they would manhandle away and come bursting through, almost falling over themselves in their shock. They were not Rekef, so had expected threats, justifications, a warning from him. If he had not started killing them as soon as they exposed themselves they would not have known what to do with him.

He let his sting speak for him, striking them down even as they tried to pile into the room. He expected that they would kill him despite his efforts, but there were only four of them in the end. He had been a four-guard threat, in Reiner's eyes. A moment later the other two from outside had crashed in, too late again, alerted only by the shouts of the first four. He killed them too before they quite understood.

He fled to the balcony and paused there, waiting. He himself would have had guards posted either side of the balcony doorway, but Reiner had positioned himself there instead. Thalric's exit was clear.

There were no running footsteps, no shouts, no alarm.

With the utmost care he stepped back into the room, eyes roving dispassionately between Reiner's corpse and those of his guards. It was over so very quickly that no word had spread. Had nobody even heard? Where were the staff and soldiers of this palace, to come running at the sound of seven murders?

The servants would normally be locals, so perhaps Reiner did not trust them. Perhaps he was right not to, given the reports Thalric had read in Tharn. As for the soldiers and other imperial officials who should be thronging up here, they were either off trying to crush a resistance that was already too great for them to get their fingers around or had already fallen victim to imperial politics. Looking down at the general's thin face Thalric wondered whether Reiner had gone a little mad, at the end, backed into a self-made corner by mounting paranoia.

There was a knock on the door and, motivated by a foreknowledge of who this would be, Thalric called, "Come in."

In came Colonel Latvoc, mouth already open to speak when he saw the wreckage. Thalric had a palm directed toward him but Latvoc made no move against him, just stared and stared. Something was melting behind his face, and it was his own future. The ship he had invested everything in, whose fortunes he had backed beyond all else and which he had clung to in the storm, was now sunk.

He fell to his knees and a noise came from him: not a word, or anything that Thalric had ever heard uttered by anyone before—just a small, thin noise of pure grief. It seemed to Thalric that, in that same moment, Colonel Latvoc suffered more over the loss of his general than did Felise Mienn over the deaths of her children.

Thalric felt no sympathy, finding again that he was a Rekef officer at heart. In the end he cared only for the Empire, and the Empire's worst enemy, right now, was itself. It was men like Reiner and Latvoc here, yes, and Maxin and all the other conniving generals and colonels and governors who were tearing out pieces of the Empire for their own fiefdoms, behaving no better than the criminal gangs of Helleron. Even the Emperor himself, if he tolerated or encouraged such practices, was no longer exempt from Thalric's contempt. Such a weight was suddenly lifted from his shoulders with that thought, for he had done something truly good for the Empire at last.

He hardly even had to make the decision. His hand seemed to flash fire of its own accord, searing into Latvoc's slack face and smashing him to the floor.

Now he could go, his work here done. He went to the balcony and looked out across Myna, a city on the brink of uprising. In the circumstances, what should the good officer do?

Or what should the turncoat Lowlands agent do? Or the sometime companion of Che Maker?

That thought still rankled: he should not have left her. Worse, he should not even have put her in the situation. Che was in the hands of the resistance, that seemed certain, and they might already have killed her. They might, on the other hand, have believed her. Of course he, Thalric, had news now that the resistance would covet. How would the officers here cope now, now that the governor and his Rekef general master were both dead?

It took him only a moment, poised there on the balcony's brink, to see it: the Wasp garrison would lash out. They would see this as a political killing and they would retaliate blindly in the heavy-handed way that Latvoc had taught them. Without precise targets, they would bludgeon the whole city in their wrath. Myna was about to feel the whip, but the slaver might yet find the slave snatching the weapon from his hand.

Wings flashing into life, he vaulted off the balcony, stepping out over the city. He would find the resistance. He would find Che. He owed her that much.

◊

They were within sight of Hokiak's Exchange when Kymene signalled a halt. Che stumbled, blundering into Chyses' back, and he cuffed her hard with a hiss of annoyance. She was pinned between two of the Mynan Red Flag dressed as civilians, cloaked and hooded as if against a blustery day.

"Kymene?" Che asked. Chyses glared at her, but he was just as uncertain.

"Something has changed," Kymene said, though there was no obvious reason for the remark. She might as well have made the declaration after just sniffing the air. Still, the men with her took her seriously. Chyses carefully drew his blade from its sheath, hiding it along the line of his arm. Ahead of them, a squad of Wasp soldiers crossed the street, from alley to alley. To Che they seemed hurried and yet uncertain, dashing most of the way before dawdling for a moment, then dashing on.

"We should go back," Chyses suggested. "Or send for more men." Che's two guards were their only escort. Kymene was not a leader to hide behind walls, Che gathered, but it was a two-edged sword. Her followers loved her for her bravery in taking the self-same risks she asked of them, but of course the Wasps would give a great deal to catch her. Che understood from Chyses that there had been some close calls since Kymene's release from the palace, attempts by Wasps and mercenary hunters both to recapture the resistance's leader.

Kymene gazed thoughtfully at the front of the Hokiak Exchange thoughtfully. Hokiak was more than capable of double-crossing her, and it would have been entirely in character. He would have done it differently, though: the trap would be elsewhere than his own den, and more subtle than sending a simple message that the very Thalric she wanted to see had just walked into the Exchange and given himself up.

A trap of the Empire, then? She and Chyses had made what examination they could of the Exchange's exterior. They were used to spotting ambushes after long years of setting them. If there were Wasp soldiers waiting to drop on to Hokiak's Exchange then she saw no sign of it. Furthermore, she was sure that Hokiak kept a few eyes of his own out, and she knew for certain that those venal Wasps who used his services to bring in contraband ensured that he always had warning of any intended raids. There was the alternative, unlikely as it sounded, that Thalric was exactly what Che said he was, and therefore a useful man to talk to.

But something is wrong. Not a simple betrayal, but my city has changed in some way. She would recognize Thalric, while her men would not. So she had to go in herself. Chyses was all for burning down the Exchange, with both Hokiak and Thalric inside it, but she wanted to see the man and speak with him.

"He killed the Bloat, remember," she murmured.

"Not for us, he didn't," Chyses shot back, and that was true.

"We go in," she said.

He hissed in frustration, but he nodded in the end. They had not always been allies, the two of them, nor had he always been willing to take her orders. It was only after her capture that he had realized how much Myna needed her.

They found Thalric playing a game of dice and counters with one of Hokiak's followers. The old Scorpion himself was lurking at the bar of his back room, which was inhabited only by his men and by Thalric. Chyses went in first, the drawn knife still hidden by his cloak, peering suspiciously at every face in turn. Hokiak's men, a half dozen of them, watched him just as carefully in return.

There was a change, though, that went through them when Kymene entered. They were mostly locals and, though they had given their pledge to gold rather than city, they knew her. When she lowered her hood, the Maid of Myna, both beautiful and stern, their slouching arrogance straightened up into something more respectful.

"You took your time." Hokiak came hobbling over toward them, immune to all that. Across the gaming table, Thalric's eyes found Che's own.

"Tell me what you're playing at, old man," Kymene said. "You said he was your prisoner."

"He ain't going nowhere," Hokiak said. "As for games, what have you got? You been list'ning at all out there? It's like the start of a sandstorm, just beginnin' to blow. You hear that?"

"What's changed, Hokiak?"

"*He'll* tell you." The Scorpion chuckled. "Gryllis, how's it going?"

The voice of his Spider accomplice drifted in from the shop front. "Everything worth taking is boxed. The boys are moving it right now."

"Taking a trip?" Kymene inquired. When the Scorpion just leered at her, she reached out and grabbed his collar, twisting it. His men moved, but uncertainly and without direction. In that moment it was clear, as it had not been before, that they would not attack Kymene even for their employer.

"This city is like a keg of firepowder, and it's just about ready for the match," Hokiak said casually, as though she did not have him by the throat. "I deal with all sorts here, you know that. I do good business with your lot and the Wasps, and with anyone. Ain't no matter to me, so long as there's business in it. I seen what's coming, and I ain't going to have no looters gettin' their hands on my valuables. Just taking care, that's all."

"What's happened?" she asked. "Why now?"

Thalric stood up. "I remember you," he said. "From the palace. You were Ulther's prisoner."

Kymene nodded. "And you his executioner." She saw him flinch, however hard he tried to hide it. "You did me good service, Major Thalric. I remember you too."

Hokiak chuckled, tugging his collar from her fingers and sloping back toward the bar. "You ain't heard nothing," he said.

"Speak to me, Thalric." Kymene approached him. She caught Che's wrist as she went, pulling the Beetle girl after her. "This one says you've turned traitor to your own now. I don't believe it."

"It's a philosophical question," Thalric replied with a bleak smile. "I still believe that I am a good imperial officer. It's only that the Empire doesn't seem to be what it should be."

Her lip curled. "And so what?"

There was a sudden banging at the front door of the Exchange, and abruptly Hokiak's men were on their feet, reaching for crossbows or drawing swords. Chyses' knife flashed in the lamplight. A moment later Gryllis appeared in the doorway.

"Empire or her lot?" Hokiak demanded.

"Empire!" Gryllis proclaimed. "Two whole squads of them." He ducked back out front as the splintering sound from the shop front told of the door being smashed in. The old Scorpion leant forward stubbornly on his cane.

"Why Lieutenant Parser, my old friend!" they heard Gryllis cry, all fake cheer. "You know you only had to knock—"

"Out of the way, Gryllis," a Wasp voice snapped.

"But listen, whatever you want—"

"We're here to search your place, old man. Nothing personal. Everyone gets turned over tonight. Everyone but everyone. You just stay quiet and you can walk away."

"What did you do?" Kymene demanded in an urgent whisper.

"I killed Colonel Latvoc," Thalric replied. "I killed General Reiner and I gave you your revolution. Enjoy."

Abruptly there were Wasps in the room, pushing into it with their swords drawn, hands outstretched. Kymene flicked up her cowl.

Thalric counted a score of Wasps: not a targeted raid, just a fiercely punitive one. Because of him, bands like this would be kicking in doors all over the city. "Lieutenant, hold!" he snapped out. With the automatic reflex of a soldier hearing orders the officer held up his hand to stay his men.

"Who are you?" The lieutenant was a young man, but no fool. "If you're a soldier, you're out of uniform."

"What are your orders, Lieutenant?" Thalric asked him. "What's the news from the palace?"

"We're rounding up every known rebel we can catch," the officer replied instinctively, and then, "And we're not answering questions from a stranger!" Thalric sensed the frayed nerves there, meaning the news had already got around the garrison, for all the efforts the senior officers might have made to keep it quiet.

Thalric glanced at Che, then at Kymene. *Oh, they picked the right place, for all that they don't know it. A prime Lowlander spy and the leader of the resistance. The Rekef would have a field day.* He looked over at Hokiak and saw the same thoughts written on the old man's lined features.

And I could sink the resistance right here, and save Myna for the Empire, Thalric reflected. There were swords drawn on both sides, the numbers weighted in favour of the Wasps, but then he heard the sound of even more soldiers entering the shop front.

He nodded to Hokiak.

"Che," Thalric signalled briefly. Abruptly there were Hokiak's men on either side of him.

"Thalric?" Che asked, even as the lieutenant ordered, "Arrest the lot of them. Search the back, too."

"I'm the one you want," Thalric announced calmly.

"Oh, and why's that?" the lieutenant asked.

"Because I killed the governor."

They froze, every one of them. The news obviously had trickled down to the very rank and file of the garrison. Every man among them was staring at him, and the mixture of expressions amused him, in a brief moment of clarity. They were making sure they looked as though they hated him for what he had done, but clearly Latvoc had not been loved.

"Say that again," their officer said slowly.

"Lieutenant," Hokiak began softly, "you know me. You know me well. I do good business for the Empire, right? You don't want to come and smash my place up, on account of I got stuff here that it ain't . . . politic to find, see?"

The lieutenant looked from him to Thalric, and back.

"I kept this fellow for you, right? I was going to send news to your lot. He's yours, so take him. Just let me and my people here keep on doing business."

From his thoughtful look, Lieutenant Parser was obviously no stranger to Hokiak's services, and a few of his men had shown a similar interest in the old man's words.

"Nothing else to declare, is there?" he asked, staring at Thalric again.

"Is the governor's murder not enough for you?" Thalric asked.

"You're remarkably flippant for a man about to die."

Thalric sensed Che tense beside him. *Not for me, stupid girl, and certainly not here.* "You won't kill me, Lieutenant. You're a clever man. There's a man named Maxin back in Capitas who'll be very interested to hear that I killed General Reiner and his pet flea."

The lieutenant was a good officer and he had a sense of his own political future, even here and now. "Bring him," he ordered brusquely.

"Thalric—" Che protested.

"Quiet." He looked down at her, putting a hand to her cheek. *Stupid, clumsy Beetle girl, you should be dead a dozen times over.* And yet here she was, and he knew, as he had known for a long time, that he liked her. *Her Moth-scholar is indeed a lucky man.* Before she could react, he ducked and kissed her briefly, watched her eyes widen in shock, though she did not pull away. Then the soldiers had him.

"You keep yourself quiet down here," the lieutenant was instructing Hokiak. "If they tell me to come back and torch this firepit, I will do."

"Of course," the Scorpion said humbly. "Me and my people will keep our heads down, don't you worry."

The lieutenant's eyes passed over the others gathered there with a hint of suspicion. "They're all yours? You can vouch for them?" the officer asked.

The sweep of Hokiak's broken-clawed hand took in Che, took in Kymene and her escort, cloaked them with the anonymity of his own surly bodyguards. "Like my own flesh and blood, Lieutenant." This was his token gesture of taking sides, as much as he ever would.

EIGHTEEN

"**I** have considered your proposal, General," the Emperor Alvdan the Second declared. The last of his advisors, slow old Gjegevey, was just shambling out of the room, leaving the Emperor still slouching on his central throne.

"Your Imperial Majesty," said Maxin neutrally. The Emperor's face gave nothing away, he did not even look directly at the Rekef General, but Maxin's mind was busy straining the possibilities. The "proposal" now referred to could mean only one thing: the future of the Rekef.

"I have sent for General Brugan. I understand he is still in the capital."

He was, and that had been cause for some disquiet as far as Maxin was concerned. Brugan was every bit the dutiful soldier: his achievements in the East-Empire had been numerous but untrumpeted, accomplished efficiently and without fanfare. He had put down rebellions and infiltrated cities, but he had been long away from Capitas and word of his triumphs had not spread far. Now he was here, though, and Maxin had been watching him closely even as he went about mundane and expected business. Maxin was never the trusting sort.

"I have also sent word to General Reiner," Alvdan said. Now he was watching Maxin keenly, though Maxin's expression was merely one of polite interest.

"Your Imperial Majesty?"

"I have asked him if he would have any objection to your reorganization," continued Alvdan mildly. "He has sent me no reply."

"I am not surprised, your Majesty." *Because he's dead, dead, dead.* Maxin trusted himself to be ahead of the Emperor in any news. After all, was he not the man supposed to keep the crown informed? Oh yes, Reiner was dead, and there was at least a chance Alvdan had not yet discovered it for himself. The unexpected executioner was in the hands of Maxin's agents and on his way to Capitas even now. *I should thank him, really. I should give him a medal.* Instead the culprit would be executed in some very public way, this blessed assassin, as befits the murderer of an imperial general. One could not allow such a precedent to be set.

"May I enquire," he said carefully, "what decision you have come to?"

Alvdan gave him a wintry smile. "You have omitted an honorific, I think, General."

"Your Imperial Majesty."

"Do not take me for a fool. I know your schemes only too well. I have an Empire full of plotters, and every man after his own profit. Well, I can use that, nevertheless. I am still Emperor, and though my subjects twist and turn, all that they achieve is advancement for the Empire, would you not say?"

"Of course, your Majesty." Maxin watched him closely. The Emperor seemed in a flippant mood, which seldom boded well.

"You have done your best to cripple General Reiner." Alvdan studied him, abruptly stern. His posture on the throne was suddenly that of a severe Emperor addressing a mere subject. "His silence we find ominous, but time shall tell. You have continued to keep General Brugan far from here, where we should not notice him. But know that his acts have been noted. He has been a good and loyal subject, and all the more so for his distance."

Maxin found his palms opening reflexively, where a man of any other kinden might have clenched his fists. Alvdan currently regarded him with so little love that it seemed any moment he must call for his guards to take the general away.

Then the Emperor smiled, and the moment of suspense broke. "The Empire rewards service ably performed. The Emperor, in particular, rewards service well done. Do not think that I have forgotten who removed all those troublesome siblings . . . Ah, General Brugan."

Maxin turned to see the younger general walk in and kneel before the throne.

"Rise, General. You have enjoyed your stay in Capitas, we hope."

"I have, your Imperial Majesty."

"We have a proclamation for your ears, General, concerning the Rekef and its structure."

Brugan did not even look at Maxin, but fixed his eyes at a space immediately before the Emperor.

"We have decided that our father erred," said Alvdan, clearly savouring the words even as he spoke them. "Three men to wrestle for the future of the Rekef? No, for once, and in this one matter, he erred. There must be *one* man only leading the Rekef against our enemies."

Brugan still made no reaction, only waited.

"We are therefore appointing our General Maxin here as lord of all the Rekef. Since we cannot very well demote yourself and General Reiner, he shall henceforth be entitled Supreme General, second in rank only to the crown itself. I trust you have no objection to our will."

Maxin was watching the other man with all the practice of a spymaster. There was no defiance in him, no anger, but there was simply . . . *nothing*. General Brugan did not kick against the imperial edict, he showed no resentment whatsoever. That was the unnatural part of it. Maxin knew that Brugan was always the dutiful soldier, but to be put down thus, passed over, and show absolutely *no* emotion . . . there was something more going on here, that Maxin was not aware of. For a man in his position it was an acutely uncomfortable realization.

"I shall do in all things as your Majesty directs," replied Brugan simply, and he then looked sidelong, and very briefly, at General Maxin, but still without any expression that could be read.

"You are dismissed now, General. We anticipate that, after the celebrations for the anniversary of our coronation, you shall be returning to the East Empire."

"Of course, your Imperial Majesty." Brugan bowed again and then departed smartly.

"You appreciate why we are doing this, we are sure," Alvdan informed Maxin. "A sundering of the Rekef weakens us all. I have given you command because, now that you've forced matters to a head, who else is there?"

Maxin noticed the lapse into informal speech and relaxed a little. "Your Imperial Majesty," he acknowledged, to be safe.

"I warn you, though," Alvdan said, "I want it all reined in. You've let it go too far in your seeking this. Szar is in open revolt now, and now I understand that the Mynans are bucking as well. I want troops into Myna, enough to crush the entire city. That is, if they're still so interested in fighting after they see what we leave of Szar. Crush them, Maxin, swiftly and thoroughly. We must concentrate all our forces on the Lowlands campaign. I feel a need to expand the imperial borders."

"Yes, your Majesty."

Alvdan's eyes narrowed. "And fetch me the Mosquito. All his wretched protests can go hang. I want to know *when*."

"I have told him that the ritual shall be performed *after* his coronation festivities," explained Uctebri dismissively. "He wanted something public, and so I explained why that would not be appropriate."

"And why is that?" Seda asked him.

From beneath the cowl, Uctebri smiled slyly. "Well, now, the reason that I gave his Imperial Majesty was that his people would perhaps not readily accept a ruler seen to be dabbling in such arts as I can peddle. However, the reason that I now give you is that our own plans shall come to fruition quite publicly enough, and somewhat sooner."

"During the anniversary celebration itself."

"Precisely." The Mosquito steepled his bony fingers. "Timing will be essential, and I have a great deal left to accomplish if we are to succeed. Who would have thought that in just three short generations the Empire would have built up a tangle of politics quite so complex? Would you not agree, General?"

The third conspirator present in Seda's chambers eyed the old man with patient loathing. General Brugan despised Uctebri as a slave and as a charlatan, and made no secret of that. He understood nothing of the arcane schemes that the Mosquito spoke of, only that it was treason. It was a treason he had cast his lot with, however, for Seda had wooed him, and he knew that it would be through Uctebri's machinations that she triumphed over her brother. That Brugan would do his best to have this pallid creature killed thereafter was quite obvious. That Uctebri was blithely unconcerned by the threat was just as plain.

"General," Seda addressed him. "I trust you are not having second thoughts." She already knew that he was not. Between Uctebri and old Gjegevey, she knew a great deal these days, both natural and otherwise. She wanted to give Brugan the chance to make his own decision, though. That way he would be less likely to change his mind later.

"I have been told I'm passed over for Maxin," Brugan said flatly. "I know General Reiner's dead, and it seems to me that I won't live long when Maxin commands the Rekef." He shrugged, the bluff, honest soldier with the secret schemer plotting invisibly beneath. "I'm best served by making sure you succeed, and I have my people in place. They will be ready to move, assuming you can achieve all you boast of." This last remark was directed at Uctebri, who grinned at him with needle-sharp teeth.

"The Emperor wishes a spectacle for the anniversary of his coronation," he said. "I can promise a show the like of which no one in the Empire has ever seen."

In Uctebri's mind, the pattern was coming together. He was a man lying in wait, seeing fate's pieces pass back and forth, lunging suddenly to change a certain course, plant a thought, poison a mind. Still, as he had said, there was a great deal to do. He presented only certainty to Seda and her allies, but there were still gaps in his logic.

But here came a new part of the pattern, drifting into place with such neatness that he should have been suspicious. Still, he seized it, as a means to his end.

So little time now until the end of an Empire and the beginning of something new: the rise of the Mosquito-kinden, the first bloody ember of their new dawn.

It was just a matter of getting all the guests to the party.

⟨⟩ ⟨⟩ ⟨⟩

Thalric's transit had been swift. He had been out of Myna within two bells, leaving the racked city behind him. The automotive they had put him in was now making all speed to deliver the traitor into the Emperor's own hands. For certain crimes, provincial justice was not enough. They therefore travelled all day, and some nights.

How often have I travelled like this, and also had the chance to admire the scenery?

It was a strange thought, but Thalric had been given a lot of thinking time recently, and he was making full use of it. It seemed to him that he had spent all the years of his life chasing about the Empire, or to points beyond, and always with a timetable weighing on his back. His service to the Empire had involved a constant race from one town to another. When he had been alone, he had been running ahead of the tide of imperial expansion, preparing the way so that its wheels might roll smoothly over the foreigners. When he had been in company, he had been constantly hauling on the leashes of his underlings, packing them off to where they were supposed to be as if they were reluctant children.

But now he could sit back and relax. The road to Capitas provided a reasonable vantage point to watch the Empire go by, and it was only a shame that there were bars between him and the view. A further irony, for he had ridden with these prison automotives several times before—boxy, ugly, furnace-powered vehicles that jolted and juddered their way across the imperial roads on solid wheels—but he had never before been a passenger in the back.

Tonight they had stopped at a waypoint, one of the hundreds of little imperial outposts that existed solely as a place to rest for messengers and other individuals travelling on the Emperor's business. From overheard conversations, old habits dying hard, Thalric knew that they were now only a day away from Capitas, since they had made swift time on the imperial roads, and those leading to Capitas were always kept in the best repair.

In truth all the days since Myna had been days he was not entitled to. He should have been executed out of hand, but he realized that his crime was so immense, so unthinkably bold, that someone more than a mere major—the highest-ranking officer left in Myna—would now have to deal with him.

And the chequered course of his career had given him insight into the might of Rekef politics, and General Maxin especially. Maxin would undoubtedly want to see the man who had removed General Reiner from the equation. There would be no handshakes or medals, however, and Thalric was under no illusions about that. He had done Maxin a greater service than perhaps any of the man's actual underlings, but it was still not something that could be rewarded. Maxin would conveniently be able to wash his hands of the affair, luxuriate in the death of his enemy while condemning the executioner. Thalric guessed that this unexpected good fortune would put the man into a sufficiently indulgent mood to at least talk to him. Irony the third: *If I had killed Reiner on Maxin's orders, he would be forced to have me killed before I got back, in case I spoke aloud.* There was absolutely no link between them though: no incrimination that Thalric could substantiate. Reiner's death was a gift dropped unexpectedly in Maxin's lap, and therefore so much the more to be relished.

I am at least still alive, so I have that much. And in the Rekef they taught you to be resourceful.

He became aware that a soldier was peering in at him through one of the barred windows.

Thalric stared right back. "What?" he demanded. His escort had remained oddly coy with him, staying clear and never speaking. Thalric guessed that this one man left on guard had seized his moment to satisfy his curiosity unobserved.

"They say you killed a general," the man said, so quietly that Thalric had to hunch forward to hear him. That took him to the end of the chain that led from the locked shackles on his neck and wrists to the interior wall of the wagon.

"And a colonel too," Thalric replied calmly, seeing the man flinch at the . . . at the what? The sacrilege of it? Had the imperial hierarchy become a form of sacred mysticism now, like the mad obsessions of the Moth-kinden?

What is a religion, after all, but blind faith in something entirely unproven? Yes, that theory seemed to fit.

The soldier was still staring at him as though he had two heads, so Thalric clarified: "A Rekef general and a Rekef colonel, to be precise. What of it?"

"Why?" the man asked him, horror struck.

"Well, I'm a Rekef major myself. Perhaps I wanted a quick promotion," Thalric drawled. The utter shock on the wretched man's face was quite enjoyable. "Come now, soldier, have you never wanted to kill your sergeant?"

The sudden guilty flicker only betrayed what Thalric already knew, because of course every soldier in the Empire had thought about it, and no doubt others had put it into practice, but it was never *admitted*. The Empire had reserved a traitor's death for any philosopher who pointed out that they were all still barbarians at heart, that the whole machinery of military hierarchy was not—as with the Ant-kinden—to complement their essential nature, but to restrain it.

"It's just the same," Thalric told the man. "It's just a matter of scale."

The soldier was already backing away, shaking his head, as though insane treason was a disease he might catch.

Thalric settled back. For a man with nothing but his continued existence to recommend him he felt curiously at ease, as though some old debt had at last been paid off, for all that it had taken up all the credit he had in the world.

NINETEEN

Stenwold was unsure whether to be impressed by Collegium's response or to laugh. Certainly it had all the hallmarks of people desperately doing the right thing without any real expertise, or even a clear idea regarding it. As the *Buoyant Maiden* drifted into the skies over the city, there arrived a succession of visitors to the airship: first a handful of Fly-kinden wheeling past it, ignoring Stenwold as he waved at them, and darting away to get out of range of any notional attack. But the customary curiosity of their race kept them in the air to watch, rather than returning to the ground to report, and so the next wave of airborne defence turned up spoiling for a fight. This was a dozen armoured Beetle-kinden with mechanical wings buzzing away in a blur, moving through the air with a surprising speed and grace. Stenwold recognized the design: namely Joyless Greatly's one-man flying machines that had done such sterling service in the Vekken siege. At least one of them had survived the conflict, and Collegium artificers had since been industriously copying the design and improving on it.

The leader of the heavy airborne, as he proclaimed his troops to be, landed on the *Maiden*'s deck with a sword in one hand and a cut-down repeating crossbow in the other. He looked as ferocious a figure as any Beetle-kinden had ever cut, and instantly demanded to know who they were. Jons Allanbridge, who found this reaction from his native city somewhat galling, proceeded to get straight into a row with the man and the exchange became sufficiently heated for the passengers packed below to come up to see what was going on. Because they were who they were, and in a foreign land, they came up fully armed and expecting trouble. There was very nearly a diplomatic incident as a dozen of Collegium's new heavy airborne faced off against a score and a half of Dragonfly-kinden warriors with every apparent intention of hacking fearlessly through them. It was then that Stenwold was able to intervene and, thankfully, at least one of Collegium's defenders now recognized who he was.

Of course, in all the confusion, nobody had informed the city what was going on, and so Stenwold had just managed to make peace with the airborne when a long shape slid alongside the *Maiden*, and put it entirely into shadow. It was another airship, and not much smaller than the colossal *Sky Without*, but this one was brand new, coming straight from the Collegium foundries. Stenwold later discovered that the design of it had been kicking about Helleron for ten years, and had been repeatedly turned down on the basis that nobody in their right mind would have need for such a thing. It had finally been brought to Collegium by a Helleren exile, whereupon somebody had realized just what they were looking at.

They called it the *Triumph of Aeronautics*, and they called this type of vessel a Dreadnought. The craft's individual name spoke truest, though, for the city's chemists had needed to concoct an entirely new kind of lighter-than-air gas just to keep the weighty thing in the sky. It was an armoured dirigible, a great wood-reinforced balloon beneath which lay a long, narrow gondola plated with steel. From his privileged vantage point on the wrong side of it, Stenwold could see two dozen open hatches, with a leadshotter behind each, and he guessed there were other hatches in the underside to bombard any enemy on the ground. Meanwhile the rail bristled with mounted repeating crossbows and nailbows. It was certainly a magnificent piece of engineering, and it sent a shiver through him to think that it was something his people had made.

By that time, the officer of the airborne had explained what was going on to the captain of the *Triumph*, and someone had the presence of mind to send a Fly-kinden messenger down to the city to stop them sending anything *else* up. It was in such august company that the *Buoyant Maiden* touched down.

The city walls were lined with engines, Stenwold observed, and everywhere they went, every step of the way from the airfield to the Amphiophos, there was armed militia evident in the streets. The same kind of people who had been sent off to help the Sarnesh were now distributed all over Collegium, and most especially on the walls.

She met him before he was three streets into the city: Arianna, rushing out of the crowd so swiftly that several of the Dragonflies drew their swords on her. Stenwold flung his arms about her, noticing her stricken expression.

"I didn't know," she got out. "The news has been so bad, I didn't know if I would ever see you again."

As he looked at her face, Inaspe Raimm's prophecy came back to him, and he said, "There are no certainties." There were a lot of people waiting for him to move on, but he did not care. "I've missed you. I have missed you, but I'm glad you stayed here, safe."

"War Master, the Assembly—" interrupted the commander of the heavy airborne. Stenwold shrugged him off.

"Safe?" Arianna asked him, and laughed, a wretched and unwilling sound. "I'd ask you where you'd been, if I didn't already know. Sten, there's a Wasp army marching east of here. It's no more than three days away."

Passing into that familiar great chamber, he was at least relieved of one fear: there were not hundreds of Assemblers waiting there to pick his own news apart. That would come later, no doubt. In his mind, the Assembly of Collegium seemed a worse prospect even than the approaching Wasps. Instead there were only two people there, in that great amphitheatre: a fat Beetle man and a Spider-kinden Aristos.

"Hello, Stenwold," said the Beetle, with a faint smile. His name Stenwold now recalled as Jodry Drillen, and instead Stenwold had expected to see the Assembly's Speaker, old Lineo Thadspar. After a moment, Stenwold decided that question could wait.

"Master Drillen," Stenwold said, and then, to the man next to him, "Lord-Martial Teornis."

The Spider nodded. He was wearing sombre colours, his features drawn, as if that indefinable varnish of Spider grace and charm had rubbed off in places

"May I introduce Paolesce Liam." Stenwold gestured at his companion. The bulk of the Dragonfly-kinden were, he hoped, being billeted even then, but he had brought their leader along with him. Paolesce was a tall, slender man whose age was hard to tell at a glance, but whom Stenwold had pinned, after speaking with him, as being around the Beetle's own years. He wore his gleaming armour still, standing with feet apart, gazing about with apparent equanimity at a city that must seem overwhelmingly strange to him.

"Master Liam is . . . ?" probed Jodry Drillen.

"Master Paolesce," Stenwold corrected, "is here as . . . as a gesture of solidarity. He has brought thirty soldiers. The Commonweal will, I hope, be raising a force to trouble the Wasps on their own border, but—"

"But you thought we had more time," Drillen finished for him. "Didn't we all."

"How . . . ?" Stenwold looked from him to Teornis. "The Wasps have come by ship?"

"They came by land," the Spider said. "They simply didn't stop for anything. Egel and Merro rolled over, as we knew they would. Kes declared itself uninterested in war, and most of the surviving population of Felyal is here, within Collegium's walls, or north with your Prince of the Wastes."

"And," Stenwold frowned at the Lord-Martial, "what about your own people? What about the Spiderlands?"

Teornis gave a smile, but it was painful. "Why, when their army was sufficiently far west, we sallied forth and attacked the garrison force they had left behind. We had a battle and, in short, we lost. We lost in a sufficiently flamboyant manner that enough of our army got back to Seldis to man the walls. Some of the mercenaries we hired fought a bloody enough rearguard that I managed to save my own hide. Seldis is currently under siege. We're having *our* turn on the rack right now."

"The Sarnesh are probably fighting even as we speak," Drillen said softly. "If they fall, then the first we'll know is another Wasp army marching south on us. We are now where the metal meets, Master Maker. The war, the real war, has finally come to us."

"And how far is this south coast army from Collegium?" Stenwold asked hollowly. "Three days? Is that accurate?"

Teornis' smile was sad and genuine. "At the pace they are capable of, that may even become two. War Master, you have arrived just in time for the war."

Stenwold stared down at his hands. It was something he had been doing a lot recently. He had always considered himself a practical man, a trained artificer who belonged to a kinden that made and built things, whether those things were machines or trade agreements. But he was beyond his range of ability now. He could not repair this crisis, or even patch it. Events had overtaken him, as he now sat at the bedside of a dying man, and waited.

The man was Lineo Thadspar, still nominally Speaker for the Assembly of Collegium. The old man had weathered the Vekken siege but, with that conflict over, he had been fast fading. He had taken to his bed a few days before, barely a few hours after the scouts' reports had come in.

You knew, Stenwold surmised, *and you couldn't face it.*

Lineo was asleep and, without the energy that had burnt in him until very recently, he looked as old as his years at last. Stenwold did not have the heart to wake him. What would be the point, save to put more weight on a life already burdened and failing?

Out of respect, the Assembly had not chosen a new Speaker yet. They would not, in any event, choose Stenwold. His much-loathed title of War Master had instead been confirmed once again.

He smiled in relief at that thought. He did not want to head up the Assembly, for the very notion of tying his future to that room full of squabbling merchants and academics made him shudder. Yet they were frightened he would demand it. A War Master, however, was something that could be made and unmade at will. At the end of this business, if the Assembly was still in any position to do it, they would cast him off. He could not say that he minded very much.

Just now his responsibility felt very heavy, and it seemed he had no shoulders to share it with.

He stood up just as Arianna came in. One look at her face told him the news. "They're here, then?"

"Within sight of the walls. People want you to come and look. And yes, I know it's not as though that will make any difference."

"Perhaps they think that I'll see some vital flaw in their strategy just from how they pitch their tents," Stenwold said. "And I suppose if I was an Ant-kinden tactician, that's just what I'd do."

She had asked him, only the night before, if he felt so very bound to stay here. She had known the answer, but she had asked him. It was not too late even now, her look said, for them to go.

Go where? Where does the Empire stop, if not here?

As he followed her out of Thadspar's house, the sun shone very bright, endowing the white stone of the houses of the wealthy with a special radiance.

There were a lot of people just standing about in the streets, as though they had all received a summons from some city magnate who had failed to appear. When they saw Stenwold, he realized that he had apparently become that magnate. They pointed at him and told each other that, now War Master Stenwold Maker was here, everything would be all right. He assumed that was what they were saying, anyway. Possibly they were telling each other that he was the wrong man for the job, and would doom them all. Possibly they were just commenting on the Spider girl who was young enough to be his daughter. On balance he would have preferred that.

Up on the walls he found Teornis, who had yet to return to his own people despite sporadic reports received regarding the ongoing siege of Seldis. The Spider-kinden noble looked every bit as though the city at his back was devoted to his service, and the soldiers appearing along the east coast road were a parade in his honour. Stenwold envied him his poise.

"We've come to the sharp end, then," Teornis said, quietly and for Stenwold's ears only. On his other side were some members of the Assembly who fancied themselves as strategists, as well as Paolesce Liam, commander of the small Commonweal detachment.

The Wasp army was not looking hurried. Detachments of airborne were lazily spiralling down and taking up position, and Stenwold could make out what must be automotives and beasts of burden following them up. The first few tents were being set, but if there was any great tactical lesson to be learnt from these activities it was lost on him.

"Reports suggest their numbers to be in the region of eighteen thousand, with slaves as extra," Teornis said. "They came out of Felyal a little grazed, but nothing serious."

"You should leave now," Stenwold advised him. "You have your own battle to fight."

"It's all the same fight in the end," Teornis replied. "Moreover, the Kessen navy has decided that the current political situation makes all Spiderland ships fair game for plunder. I don't honestly see that I'll be getting away from here in the near future."

"War Master," began one of the Assemblers, who taught engineering at the College, "they've come too close to establish their camp I think. If we let fly with light loads, we could bombard them. Just give the word."

Stenwold looked at the industrious Wasp soldiers, just starting to pitch their camp.

"Let them get all their tents set up first," he suggested. "Then, if we decide to do it, we can put them to the most trouble possible. No point in making their lives easy."

"Someone's coming to talk," Arianna observed, and Stenwold saw a party of soldiers heading toward the Collegium gate.

"I can't imagine that we have much to say to one another," Teornis drawled, his casual pose seeming for a moment too obviously studied.

Stenwold shrugged. "We're Beetle-kinden, so we always talk first—and plainly. We need to know exactly where we stand."

The leader of the Wasps introduced himself as General Tynan. He was a broad-shouldered man who must have matched Stenwold year for year, although those years had left him thinner and with even less hair. He and his escort were received in one of the gardens abutting the Amphiophos, an open space that was complete with mechanical fountain, tiered pools and a dozen antique statues representing virtues. By the fashion of that time, the said virtues were all young women wearing too few clothes, which inevitably inspired thoughts that were less than virtuous. The tastes of the time had clearly also favoured undergrowth, for the garden was thick with ferns and moss and creeping skeins of ivy. General Tynan took his time in examining his surroundings whilst his personal guards and officers, some two dozen in all, stood impassively nearby.

"You're not Lineo Thadspar, I take it."

"He is indisposed. My name is Stenwold Maker."

"Acceptable." Tynan nodded briskly. "My intelligence suggested that you would be managing the defence. You performed well against the Vekken, I am informed."

Stenwold shrugged, indicating with a gesture that the city was still here, and the Vekken were not.

Tynan smiled. "We are not the Vekken, of course."

"I had not thought for a moment that you were, General."

"We have a sound record of defeating the Ant-kinden whenever we meet them," Tynan added. "Our forces have routinely proved themselves superior."

"We are not the Ant-kinden either," Stenwold pointed out. Somewhere hidden in the foliage, a clock began to sound the hour with intricate chimes.

Tynan's smile returned. "Remarkable," he said, strolling over to the mechanical fountain. "I am impressed by your city, General Maker."

"Really."

"Do not think that I am just some brute with an army. I read. I admire art. Your city here is beautiful, both in its society and its construction. Collegium will be a worthy addition to the Empire." The Wasp turned, his face now hard. "I have my orders, General Maker. Your kin in Helleron, when faced with this decision, became willing partners to our imperial rule. I am now offering you the same choice."

"That we surrender?" Stenwold clarified.

"Even so." Tynan made a small gesture that encompassed Collegium and all of its futures. "This city will not be able to stand against us. You will have hosted sufficient refugees from Tark to know how thorough we can be in bringing a people to its knees. I do not wish to see Collegium thus consumed by bombs and incendiaries. That would be a waste."

"We must decline your gracious offer," Stenwold said heavily, "or what did we fend off the Vekken for?"

Tynan's pitying expression suggested that domination by a provincial Ant warlord was an infinitely different prospect to inclusion in the all-powerful Empire. "General Maker," he said. "I will welcome any embassy from you, and I would advise you to send one soon. You will surrender, in time. Consider how much of this city you will see laid waste before you do."

The imperial bombardment of Collegium had begun that same evening, just an introductory barrage delivered before nightfall. The walls had held firm: even the Vekken had done worse. Collegium artificers had already made their measurements for a nocturnal retaliation, but the Wasps must have had some reports from Vek because they moved their siege engines out of range at the end of the day, rather than leave them at the Beetles' mercy. It would slow their artillery, having to find the ranges afresh each morning, but at least it would preserve them. General Tynan was clearly playing a careful game.

The next day the air war began. Whilst the artillery of both sides thundered loud around the walls, the Wasp airborne commenced attacking the city. Stenwold recalled the words of Parops, about how the Wasps had drawn out the Tarkesh air support before firebombing the city into submission. He hoped here they could put up a sterner aerial defence.

The snapbows helped, of course. Collegium soldiers, half trained and untested, stood ready at the walls and on rooftops across the city, and shot at the Wasps as they dived overhead. Each neighbourhood and district deployed its own little force, though the College itself was the heart of the defence. Totho's weapons, more accurate and far-reaching than crossbows, broke apart the first two Wasp assaults, but the afternoon saw a redoubling of the imperial offensive. The Empire committed two score of orthopters and heliopters to the fray to complement their innumerable soldiers, and the houses of Collegium began to come under direct bombardment. To counter them, Collegium launched its own flying machines, its heavy airborne and Paolesce's Dragonfly-kinden.

The *Triumph of Aeronautics* had positioned itself directly above the College, thus making itself the bastion of the city's air defence. From its vantage point its heavy weapons thundered away at the orthopters and the enemy siege emplacements, whilst scores of snapbowmen and repeating crossbows picked continually at the light airborne. The airship's wood-reinforced canopy shrugged off shot and sting both, and Collegium saw out that first full day of siege without the enemy gaining an inch of Beetle soil.

The next day General Tynan unleashed the full force of his army. He brought in the remaining half of his artillery and flooded the sky with men and machines and 500 Wasp-riders. His heavy infantry marched in under their cover, alongside automated rams and drills. His Mole Cricket-kinden engineers rushed ponderously at the walls, holding great pavises over their heads to ward off the defenders' shot. His Skater-kinden Auxillians attacked along the river banks, penetrating all the way into the heart of Collegium, there spreading terror and confusion, setting fires and killing anyone they could catch.

Stenwold took the command of the eastern wall, which was most heavily under assault. It was not because he desired the glory or did not fear the danger. It was because it meant he did not have to think about anything else while he bellowed commands at the defenders there. He spent the day with a snapbow in his hands, which he never loosed, but he directed the shooting of five thousand Collegium irregulars onto the encroaching enemy. They loosed their snapbows at the infantry, the short bolts penetrating heavy armour without pause; they launched leadshot and explosive bolts at enemy automotives and siege engines; they dropped rocks and grenades on the Mole Crickets.

Toward the end of the day, one of his officers came toward him, pointing and shouting. The *Triumph of Aeronautics* was moving.

That was not the plan, and the *Triumph's* captain had been at the war council. Stenwold watched helplessly as the monstrous airship drifted away from its mooring above the College.

"Hammer and tongs," said the man beside him helplessly. "It's coming down."

The *Triumph of Aeronautics* was on fire, was losing height even as they watched it. Those crew that could fly were bailing out, but most were Beetle-kinden and could not escape. The Captain was amongst them, still guiding the huge dirigible on its final flight.

He took it beyond the city walls, out over the besieging army, and here he brought it low and then fired its powder magazine.

The explosion almost hurled Stenwold off the wall. A great host of Tynan's army had also been caught by it, scythed down like wheat, their siege engines broken to matchwood and their automotives sundered, the entire heart of the Wasp advance consumed in one terrible moment.

In the concussive quiet after that explosion, the Wasps ended their assault for the day and returned to their camp.

TWENTY

"**D**on't you worry that I might kill you?" Tisamon asked. He stretched himself, flexed the metal claw of his gauntlet. The sand beneath his feet was newly spread. Across from him, Ult looked over a rack of weapons, finally choosing a pair of Commonwealer punch swords, short blades that jutted from circular guards protecting his knuckles.

"If you were a prisoner and I were your jailer, old Mantis, then I'd not be doing this without a few guards at hand, but we both know that ain't so." Ult turned to him. This early, they had the little practice circle to themselves, for it was two hours before even the servants would wake. Beyond the guttering light of the torches Ult had distributed about this underground cell, it would be dark.

"I might try to escape," Tisamon said, without conviction.

"I might surprise you," replied Ult. "If you wanted out, though, probably you'd manage it. But you don't." He stretched. Bare chested, his hide was a lace of scars, some charting wounds which looked as though they should have killed him. His stance admitted nothing of his true age.

"Do you think I want to be a performer in your circus?" Tisamon growled.

They had already talked about the way that most fighters, those who survived at least, came to love the sport and the approbation of the crowd. It could turn a criminal, a deserter or even a slave into a brief hero of the Empire.

Ult advanced on him, carefully but not hesitantly. "You want to kill the Emperor," he said bluntly. In the beat of surprise following his words he lunged at Tisamon, getting in close, jabbing with both swords, then trying to bind aside the Mantis' claw with one weapon. Tisamon gave ground, his blade cutting his opponent's attacks out of the air as they came for him, then bringing Ult up short with a feint that gave him space to get sufficiently clear, out of the reach of the other man's short blades.

"And you yourself have no problem with that?" Tisamon demanded. "A good imperial citizen?"

"Only thing I'm good at is what I do," Ult said. "I don't get myself involved in politics. You wouldn't be the first who saw this business as a way to force an audience with an Emperor. It's already been tried."

"Not by me, not yet." Tisamon started forward, whipping out his claw at the Wasp, forcing him back. Ult parried calmly, hands just a blur, giving only as much ground as he needed to keep the blade away from him. He was better than Tisamon had thought, and with the advantage that the old Wasp had seen Tisamon fight a dozen times and measured his style.

"I got no problem with putting you in that arena if I could, whoever you reckon you're there to kill." Ult was breathing slightly fast as they disengaged. "I reckon if the man's fool enough to let a pit fighter get near to him, maybe it's time for someone new."

"That's treason, surely."

"So what would they do with me? Stick me in the ground with a bunch of animals and slaves?" Ult changed his stance, blades out but held back, inviting attack. "You ain't going to get him, 'cos it ain't that easy. You think you're good enough, but I reckon nobody's that good."

Abruptly, Tisamon stepped out of his own stance, claw lowered. "And I'd prove you wrong if you'd only give me the chance. Is that the other way the Emperor protects himself? By not letting the best of us fight in front of him?"

The old Wasp shook his head. "Most of those who ever had a go were Wasps. Politics, right? You foreigners don't get involved in that so much."

"Your Empire's mad."

"It ain't my Empire." Ult replaced the Dragonfly blades on the rack. "Fine, so you're very good. Maybe I've not had anyone better down here. Doesn't mean you're good enough to kill the Emperor. They'll just end up seeing another foreigner put down. Why not? It's what they go see the fights for."

Tisamon regarded him doubtfully, his clawed glove now gone from his hand. "You are an unusual Wasp."

"Not so much." Ult shrugged. "We ain't all like what you've been dealing with—Rekef spies or army officers. You find after a while that it's what you do, not what you are, that matters. When I did my time in the army, I had more in common with the rank and file of the other side than I did with the officers above me. Now I keep fighters for the pit, and I got more in common with them—and with you—than I have with them people who put me here. That's why you ain't going to kill me."

"I could," Tisamon said firmly, but his voice sounded hollow to his own ears, as though he was trying to convince himself. "It would not be easy, perhaps, but I could."

"Sure you could," Ult told him, seeming unconcerned. "But I *know* people like you."

"Put me in front of the Emperor," Tisamon said quickly. It was pleading, he knew, begging. He forced the next words out before his pride could intervene. "I must have come here for a purpose."

"World's short on purpose, to my mind," said Ult, regarding the Mantis with sympathy. "I only get told what the Emperor wants to see. He doesn't want to see any unbeatable Lowlander killing dozens of his men or hacking the legs off beasts. The anniversary fight is for him, for his pleasure, so if he don't like it, it's the end of me, far more than if one of the slaves takes a leap at him. What am I supposed to do, anyway—get you to fight yourself?"

Laetrimae, thought Tisamon. Since sending him here, that shadowy and tortured woman had not reappeared to him. Could she have abandoned him? It seemed entirely possible, for perhaps she had simply sought to punish him for his pride. *Laetrimae, you brought me here, and it must have been for* this *purpose or none at all. If you wish me to accomplish anything, you must give me the means.*

The thought echoed in silence.

I care not how. He felt, abruptly, the oppressive weight of stone above, the walls around them, the fact that he was a prisoner, of his own making. He had put himself in the hands of fate, and it had let him fall.

"Take me back to my cell," he said quietly. Ult nodded, saying nothing. His old face was all understanding.

It was on the way back to his cell that Tisamon saw the key that fate had provided, but instead of triumph it plunged him into the depths of black despair. He was still reeling from the sight as Ult got him to the door of his cell, but there he stopped, unwilling to step inside.

"Ult . . ."

"What is it?" The Wasp trainer's eyes narrowed, aware that something was wrong.

"Your new prisoner . . ."

"Which one? We've all kinds of new faces here."

"The Dragonfly woman," said Tisamon, feeling something hollow in his chest.

"Oh, the mad one," Ult replied dismissively. "What about her?"

"Let me see her," Tisamon requested, and his voice shook.

Ult stared at him suspiciously. "What's got into you?"

"I . . . know her. Let me see her," Tisamon insisted.

"You know her? I don't like this," the Wasp said. "How can you know her? Unless this is some kind of trick?"

"No trick," Tisamon said. "It may not even be coincidence. She may have tracked me here, followed me. She's good at that. I must speak with her." Suddenly he felt himself genuinely a prisoner, being denied this one request. Up until then the bars, the guards, the tasks, none of it had really confined him, because he had no wish to be elsewhere or do otherwise. Now he had a desire that only Ult could grant, and he was a *prisoner*.

Ult let his breath out. "Not in the same cell, and not alone. I'll be there too.

You want to speak with her? You do it so I can hear. I'll put you in the cell next to hers."

"That will suffice," stated Tisamon, as calmly as he could. Something was turning over in his stomach, though. *I am being brought to trial, at last.* It was his own doing, of course. He was the master of his fate, and his hand alone had piloted his life on to these rocks. Even now he could have ignored this grotesque turn of events, but he had already put his hand into the jaws of the machine, waiting for it to bite. Why spare himself now?

She did not look up as they reached the cell beside hers and Ult unlatched the door. The current occupant, a scarred Ant-kinden man, was taken out. He stood tensely, looking down, like a mount being readied for riding. Tisamon stepped into his place, holding to the bars that separated this small piece of captivity from hers.

They had taken her armour from her, and her blade, and instead they had dressed her in slave's clothes just as they had with him. He wondered if she had submitted to it so readily. *Why was she here?*

"Mienn," he began, and then again, "Felise Mienn."

From beyond the bars, in that part of this underground realm that was nominally free, Ult watched them both. It was a long time before the seated figure looked round but, even when she glanced back over her shoulder, she said nothing. She did not need to. Her expression was wounding enough.

"How did they catch you?" Tisamon asked her softly. He forced himself to meet her gaze, and knew that her imprisonment had been by her choice just as it had with him. "Why are you here?" he asked her. "Why did you let them take you?"

The slightest, bitterest smile touched her lips, and she said, "You think I came here after you?"

He had been so ready to now take responsibility for her that it was as though he had suddenly stepped into thin air. He held on to the bars to keep on his feet. "But . . . why? If not that, why?"

The smile was widening, like something tearing. "Why, Tisamon, because I had nowhere else to go. I cannot be with my own people. I have been told as much from the highest authority. I would have gone to the Lowlands, but . . . what have I left to me there?" Her voice shook while uttering the last few words. Abruptly, she was on her feet and facing him. Her beauty, her grace of movement, stunned him as on the first time he saw her.

"I *know* what I am," he said. "You cannot understand . . . I have betrayed so many . . ."

She cut him off silently with just the slightest movement that, for a moment, he could not identify. Then he realized that her thumb-claws had flicked out, ready to fight.

"Do you think I care about your history of self-indulgence?" she asked him quietly. "Do you think anybody cares, apart from you? Do you expect me to understand? Yes, I know—you lay with some Spider-kinden, and then she died. How is that my burden to bear? How am I now the victim of your desires?"

"I know what I am," he heard himself say, again.

"You do not know what you are," she spat at him, approaching the bars that separated them. "You are beautiful, Tisamon, you are beautiful and deadly and bright, but you are cold and barbed like an arrow, that hurts most when it's drawn out." She was so close that he could have touched her, had the bars suddenly lifted away.

Oh I have done this badly, he reflected, and for just one moment the mists of his own pride lifted and he saw how he could have been quite happy, just in staying by her side. *Atryssa would not have understood*, but of course Atryssa, being dead, would have made no comment.

"You wish to fight with me again," he said, and it fitted so neatly into the plan that he looked around for that other woman who had entangled herself inextricably with his life.

She was there, like a writhing dark shadow in the corner of his cell. Laetrimae shuddered and hung there as though suspended on hooks: woman and mantis and savage thorns all intertwined. He glanced quickly at Felise, then at Ult, realizing that neither of them could see her. Laetrimae was present for his nightmares only and, when he looked back at her, she nodded once.

"No!" he exclaimed, suddenly rebellious, startling Ult, who put his hand to the cell's door. *Is this it? The final turn of the knife?*

"You came here to fight me?" he insisted.

Felise was still gazing at him with an expression that spoke in equal parts of love and hate. "I did not come here for you. You know what I came here seeking. However, since you are here, perhaps you can help me find it." Her smile was pitiless. "Perhaps we can find it together."

We are being used like pieces of a machine. He felt her hand touch his as he clung to the bars. He half expected her claw to lash out and to sever a finger or strike at his face, but her hand was warm, and when she covered his own it was a lover's gesture.

If we are pieces of a machine, we are broken pieces. He knew how she must feel. He had come here without hope, and then Ult had given him a purpose by mentioning the Emperor.

Kill the Emperor. Would that make sense of it all?

"Enough," grunted Ult, behind him. "Enough time." A glance at the Wasp showed the old man was not devoid of sympathy, shuffling a little in embarrassment. "You need to go back now, old Mantis. Your time's up."

He felt her sudden presence in his dreams, Tisamon thrashing in brief nightmare before he leapt, kicking and fighting, into wakefulness.

"Felise?" he got out, but he knew, even before he opened his eyes, that it was not Felise Mienn who had come to visit.

She coalesced out of the darkness, there beneath the arena, where a few smoky torches were shared across the whole labyrinth of bars and cages. She was strangely lit by light from elsewhere, so that he could see her more clearly than he wanted to.

"Are you happy now?" he asked softly, wishing he could strike at her, but there was nothing to strike at and, besides, it would be blasphemy.

She stared down on him, nothing but that taut knot of pain and hurt that was left when the mortal woman Laetrimae had been ripped from the world of the living. *Happy, Tisamon? The words came to him unspoken. Have I cause to rejoice?*

"Your plan has its hooks in me," he accused. "I had thought these bars would be the worst of it, but there is always something worse—and you have found it."

She shimmered and blurred for a moment, as the thorny vines continued to crawl their bloody tracks across her skin. *It is not my plan, nor your place to complain.*

"You brought me here," he argued weakly.

I was brought here against my will. You guided yourself here.

He became aware that some of the neighbouring prisoners were now listening, and wondered what they could make of this one-sided conversation. Perhaps such muttered ravings were not uncommon down here.

"So you are just a piece, then? Just another broken piece?" he suggested.

Just another broken piece. There is always something worse, as you say, and I have found it.

For a moment the voice in his mind had sounded like that of a real woman, one alone and in great pain, and he glanced up at her.

"So I must fight poor Felise Mienn, spill her blood to open the way to the Emperor, if I can manage it."

There came a noise that chilled him all the way through and made his skin crawl. It was, he realized then, Laetrimae laughing.

Is that what you think your purpose is? Your pride is not yet sated then?

Tisamon stared at her blankly.

You cannot kill the Emperor, Tisamon. You are not as invincible as you believe. Try it, and you shall fail—as you have always failed in those things most important to you. You must set your sights at more realistic targets.

He was on his feet abruptly, his clawed gauntlet already covering his hand. She shimmered and glowed in the darkness and he wanted to drive his blade into her heart. Except that he knew she was not truly there and had no heart left to her.

The look she gave him, before she vanished away, was sheer contempt.

TWENTY-ONE

The cards were slapped down on the wooden board, and Balkus cursed, not for the first time. Plius chuckled and scooped them up, adding them to his already considerable hoard.

"Must have taken years of practice for you to get that bad, Sarnesh."

Balkus glowered at him. He had been losing steadily throughout the evening, and mostly to this fat Ant with the bluish skin. "Just deal again," he grunted.

Plius laid out the next three centre-cards, and the players retreated to study their hands and decide what to play. The problem with the game of Lords was that the winner tended to keep on winning. It was a Fly-kinden import to Sarn, and Balkus didn't think much of it. Being a poor player, he preferred games with a greater element of luck.

The third player, Parops, had already placed his cards down, not to be drawn further into the bickering of the two men. He had not come across card games before, for, alone of the three, he had lived close to a normal Ant-kinden life, before the Wasps had come to his city. Ants did not play card games with each other, for when they were amongst their own kind it was against their very nature to bluff. Amongst those from other Ant cities, they fought.

Except not here, not now, and it was one of those little pieces of history so easily trampled over and lost after the fact. The great bulk of the army camped about them was Sarnesh, of course, but here on this flank were the exceptions. Here, Balkus had his mob of Collegium volunteers, who were were audible across the entire camp with their drinking and singing and *talking out loud*— unthinkable! Parops had with him his pale Tarkesh, the exiles who had been left with nothing to do but spill imperial blood. Their chances of ever seeing home again were brittle and slim: they were renegades now in all but name, forced out of a conquered home and into mercenary life. Some Ants chose that willingly, even whole detachments of them, but Parops and his men would have preferred a set-tled existence back home had they been allowed.

Then there were the Tseni that had come, at Plius' call, from their faraway city. They kept their distance from the others here in a land normally identified as hos-tile on all their maps. They were Ant-kinden, too, but foreign, wearing scale armour rather than chain mail, carrying oval shields and swords with a back hook jutting from the blade. They might have seemed primitive, except that they came with superior crossbows: heavy pieces equipped with a long-handled winch to recock them at a single turn. *They're just different*, Balkus had decided and, anyway, Tsen was far enough away from the other Ant cities not to have to fight them regularly. They had not followed the Lowlands' curve of history but kept themselves well apart out on the Atoll Coast.

Those three Ant-kinden officers had become, not friends exactly, but enforced allies against the great sameness of the Sarnesh: two outsiders and one insider trying to remain outside. They kept to each other's company and played the games that Plius had learnt from his days spent in the Sarnesh Foreigners' Quarter. Ant-kinden needed peers and, from their positions of unwilling command, they had only each other as equals.

It had been hard enough, going on the journey east. They had not known if they would run into the Wasps before schedule, with nothing more than some panting Fly-kinden to warn them of it. Instead they had covered more distance than anticipated, the Wasp advance running well behind time. This suited the Sarnesh, who were thinking about what would happen if the coming clash became another Battle of the Rails. They wanted proper time to prepare their city's defences.

The artillery, Balkus thought glumly. That was Stenwold's boy's job, of course, and he had done his best not to think of the young Dragonfly and his impossibly suicidal task, but right now it shouldered its way to the forefront of his mind.

The Wasp army was now encamped within sight. The talking and shouting amongst the Collegiate soldiers had become strained and over-loud due to the proximity of the enemy. General Malkan's Sixth and Seventh Armies, the Hive and the Winged Furies in all their mortal strength, were scarcely three miles away. Before evening had darkened the sky, they had been in plain view, and Flies could spy on them with telescopes. Malkan was making no attempt at hiding his numbers, but instead displaying to the utmost his military strength, which exceeded everything the Sarnesh had gathered against him by two or three to one. The morning would see some bloody work.

Balkus stood up. "No more for me," he informed the other two. "Going out to walk amongst the soldiers."

For of course an Ant commander would not need to do that. Parops and Plius did not have to do that. They were always amongst their soldiers, mind touching mind in a net that supported each Ant and bound the whole together. Not Balkus. Balkus had his detachment of deaf-mutes, their minds single and separate, and in his brain instead there was always the murmur of the Sarnesh camp around him, no matter how hard he tried to blot it out.

The march here had allowed him his one moment of amusement when, in the midst of all the great voiceless march of Ant-kinden, a Collegiate woman had struck up a song in a single quavering and slightly off-key warble from the midst of the out-of-step merchant companies. A few others voices had risen to join her, and then half of the rest of them were chorusing the words, or loose approximations, using this simple rhythm to keep their steps sufficiently coordinated to catch up a little with the stoically silent Ants.

Balkus had enjoyed that. He had particularly enjoyed it because of the utter sense of horror that had arisen in his mind, transmitted there from each and all of the Sarnesh, that these shopkeeper soldiers should be going to war making noise, flapping their lips in some pointless and mostly tuneless song. Balkus had *felt* the minds of his kin, and known them to be scandalized and disgusted, and he had enjoyed that a great deal.

Then his soldiers had begun on a new song, the words of which he managed to catch:

Well, my old farm was a good old farm, the neatest you did see-o
With aphids, sheep and fields of wheat, that all were dear to me-o
But came a man in College white, the smartest e'er I saw-o
Who looked me o'er and ordered me to fight in Maker's war-o

And Balkus had considered just exactly what Stenwold Maker himself would think of that, and had chuckled to himself over it for a good hour.

Now he passed amidst the campfires of his men, pausing occasionally to look out at that distant constellation of fires that indicated the enemy. At least there was no fear of a night attack, for the Wasps were not night fighters—but the Mantids and Moths the Ancient League had brought were. Any force of Wasps that tried to use the cover of darkness would find that cloak soon stripped from them. Indeed it would be hard enough to stop the Mantis warriors going out tonight to kill as many Wasps as they could catch unawares, but that was emphatically not the plan.

The plan, the wonderful bloody plan! It was all the King of Sarn's work, he and his cursed tacticians. The Ancillaries, as the Sarnesh had taken to calling their foreign hangers-on, had not even been consulted, merely instructed.

At least they're not sticking us in front. That had always been the fear: that the Sarnesh would see their unreliable foreign friends simply as fodder for Wasp bolt and sting to cover their main advance. *At least we're only being given a fair share of the load.* But Balkus knew who the load was really resting on. *Stenwold's boy.*

Somewhere out there was rabble of bandits and refugees who would be readying themselves, even now, for what must look like certain death. At least it looked like certain death to Balkus, and he wasn't even going.

"We're sure this is going to be a surprise?" Phalmes asked. "If this isn't a surprise, then it's not going to go well for us."

I'm not convinced it's going to go well for us in any event, Salma thought, but Phalmes would know that already. After all, the Mynan was an old campaigner. He knew the odds.

"Every scout that comes this way gets disappeared," said Chefre. The Fly-kinden woman sounded dispassionate and businesslike about it. She and her gang had been criminals in the Spiderlands before this and, as far as she was concerned, it was just the same war with bigger gangs. "Also, we're disappearing scouts all over. I've got everyone who'll be no good for this game out hunting Wasps in the dark." Her smile was neat, surgical. "Of course, most of our lot *can* see in the dark. Or more than they can anyway."

Salma nodded. It was a weakness of the Wasps that the Empire could do little about. There was scarce moonlight tonight, the clouds hanging heavy about the sky. It was dark even for him and his people, so for the Wasps, the only light would be what they could make themselves.

Phalmes, who could not see in the dark either, grunted unhappily. "I don't think we've got men enough." It was not the first time he had said this.

"Probably not," Salma agreed, "but what are you going to do about it?" He saw Phalmes' shoulders rise and fall. "Your fliers are ready?" he then asked Chefre.

"Chief, if we don't give 'em the word soon, they're just going to go off and do it on their own," she told him cheerfully. She had at least four hundred under her command, mostly Fly-kinden but with Moths and others amongst them. They had bows and, where the Aptitude ran, they also had crossbows, snapbows and grenades. Salma would have been happier fighting along with them but he was needed here, at the point of the lance, where his army met the enemy head on.

Every horse, every riding insect that his people had been able to steal, capture, beg, buy or inherit was here, till he had a cavalry force that was nearly half again the number of Chefre's rag-tag airborne. They had trained and trained again, a rabble that the Commonweal would cringe from. They had got on their horses and fallen off and broken legs or ridden the wrong way. The mounts had been just as bad. It was, he knew full well, a stupid idea, and nobody in their right mind would have thought of it.

The Wasps would not have thought of it. In fact it would be something most Wasps would never have seen, or at least not since the Twelve-Year War. It would come as a surprise, and in war surprise could be fatal. He was attacking a full imperial army, tens of thousands of men. His people would be outnumbered fifty to one, but . . .

They would anticipate an attack, but he hoped it was just skirmishers, infiltrators, saboteurs, that the Empire was expecting. He would not be sending such, however. He had decided already that General Malkan's camp could not be opened up by a stealthy few. The scalpel must give way to the hammer.

When Malkan had overwintered his forces after the Battle of the Rails, he had built a palisaded, fortified camp protected against land and air attack, reinforced with artillery. Now his army was on the march, he was forced to rely on a torchlit perimeter and sentries. Where an Ant-kinden army would have dug in every night, if they knew that someone like Salma was out there, the Wasps were not quite so organized. It was the same mistake that General Alder and the Fourth Army had made, when the Felyal Mantids caught them unawares. Salma realized that Malkan would have learnt from that, and would surely have a force on standby, ready to spring to the camp's defence and give the main army time to organize. Cavalry, though . . .

We must punch through whatever they throw at us. We will give the Sarnesh artificers time to finish their work.

Or we will die.

It was at least a plan. He did not feel particularly proud of it, but at this late stage it was the only one he had.

"Morleyr's people must be in place by now," Phalmes decided. His horse shifted, picking up his unease.

"You're right," said Salma. The Mole Cricket, Morleyr, would be leading a feint attack on the camp's far side, but Salma had not been able to spare the giant much in the way of manpower, and it was unlikely to deceive the enemy for long. He looked down at the Sarnesh standing beside him. "It feels like time," he agreed.

The man held a little device in his hand, and Salma knew that there was another such device with the Sarnesh army. In some arcane way wholly lost on him, these instruments told the Sarnesh how much of the night had already passed. They were waiting for the Ant's mark, and he had been watching the little dials and wheels of his device closely, with a tiny lamp cupped in his other hand.

"You have a good sense for these things," the Sarnesh observed, "and it . . . is time, indeed." Salma knew that the man would be simultaneously speaking with his mind to others of his kin accompanying Morleyr, or to the Ant-kinden soldiers and artificers ranked up behind Salma's makeshift cavalry.

"Chefre, over to you," he said. With no access to the Sarnesh and their mindlink, once Chefre's airborne took off they would be cutting themselves loose from Salma's command, operating on their own initiative. "Go," Salma told her, and she went.

The wait was something he had not thought of, before. There was an appalling, stretched-out moment, between Chefre's people taking wing and his hearing their signal, in which he sat in his saddle with nothing to do. Prince Salme Dien, the commander of armies, had finished his shift, and Salma the warrior, the battle leader, had yet to go on duty . . . and he now waited while the horses stamped nervously, feeling his men around him shift and try to even out their breathing.

"Salma." The faintest touch at his shoulder, and he turned in the saddle.

She was there, his luminous lover. He had told her not to come, but she, of all his army, took no orders from him. She hung in the air, her skin streaked with colours, radiant wings beating.

"You should not . . ." he started.

"How could I not?" she responded. "I know what you go now to do."

"Please, this is hard enough . . ."

She reached out, took his head in her hands and darted in to kiss him as he leant down in the saddle, her lips soft against his. He felt her tears on his cheek. They ran down her face and glinted and sparkled over her faintly radiant skin.

"I will never abandon you," she assured him. "*Never.* As you were there for me, I shall always come for you."

He shook his head, with no words to express what he felt. *I love her so much*, he thought. *How can I do this to her?*

The Butterfly-kinden gazed along the line of nervous animals, the horses, the beetles, the crickets and spiders, the miscellaneous grab-bag of rideable monsters that they had drawn from everywhere. She looked at their riders, too: untested, awkward, half-skilled.

"I feel your belief, my prince," she whispered. "It is the strongest thing here."

"Then it will have to suffice," he said, his cheer sounding slightly fragile, his face expression brave for those around him. She laid a hand on his, where it rested on his saddle pommel.

"Share your belief with me," she told him. "Make me believe."

Salma sensed her presence as a halo that reached out from her, imbued with her gentle magics. She had enchanted him before, but she needed no such arts to secure his love now. Still, though, she touched his mind, the essence of him, and she brought her other hand up to the muzzle of his steed.

"Be strong," she whispered. "Share the faith and be strong," and he knew that she was speaking not to him but to the horse.

Speaking to all the horses, to every riding animal standing and stamping or chittering there in the dark, waiting for the signal. It was not like his people's magic, but the Butterfly-kinden had their own arts, born of the sun, born of light and hope.

"Be brave," she murmured. "Be true. You will not lose your way. You will not turn aside from danger." She was shining now, despite the cloak she wore, so that he was terrified that the Wasps might mark her, but still she spoke softly to his horse, and he felt the animal shift its stance beneath him, something strong and iron-like entering it. All down the line, to either side and also behind him, the nervous shuffle of animals quietened, replaced by a watchful patience, an *anticipation*.

And at last she again looked up at him, with her face like a sunrise. "Come back to me," she whispered, and stepped aside from his mount.

He heard the first bang even as she did, the first firepowder charge exploding. Chefre would be coming in from the side, her airborne rabble streaking over the Wasp camp, attacking indiscriminately, dropping ignited grenades, loosing arrows, crossbow bolts and fire arrows, even slingshot. The Wasp soldiers on duty—he could almost see them in his mind's eye—would streak into the air, their stings lighting up the night with a network of gold tracery. Some of Chefre's people would die but the rest would keep moving: a great, chaotic cloud passing back and forth over the vast Wasp camp.

There was no more time for thought, nothing to wait for now. He kicked his heels into his mount's flanks and launched forward, the first man to the battle, forming the point of the wedge. False heroics, he knew, for in this fight it would be those at the rear who would be most at risk.

But they had formed a decent wedge after all, which was something that had never quite come together as he drilled them. He saw the flames of the Wasp perimeter straight ahead of them. Somewhere behind him, there was the scream of a horse missing its step, going down. They were charging in the dark and some of the other riders could not see as well as he could. It was something he had anticipated and been unable to solve, and he knew that his plan could not survive too many unsolved problems.

Behind the cavalry came the infantry, running as fast as they could: and hiding amongst their number were the Sarnesh engineers whose skilled job would be the point of all tonight's festivities. It had been their arrival that had finally decided Salma. It meant that Sarn was not throwing his own people away needlessly as an expedient way of whittling down the enemy. Sarn had sent almost one hundred highly trained artificers, who would almost certainly not survive the night. Sarn was allowing him the responsibility of a true tactician.

He had a brief view of a Wasp sentry standing almost exactly in his path, turning from the confusion within the camp behind him—several tents already ablaze, swift work on Chefre's account—to see 500 of horse and other beasts thundering down on him. The man's wings flared instantly but he was only at head height when Salma's first lance drove into him, the weight of his dying body ripping the shaft from the Dragonfly's hand. Salma and his men were fortunately armed to the teeth, much of it through the unintentional benevolence of all the Wasps they had caught and killed. Most wore repainted Wasp armour, and they carried two or three lances each besides crossbows and swords. Salma himself had a holstered shortbow, ready strung, that he now hooked out into his hand. To either side of him the lance-wedge was driving itself through the scattered Wasp watchmen, but ahead of them the main force was mustering, men rushing into place both on the ground and into the air. The Wasp airborne were meanwhile being harried by Chefre's utter shambles of a squadron, their formation constantly being broken and re-forming. Chefre's Flies and Moths were not real warriors, their attacks causing more nuisance than real threat, but they were too insistent to be ignored. The Wasps already in the air kept trying to pin them down, but they were not a force of soldiers to stand together. They were individuals, and had to be chased and caught one by one. It looked as if that would take all night.

Spears were now levelled amongst the Wasp lines, firmly grounded against the charge. Salma sent off his first arrow but, even as he did so, was beaten to it by at least a score of his men, shooting crossbows and snapbows into the massing enemy. Sting fire came right back at them. Salma knew that many of his soldiers were falling but, so long as they were not stopped, so long as they kept moving, then they were not beaten.

The archery from his riders had been concentrated toward the point of the wedge, and Salma saw a good number of Wasps go down before it. Was it enough? Only one way to find out. He took up another lance, bow clutched for a moment in his reins hand, and let his mount dictate the timing of its leap, plunging down on to the Wasp lines with thundering hooves and lance and a great shout. An enemy spearhead streaked past his face, his second lance was torn from his hand on the impact, and then he had smashed past the front rank, broken the Wasp order, and there were 400 and more riders following right behind him.

He pulled his sword out, a heavy Hornet-kinden blade with the weight loaded toward the tip, and simply laid about him as his horse charged on, feeling the jarring shocks as men fell beneath its hooves. Others tried to fly at the last moment, nerve failing them. At every split second he was fighting a different man, just time for a single strike, whether hit or miss, and then was carried past them, galloping deeper into the camp. The enemy spears tilted and skewed, the sheer weight of thundering cavalry breaking the Wasps' will to stand. Hooves trampled them remorselessly, while the mandibles of insects sheared and cut. They were scattering even as the cavalry struck them, and those who could not take to the air in time were simply ridden down.

Salma was clear of the Wasp lines without warning, charging down a thoroughfare between tents, and the soldiers he saw were half dressed or unarmed, coming out to see what was going on, and then throwing themselves up into the air or just to one side in utter panic. All the while Chefre's scattered airborne were taking every opportunity to evade their pursuers and bombard the ground again.

From across the camp a thunder roared, and for just a second the entire place was like day, lit up bright white and then red. Salma closed his eyes against it, trusting his horse would manage. He himself had no idea what had happened.

Time to turn, though. He wheeled his mount along another avenue of tents, safe in the knowledge that every Wasp possible would be watching him, believing that *he*, Salme Dien and his cavalcade, formed the attack. Beside him, Phalmes was grinning fiercely.

"Firepowder store!" he screamed over all the noise, though Salma could still barely hear him. "Chefre must have hit it!"

Behind the cavalry, his infantry must have already fallen on the broken Wasp defenders, taking them apart in savage desperation. Time was everything, now. Salma and Chefre and Morleyr's little force had been all simply to catch the eye, like a flashy brooch, whilst the infantry got the engineers to the engines and then let nature take its course.

He did not even turn to look back at his riders, as he twisted in the saddle to loose another arrow. He knew that they would be falling, shot from both sides, from behind and above, by Wasps who probably did not realize quite what was happening but knew an enemy when they saw one. His people were busy dying, and his only hope was that they had all known, as he had, what they were getting themselves into.

Many had families and friends who were under the care of Sarn now. Their safety was what this was about, and surely it was a nobler aim than personal survival.

They were running out of room, though. Enough of the Wasp camp was now aware of them and was trying to box them in. Salma turned this way and that, knowing that with each turn he had fewer riders behind him.

Time for a last-ditch attempt to escape, he decided. He would just have to hope that by now the Sarnesh engineers had got their work done.

The next clot of soldiers that barred his way he did not turn aside from. With his last lance couched in his arm he simply rode straight into them. They scattered at the last moment, many of them too late. One man, in his hurried flight, slammed a knee into Salma's shoulder, rocking him back in the saddle. The lance, unbloodied, flew from his hand, but he managed to stay on horseback, charging in what he hoped, after all the twists and turns, was the direction of the camp's closest perimeter.

At least they all know this part. From this point on, their work was done and it would be everyone for himself. Wasp sting bolts crackled and danced past him, each one lighting up a single strand of the night.

One struck his horse.

He felt a lurching shock run through the animal's very frame, not the shock of impact but the animal's own pain and fear. It reared up, and he had a brief sense of other riders flashing helplessly past him, and then another shot struck the wretched beast, whether sting or bolt he never knew, and it pitched sideways. He knew enough to get himself out of the saddle and into the air as the animal crashed to the ground.

The air was full of fire and light, but a calm voice in his head reminded him *We have been here before.* That had been the camp outside Tark, but the principles were the same. In the air he became a target for every man within thirty yards. He nevertheless tried to ascend, but then found that there were Wasps all about him and no sign of Chefre's people. *Fled. I hope they fled.* He had his sword out, wounding the three closest to him, and then a blade coming from behind and below opened a shallow cut on his leg and, with the sense that he was totally surrounded and about to be cut apart, he dropped from the air.

He landed running, forcing away the pain, knowing that he was too far now from the camp's edge to escape. There were Wasps all about him, but most were too surprised at the sight of this single running enemy in their midst to react. The rest formed a growing tail of pursuit, hounding him through their camp. Despite the pain, the deaths, the certainty of his end, he was grinning because the situation was so utterly ridiculous.

Amid all the noise, he missed the voice shouting his name. It was only when Phalmes' horse flashed in front of him that he realized that someone was trying to rescue him.

"Away!" he shouted. "Just go!" but Phalmes was returning for him, riding back toward the pursuing Wasps with his sword raised, a mere black silhouette now against a backdrop of leaping light.

And Salma skidded about the corner of a tent and saw the flames. The sight stopped him: a field of fire, a whole quarter of this tent city roaring in conflagration.

"Salma!" shouted Phalmes again, as he must have been doing for some time, and he was reaching down from his mount when a sting caught him in the chest. Salma saw his face contort, the force of the blow punching him out of the high-ended saddle. The horse slewed about, dragged by the reins, and then Phalmes released it, and it fled.

As the Wasps arrived, Salma knelt beside him, the thunderous flames fierce against his face. He would have liked a last word, for the Mynan bandit had been a good friend to him. Phalmes' words were done, though. He was gone.

He was in good company, at least, for the ground was covered with bodies. Salma saw dead Wasps, in and out of armour, occasionally the bodies of his own motley following, and the scattered forms of the Sarnesh engineers. The fires ahead leapt and roared about complex skeletons of wood and metal, about the wagons of parts and ammunition, all the paraphernalia for bringing a city's walls down. It was like a forest on fire, but it was a forest of engines, burning their wood, their fuel, their firepowder. The Sarnesh had done their work, and only the morrow would tell whether they had done it well enough to justify all this waste of life.

The Wasps approached him carefully, but he put down his sword, laying one hand on Phalmes' chest. He suddenly felt very tired.

TWENTY-TWO

There was a certain status to being brought in alone. Prisoners who came to Capitas in droves, such as escaped slaves, prisoners of war or manpower tithes levied on the subject races, were processed as a commodity, consigned to a group fate, enslaved, executed or sent to the fighting pits, recorded in quantities rather than names. How many thousand lives and dreams had been buried in such a manner, Thalric could not even begin to guess. That fate was not to be his, though. He had come in as a celebrity, a single prisoner with a heavy escort, flown in for the last tens of miles at great expense and with indecent speed. He was being accorded the treatment he had earnt.

Those prisoners whose circumstances merited something more than a humble clerk signifying their doom with a woodcut stamp were brought to the Armour Square, far enough into Capitas to be within easy sight of the top tier of the imperial palace. The square itself, which would have made a very serviceable marketplace, was instead lined with buildings commandeered by the imperial government. There were factor houses for the merchants of the Consortium, offices of military administration and requisition, the chief stockade of the Slave Corps, and this place: the Justiciary. It was a low, uninspiring edifice, staffed by slave clerks overseen by Wasps whose careers were dire enough to see them end up there. It dealt with the disposal of prisoners.

The building itself was not the point, though. The Justiciary was the basis for a fond tradition of the Empire, and thus the reason that Armour Square was a stopping point for anyone touring the city. Well-to-do Wasps brought their families there for entertainment, or their slaves as a warning.

The free-standing posts that lined each side of Armour Square, making a smaller square within the large, had been used once for displaying suits of mail, a relic of the Wasp-kinden's tribal past when warriors had shown their readiness for battle by exhibiting their war gear. More enlightened generations had found a better use for them. At noon, most days, almost every post had a prisoner hanging from it, hauled up high enough to make them balance on their toes, stripped naked for lashing if need be but, most of all, exposed for public ridicule.

There were guards, of course, for prisoners were a resource of the Empire and therefore not to be wasted needlessly. The citizens took the importance of tradition seriously. The Grasshopper-kinden three posts down from Thalric had just had three Wasp youths beat him bloody with staves, as the guards had watched with indulgent pride in such pranks and games.

Thalric shifted his weight again, despite his discovery that there was no easier position to find. Whoever had strung him up had known what they were doing. He tried to relax into it, but his body, which had put up with a great deal recently, was starting to fray. He knew from experience that he could be here for over a day before anyone decided what to do with him next.

Well, think of it as training for the artificer's table. They would want to put him to the question, sooner or later, to find out why he had killed General Reiner and who had put him up to it. His own experience of operating on the other side of the table was not helping, either, and the mental pictures he recalled were too exacting and accurate for comfort. He had no illusions about being able to withstand such questioning. Nobody ever did. It was not some kind of competitive sport between the practitioner and the recipient. You could not *win* it.

Myna should be in arms by now. The thought sent an odd shiver through him, for he had taken a hammer to the Empire and cracked it. Myna would already be in arms, and then there was Szar . . . if Szar was still fighting, and Myna rose up, then where would the Empire choose to deploy its soldiers? And then it was not so far to the occupied Ant-kinden city of Maynes . . . who could have thought that an Empire could be such a fragile thing?

"Well, look at you," said someone next to him, and his first thought was, *Time for a beating.* When he identified the voice, his expectations did not alter. Painfully he shifted round to see her properly.

"It *is* you, isn't it," she said. She was standing beside him, quite free and unfettered, as though this was her city and not his own.

"Tynisa," he got out.

The Spider girl examined him, seeing no doubt the latticework of scars across his naked torso, some of which were older than she was, and all set within the colourful backdrop of the recent bruises that had yet to fade. In turn, he saw that she was wearing the clothing of a well-off Capitas woman, with the cut modified by just inches to turn demure into sensual. If he had encountered her as a stranger, on any Capitas street, he would have taken her for an adventuress or even a prostitute, and probably taken her home with him for that matter.

"I see," he said, "that you're making yourself at home here. Thrown in the fight, have you? Or has Stenwold become a little optimistic about where he can plant his agents?"

"On my father's business."

Tisamon? Thalric could not imagine the Mantis stalking about the city dressed in Wasp clothing and pretending . . . no, of course, he had run away. "Tisamon's here?" He craned about, looking at all the other posts. There were plenty of fellow sufferers but no Mantids among them.

She stared levelly at him. "That looks painful, Major Thalric."

"Well spotted."

"I'm allowed to strike you, I believe?"

He closed his eyes. "That depends on who you're supposed to be, Tynisa. Go on, try it. We've been at daggers drawn long enough and you've not laid a straight blow on me yet." That was not, of course, true. She had nearly killed him outside Helleron. Furthermore, it was a foolish thing to say because she took his provocation in the spirit it was meant and punched a fist into his abused ribs hard enough that he felt them creak. He made a short, choked sound of pain, hearing some of the spectators murmur appreciatively. Needless to say, the guards just watched.

She leant close to him. "You've earned that, and more," she murmured, "but right now we're in a position to help each other."

"Your negotiating techniques leave something to be desired," he grated.

"Do they?" Before he could say anything to stop her, she had stepped back, and then the back of her hand cracked against his cheekbone and whipped his head round. *My mouth is going to get me killed.* This time when she leant close, he said nothing.

"That was for the crowd, Thalric. And for me, a little—but mostly for them. Now, listen. I've made some friends here in Capitas. Well, maybe friends isn't the word, but a chain of people who'll do things for me if I ask them nicely. What they won't do, though, is let me down to the cells beneath the palace."

"The pit cells," Thalric recalled. "And that's where they've got Tisamon, is it? Right place for him."

He felt her tense, but she did not strike him again. "I can get you down from your post here this afternoon, instead of tomorrow, seeing that my friend of the moment is an overseer of your Justice place here. If I ask him very nicely indeed, maybe he'll have you sent to the pit cells, just like Tisamon."

"If you lead him on, you mean."

"Jealous?" There was a edge to her voice. "I can't fight an entire Empire with my sword, Thalric. There are just too many of your wretched people. I could stab at your kin all day and still not get anywhere. So I use other weapons. I got here, didn't I? I'm not proud of my methods, but they work."

"And if I'm really good, your methods will now see me condemned to the pit cells. Thank you very much."

"Just to hold you there, until they decide what to do with you. You'd rather be sitting in a cell than hanging from a post, I assume."

"And in return . . . ?"

"Take a message to Tisamon." Her hand was in his hair, abruptly, dragging his head back, to the further appreciation of the spectators. "Tell him I'm here for him, that I will find some way to get him out."

He thought about that slowly, long enough for her to yank at his hair again. "What," he asked, "if he doesn't want to get out?"

She went very still. "I don't know what you mean."

"Yes, you do. How do you capture Tisamon, the Manti-skinden Weapons-master? Either dead or not at all, surely, and yet you say he's malingering in the cells beneath the palace—"

"Shut up," she hissed at him. "Shut up or this crowd will see me put your eyes out, Thalric. That's not your problem. That's my problem and I . . . I'll deal with it." She stepped back, and he braced himself for further injury.

"Nod or shake, Major," she told him. "Do what I want now, or I'll make sure you hang here for another three days before they work out where to send you."

He let his head sag. It could be taken for a nod. Then she punched him in the kidneys, and this time he could not stop himself crying out.

"You move too fast," cautioned one of the cowled shapes around him. Uctebri saw all his reflections in the polished walls nod and nod, out of time but in agreement. He bared his needle teeth at the speaker, stalking across the room and making the candles gutter, so that all that assembled host within the mirror-shiny walls momentarily bobbed and flickered.

"It must be now," he said. "I have wrestled with fate too hard just to get my players to the wings. I cannot stand back and let it all go to ruin."

"The risks are too great," said another, a whispering woman's voice. "The Empire . . ."

"Is the prize, in case you had forgotten," Uctebri supplied. "Temporal power, at last, and after so long," Uctebri said.

"If they uncover you . . . if you fail . . . we have not the strength or the numbers to resist them or to survive another purge."

"They are savages," Uctebri snarled. He could feel his blood, that borrowed and mingled commodity, rising inside him: only his own people could ever provoke him so. "How would they find us? These are not the Moth-kinden, to understand our hearts, or the Spiders, to ensnare us. They have no understanding of the old days. If they recoil against us I shall pay the price, I alone."

"You cannot be so sure of that," another said. "The girl, she may know more than you realize."

"You have taught her too much," said yet another. Uctebri glared at them all. For a moment he saw them as they would seem to an outsider: a conclave of thin and twisted creatures, sickly and cowardly after so many centuries of hiding.

"I have come too far now to cry 'Hold.'" he hissed at them. "So what would you have me do? Wait another year, perhaps? Burrow into the Empire like a maggot into rotten flesh, never to find the heart? You have been too long in the dark. The girl is mine, and all that she possesses is my promise. She has lived under the shadow of her brother's knife all her life, so she will take what I give her, and do what I say, just for a chance to be rid of that doom. What is she, but a woman in a race where the men lead? She will not be able to rule without our aid. We will make her our puppet, and the Empire, all its youth and strength and blood, will be ours to tug at." Greed was the key here, he knew. His was a greedy race, and it had always been so. "What might we do, with such a beast under our spur? Do we not have scores to settle with the world? Are we not *owed*? What vengeance might we exact on our old foes, with all the armies of the Empire at our disposal?"

They shuffled and turned to one another, and he felt his fingers crooking into claws with frustration.

"If we had known—"

"You knew," he addressed them all. "My plan has been years in the making. You all knew what I intended, and for the good of us all! Only now, when I am on the cusp, do you cringe away from grasping it." He drew himself up straight. "It matters not," he decided. "I do not need to care what you all think. I am in too far, now, to draw myself from the wound. I needs must suck it dry. If you will not share the feast, so be it. But I have no doubt that when I have the Empire in my hand, you shall come begging on your knees for a share."

They fell very silent then. The Mosquito-kinden were close knit out of necessity, surviving by mutual conspiracy. The censure of the many was always enough to govern the few, or so it had been for longer than any of them had been alive.

"You will bring ruin on us," one of them said slowly. "You are become too proud."

"And you are not proud enough," Uctebri retorted. "Where is the race that once battled with magi and great scholars to be the masters of the world? Is there nothing left of that ambition? Has our defeat so long ago crippled us, even until today? Well, not I. I shall grasp the Empire with both hands and make it do my will. I shall be shadow-Emperor behind the girl's throne, and in a hundred years from now—three generations of theirs but within a single lifetime for us—we shall walk openly in their streets, and speak counsel to their leaders, and perhaps we will no longer remember what craven things we had once become."

With an impatient thought, he severed his link to them. Worms, all of them, pallid, soft things hiding away from an enemy that had suffered its own catastrophic reversals some five centuries before. The world needed a stronger hand to master it, and that hand was his. He considered his protégée, the Wasp princess. At this moment he felt she showed more promise than all the rest of his kinden put together. *And you will be mine, heart and soul. You will sell your people's future, your own will, in exchange for the empty reward of a throne.* The thought cheered him, the nearness of all he had worked toward. His puppets were now all in place and ready to dance for him.

◊ ◊ ◊

That she was so reliant on others was frustrating to her, but then it had always been so. To compensate, Seda had developed the ability to persuade others to do those things for her that almost any other member of her race could simply have reached out and accomplished in person.

This room, however, she had found for herself: an armoury on the third floor of the palace, stripped of its contents when the new garrison quarters had been built elsewhere in Capitas. No alternative use for it had yet been found. It had one main door and one hidden door, as was the case with most of the military rooms in the palace, for Seda's father, the late Emperor, had been a man given to surprises and ambushes—and so had his chief advisor, the infamous Rekef, whose name lived on in the force of spies and agents that he had fashioned.

The secret entrance was crucial. It was of the utmost importance that nobody realized just how many people she was meeting here. Otherwise it would be so easy for word to get to her brother Alvdan, and then everything would be thrown into disarray.

Already, General Brugan had his men posted nearby, watching all approaches, turning passing servants away. Alvdan and his lackey Maxin need never know what had transpired here.

She wondered if Uctebri would, however. The Mosquito had ways of spying on her that she could not control, just as she could not control him. His invisible eyes could be present here, in this very room, as she received her fellow conspirators and told them what they must do for her. Like all the others, Uctebri had missed discovering the real Seda. She had grown up in continual fear for her life, and her one defence was to seem vulnerable and helpless. She had lived with Maxin's knife poised over her, and Alvdan's temper always ready to give him the word. She had made her way through the world with meekness as her only shield. She had cultivated it assiduously, seeming a willing tool to every purpose. When she was young, she had feared that General Maxin could read minds, that he would register even the slightest flicker of rebellion or resentment.

But now she had as her doubtful ally a man who really *could* read minds, and she was practised enough to place there in front of him just what he wished to see. Even the master-sorcerer himself would have to dig very deep to find the real Seda beneath her camouflage.

He was clever, was Uctebri the Sarcad, clever enough to plot the downfall of an Emperor, but she hoped that, like so many clever men, he underestimated the intelligence of others. She now gazed about the room at her assembled allies. They included General Brugan, of course, solid and dependable and very much hers since her brother had made Maxin the lord of the Rekef. The suspicious death of General Reiner looked enough like a precursor to his own that he was now entirely Seda's to play with. She liked him, too: in face and body, here was a man to be admired, and with an uncommon streak of integrity that she found intriguing. She knew what he hoped from her, and she had given him nothing to dispel those expectations. They would prove useful to her.

She also had three of the Imperial advisors on her side now: there was old Gjegevey, who saw her as a victim who needed nurturing, and two of the older Wasp councillors who could feel their seats beside the throne being prepared for younger men now dearer to the Emperor. Two years ago such treason would not have been thinkable, but the war within the Rekef had made men fearful for more than just their station or reputation. General Reiner's death had scared a great many powerful people.

She had both of the palace stewards in her party: considered lowly menials who ordered the servants and slaves about, nobody cared much about them; one was a Wasp woman, the other a Grasshopper slave. Being strictly civilian, they were firmly under the heel of the Empire, and nobody save Seda had realized quite how much power they wielded and what they could accomplish. Beyond that, she had several military officers: a colonel and two majors from within the Capitas garrison, and a scattering of others from outside it. They were disaffected men that Brugan had been watching, and normally he would have caused them to disappear, thus increasing that fear of the Rekef that kept ambitious officers throughout the army in line. But now he had made them her offer.

From face to face she looked in turn, seeing there her own fragile empire ready to set against her all-powerful brother—and against the unthinkable Uctebri.

She smiled at them warmly, and set about explaining precisely what they must do for her.

◁) ◁) ◁)

"You've got another visitor," came Ult's voice. Tisamon opened his eyes, his mind falling back from dream-tormented sleep to the gloomy confines of his cell.

"Keep your visitors."

"What can I say? You're a popular man." Ult grinned mirthlessly. "Never had a prisoner get so many visitors wanting to see him."

Tisamon shrugged. "To the pits with them."

"Don't be like that. You're denying me a chance to make a fortune."

Two nights ago, the Mantis had fought in one of the smaller private arenas, after which word had spread. This last day alone there had been over a dozen people escorted down into the gloom to see him, almost all of them women of good family. It was a tradition, Ult explained. So many menfolk were away with the army, it was only natural that their wives became bored. A little excitement, a little titillation, and of course most of the fighters were glad of the attention.

"But not you," Ult noted. "We'd do well out of them, if you'd let them touch you."

"What if I killed them instead?" Tisamon asked bitterly.

"Then you'd be stung to death in your cell," Ult said with equanimity. "Don't think that hasn't happened. It's all part of the thrill."

Tisamon sat down with his back to the bars, his arms wrapped about his knees. "What is it they really seek, Ult?"

"Death, Mantis. Surely you know that rich people love death."

"In Capitas perhaps."

"It's because they live safe lives, the rich and powerful. Oh, some of them go off to the army, and that ain't exactly safe for anyone, but there's a load of people with rank and medals who just sit behind their desk and do their marching on paper. And there are the officers' wives, of course, with all the time and money they could want, and nothing to do with it. . . . And here you are, a bit exotic, a bit rough and dangerous, and not bad looking for all that, and you move like you do—bound to catch their eye, yes?"

"It's disgusting."

Ult laughed at him. "You got cursed high standards for a pit fighter, Old Mantis. Look at your fellows here—they'd give a lot to be where you are. Think of it as a recognition of your skills, if you want, and the more people want to see you . . ."

The Wasp left the words hanging, but Tisamon heard the rest in his head: *the more chance you'll get what you want.*

"So who's asking for me now? The queen herself?"

"Something a little different. Something you can say 'no' to without me thinking you're a fool for refusing. Got a fellow wanting the cell next to yours, just for a bit. He says he can point me in the way of some money in the city, if I do it. But it's your call in the end."

"Another prisoner?"

"He'd like me to think so," Ult sneered. "They reckon you got to be stupid, to work down here, but I seen most types. This fellow, he's a spy. He's got that look to him. He's Rekef, more than likely. He's here to take a look at you. Maybe the Emperor's heard of you, and wants you checked out."

"Then bring him in. I'll play the abject slave, shall I?"

"You ain't got it in you," Ult told him. "You carry yourself prouder than a battlefield colonel, you do. I'll bring him over, though. If you end up gutting him through the bars that's your business."

Tisamon waited in the dark, listening to the other prisoners all around him. *Am I so proud, still?* Perhaps he should have given those Wasp women what they wanted: one more debasement, the last step in his descent. *But she is out there, somewhere*: Felise Mienn whom he would have to kill—or else she would kill him.

He did not even look up as Ult and a pair of guards returned, and his latest visitor was slung into the cell next to him, which had been empty since the previous evening.

"What do you want?" he growled.

"Is that any way to greet an old friend?" There was more weariness than humour in the voice, and it took a moment for Tisamon to place it.

"Thalric?"

"The same." The Wasp looked haggard and bruised. If he was a Rekef spy once more, he was certainly well disguised as a man to whom life had not been kind for some time.

"You've come home, then," Tisamon observed, finding that the sight of the man raised no particular emotion in him.

"The Emperor called for his errant son," replied Thalric, and leant carefully back, wincing in pain. "I've not been this comfortable for a while, believe it or not."

"Why are you here, Thalric?"

"The consequences of a piece of fairly severe insubordination."

"I thought you'd left the army."

"Ironic," Thalric laughed. "They let me back in just beforehand. You've never trusted me, have you?"

"Any reason that I should have?"

"No." Thalric's smile was small and bleak. "So in that case you can decide whether I'm faithfully passing on a message or merely taking pleasure in putting the knife in."

Tisamon regarded him. "I don't cut easily."

"Excellent. Well, your daughter is in the city and she wants to rescue you." Thalric closed his eyes. "For some reason she wanted me to tell you and, although I can hardly say that I'm ever as good as my word, here I am, and the words are said."

There was a long silence, which gave Tisamon every chance to consider Tynisa's likely fate if she attempted to free him, until eventually, eyes still closed, Thalric said, "Tisamon? You haven't died, have you?"

"Felise Mienn is here," Tisamon said, out of some obscure desire to strike back. "She will probably kill you, if she gets the chance."

Thalric's smile actually broadened. "Then tell her to stand in line." He gave a sigh, which ended up as a wheezing kind of laugh. "Don't you love it when old friends get together?"

Thalric was asleep the next morning, when Ult came to fetch Tisamon. If the former Rekef man was playing a role now, he was playing it to the hilt. Even at rest his face looked haunted by past decisions.

"Whose blood am I shedding?" Tisamon asked.

Ult shook his head. "Not this time, old Mantis. This time you're indulging me."

"Is that so?"

"I want to see you fight her."

Tisamon was on his feet instantly, and something caught inside him, like a hook. "Felise?"

"The Dragonfly woman, right." Ult unlocked the cell and Tisamon stepped out. He felt unsteady, unsettled within himself. It was anticipation, he realized. The moment's thought came to him, not of their sparring bouts in the Prowess Forum, but of their very first meeting when she had been trying to kill him for real, both of them tested to the very edge of their skill. He felt his heartbeat speed up just at the memory.

Ult led him to the practice ring beneath the palace, where a dozen Slave Corps guards were sitting around the periphery of the room. In the centre stood Felise Mienn. Ult nodded to her, warrior to warrior, as he came in, before heading for the weapon racks.

"We generally use these for the comedy matches," he explained, weighing a short stave in his hand. "Good enough for practice, though. I want to see the pair of you go at each other."

Tisamon did not even look at him. His eyes were fixed on Felise. They had not given her back her armour but, standing there with the three-foot length of wood in her hands, she had regained every semblance of the warrior.

"Comedy matches?" she repeated emptily, but her eyes were just as much for Tisamon. She spared no glance for their jailer, or for the Wasp soldiers that ringed this little private arena.

"Oh, you know, half a dozen Fly-kinden up against a big scorpion, civilians against the reaping machine, that kind of thing." Ult shrugged, looking between them. "I keep telling them that if I was allowed to properly train the prisoners I get down here, get them practising, the shows would become that much the better, but they don't like the idea." It was clear that his mouth was simply making the words while his mind considered the problem these two represented. "Right then," he said at last, handing a stave to Tisamon. "Remember, this is just a friendly."

Felise's eyes narrowed and she dropped back into a defensive stance, weight on her back foot, weapon held low and forward. Tisamon found that his own stance came on him without thinking, the stick cocked back behind, one hand ready to beat aside her weapon, a stance that invited attack, yet not at all the best for dealing with her own pose.

Their eyes met almost with a shock. She wanted to kill him, and she would do so unless someone stopped her, wooden stick or no. Dirt-smeared and haggard as she was, in that moment she was as beautiful as he had ever seen her.

She went for him, the defensive stance becoming something else without warning, a sudden darting lunge. They had bound leather across her back to stop her calling up her wings, but she seemed to fly at him anyway. A swift downward strike, which he avoided, was cover for a lunge at his midriff that clipped him, the slightest contact, perhaps the pinprick of a splinter from the stave. With a quick turn of her wrists, she spun the wooden blade in a circle to catch his inevitable counterattack, but it did not come; instead he moved back and back, weapon still poised to strike.

She halted, evaluating, watching, turning as he circled her. Something inside him had told him at the start that he could not strike at her. After all, he was the betrayer, so he had no right to fight to win. But as soon as the fight had begun, he had shaken that off. The old fierce fire came back to him, as though the whole of his recent past had never occurred. It was as though he had now stepped sideways into a different word: a pure, plain world of light and air and the uncorrupted elegance of combat.

He struck, a sudden whirling of the blade toward her to draw her out, but she just swayed back. Her own stave drove at his face, and he put it aside with his free hand, bringing his mock weapon down on her shoulder. She caught it with her offhand, bending at the knees to absorb the force, and cast him off, and he spun away, dancing across the arena floor, every line become a circle within that closed space, so as to lead him back to her.

He took no pause, lashing down at her, and their sticks met a dozen times in a rapid patter, instinct taking over where the eyes were too slow. Then they were past each other, without a strike scored. He slung the stave back, arcing it at the back of her head, but she dropped to one knee and her own weapon skimmed his side and caught the cloth of his slave's shirt.

They parted again, circling. Ult and his men might not even have been there. They now had their small and hermetic world entirely to themselves.

She was smiling—as he realized that he was, too. Their expressions must have seemed a perfect match.

She was at him then, striking down at his head, sideways at his neck, blows swift and hard enough to break bone if they landed. He skipped back, swayed aside, dragged the stave across the front of her body to slash her open as though it was a blade indeed, missing only by moments. Her own stick blurred overhead as he dropped down. She had struck one-handed, and her left hand came in, ripping a bloody line across his shoulder with her thumb-claw. He felt the pain only as a distant voice urging him on. His own arm spines grazed her hip, and then cut at her stomach as she gave ground, and all the time his stave was moving, meeting hers again and again, as though they had practised the fight for months or even years. They were closer and closer together, well inside each other's reach, the deadly work being done with the off-hands, the useless staves only a distraction. She gouged his cheek, aiming for his eye. He raked three lines of red below her collar-bone, looking for her throat.

They broke apart, six feet of clear ground between them in an instant, poised in their perfect stances, waiting. Although she still gripped it like a sword, Felise's stick had been sheared in half.

Ult made a small sound into the silence. The soldiers were on their feet in shocked silence, hands out and open ready to sting.

Tisamon looked at Felise, seeing the few lines he had managed to score on her, and feeling his own blood where she had drawn it. He met her eyes, took a step toward her. She cast the halved stick away, her thumb-claws flexing and out, while moving in toward him. Ult was saying his name, but he did not care.

Another step, and almost within reach of her hands. He knew now that, where his stick had been, his clawed glove was now buckled about his hand and forearm as though it had always been there, the short, deadly blade drawn back to strike. He had not even realized that he had called to it.

He looked into her face, golden and savage and beautiful, and, even as Ult called his name again, he said, "Forgive me."

Even as she tensed to spring, her lips moved, and what she said was, "Of course."

He let his arms fall to his sides, but she did not kill him. Instead, the soldiers had grabbed her, hauled her back, even as others were reaching for him, reaching to take away the weapon they had seen, but that was no longer there. He held her eyes, and felt at the same time a crippling joy and a wrenching bitterness that he should realize only now, at this waning end of their time together, that he loved her. It was only when they fought that he could see it clearly.

Ult was staring at him—indeed all the Wasps were staring at him, but Ult's expression was different. He was the only one there not busy convincing himself that he had been mistaken. He signalled for some of his men to lead Felise away, and Tisamon watched her until she was gone. Only then did he turn to his keeper, expressionless.

"If your badge got taken from you, I can get it back," Ult said, studying him. Tisamon raised his eyebrows, and the Wasp continued, "Oh, they had me in the

Twelve-Year War, early on, so don't think I don't know your kind. We were fighting plenty of Mantis as well as Dragonfly back then, and I saw some pull tricks like you just pulled. Don't assume I don't know anything."

"I abandoned the symbol of my order by choice," Tisamon said. *Because of her, and my own pride.*

Ult nodded slowly. "Well," he said, "I reckon I was just quick enough to keep you alive until next time, Mantis. I just hope the Emperor will appreciate the pair of you as much as I do."

⟨⟩ ⟨⟩ ⟨⟩

It was the middle of the night, so far as he could judge, when they came for Thalric. Four guards opened up his cell, chained him up and hauled him off. He was conscious of Tisamon's wry gaze on him as he left.

They took him to a windowless room, lit by a dim gas lantern fixed on the wall. For all he could see of the sun it could just as easily be noon outside as night.

It was an interrogation room. Not a room with that trade's machines and artificers but a little booth of an office that, in the great scheme of questioning through excruciation, preceded the main event. A big man was standing there behind a desk, an officer from his bearing, but Thalric noticed no badge of rank. Sitting at the desk itself was a woman.

He was surprised at that because, in Capitas, even the Rekef—which elsewhere used whatever tool best fit the hand—was intrinsically a conservative force. Women were considered servants or perhaps clerks at best, but not put in charge, as this one clearly was. Even the officer, who had authority enough to be at least a colonel, was deferring to her.

She was young, fifteen or twenty years Thalric's junior at least, and the dim light showed that she was attractive. Her hair was long and golden, tied back neatly. She wore clothes that suggested wealth—some rich officer's wife? Her gaze was very steady.

"Major Thalric of the Rekef," she began, but not as a question. The guards were still watching him narrowly despite having bound his arms painfully tight behind his back. He waited, understanding that this was not an opportunity to better his lot. He would just have to weather whatever came.

"So you killed General Reiner," she noted.

Is she his wife? That would make sense. He had no other theory as to who she might be. She would make a very young wife for Reiner, though, surely? He had never thought of Rekef generals as being the marrying type, but then he himself was still married to a woman he had not seen in years. The Empire needed sons, but it was a duty only, and sentiment did not come into it.

"Major Thalric . . . or perhaps just Thalric." Her smile remained bright and unreadable. In fact her eyes glittered with a hard-edged mirth, and if she was a widow there was little enough grieving in her. "General Brugan, here, has shown me your records."

Thalric blinked, glancing up at the big officer. *General Brugan?* So the Rekef really was ready to take him apart, was it? But if that was the case, who was this wretched woman? Where was General Maxin?

"A remarkable piece of patchwork, your career," the woman noted. "Remind me of it, General."

Brugan stared bleakly at Thalric, like an artificer studying a broken machine. "Anti-insurgent work, after the conquest of Myna. Referred to the Rekef by Major Ulther, as he then was. Behind the lines during the Twelve-Year War with assassination squads. Then the Lowlands business, Helleron. The strike against Collegium by rail."

The woman's smile was cutting. "That didn't go very well, did it?"

I was outmanoeuvred. The army gave insufficient support. My chief spy betrayed me. "No," Thalric said simply. *If I am to be racked, let it be for my own failures. I will not die blaming others for my misdeeds.*

"Neither did the Vekken campaign," General Brugan added darkly.

Major Daklan was in charge of that, you bastard. A brief memory, of Daklan's blade driving into him, made him twitch.

"And then you went rogue, I'm told," the woman noted. Her face told him that she knew to the last detail all the circumstances, and that he would be able to use none of them in his defence. He did not feel up to singing the old tune: *you sold me out before I sold you.* It was not as though it would make any difference.

"Collegium, Jerez, and then you turn up in Myna and kill General Reiner. And then you surrender to the army, who bring you here. Why, Thalric? Tell me why."

"Why to which question?" he asked. "There is no one reason for all of it."

"What a complex man you are." All the humour was gone from her face. "So tell me why you killed the general, Thalric."

A hundred flippant answers came to him and he brushed them all away. *Let them kill me for the truth, why not? Let them rack me and crush me, and find in the end only what they had at the start.* "He cast me off. He let them send men to kill me, simply because of politics," he told her. "I had always served the Empire faithfully, and yes, I have not always triumphed, but the Empire was all I ever cared about. He cast me off. He let them take me. Then, when I was caught in Myna, he took it all back. He gave me back my rank and my place, and said he needed me again, but not to serve the Empire, just for his own private schemes." The rush of emotion he felt now putting it all into words thoroughly shocked him. "And do you know what? He got on my nerves. All the things I had done for him, that at the time I thought I had been doing for the Empire. All those muddied waters, the children I killed and the friends I betrayed, and was it for Empire, or just for Reiner? I'd never know. I'd only know that Empire's good and general's ambition were not the same thing any more. And he sat there, taking it all back and about to give me orders, and I just couldn't take any more of him. And so I did it, and I defy anyone to honestly claim they wouldn't have done the same. He was an *irritating* man."

General Brugan's mouth twitched just the once.

"I killed Colonel Latvoc as well," Thalric added, as though this was some obscure mitigation.

The woman's hand waved, consigning Latvoc to the oubliette of history. "And you really expect us to believe you did it all for the Empire?"

"Not for a moment," he said. "But it doesn't make it any less true."

"You're a presumptuous man. For the Empire? Most would be glad enough to do it for a superior officer, for their general, for their own self-interest, for the Emperor even. The Empire is a large master to claim."

"That is why it is fit to be served," replied Thalric. The evident sincerity in his own tone surprised him.

The woman stood up, still looking at him.

He shrugged again. "What do you want from me? You may as well just take it. I'm in no position to stop you, whoever you are."

"I will have to think about what I want from you," she said, and stepped neatly from the room, leaving him for the guards to manhandle away. Only later, after he had been cast back into his cell, did some thought of who she might be occur to him.

◊ ◊ ◊

It had been a long night, and sleep was slow in coming. Tisamon suspected that he was staving it off because of the unsettling dreams. In his dreams he saw Laetrimae in all her riddled detail. That was all the dream consisted of. He was made to stare and stare at her despoiled flesh, her hybrid carapace and the constant piercings of the vines. He was a prisoner even in sleep now, and the blood he shed in the fighting pits was more wholesome than the sight of that mangled but undying cadaver.

The failure of all our kinden. Laetrimae and he, they were well matched in that. They had both led ruined lives, bitter ones, twisting inward and inward until they stood face to face in this sunless cell. The only thing that stood between them was five hundred years of torment, but he felt as though he was rapidly catching her up.

They brought Thalric back to the cells eventually. The Wasp had no words for him, although his skin looked as intact as it had done when he was dragged away.

Thalric could make out the long scar that Tynisa had given him in Helleron, but it was only one amongst so many. The world had done its best to kill Thalric. *And he has survived, for this?*

Ah, Tynisa. And was she captured yet? Dead yet? And, if not, then surely the sands were running out on her. She would come stalking into the palace to find her father, but she was not skilled enough, as Tisamon well knew, to survive it. He had taught her all he could, but it was an errand he himself would have died in attempting.

And yet I might have tried it, even so. She is my daughter, yet.

It was a curse he would not wish on anyone, to possess his tainted blood in her veins. *Instead I would tell her, look to Stenwold. There is your model for a proper life, a life of meaning.*

He wondered if, somehow, it would have been possible to sever that twisted, self-hating part of himself, cut it away, cast it off. What manner of father would he have been to the girl then? A better one, surely.

When yet another stranger came to stare at Tisamon, the Mantis did not even look at him, at least not at first. He did not mark Thalric's abrupt flinching away, nor did he care much about the two armoured sentinels that stood behind the visitor with spears at the ready. It was Ult that Tisamon finally noticed: Ult's peculiar response to the newcomer. The visitor himself never glanced at the old man but Tisamon read it all in his reaction: here was a man that Ult feared, and revered, and hated so fiercely and intensely, all emotions melted together in the same pot. It told Tisamon who the newcomer was more eloquently than words.

He was young, this man, or at least younger than Tisamon: young and clean-featured and handsome in the Wasp way, fair haired and well dressed. His style was that of rich Wasp men, favouring garments that were loose cut and intricately embroidered, yet with a military stamp still very much in evidence—and the fashion was so *because* this man dressed in such garb.

Tisamon finally turned to look with curiosity upon his Imperial Majesty Alvdan the Second.

"This is him, is it?" Alvdan asked, eyeing Tisamon without much interest. "This is your killer Mantis."

Ult murmured something that might be, "Yes, your Imperial Majesty."

"We have heard that he fights well, and we hope we have been correctly advised."

Again Ult murmured some confirmation.

Alvdan met Tisamon's gaze and the Mantis saw that here was a man to be reckoned with: not vain or foppish but insecure and intelligent, the two qualities that ever honed the tyrant.

"What will he fight?"

"I've not made my final choice for the warm-ups yet, your Imperial Majesty,"

Ult mumbled. "A beast first, probably. Then I was thinking a bare-hand match, since he does that well."

As Alvdan made a slight, dismissive sound, Ult hurried on.

"Then for last we've got a Commonwealer."

Alvdan smiled at that. "The best of the Lowlands against the best of the Commonweal. That may indeed entertain us. This Commonwealer is skilled?"

"She's something very special as well," Ult confirmed.

"She? One of their fighting women? Yes, that will be appreciated," Alvdan remarked, with a dry smirk. Looking straight into Tisamon's face, his eyes suddenly narrowed.

"We do not like this Mantis," he decided. "His people have been a considerable obstacle to our armies, we understand."

Ult said nothing, just waiting.

"When the fight is done, between this one and the Commonwealer, the winner shall be executed on crossed pikes, in the arena."

Ult pursed his lips but said nothing.

"Our people shall see that our enemies do not prosper, even though they entertain us. Arrange it."

The Emperor strode off, his guards in tow, and Tisamon watched Ult staring after them, the hatred naked on his face. He saw that a man who lived as Ult lived, with the lives of all around him passing like water through his hands, must come to grief eventually. When he did he would have two choices: he must despise the wretches that he sent to their deaths, day in, day out, or he must despise those who command it.

TWENTY-THREE

Colonel Gan was still governor of Szar, but merely by a knife edge. More than half of the city was denied to his troops, for over thirty of the city's orderly little streets had been barricaded, and these barricades were made of metal riveted to metal, dug firmly into the earth. They would not stop the Wasp airborne, of course, but they had already made wrecks out of several of Gan's automotives. The Bee-kinden had always been notable craftsmen.

In this way a line had been drawn across the city. There had already been several hundred dead Wasps, and three times as many locals, in skirmishes along the barricades. The Bees had meanwhile captured two of the arms factories that for the last decade had happily been providing the Empire with its weaponry. They wore Wasp armour painted over in russet, bore pikes, swords, crossbows and a scattering of more sophisticated weapons, while some of the barricades had ballistae to back them up. The Bees fought without flair but with a solid determination that made it almost impossible to wear them down. Yesterday thirty of Gan's men had pinned three of the locals within a makeshift shelter and called for their surrender. It had not been forthcoming, for the same blind devotion that had kept the people of Szar docile under imperial rule while their old queen still lived now gripped them with a spirit of rebellion under Queen Maczech.

I could break them, Gan liked to think, *with enough men.* The Bee-kinden fought with a cold fury, though. They were not the natural soldiers that the Imperial Army were but they would simply not give ground without blood spilt for every inch. When cornered, they fought with a savage, fearless fury, and they made every action, even those guaranteed to succeed, absurdly costly in lives and in time.

And then there was the problem of the Colonel-Auxillian. In the last tenday, Gan's life had become a twisted nightmare: his command usurped, his men intimidated, his very grasp of warfare ridiculed, and all at the hands of an arrogant half-breed. *I should have him seized and whipped. I should have him made to disappear.* But the Emperor himself had signed the orders that brought Drephos to Szar. He made no secret of how much he loathed being here, and Gan made no secret of returning that loathing in full force. But the man was here now, and Gan could only step back and watch as the newcomer's men stole away the existing garrison, put them to work, berated them and monopolized Gan's engineers. Gan himself was becoming a recluse in his own city. Every time he gave an order he discovered that Drephos had already been there. And what was the man doing, anyway? Being no artificer, Gan had no idea. At those points where Gan would have been mustering men for an assault on the barricades, Drephos was instead setting up great machines.

To Totho's eye, they were something like leadshotters, but more delicate and longer in the barrel, cluttered with mechanisms to give their artillerists as much control over force and aim as artifice could provide. Instead of volatile firepowder, they housed steam engines for a less violent discharge of their ammunition. There were high watch platforms built beside them, from which engineers could see the lie of the city and thus make precise calculations of their exacting trajectories. When these engines loosed their loads, the shot would sail serenely overhead to land far inside the rebel-held districts of the city. Beside them sat canisters of the same stuff that had killed the soldiers, an invention of the Beetle twins, the dreadful potency of which had driven them to suicide. In assisting with the construction, Totho had seen enough to understand the plan. True to his stated aims, Drephos had taken war to a new level.

They had not been meant for this eventuality, however. Drephos had intended to deploy them against the defenders of Sarn, or the Sarnesh field army if it was foolish enough to venture forth. However, little adaptation had been needed to comply with the Emperor's present wishes. Drephos had done most of the work himself with almost indecent speed, eager to return to what he saw as his true place on the front line itself.

The Szaren resistance assumed that there was a stalemate, and meanwhile the Bee-kinden were gathering their forces, making themselves strong. Scouts' reports came back now with news that, as well as the stolen arms and armour of the Empire, more and more of the Szaren were wearing their own traditional styles: breastplates and helms freshly painted in russet bands, or great, intricately articulated suits of sentinel plate. Some of these had lain in storage these past fifteen years, waiting as patiently as their owners for the call to arms, others were newly smithed. The Bee-kinden were rediscovering their heritage.

But there was no stalemate, of course, as Totho knew well. There was just a peculiarity of the weather, for the wind was currently adverse. The breeze was gusting against the imperial forces, enough for them to hear the clatter and scrape of armed locals from ten streets away. The engines only sat idle while Drephos waited for a favouring wind, and he would not have to wait long.

The thought of what would then happen made Totho tremble. Even stretching his mind, he could not quite fit the concept in. There were hundreds of thousands of Bee-kinden here in Szar. It was formerly one of the industrial workhorses of the Empire. The Emperor had taken its rebellion personally, and he wanted an example made.

There would indeed be an example made, and it would be Drephos' example of how war would be fought from now on. For Drephos had invented a war that needed no soldiers, only artificers, and his machines would soon make full-scale armies obsolete. The very concepts of war would change. Conquest would become devastation, attack would become annihilation: cities turned to cemeteries, farmland to wasteland. What would be seen here in Szar would stop the world in its tracks. In the wake of it, every artificer, every military power, every Ant city-state would be striving to copy what Drephos had done, and without possession of such weapons there would be no chance of continued liberty, or even survival. It was not simply a case of an improvement on an old idea, as the snapbow was to a crossbow, the crossbow to a thrown spear, the spear to a rock. It was a whole new method of warfare.

Totho sat in a corner of a workshop that he had marked out for himself, and tinkered with his new snapbow design, feeling obsolescence creeping over him already. This was not a war that he understood any more.

Kaszaat was kept under watch most of the time. This was not by Drephos' orders but those of Colonel Gan, who could not accept that she was Drephos' creature and not a spy of the rebellious locals. Totho knew that Gan was right to doubt her, and he was only thankful that he himself remained trusted enough that the spies would keep their distance when Kaszaat sought him out.

He had expected her to try to recruit him in her own tiny rebellion but, when she was with him, she made no mention of the great engines, of the poison or of Drephos. He did not know whether it was because she was uncertain of what move to make next, or whether she simply did not trust him.

I do not care what the history books will say.

But that was not entirely true, because Drephos had not managed to cut himself off from ordinary human feelings quite as thoroughly as he might have wished.

Colonel-Auxillian Dariandrephos now stood atop one of his observation platforms and looked out over the city of Szar, all those little low buildings, those innumerable factories and workhouses. It was evening now, late and getting later, but a strong breeze was predicted to begin before dawn, blowing in from behind him. Daylight would then see the engines begin their work.

In his mind's eye, which was always sharper and more vivid than his actual sight, he could see it all: the canisters, full of poison held under immense pressure, would be hurled almost gently, tipping end over end into the sky. The locals would look up and wonder, at first. Only on impact would their casings crack open, their tight-pressed contents escape.

With Drephos' arrival, Colonel Gan and his soldiers had ceased trying to break the rebel lines. With typical Bee-kinden thinking the locals had simply hunkered down and refortified, defensive to the last. They were a simple, industrious and inoffensive people, strong in their unity but in little enough else. That was the reason the world was not overrun with them. They were now waiting for the anticipated Wasp reinforcements to come, having heard there were ten thousand soldiers marching from the Capitas garrison. Drephos knew those men had now been diverted, however, redeployed to keep the lid on the situation at Myna, which he heard was deteriorating.

Let them first hear the news from Szar, and then let them think about their revolution, he reflected, but he felt oddly uncomfortable with the concept. *This is war simply for politics' sake. I prefer the reverse.*

The canisters would burst asunder, and the gas would be let loose in the city. The natural breeze would keep the heavy gas from spreading back toward the Wasps, and the chemicals would pass through every window, into every cellar. Death would be relatively swift, but agonizing. The gas, once taken into the lungs, began to dissolve the very tissues, so that the victims died while trying to inhale the fluid of their own bodies. The Beetle twins had been great innovators in the field of alchemy, and Drephos had been lucky to have grabbed them for his own service.

Dead now, of course. He was disappointed in them for that, but he always failed to allow for basic human sentiment. It was such a weakening force. Besides, when it came to culpability, it would not be their names written in the history books.

Perhaps the Bee-kinden would seek shelter underground, considering so much of their city was dug into the earth. It would avail them naught since the gas, to be effective at all, needed to be heavier than air. It would sink inevitably into every cellar and tunnel and crevice, and if the Bees managed to board themselves up so tightly that the poison could not get in, well, neither could the air. Colonel Gan had already planned to send men in straight after the gas, to "clear up any remaining resistance." His comprehension of what was about to happen was so blatantly limited that Drephos had not even begun to explain. He had simply warned that, wherever the gas lay, in any depression or hole or bunker, it would remain potent for many tendays.

"But I will have a city to run," Colonel Gan had protested. Drephos had merely turned away from him. Gan would have no city, would no longer be a governor, after this. Drephos had an uncomfortable feeling that a great many careers would die here along with Szar. Even the Emperor himself, who had given the order for Drephos to come here, had not known what kind of war he was unleashing.

Drephos had designed protective masks, to filter the worst of the poison from the gas. There were enough of these for his people only, and he suspected that inhaling even the air thus filtered would make them all ill. If the gas was blown back by errant winds, at least his artificers had a chance at survival. Gan and his garrison would not be so lucky. After tomorrow, the whole Empire would come to know the name of Dariandrephos. Within a month his fame, or his infamy, would spread to the Commonweal and the Lowlands, and beyond. He had never objected to either fame or notoriety so long as either was justified.

After tomorrow the world would know Drephos for one thing. It would not be as a genius artificer, inventor of machines, paragon of progress, the man who drove the mills of war. They would know him as *the man who killed Szar*. They would overlook the technical achievements he had made in bringing it about, citing him only as a butcher, the pedlar of atrocity. The Empire, that had given him such opportunity, would have made him its scapegoat, the focus for the world's scorn and hatred. The Wasps would keep him around, keep him working, but the world would never know the truth for which he had worked all his life, his ideology and his ethos. Anything he put forward henceforth, be it philosophy or technology, would be tainted with that reputation.

He heard movement below him, where nobody should be trespassing, then a sudden shout of alarm as Big Greyv, the silent Mole Cricket, loomed massively from the shadows to accost the newcomer.

"It's all right, let him come up," Drephos called down. "Come on, Totho. I've been expecting you."

It was the sudden unfolding of Big Greyv from the shadows that had given Totho such a turn. Of course he knew that the Mole Cricket could see perfectly in the dark, just as Drephos could, but that someone so huge could lurk totally unseen shook him badly. Greyv held an axe casually in one hand, the weapon dwarfed by its wielder. Totho himself would barely have been able to lift it.

He weighed his own burden in both hands while looking up at the watchtower beside the new engines. The lights of the engineering works behind showed him the robed figure standing atop it.

"You are here to talk to me, are you not?" the voice of Drephos drifted down to him. "Then climb up here. I dislike shouting."

Totho cast a look at Greyv. The Mole Cricket's dark face was unreadable but the set of his body said that he was unhappy, and that he did not trust Totho alone with their master. It was, Totho reckoned, a fair enough assessment.

He slung his burden over one shoulder and walked over to the metal rungs. One was missing and some were loose, and he therefore divined that this must be a tower constructed by the garrison engineers and not Drephos' own people. He paused for a moment beside the deceptively small cask that was crammed full of the poison. It looked manageable enough to be carried easily by one man but the material within was so compressed and concentrated that it would have taken all

Totho's strength to shift it. He glanced up to see Drephos peering down at him, his half-breed, iris-less eyes calmly curious as to what Totho might do.

What he did was climb on up to join his master. He wanted to talk.

"I anticipated I would be seeing you at some point tonight," Drephos said. "You have brought another sample of your work, I notice." He held a hand out and automatically Totho unslung his piece and held it out to show him.

"You have perfected the loading mechanism, I see," Drephos remarked.

The repeating snapbow lay slender and silver in Totho's hands. "I adapted one from a nailbow," he explained. "It's too complex for mass production, though, and it jams too easily. It needs more modification."

"Even so, I am impressed. Good work." Drephos' hand touched the weapon briefly, but he made no protest as Totho reslung it, continuing, "I know why you're really here."

"And why is that?" It had been an unexpectedly hard climb, or perhaps Totho's own nerves were running him fierce and ragged.

"You are not yet one of my cadre, not fully. That is only to be expected. Everyone needs time to settle in and learn the routines."

"Routines?"

"Both physical and ideological."

Totho grasped the rail, looking out toward the Szaren barricades. *How many thousands of people . . . ?* "And the Twins?"

Drephos shrugged unevenly, joining him at the rail. "I was surprised by that," he admitted. "I had not judged the limits of their stresses and their tolerances as well as I might."

That brought a bitter smile to Totho's lips. "So they were just a piece of your machine that failed."

"After their task was done, thankfully." If Drephos had heard any accusation in his underling's words there was no sign of it.

"They killed themselves rather than see you do this." Totho knew that he had to force a confrontation now, before his own nerve failed altogether.

Drephos' hands found the rail, one of them with a subtle scrape of metal. It looked for all the world as though he and Totho were simply sharing the view. "If that was the choice that they set themselves," the Colonel-Auxillian replied, "then I am disappointed, but it was their own choice to make." His voice hardened slightly. "You will note that they did not attempt to interfere with my work. Is that the choice that you have set yourself, Totho?"

Totho took a long breath. "I have merely come to ask you to reconsider." It sounded absurd to him, a pathetic anticlimax, but Drephos was nodding.

"Good. Rational debate, I never tire of it. I always knew that you were trying to install yourself as my conscience. I am glad that you felt you could bring your problem to me rather than dwelling on it in silence, as the Twins did. You have already learnt your lesson, after the issue with the girl."

The girl: Che. The mention of her jarred in Totho, wrong-footing him. "I cannot believe that you would willingly do what you are about to do, if you had . . . if you had properly considered the consequences," he got out.

"Consequences," echoed Drephos. "Do you mean political? Technical?"

"Moral," Totho blurted out. "What you're about to do is immoral. It's *wrong*."

"Why?" Drephos asked. Totho just stared at him. After a beat had passed without an answer, the master-artificer added, "There is a matter of scale, undoubtedly. I have found certain . . . obstacles within my own mind. Morality does not enter into it, but there are other matters that have given me pause." For the first and only time in Totho's knowledge, he sounded uncertain.

"You are a war-artificer," Totho said, "and you know it is not flattery if I say that you are the greatest I have known. This is not war, however. This is beneath you. You constructed these weapons for the battlefield."

Drephos smiled with the pure, simple expression of a clever man who is understood. "I have considered this myself. War, though—war is not a static thing. A war is not just the sum of its battles and skirmishes, Totho. It is the same as the difference between strategy and tactics: the great war and the little one. This is the great war."

"But most of those people who will die tomorrow will not be warriors," Totho pointed out. "They will be . . . just citizens of Szar: the young, the old—"

"And on the field against the Sarnesh, my opponents would be soldiers?" Drephos finished for him. "Yes, I asked myself that. What is the *great* war, though, if it is not the Empire against the world? That world is not built on soldiers. The soldiers are merely the sword, not the hand that holds it, nor the body to which that hand belongs. Those people out there, you consider them as innocents in war? Mere bystanders, detached and uninvolved? Surely you were better schooled in logic than that."

Drephos' manner made Totho think of his studies at the College, the same dry approach to theory, and here it was trotted out with a whole city's fate resting on it.

"Have they fed a soldier? Then they are the war," Drephos elaborated. "Have they clothed one? Taught one? Given birth to one? Will they grow to be one? Have they lived their lives fed and aided by the achievements of the soldiers gone before? You cannot say that they are not the war, Totho. The soldiers themselves are merely the tip of it, but beneath the waters is a great mountain building toward them. You see, Totho, I have already considered all this. I am not some irrational tyrant."

"Yes, but—"

"If they survive, they shall rise up again, the next generation, or the next. If they are whipped down by main force, they shall merely nurse their wounds and resharpen their blades. If a single Szaren still stands after tomorrow, then the Empire is doomed sooner or later, for inevitably the war will be lost, in ten years or a hundred or a thousand. If we wish to win the war, then we must make war on all our enemies—not only those that now present themselves with a blade in their hand. Can you honestly refute my logic?"

"But there are other ways to solve a problem, surely?"

"Now that is an old argument, and you are merely echoing it," Drephos replied, as mildly admonitory as a schoolteacher. "Yes, there are truces and treaties and accords and concords and all of that, but they are merely games, Totho. They are games to give both sides time to prepare for the real thing, and that is *war*. Treaties can be broken. In fact most are made with that in mind. There was a philosopher of Collegium a hundred years ago who thought that, instead of wars, your Ant cities could resolve their differences by playing games, thus saving the loss of countless lives. You must see the inevitable flaw in his idea, for what if the losing side refused to accept its defeat? In war there is no such uncertainty. The bodies left on the field give a finality to what happened, however each side dresses it up in its reports. And in this war, my new war, I will expunge even the most lingering doubt. The Empire will win and Szar will lose, and the proof of it will be that there will be no Szar left, no Szaren people, no trace of those who defy the Empire."

"So that the other cities, Myna and the others, they'll never rebel again, is that it?" Totho asked him. "Surely—?"

"Surely I can see that it isn't the case? Yes, the Maynesh and the Mynans and the rest, they will rise up again, and, when they do, do you know what they will have? They will have weapons of their own to counter this one, to bring a new war against the Empire, and we will have to find weapons more terrible still to defeat them. Don't you see, Totho? That's the point. This is *war*, and it is also *progress*, the living, breathing engine of war. Your snapbows, the incendiaries that took Tark, they're just stopgaps. This is the next step, and that, beyond any other reason, is why I must take it. One cannot deny history its prize, Totho."

Totho opened his mouth, once or twice, but no words came out. Drephos' smile, kindly enough in its way, broadened.

"If you will be my conscience, well and good," he allowed, "but from where do you derive yours?"

Totho stared down at his hands as they gripped the rail, realizing as he did so that he was now copying one of Stenwold's mannerisms, when the old man felt harried on all sides and beset with unsolvable problems. "From her," he replied, and it was true. "From Cheerwell Maker. I always ask myself if she would approve, and if she would not, then it's wrong. But then I've already done so many things that she would not approve of, so where am I now?"

"Quite," said Drephos. "Be thankful that reason and calm thought can prevail over such vague notions." Abruptly his head turned, and he was looking past Totho at something below them. "And here," he said, "is my other expected guest."

Totho turned to see Kaszaat herself being led toward the engine, firmly pinioned between two Wasp soldiers.

TWENTY-FOUR

They had chosen the island of Findlaine as their staging point. The Wasps, still focused on holding on to a turbulent Solarno, had not further expanded their influence out over the waters of the Exalsee. But Findlaine was close enough to undertake the flight and still have fuel and fire to do battle over the city itself; far enough that the flying machines and beasts could muster there without sharp eyes from Solarno's garrison spotting them.

There was an old tower on Findlaine, its provenance lost after successive changes of ownership. The style was Spider-kinden of centuries before, a delicate once-white spire that the years had brought down so that only a stump still remained, rising mutely out of the screen of surrounding trees. Taki had taken it as her vantage point. Looking north, she could see the pale blur on the shoreline that was Solarno, while looking south, down into Findlaine's broad and shallow bay, she . . .

They were now gathered there, every flying machine that the free pilots of Solarno could muster, as well as a contingent of pirates and freebooters from Chasme, with some concerned mercenaries and a flight of dragonfly-riders from Princep Exilla. She had never seen so many pilots in one place, and it was all she could do to hold them together. They were at each others' throats all the time: no natural allies but bitter enemies and rivals reluctantly pressed into service side by side. When the time came, they would fight as they always had, as individuals. She only hoped that they would concentrate on fighting the Wasps.

In her hand was a crumpled note recently brought to her by a messenger who was even now skimming back in his little sailboat toward the city. It reported that Nero had organized what resistance he could. The Wasp governor's ceremonial confirmation was nigh. The entire Wasp garrison would be out on the streets, waiting for trouble. They would certainly not be disappointed.

One single strike, to shatter their power. Very little word had come from the west, but Taki knew that the Spider-kinden were engaged in fighting up on the Silk Road, at places she had barely heard of, seen only briefly in passing.

She spared a thought for Che: *I hope your plight is not as bad as ours.* She also hoped that, in making this push against the Empire, she would be aiding the

Beetle girl, just as she hoped that whatever trouble Che was in would take some of the pressure away from Solarno. *Even the Empire only has so many soldiers, so many armies.*

That was the theory, at least.

She consulted the little pocket clock that had been a gift from her brother, years before. She angled it at the sun until the little shadow told its tale. It was telling her that she would have to get started.

Without giving herself time to think, Taki sped down the slope toward the bay. *Nero had better have his end of this action in hand.* Even the thought of the man made her uncomfortable, because she knew he was not really here for any love of Solarno or hate of the Empire. A man ten years older than she was, and bald and not well favoured and, most of all, not a pilot. She could have overlooked the rest but she had never glanced twice at a man who wasn't a flier. It was something in her heart and blood, needing a man who would share in the places that she really belonged.

Old fool that he is. She still hoped he would be all right. She wanted no more guilt on her shoulders than was there already. *There will be a great many people by sunset who will not be "all right."*

Freedom, though—freedom for Solarno and the Exalsee and perhaps, just perhaps, for the world. *We cast our little stone now in the hope of a landslide.*

"To your vessels!" she shouted as she descended the slope. She saw men and women starting up from their card games and campfires, and mechanics make a final twist or turn, then scrambling out from beneath or within a machine. Niamedh flipped her a salute before vaulting up to the cockpit of her sleek *Executrix*. On the water, the bulky *Mayfly Prolonged* already had its propellers moving sluggishly as Scobraan started up the engines.

A big female dragonfly some thirty feet long lifted out of the woods with an armoured rider perched on its back. She marvelled at the sight, viewing it from the ground like this, and for this fragile moment as an ally not an enemy. They were fleet, jewelled anachronisms, those beasts—far nimbler than a flying machine, but what could the rider's lance or bow do against Taki's vessel's metal hide?

There were more insects in the air by now, all circling and hovering. She saw Drevane Sae's own mount take flight, identifiable by the emerald banner streaming behind his saddle. From the water the ugly, blackened hulk that was Hawkmoth's *Bleakness*, most infamous pirate vessel of a piratical age, was planing over the wave-tips, fighting for height.

"Luck." The word was spoken briefly by its owner passing her by. It was the Creev, the slave-mercenary of Chasme. She watched him climb up the spiny hull of his vicious-looking new fixed-wing *Nameless Warrior*, his previous *Mordant Fire* having been lost in a duel with the Wasps. Beyond him she saw the flash of the Fly-kinden te Frenna's red scarf as she dropped into the seat of her slender heliopter, the *Gadaway*. It came to Taki that this might be the last time she saw many of these people, whether friends, foes or strangers. She had brought them together and now she was sending them into war.

She let her own Art wings bring her out to the *Esca Volenti* as it bobbed just off the shoreline, and then started the clockwork of its engine determinedly, trying to lose such mournful thoughts in the comfort of her old routines. Her elegant orthopter leapt from the waters in a spray of silver, passing up and up through the strata of carefully circling machines and beasts, and flung itself like an arrow across the waters toward Solarno, with a train of others following immediately in her wake.

The Empire had found a scapegoat in the local branch of the Demarial family, former supporters of the Path of Jade. With most of that family's Aristoi having fled to Porta Mavralis, the Wasps had simply seized their expansive townhouse with its prime view over the Galand Square and the bay. The new imperial governor himself intended to live there in style, it was clear, and the gesture had even brought a measure of approval from the Solarnese.

Galand Square was full today, the people of Solarno jostling shoulder to shoulder and Fly-kinden roosting on the three outsized martial statues that the square was famous for. One of those trespassing Flies, a bald, lump-faced creature, was doing his best not to keep glancing behind him at the glittering waters of the Exalsee.

Nero felt as tense as he had ever been. The hammer was about to fall—or at least that was the plan. He had to take it on faith that the hammer was poised at all. There were so many pieces to come together and, although he was high up here, sitting like a privileged child on the shoulders of the great stone soldier, he could see none of them. Even the Wasp governor had yet to show himself. The balcony—and perhaps the confiscation of this house had been solely to acquire that great balcony, so suited to public declamation—currently hosted a half dozen soldiers in heavy sentinel armour and two Fly-kinden slave-scribes, but nothing that resembled an officer, let alone whichever imperial colonel would be governing here.

Finally the game was about to begin. Nero had spent the last two days urging people into position by sheer force of will. Jemeyn and Wen, and the other Solarnese who were willing to take up arms, were split into bands of ten and twenty now within a quick dash of the square. Odyssa and her Scorpion mercenaries were on ships out in the bay, equipped with a telescope and a Solarnese artificer to use it, closely watching Galand Square for the signal. Somewhere out across the waters, Taki and the other free pilots were waiting. The frustration in *seeing* none of it was maddening.

Nero, old boy, you're only an artist. What are you doing starting revolutions?

Then there was Cesta, of course, who must already be lurking somewhere close, ready for whatever he intended to do to light the fuse here. A blade thrown from a good distance was Nero's guess, but first there would have to be the right target.

By now there were soldiers lining the square, marching forth with black and yellow pennants on their lances. Nero shifted his balance on the statue, resisting the urge to glance back toward the sea (were there black dots he could see, in the distance over it?) or to check that his dagger could be easily drawn through the buttons of his breeches. The incoming crowd, hustled together by roving Wasp soldiers to witness the new governor's inauguration, had already been searched for blades, but few Wasps were diligent enough to feel up the inside of a Fly-kinden man's thighs, especially one as grim looking as Nero.

The mood in the square was very quiet. Some spoke together in low voices, but many simply stared up at the imposing balcony or at the encircling soldiers. They were not taking their subjugation well, and today would be either kill or cure. Nero was willing to bet that there were more than a few hidden weapons among the crowd. The Wasps had not won any great love amongst the people here, nor was Nero the only player whose pieces were out of sight. Only the day before, a third of the Solarno garrison had simply packed up and marched north again. Rumour said that the siege of the Spider-kinden city of Seldis was dragging, despite the Empire's mechanical might. Nero himself knew how the Spider-kinden dealt with sieges: assassination, mass poisonings, sabotage, infiltration and incitement, and all the time there would be mercenaries and Spider levies gathering to the south, along the Silk Road. The news had helped stoke the smoulder that was Solarno and he reckoned it was all about to catch ablaze.

Myna all over again. But of course he had not been there at Myna when the gates came down. He had carefully weighed up the odds, and then told them— Stenwold and Tisamon and Marius—that he wasn't game for it. After all, Fly-kinden were not noted for their warlike tendencies. It was the nature of his small kinden to bend before the storm. That was why they fitted in so well, why they had settled everywhere from Collegium to the Ant city-states and the heart of the Empire. But here in Solarno he had met a different breed of them: fighting Fly-kinden amongst the free pilots. One in particular, actually.

All this for a pretty face. But it was a very pretty face, and a lively manner, and though she was young enough to be his daughter, still he had been drawn to her like a moth to a flame. *I am, let's be honest here, too old for all of this, so if I'm going to start playing the young man in going to war, why not play him elsewhere too?*

The thought put a smile on his face, but it vanished as the governor appeared.

There were abruptly a dozen Wasp officers up there on the balcony, looking interchangeable in their armour and peering down at the resentful mass of their new subjects with disdain. Amongst them, only the governor had dressed for the occasion. Over his banded hauberk he wore open-fronted robes of black with gold trim, and from somewhere, doubtless some pillaged loot of a Solarnese Aristos, he had found himself a golden circlet.

Drama, Nero thought. *I can't deny that the man has drama.* He then realized that he did not even know the governor-to-be's name. *But you shouldn't be wearing that crown just yet . . .*

The governor was a broad-shouldered man, with greying hair, an imperial colonel whose loyal service had earned him this prestigious post. He went over to grip the balustrade, visibly scowling down at the brooding Solarnese below. His officers stood back, giving him the moment. Was this because they respected him as a commander, or because they did not want to draw the ire of the natives onto themselves? Nero shifted his balance again, aware of the dagger strapped to his thigh as though it were scorching him. The crowd had gone quite quiet, even the murmur of private thoughts expressed to a neighbour had ceased. Only the pounding surf of the Exalsee and the occasional clink of a soldier's armour broke the silence.

As the governor opened his mouth to speak, Cesta was magically there.

Nero never noticed whether he had leapt from a neighbouring building, or flew there, or even pushed his way through from the interior of the Demarial house, but he was suddenly there, dressed in the loose white garments of a Solarnese citizen and cutting the governor's throat in public. Perhaps it was the world's most witnessed assassination. Nero felt his jaw drop, and a shock eddied through the crowd as if recoiling away from the spray of blood that spattered the front rows of those watching like a benediction.

In his artist's heart, Nero yearned to capture that tableau: the colonel—never now to truly be the governor—arched back, the glitter of red hanging in the air, the lean man of uncertain race poised beside him on the balcony rail, the utter blank shock of the officers behind. Even as he appreciated it, the moment was gone, to be succeeded by the next.

With the governor's blood spotted across his pale clothing Cesta cried out "Solarno!" and his hands sprang alive with metal, hurling his blades even as the shocked sentinels lumbered toward him. Nero saw two men fall back, all their weight of armour no protection against a narrow dart through the eyeslit. A lance drove for the assassin, but he used it as a step to cast himself upward and forward, toward the retreating officers. Nero saw a scatter of sting blasts explode around Cesta, at least one of which struck down a Wasp major by mistake, and then the assassin was amongst them. His blades sprang from his hands like steel rain, but it was the hands themselves that dealt death. Open, empty hands, yet some Art of Cesta's lost kinden made them killing things, passing through armour without a mark, slicing flesh like razors.

The crowd took over at that point. No swords but a sea of daggers, walking sticks or Art-bladed fists, and abruptly they were rushing the cordon of soldiers around them. The Wasp-kinden still possessed lances and stings, and the mob in Galand Square fell back from them and their wall of steel points, but a moment later Jemeyn and Wen, and all the others, had appeared at all the exits to the Square and immediately the Wasps were a thin line of men fighting on two fronts.

And word has gone to the garrison already, Nero knew. *More soldiers are coming, but let's hope they aren't the only ones.*

The fighting was all around him now and, though he had dragged his dagger out of concealment, he stayed clinging to the statue's stone head. The front doors of the Demarial house burst open and a wedge of imperial heavy infantry tore out into the crowd; just as the Wasp cordon on the east side of the square disintegrated entirely, and whole bundles of Solarnese curved swords were passed over into waiting hands—and still Nero had eyes only for Cesta.

Over half the Wasp officers were dead now, and most of the rest retreating into the house, frantic to get away from this madman and his bloody hands, but Nero was there to see the sentinel's lance drive into the assassin's back, finding a gap that no amount of luck or skill could quite cover. Cesta was slammed into the doorway and, even as he convulsed on the pike's end, his hand flicked out a knife that snapped the sentinel's head back, collapsing him to his knees.

He died in the doorway, did Cesta, his back turned to the great fighting scrum of people that he had set alight: impaled and scorched with Wasp fire, but still casting one last blade before he fell. In his mind was the sad knowledge that his kinden, his whole race and heritage, might wink out the moment he did.

Nero shuddered at the sight, and only then looked back out over the Exalsee, hearing in the very back of his mind the drone of engines. There he spotted the dark dots that were the flying machines of the free pilots casting themselves across the waters toward the beleaguered city of Solarno.

When the first message had reached the imperial garrison it was so garbled that they had not known what to make of it. Men were sent out on to the streets, others toward the governor's coronation. Then more word came in, and units of the Wasp army began to form, a coordinated march to clear Galand Square.

Lieutenant Axrad cared nothing for that activity. The moment word came, he had rallied his pilots and rushed for their commandeered airfield. He had sent word to the captain of the *Starnest*, still up above the city, to expect attack, and then he and his people had leapt to their machines. Some of them were being lifted aloft by the airships, able to drop gracefully into the air. Others, the better fliers, were making their awkward takeoff from the ground. Axrad flew to his own cockpit, there starting the engine and feeling the wings thrum so that the machine lurched and lifted as though hastily woken from sleep.

The ground fell away from him and he was free.

Axrad was not a model officer, but things were different in the flying corps. Five years earlier there had not even been such a division, but the Imperial Army was evolving rapidly. Three generations before they had been nothing but barbarians with spears and war cries. How they had evolved since then to produce Lieutenant Axrad, pilot, aerial duellist and sophisticate. Some foreigners thought that the Wasp's assurance of their own superiority would prevent them ever learning from the conquered, but that was not so. They saw the achievements of their subject peoples, and they thought: *We are superior to them, so we can do better.*

The rebels' attack had been sudden, but the assault force on Solarno was not composed as a normal imperial army. The need for a sudden strike to secure the city, once the Rekef operation had foundered, had required a conquest far swifter and more mobile than all that grinding artillery and slogging infantry. Launching an aerial attack had been a glorious and successful experiment.

Now let us see if we can hold on to what we have gained. The lifting blimps were now in the air—they had been held ready since the invasion, although it was originally anticipated that they would be carrying the airforce west toward Seldis and the Spiderlands to support the army there. Much of the infantry, which had come stomping into Solarno already too late for the conquest, had already stomped right out again, heading to reinforce the besieging of the Spider cities.

There were wings everywhere over the city. Axrad tried a quick count. *More than forty flying machines* he saw. The numbers would be tight. Under normal circumstances, the air fight would be over by now, the imperial machines destroyed in their hangars by the sudden strike but, as the airforce had been kept ready to leave the city, every machine had already been in a position to launch.

Behind and above him the sleek and massive bulk of the great dirigible *Starnest* blotted out the sky. She had nowhere near her complement of soldiers, for they were on the ground already or had marched out days ago, but there were enough engineers to man her weapon emplacements: leadshotters and bombards to thunder into the city, and nimble repeating ballistas to take on the Solarnese aircraft.

Axrad himself had been busy these last few days, not through conquering zeal but from professional curiosity. Flanking the nose of his craft were two rotary piercers, the firepowder weapons that the Solarnese pilots preferred, which were more powerful than the mechanically assisted ballistae the Wasp vessels normally sported.

The Fly-kinden Taki would be amongst that crescent of fliers that was even now sweeping over the Exalsee. He hoped he would spot her *Esca Volenti*. He owed her a final duel.

If she falls, it should be by my hand, and with respect, he thought. *If I fall, I would rather it be due to one of her skill.* Axrad had no room in his own head for the mantra of racial superiority that drove the Empire to conquest. He was one of that strange new breed combining soldier and artificer and aviator, a fighting pilot. Skill in the air was the sole qualification for respect in his world, and he did not care what colour of skin or physical frame came with it.

They were all in the air now, clawing for height or already dropping from the lifting blimps. The Imperial Airforce, the daring innovation that had taken Solarno, was about to defend it against all comers.

The free pilots came barrelling in from over the Exalsee with engines ablaze. The battle for the skies of Solarno had begun.

Below them the battle for the streets, the houses, the city proper, would have to be left to the amateur forces of the resistance, the Path of Jade, Odyssa and her Scorpion-kinden mercenaries. They and the Wasp heavy infantry would now grind through Solarno, skirmish after skirmish, until either the spirit went out of the locals or the Imperials cut their losses.

If the Empire gained control of the sky then the rebellion would be over before it began. Just as with the invasion, the Wasp airborne would then be able to descend anywhere across the city with sword and sting, picking the resistance off bit by bit, stopping the Solarnese from unifying. It was Taki's job to contest the skies with them.

An airborne Empire. She saw now what she should have seen before: how it was that the Wasps had grown so powerful. They had all the fighting spirit of the Solarnese or the Ant-kinden, but they had the air as well, in which to give full rein to it. *If only we Flies were fighters by nature, we'd be masters of the world.*

Ahead she saw the long grey bulk of the *Starnest*'s airbag as the great vessel lifted higher. They had all agreed that it must be their target, beyond all else. They even had a plan, or at least some cobbled-together flimsy sort of thing that passed for one. What with the natural enemies that Taki had under her command, it was the best that they could manage.

She was approaching it fast, but it just kept growing. She had not appreciated the sheer scale of the vessel as it rose sluggishly into the air. The smaller carriers were already well above it, and she hauled back on the stick to take the *Esca Volenti* up toward them, meanwhile starting the motor of her rotary. In order to down the *Starnest*, they would have to cut through the enemy flying machines, and that was what she and the nimbler of the pilots would now be doing.

The air shuddered, a thunder felt in the sudden tremor of her controls before she actually heard it, and the weapons of the *Starnest* opened up on them. She saw gouts of powder smoke from the leadshotters and, to her left, one of the Creev's mercenary pilots was smashed to splinters, going without transition from a darting heliopter to a . . . a nothing, within a mere second. It was a lucky strike for the Wasps, since the leadshotters had never been meant as weapons against fliers. There were rapid-firing ballistas there, too, swivel mounted to cover all angles, and, although they were still clumsy hammers to bring to bear on a swift flyer, Taki knew there would be losses to them also before this was out.

She was now coursing up across the grey vastness of the *Starnest's* flank, while above her were Wasp flying machines dropping from their carriers and falling toward the Solarnese vessels.

Right.

Her first target had not even seen her, simply an unwary pilot who still thought he was the predator and not the prey. Just as the Wasp jockeyed his orthopter into position for a shot at one of her colleagues, Taki let her rotary spin and simply ripped the underside of his vessel out from under him. He lurched in the air, dropping sideways with engines still running, so that she realized that one of her shots must have reached the pilot himself. Beneath the whir of her own engines and the concussive bang of the rotating piercer his descent toward the city was silent.

All around, her attacking fleet of fliers had split off to tackle the Wasps in individual duel. In the moment's grace before she found her next target, Taki saw the iron-clad bulk of the Creev's *Nameless Warrior* clip one of the Wasp fliers in passing, suffering barely a shudder but sending the smaller enemy ship spinning. Meanwhile Niamedh's *Executrix* lanced through a scatter of circling ships with rotaries blazing.

There were men in the air as well, for the Wasps had sent up some of the light airborne to support their airships. That was a tactical mistake, Taki knew. Men and machines did not go well against each other, pitching small and agile targets against swift hulls that were proof against their little weapons. She was glad of it: the more soldiers despatched impotently into the sky left fewer that could do real damage on the ground.

She flung the *Esca* straight through a crowd of them, scattering Wasp soldiers left and right, but then a shadow swept over her and, craning back she spotted a gap, a hole in their formation that the others were still reeling away from. Just then a second shape passed her, and she recognized the sleek lines of a hunting dragonfly, a creature that was born to take live prey in the air. A red and gold banner fluttered alongside the arrow-straight length of its tail, and she caught a glimpse of its rider, one of Drevane Sae's people, turning back to loose an arrow even as the beast clutched a victim to itself.

Taki sent the *Esca Volenti* across the sky, leaving the plume of a failing Wasp flier to fall behind her. It was as if her mind was split in two. One part continued to grip the controls and sent her darting through the cluttered skies, hunting targets, striking at Wasp pilots and evading their reprisals, and all the time trying to find a clear path toward the *Starnest* in order to bring the giant dirigible down. But there was another part of her that had gone numb, for she had never seen aerial war conducted on this scale. It seemed unthinkable.

Te Frenna's elegant *Gadaway* lay shredded across a forty-foot extent of the city, unrecognizable now, the fate of its pilot unknown. A downed Wasp craft had rammed the five-hundred-year-old Celenza gallery, which was now in flames, only one of a dozen fires across the city. The fighters on the ground were in constant danger from a sporadic rain of broken machines, dead men and crippled insects. This was a horror surely never meant to be inflicted on her poor home.

The *Esca* turned on her wingtip, and she found another Wasp vessel cutting through the air before her. Its twinned repeating ballistas were already loosing, and she saw a Solarnese fixed-wing abruptly shudder in the air as the bolts struck. It was Scobraan's heavy *Mayfly Prolonged* and Taki realized that her friend was making his own run at the *Starnest* now, either tired of waiting or spotting some chance she had overlooked. She unleashed the fury of her rotary on the Wasp, seeing her enemy falter, then dive and dart away to try and escape her, abandoning its prey. She swung into line behind it, matching swoop for swoop, unhurried and cool-headed, whilst her stomach sank in worry over the fate of Scobraan as he dived in toward the gigantic airship.

One of her bolts struck the enemy engine, and she saw the smoke start to billow. The Wasp began to lose height as quickly as he could, and then she saw the pilot kick the cockpit open and throw himself over one side, wings unfurling to catch him. She broke off immediately, and just then the *Esca* took three solid strikes from behind, two piercing the canvas of the craft's wings, and a third slamming into the fuselage two feet behind her. Taki dived low, almost clipping the tumbling ship she had just dispatched, but a quick glance back showed that her pursuer was still with her, its ballistas ratcheting out bolts with mechanical precision. She hauled the *Esca* up into the sky, as steeply as she dared, knowing that she was thereby making a target of herself. Another bolt nipped past her, causing her to flinch.

Taki released her first chute, cutting it free entirely and sending the *Esca* wide. The Wasp was too close behind her, and the silk of the chute was in his wings before he could avoid it, snarling them, stopping them, and turning him from a flying machine into just another weight to plummet into Solarno.

She looked desperately around for Scobraan and spotted the *Mayfly* as just a small shape against the grey wall of the *Starnest*'s airbag. She sent the *Esca* scudding across to help him. Airships were notoriously difficult to bring down and, unless the Wasps were notably bad at their craft, it would take a thousand little bolts to pierce that bag enough to make the ship lose even a foot of height. The material would simply contract about each tiny puncture, every needle wound nearly sealed almost in the moment of its making.

Scobraan's *Mayfly* hurled itself straight at a Wasp orthopter, breaking the nerve of the pilot, who let his machine drop away rather than clash head-to-head with the big, armoured fixed-wing. Scobraan brought his craft as close as he dared to the *Starnest*'s fabric, until it seemed to Taki that he was skimming across it, that he should be leaving ripples in his wake.

Flame gouted from the *Mayfly*'s aft, indicating the firethrowers that Scobraan was so proud of, for what punctures could not do to damage an airbag fire would invariably accomplish, shrivelling the material to nothing. Taki felt her heart leap for joy at the sight.

But the *Starnest* remained untouched, no more than a long soot mark to tell of Scobraan's passage. *Some new material*, she reflected numbly, some stuff that would not burn. It seemed the Wasp artificers had outmanoeuvred them.

Then there was a Wasp pursuing Scobraan, darting around the *Starnest*'s bulk to fall in line behind him. Taki saw the *Mayfly* break off quickly, trusting to its armour to shrug off the shot of the nimbler craft, but then the Wasp opened up with its paired rotaries—pillaged Solarnese weaponry—and the *Mayfly* jerked in the air, losing height.

Taki was already diving to intervene, sending the *Esca* in as fast as her wings could beat, but the Wasp kept his line perfect, sending bolt after bolt punching into the *Mayfly*'s frame as Scobraan tried to throw him off. Then abruptly Scobraan was not trying any more, and the *Mayfly Prolonged* was simply dipping, nose-heavy, toward the ground.

Axrad, Taki realized. The Wasp fliers were all painted alike but she recognized the way he moved in the air, his unique style and skill.

She slung the *Esca* toward him. It was time to conclude their business.

TWENTY-FIVE

It was well before dawn but General Malkan had his slaves dress him in his full armour. This was a state occasion, he decided. He would be the representative of the Empire speaking with a foreign power, even a captured and humbled one, so it would do to look the part. He had unpacked his suit of partial plate mail, enamelled black and edged with gold, to go over the lightweight hauberk of fine chain made to his personal specifications by the Beetle smiths of Sonn. He had his best sword, with the gilded pommel, buckled to his belt, and held his helm beneath his arm. After all, there was no shame in appearing gracious in victory.

"Have the man brought in," he instructed, once the last buckle had been tightened. The armour was well made enough that its weight barely slowed him, distributed evenly across his shoulders as though it was nothing more than a scout's light brigandine. His slaves retreated from his tent without needing any order, and two soldiers then marched in with the captive.

Malkan studied him: a Commonwealer, which confirmed the rumours and gave cause for thought. He was a young man, with his kind's slender build and a steady gaze despite the broad bruise spreading across half of his face. His hands were bound behind him, but he stood straight and tall like a visiting officer come to inspect the troops. Malkan decided that in other circumstances he might have liked this man. As it was, he did not have that luxury.

"So you're the one they call the . . . what is it? The 'Wasted Prince'?"

"I can't vouch for what your people call me," Salma replied. He had found a curious calm within him, now his run of fortune was finally at an end. Had he not been here before, in the custody of the Wasps? Of course he had, and worse, too. He had even died outside the walls of Tark, had he not? Then all this was just borrowed time. It was all credit he had accrued with the world, and if the world now called on him to pay his debts, how could he complain? "You are General Malkan, I take it."

The Wasp general made the smallest nod but Salma, looking him in the eyes, saw the faintest disquiet there, a tiny worm gnawing at the man's contentment.

"You have a name?" Malkan asked him.

"Prince Minor Salme Dien, enforcedly at your service," Salma informed him, managing a moderately accomplished bow.

"You really are a prince, then." Malkan had witnessed the last convulsions of the Twelve-Year War, for as the youngest general of the Empire, most of that glorious, costly campaign had preceded him. He recognized the Commonwealer title, though. "Renegade, are you, then? Exiled?"

The suspicion already in Salma's mind began to solidify. "Not at all, General. Still a proud son of the Commonweal, I'm afraid."

Malkan regarded him without expression. "A little out of your way, aren't you?"

"We go where the Monarch commands."

"I don't believe your Monarch has ever heard of the city of Sarn. I don't believe it's even marked on the Commonwealer maps."

Salma was staring straight into the man's eyes, and he saw that small flicker again. *He's here in person talking to me, and he's got up as gaudy as a Spider whore, but he's not telling me how wonderful his Empire is and how defeated I am. Somehow I've thrown him off his course.* He took a deep breath and smiled casually, as though he and the Wasp were merely standing in Collegium debating philosophy. "Mercers are always allowed a little initiative, General, in how we go about fulfilling our orders."

The moment's pause told Salma that the lie, the outright abject lie, had registered. Malkan obviously knew of the Mercers, and imagined them, no doubt, as some kind of Dragonfly Rekef.

"Well, perhaps I should send your head back to your Monarch, to show him how he has failed," Malkan declared and, without that pause before, he would have sounded entirely confident.

"What failure would that be?" Salma asked him.

"Your 'Landsarmy' is scattered and mostly slain," Malkan replied. Salma knew that he must have flinched at that news, for he saw his reaction mirrored in the other man's eyes. "I have you, to do with as I wish, to enslave or kill or send to the Emperor himself as a trophy. You have failed."

"But you were speaking of the Monarch, not of myself." Salma kept his voice steady, hoping that Malkan was painting the situation darker than it really was. "The protection of the Lowlands from imperial aggression is not a task to be entrusted to only *one* man."

Malkan stopped, again just for a moment, but Salma noticed it. The thought of a dozen, a score, a hundred Mercers, infiltrating the Lowlands, raising scrap armies as Salma had done—the tactical implications unfolded in Malkan's mind.

If I can achieve nothing else now, let me crack his confidence. Words were all Salma had left in the way of weapons. He would not spare them.

"Well, we shall question you at leisure about whatever comrades you have," Malkan decided. "Being a Commonwealer, you will be unfamiliar with our methods of questioning, so I shall have my artificers introduce you."

Beneath Salma's feet, the earth shifted slightly, very slightly. He had only soft shoes on, and most likely Malkan would have felt nothing through the soles of his armoured boots. Behind his back, Salma flexed his fingers. "General?"

"You have some other vague threat for me?" Malkan asked him.

Salma's thumb claws flicked out, digging into the ropes about his wrists. The angle was awkward, but he drove them in as hard as he could. "You forget two things."

"Do I, now?" Malkan asked, irritated, but paused for just a moment more. "And what would they be?"

"You will have to discover that for yourself," Salma said, every bit the picture of the mysterious Commonwealer, and when Malkan signalled for the two guards to take him, he concentrated all his strength into his arms, his hands and his thumbs, and flexed them.

The rope sheared and his hands sprang free, just as the whole of the earth floor within the tent bucked once and then burst open.

General Malkan was thrown off balance, but already grabbing for his sword's hilt as the ground split. A monstrous form hauled its broad-shouldered bulk out of the ground, and for a moment, in the explosion of dust, it was impossible to see just what it was. The two guards that Malkan had kept to hand did not need to know precisely what was attacking their general, though. One was already raising a hand toward Salma even as the ropes gave way. The other drew his sword and threw himself forward with a kind of blind courage, not risking a sting shot with Malkan so close.

It was Morleyr, of course. Morleyr the Auxillian deserter whose squad Salma had talked into defecting. Morleyr the Mole Cricket-kinden giant who could dig through the earth with his bare hands.

His hands were not bare now, though. The soldier that rushed at him, into the cloud of dust, met the upswing of a mace blow intended for Malkan. Salma heard bones snap as its heavy iron head struck the man through the ribs. Salma was already moving, casting himself to the left as the crackling bolt of energy seared past, and then jabbing with his thumbs, going for the throat but tearing a bloody line across the soldier's face instead as he reeled back.

Malkan's sword was now clear but there were others emerging after Morleyr, coughing and choking but armed with short swords and daggers. They were a handful of Salma's people dragging themselves out of the darkness . . .

No, not dark, for there was light down there. Salma's chest contracted at even the brief glimpse he had of it.

No! Not here! He lunged forward, got a hand about the soldier's sword wrist, trying to prise the weapon free. The man backed out of the tent into the night, stumbling through the flap, colliding with another man who rushed in and just managed to say, "General Malkan—" before he was bowled over. The soldier Salma was grappling with tripped, and the contested sword was driven deep into his chest as Salma fell on top of him.

There was no time to waste. Salma got his hands around the hilt of the stunned new arrival's blade and drew it clear; easier to pluck a sword from a scabbard than from a man's ribs. The messenger goggled at him and Salma gritted his teeth and drove the sword into the man's throat. Honour was like a coat: sometimes one did not have time to put it on.

He spun back toward the tent, seeing Morleyr aim another great sweep of the mace at General Malkan. Mole Crickets were monstrously strong, but also ponderously slow, and Malkan drove his sword forward once, twice, in the time it took Morleyr to strike. The first lunge carved into the great man's side and his blade came out spilling red, but the second went up to the hilt in Morleyr's armpit, making the Mole Cricket cry out in shock. Then the huge body was collapsing, sword still deeply embedded, and by then Malkan had a knife in his other hand and had slit the tent behind him. Another man, Salma could not see which of his followers it was, lunged at the general with a dagger, but Malkan grabbed his wrist almost contemptuously and then stabbed him in the eye before backing out of the command tent altogether.

Salma darted out of the tent and pursued him with sword in hand. Within the tent, the light was growing ever brighter and he did not want to see her here in this place where death was moments away in any direction. *But of course, how else could Morleyr have found me, save by her?*

This was not the plan. A mad rescue was not the plan. We're right in the middle of their army! But the army currently seemed to have other things on its mind. Soldiers were everywhere, but they were all heading somewhere else, and most of them were running toward the western edge of the camp. It occurred to Salma suddenly that, of course, this was the plan after all.

The Sarnesh possessed their own time-keeping machine to count the moments for them. They would have sprung up, every one of them, at a single thought, and begun their approach. Dawn had not begun to lighten the eastern sky, and already the Sarnesh assault had reached the Wasp camp.

The dust-coated fighters Morleyr had brought with him were now spilling out from the tent, twenty of them at least, a chaotic rabble raggedly engaging any black and gold that they could find. General Malkan grabbed a passing sergeant, shouting orders at him, dragging the man's sword from his hand. Before the sergeant could pass on the word Salma was on them both. Distantly he heard the roar of field artillery, a leadshotter loosing its shot, the tremble of the ground as a catapult missile landed. Salma jammed his sword in under the sergeant's arm, swiftly and cleanly, dragged it clear and turned toward Malkan.

That he was amazed meant only that Balkus had been away from his own kind too long.

When the moment came, every Sarnesh in the camp had woken simultaneously by virtue of the tactician's call to arms. Balkus himself had leapt up, snapped instantly from his sleep, hauling on his chain mail by old instinct, in exact step with thousands of Sarnesh soldiers.

By the time he had the hauberk on, he had come fully to his senses. He had first kicked awake Parops and Plius, thus wrenching their entire detachments from sleep into instant wakefulness. Then he had run about amongst his own men, shouting and striking them, telling them to go and wake others. They would be the anchor dragging at the attack, he realized. The last to be ready, the last to get in line. Still, his urgency got through to them, and they strapped on their armour as swiftly as they could, readied their snapbows and crossbows and pikes. Beyond them, Balkus saw the Moth and Mantis-kinden warriors spreading out to take up their staggered skirmish line ahead of the army. By day there had been Wasp scouts lurking nearby, keeping an eye on the Sarnesh force. By the time Balkus' men had assembled they would all be dead.

The Sarnesh fell smoothly into place by their nature and instinct. Balkus meanwhile was left shouting and harassing his people to do the same, hearing them blunder into one another in the dark. Then the Sarnesh were moving. He heard the command in his mind, called it out to his men. It was still night but they were bringing the war to the Wasps.

Ant-kinden could not see in the dark, of course. They were like Wasp-kinden in that, and the Wasps knew it. Their scouts had already noted the approach of the Sarnesh force. The morrow, everyone knew, would see the opposing forces close enough to do battle.

Ant-kinden were constantly within each others' minds, though: it was a much-vaunted ability. It made them fight as one, defending each other, seeing through each others' eyes. The more obvious applications of the mindlink were well known. It also allowed for a certain degree of logistics that other kinden could not match. In this case it allowed for 10,000 Sarnesh soldiers to move out from their camp some hours before dawn, in perfect order, and march on the Wasp encampment. It had never been done before, but then the threat posed by the Empire was just as unprecedented. The Sarnesh King and his tacticians had quietly made their decision the previous day, and the entire army had instantly known and understood.

The logistics, though! Ten thousand men in the dark of a clouded night, but each one with an absolute knowledge of where his neighbours were and where his feet were going, so that not an elbow jostled, not a foot was trodden on. They had muddied their armour, smeared lampblack on their blades. For a vast mass of heavy infantry they moved absurdly quietly, not a word spoken or needed, just the gentle clink of mail.

In advance of them, in the air and on the ground, went their screen of skirmishers: scores of Mantis warriors from the Ancient League, Moth-kinden archers, Flies, men and women to whom the dark was no barrier, sent ahead to find and silence the Wasp scouts and pickets. They were utterly silent, invisible by skill and Art and the cloak of night. They were merciless, killing by arrow or blade without warning, without fail. General Malkan had not stinted on his scouts, supplementing his own people's poor eyes with the keener vision of Fly-kinden and fielding enough watchmen to give him every warning of raid or ambush, and not one of them lived to report to him.

And then there was Balkus and the other allies who were here, but whom nobody knew what to do with. After plans were laid, the tacticians had found themselves with three commanders that had no obvious place in their scheme, but whose numbers were such that it would be imprudent to leave them out. They had in the end given the right flank to Balkus: the trailing right flank that straggled back behind the main line of advance in case some Beetle loudly fell over his neighbour. Here were Parops' Tarkesh expatriates and the little contingent of Tseni that Plius had called for. Here were the Collegium merchant companies, with their snapbows at the ready, and nailbowmen interspersed throughout in case the Wasps got too close.

The Collegium contingent did not have a mindlink to keep them together and, as they drew closer, Balkus could not risk shouting at them the way an officer of such a rabble would normally need to. He was uncomfortably aware that they were getting strung out, unable to match the brisk pace that the Sarnesh had set, but there was nothing he could do about it. He would just have to trust that not too many of them would get lost. At least, back here, they were not likely to sound any alarms.

In Balkus' own head were the Sarnesh officers. He had tried to block them out, but it was a constant rattle of orders and reports, relaying information he needed to know. It had been a long time since he had counted himself a son of Sarn but the wider family had closed about him seamlessly. He was dragged along with their advance, hearing the tacticians convey out their orders to adjust the facing of the line, to increase the pace, and hearing the reports come back from the officers at the front—enemy scouts down, the lights of the camp now in sight.

When the word came to charge, Balkus found that his pace picked up instantly and without question, so that he almost left the men under his command behind in the dark. Those nearest him hurried to catch up, and so the unspoken order to run was passed back simply through people finding themselves being out-distanced by those in front of them. Out there in the dark thousands of swords had been unsheathed, while crossbows were cocked on the run.

He sensed the precise moment that the Wasp camp, as an organism, became aware of the attack, seeing a sudden, vast and unheralded rush of movement in the torchlight, the sentries already falling to arrow shot. It was as though, for just a second, the Wasps themselves partook of the great Sarnesh mind, if only to register a brief surprise.

Then the Sarnesh line thundered into the Wasp encampment, braving the first scatter of sting shot, breaking the fragile shell formed by the sentries to get at the meat within.

"All right let's go!" Balkus yelled to his people, to Parops and Plius, his whole ragged command. "Form an archery line on me!" And with that he was off, running and not waiting for them. They would have to catch up with him, and already he was sending a thought out—*Where do you want us?*—abandoning himself to the greater mind.

The general was shouting desperately at the nearest Wasp soldiers as they rushed by, trying to reestablish his authority. Salma rushed him just as another member of the dusty rabble did—a stocky Beetle-kinden woman wielding a simple work-shop hammer. Malkan rounded on her furiously, swayed aside from the heavy stroke, and then loosed a sting shot into her face, blasting her backward. Salma drove his sword into the general's side, but the man's heavy mail turned the blow. Reeling from the force of it, Malkan was spun half-around, but then his blade came lashing back at Salma, trying to gain room.

Salma kept with him, almost inside the reach of their swords, knowing that if he fell back then Malkan would scorch him. He managed a glancing gash across the man's face with one thumb, and jabbed up with his sword, though too close to put any force into it. The tip dug between Malkan's armour plates but there was chain mail beneath to catch it. Salma caught a glimpse of the Wasp's expression, twisted in fury with blood smeared across it. Then the general's shoulder slammed into Salma's chest, knocking him backward. He expected the lash of the man's sting, but instead Malkan was coming at him sword-first, the short, swift blade dancing and swooping in the gap between them. Salma fell back before the first three swings, and then caught the next on his own weapon, trying a riposte that Malkan instantly turned back on him. The Wasp kept his attack going, for a moment forgetting both his army and his rank, becoming just one duellist intent on the death of another. Salma picked up the rhythm: it had been a long time since he had fought one-on-one like this. Malkan's offence was savage, leaving almost no gap for Salma to get a blade through.

He's good, he's good. Salma flung himself up, wings flaring, arcing overhead and coming down behind the man, sword striking backward to take him as he turned. Malkan was faster, catching the blow but not strongly enough to counterattack. Salma took the lead now, lunging and cutting, always moving his feet, darting left and right or flicking up with a moment's rush of his wings. Malkan's armour, which had turned so many blows, now slowed him down. He could not match Salma for speed. Even defending, he still kept his poise, slowly turning the tide, letting Salma wear himself out against Malkan's immaculate parries until he had an opening to strike. Salma's blade pierced his guard once, to dent his pauldron and bound away, and Malkan took this opening smoothly. His blade lanced narrowly past Salma as the Dragonfly threw himself aside, and then Malkan's off-hand blazed with golden fire.

The bolt was badly aimed, hurried. It seared across Salma's shoulder and side rather than smashing into his chest, but it was enough to make him reel, stumbling over the corpse of the Beetle-kinden woman, and Malkan drove forward with a snarl of triumph.

His sword blazed with white fire, the night around them as bright as noon. The blade drove beneath Salma's ribs with all the force that Malkan could give it.

She had gone by many names already. It was the custom of her kind to don a new name as easily as a new garment, to suit fresh circumstance. She had been Free of Lilies and Soaring Fire. She had been Grief in Chains and Aagen's Joy. And most recently she had been Prized of Dragons, and the lover of Prince Minor Salme Dien.

Her kind were strange and few, living in remote places, secluded glades throughout the Commonweal and beyond. They lived off the sun's own light, and had no needs or cares save when others found them. They were coveted, taken, forced, enslaved. They were the bright cousins of the Moth-kinden, too shining and beautiful for others to contemplate without wanting to possess them. When they were enslaved, though, they brought a trail of ruin, being passed from hand to hand, stolen, bought in blood, becoming the cause of fights and murders and the sundering of friends and brothers. It was only from other kinden, and their small and greedy minds, that they learnt of such things as sadness.

Salma had been different. Salma had been an island in the raging sea of anger and fear and lust. Salma had brought back to her an awareness of the nobility of his people, the one people that the Butterfly-kinden consented to live amongst. But Salma had a flaw, in that his nobility had driven him to a desperate, violent course.

She had known it would end like this, but she had led Morleyr and the others here anyway, desperate to find him in time to snatch him from the claws of the Empire, to rescue him as she had rescued him before the walls of Tark. Freed now from the earth, from the tunnel that Morleyr had crafted with his own hands; freed from the general's tent and rising with flaming wings above the fighting that spread out from it, she saw him.

He had fallen to his knees just then, and the Wasp was dragging the blade out, and she felt, in her own soul, the life that was Salme Dien wink out—cut to the heart, dead on the instant—and beyond even her powers to bring back.

She had already learnt many terrible things from the Empire and its subject peoples. She had learnt of betrayal and need and contempt, bigotry and vice. She had learnt hate and rage, but never until now had she experienced these emotions herself. There came surging through her something monstrous, roaring and screeching. There was a voice in her mind and it was crying out for something her kind had never known before.

Vengeance! it screamed, and she was powerless against it, battered by the storm of feeling that was now blowing her from the sky down toward General Malkan.

She saw him look up, shielding his eyes. Beyond him, the Wasp soldiers were no longer rushing frenziedly backward and forward, but instead were staring only at her. She was used to that, to attracting such attention. The massed eyes of five hundred men were no obstacle to her. Her attention was on Malkan only.

She saw him take a step away, stumbling, the sword becoming loose in his hands, falling from his grip.

She *screamed*, and let her Art fly from her, all of it, using Art that no other kinden could know. So the Empire had taught her how to hate, at last, and she would teach them something in turn.

Balkus took his men forward another twenty yards, and by now they dutifully formed their two ranks of archery line around him without needing to be told. The battle was going raggedly, messily, for not even the Sarnesh mindlink could force this predawn fight to run smoothly. The Wasps had rallied swiftly along the far edge of the line, and now there was a solid block of soldiers opposing the centre, composed of imperial sentinels and heavy infantry with a circling screen of the light airborne. The Sarnesh advance had ground to a halt.

Losing our advantage. The surprise and momentum that had carried them this far was fast disappearing. The attackers' losses were mounting and Balkus was acutely aware that his detachment was due for a hammering if the Wasps actually threw a counterattack his way. Parops' Tarkesh soldiers were keeping a line of shields braced against the stings and flagging snapbow bolts that arced over, thus giving cover to Balkus' snapbowmen. However the Wasp line was growing longer by the minute, as more of their men ran to the front. Now, Balkus had Plius' men making a line down his formation's right flank, taking up where Parops' shields left off and watching the imperial lines extend ever further to flank them. The

Tseni agent, squeezed into hastily refitted armour, was white-faced and sweating. He had been a long time as a civilian in Sarn.

Balkus shook his head, whilst around him the snapbowmen of Collegium loosed their shots, scattering the Wasp line as it tried to form up. The Mantis warband that had been on his far right had been scythed down almost to a man by an enemy snapbow volley, and a moment earlier he had felt in his mind the sudden flare and silence that had signified a leadshot ball ploughing through twenty ranks of Sarnesh soldiers.

But where in the wastes is their real artillery? Apart from the leadshotter, and a lone catapult somewhere toward the rear of the enemy's camp, there had been nothing so far, not even war-automotives. *Does that mean Salma actually pulled it off?*

The order came just then. *Commander Balkus, your men to loose on the Wasp centre.*

What about our flank? Balkus demanded, but then realized that the thought had remained in his head. He could not question the order. Obedience was too deeply bred in him. The Wasps across from him were already finding the range, so that Parops' men were taking a battering. Balkus turned his attention to the solid mass of heavy infantry at the centre, and saw that they were about to press forward.

We are dead, he realized—another thought he was keeping to himself—and then he shouted, "With me!" and rushed to get in range of the Wasps, taking advantage of the space that opened up between Parops and the Sarnesh main force.

A snapbow bolt, at the limit of its range, jammed into his mail with a spark of pain but he ignored it, knowing that his men were following him, and that enough of them were bright enough to know what a bad idea this was. The Wasp left flank, which had been trading shot with his men, suddenly began to pull together, to seize the opportunity. Without being asked, Plius' contingent moved their shield wall to take the brunt of them as they came.

"Throw everything you've got into those lads!" Balkus shouted out in a real battlefield bellow. The men and women of Collegium fell into place around him as though they were professionals, and not just a rabble of tradesmen, merchants and adventurers. Their expressions, Beetle and Fly and Ant and many others, were fixed and blank, concentrating on the task in hand while blotting out the carnage around them. It was only their second battle, and this time they had no walls to stand behind.

The Wasp centre surged forward, and Balkus' snapbowmen opened up almost as one. The closest corner of the Wasp formation crumpled instantly, sending a shock from man to man, so that the far side was still moving, but out of step, and the near side was at a standstill. In this second of confusion, the Sarnesh began charging them, thundering forward shield to shield, whilst the men of the second rank loosed their crossbows and snapbows directly into the faces of the enemy line.

"They're coming!" Plius bellowed, drawing his blade for the first time. The

Wasp left wing, heedless of what was happening at their centre, was rushing them, both on the ground and in the air. Balkus watched his own people reloading all around him, and knew they would be in time for one more round.

"And loose!" and they did, raking through the spread formation of light airborne and infantry. The Tseni soldiers braced themselves, with shields overlapping, and the Wasps struck them head on. Between Balkus and the Tseni, Parops' men were ready waiting, cutting into place like the blades of shears to trap the Wasps between their shields and those of Plius' contingent. To Parops' left, there were only the Collegium irregulars to hold the line.

"Nailbows!" Balkus roared, and took his own up from its strap, emptying it rapidly into the charging Wasps. The roar of the weapons from all around him told him that his order had been heard, and for a moment the Wasp charge was down to nothing, as though a great fist had struck them still. Then they were coming on again, and Balkus had his sword drawn whilst his band of militia were taking up their shields and maces, axes and spears, with the pikes thrusting in from the second and third ranks. The Tseni line buckled abruptly, no longer enough of them left to hold. The shock of impact recoiled into Parops' shield wall, as the Wasps drove a wedge between him and Balkus' men. Plius died without ever striking a blow.

From behind the Wasps, from within their camp, came a sudden, soundless explosion.

It was light only, with no force: a monstrous wash of white light. Balkus reeled back, covering his eyes, hearing a few sounds of metal on metal, the scream of a man wounded. The Wasps had meanwhile faltered, scattering within feet of their targets, pulling back. Balkus, still blinking, saw them looking around, their officers trying to find out what had just happened.

Something was burning within the Wasp camp—no, not burning, something was *alight*. Hanging in the air was a human shape, but one so bright that it hurt the eyes. The Wasps closer to it had all turned toward it, but were now pushing away. The light was so bright that Balkus could see every detail beneath it. This was not bright like day. No day had ever been so harshly radiant.

There was a figure directly before that light, and Balkus swore in awe and fear because the man standing there was burning, flaming incandescent. His very armour was glowing white-hot with the focus of that terrible light. This was Art, Balkus realized, but Art that he had never seen before, and never wanted to see again. The man was staggering, flailing, and yet he still faced the searing, glowing creature before him, the light so excruciating that he could not draw himself away from it, even as his armour melted on his boiling skin.

And there was a flare, another tidal wave of light ripping through the Wasp army, so that those closest to the fire, those that had turned to see what it was, screamed and clutched at their eyes and fell to the ground.

And it was gone, and the torches and lanterns of the Wasp camp barely touched the utter dark, but the Sarnesh were in one another's minds and they rammed home their attack into the suddenly disarrayed Wasps. Then Balkus gave the order to shoot at an enemy he knew was there, only yards before him, unseen and unseeing, and the snapbows of Collegium shattered the Wasp left and broke them apart.

TWENTY-SIX

The rebellion in Myna had broken out all at once and yet without any unification. The news of General Reiner's death was the spark that had sent every cell of resistance fighters into the streets, but it spread faster than Kymene could control it. Whilst many bands heeded her order to wait and attack in unison, others had simply struck at whatever local target the Imperials might provide.

The imperial garrison already had its men out in force in the city. The first reaction to the deaths of both Reiner and Latvoc, neither of whom had been men to willingly share their plans with subordinates, was to round up known trouble-makers and attempt to continue Reiner's iron-fisted bludgeoning of the populace. In many cases the soldiers thus despatched ran straight into the local resistance as it, too, sallied forth. There was a score of separate skirmishes within the first hour of the rebellion, and, in most of the fights, sheer numbers overwhelmed the small punitive forces the Empire had sent out. Where they had expected to find at worst a rabble of malcontents armed with stones, knives and clubs, the imperial soldiers ran headlong into Myna's military heritage.

The Mynans were close to Beetles, cousins perhaps, but a half-breed strain that had taken in fresh blood and stabilized into a new kinden entirely. What was not Beetle in them was a core of Ant fighting spirit that had made the taking of this city such an undertaking in the first place. Eighteen years had gone by, and the people of Myna had kept their blades sharp, their crossbows well oiled. The resistance fighters currently on the streets were a patchwork re-creation of the generation before, with their black and red breastplates and helms, their short swords and long shields and heavy crossbows. As the first unwary men of the Empire broke against them, they were overwhelmed or shot out of the sky.

The news soon snapped the officers of the garrison into line. The Empire's response was swift and proportionate, calculated to ensure that, in order to stop the rot, the rogue elements at large in the city would be destroyed to the last man as quickly as possible. Without exception, those bands of resistance fighters already mobilized were either routed or surrounded and slaughtered. At the same time that the imperial response was being deployed, however, Kymene's own people, and those that heeded her—over two-thirds of the resistance total—made their own move. They struck at key buildings and positions across the city, encountering surprisingly little resistance because the forces that would normally have rushed forth in defence were already engaged elsewhere. Several imperial detachments even returned to find their own barracks overrun and in enemy hands. Others found themselves holed up and under siege in the very buildings they had just stormed. One detachment, finding itself under threat of being trapped and smashed against the city walls, retreated through the main gates of the city in the general direction of Maynes.

By the end of a single day of savage fighting, without quarter on either side, Kymene found herself in control of over half of Myna, with the Empire still holding out in three improvised positions across the city. The balance was composed of the surviving resistance groups who had not heeded her, or areas that were so devastated or heavily contested that nobody could truthfully claim to have any grasp of them. Had it not been for one factor, her victory would have seemed inevitable.

Her men had put up barricades of furniture, overturned carts and torn down buildings across two of the three routes leading toward her problem, and she stood at one such barricade now, considering the building that had loomed so large in her own life.

The palace was the late Colonel Ulther's miniature replica of the Emperor's own in Capitas, a stepped ziggurat with, as she knew, just as much space below ground as above. The majority of the surviving Myna garrison was dug in within the edifice: doorways, balconies and windows bristled with soldiers ready to shoot or sting any-thing that came within their range. There was also a small catapult that the Wasp artificers had assembled, but Kymene had the luxury of assaulting the grand building from any side she pleased, whenever she chose, and to move the cumber-some weapon around the engineers would be forced to dismantle it each time.

For now there was an uneasy stalemate. Until an hour earlier the Empire had held the neighbouring barracks building as well, but she had since heard from Chyses that his own personal guard had fired the roof and that the soldiers had evacuated into the palace itself, while taking casualties from the Mynan crossbows. It still left her with a solid building that would be a bloodbath to take.

But take it she must. As long as the Wasps were there, her soldiers were here, watching them, instead of consolidating her hold on the city. If she had time, she could starve them out perhaps, but she had an uneasy feeling that time was one of the things not allowed to her.

She heard a step behind her and, turning, she saw the Beetle girl, Cheerwell, looking sombre. She had a sword at her waist and a crossbow in her hands, and the minders Kymene had set to protect her had confirmed at least one enemy soldier dead at her hands.

"Still thinking about your Wasp friend?" Kymene enquired.

"My friends, yes. Not just him." Che looked up at the palace. "This place brings back memories," she said weakly.

"Were you tortured here?" Kymene said.

"Never," Che assured her, clambering up a little on the barricade. "So many times it seemed he was going to, but in the end it was just a cover, so that he could talk to his man regarding some plot against the governor." She paused a moment, then added, "But he could have done it so easily, if he had wanted—Thalric, that is." She was aware of Kymene's sharp eyes on her, and she shrugged. "I don't like him much, but . . . I think the Empire made him what he is. The raw material was worth something more than that."

"And what about your other friends? The ones who came to rescue you from Thalric?"

Che bowed her head, letting her forehead touch the cold iron rim of a cart-wheel in the barrier. "Scattered, gone . . ." Stenwold gone to the Commonweal, Salma rushing his army about Sarn, Tynisa in pursuit of her father, Totho . . . lost. And Achaeos sick, and hated by his own people because of her. "And here am I, back in Myna."

They heard a disturbance amongst the soldiers behind them, a shouted word and counter-word. Both women turned to watch a Fly-kinden woman wing raggedly over the waiting fighters to virtually throw herself at Kymene's feet, one hand thrust toward her, offering a crumpled scroll. Messengers like this had been coming at two or three each hour all day, but this one seemed particularly desperate. Kymene took the message and read it. There was a slight narrowing of her eyes, but nothing more.

"Get me Chyses," she snapped. "Get all my officers here *now*, my artificers as well."

Men and women rushed off to do her bidding. For a moment Kymene's eyes were focused on nothing, seeing the future, weighing her next action.

"What is it?" Che asked her.

"Szar must have fallen," Kymene replied. "There are two thousand Wasp soldiers marching here from there. They'll be here in a day's time to reinforce the garrison."

◊ ◊ ◊

"Achaeos."

He snapped awake, his wound pulling at him painfully. He felt as though he had been running for hours, rather than just lying here in a fevered sleep. He peered upward, seeing the Arcanum agent, Xaraea. There was a finality to her expression that chilled him.

"I am not strong enough for this—" he started.

"We have no more time," Xaraea interrupted. "The Skryres have observed all the omens and cast the lots of the future. We must act now, either with or without you."

Achaeos stared at her. She was not fond of him, but neither was anyone else here in what had once been his home. He was learning to live with it. Still, for that self-same reason, he possessed something they did not: a connection to the outside world.

The wound that Tynisa had given him was healing, but slowly, very slowly. It had been too close, in the end, and the conflict of treatments between the stitching and patching carried out in Collegium and the work the doctors were doing here had not helped. He could just about walk now, for short distances, and only with a stick. He could not fly at all, and most of the time, as now, he spent resting.

I think I should accept now that I am no warrior. He did seem to get his hide cut open with distressing frequency.

"Nobody has even told me what they are intending to do," he pointed out.

"It is not your place to question," she said, but he had unexpectedly touched a nerve. *She knows, and it has shaken her.* He remained staring at her, outwardly impassive, inwardly wondering how far he could force his minuscule authority and how much they really needed his help.

The pause between them dragged on past mere awkwardness but, despite the background pain that never quite left him, he did not give way. After an excruciating time, it was Xaraea who spoke.

"I . . ." she began, and that single word told him that he had broken through to something, "I have spent *years* working on this. You can have no idea the battles I have fought. Yes, we could see the Empire on the horizon, and see all the cursed machines that the Helleren so obligingly built for them. I knew it would come to this, so I worked hard to have the right man in the right place: the one Wasp-kinden who would be one of *us* and not of them. Tegrec had already made himself a seer and an officer, but it was I who made him a governor. Why did I do all this? Because the Skryres realized that it would be necessary if we were to drive the enemy out of our halls. The Empire is *your* enemy just as much as it is ours. We have our differences, Achaeos, but we can agree on that. They are as much our enemy as are the cursed Beetle-kinden."

He did not flinch at that barb, even smiled a little to show his contempt for it.

"So where has all this work led?" he asked her. *I should have been a Skryre,* he reflected, for he knew he was now running Xaraea just as the Skryres had always run him: employing pointed questions, evasive answers, making her do the work.

"A ritual." Her voice shook marginally, and he saw her fists clench. "I am not privy—"

"But you have heard," he observed. She was hating him with a passion now, but he found he did not care so long as he could continue to pull her around like a marionette and get her to tell him what she knew.

"They say . . ." Her pause, then, was not reluctance to speak so much as reluctance to even think about it. "They say that it will be the greatest ritual since the Darakyon. They need . . . they command you there. They *demand* it."

"Do they?" Achaeos had gone cold all over, and he knew that must show in his face. There was no gloating, though. Xaraea was frightened of what the Skryres were about, and he found that he was too. Slowly he swung his legs over the side of the bed. "I will come," he told her, "but it may take a while."

She nodded briefly and was gone in an instant. No doubt she had a great deal else to do. The Skryres seemed to have made her their personal agent in this business, and he had no idea whether that was intended as a reward or not.

As great as the Darakyon, is it? he thought sourly, hearing in his mind the tortured, whispering voice of that haunted place. *We all know how well that went.* The great renegade ritual, five centuries before, intended to drag down the newly arisen Apt-kinden, to consign them to fear and barbarism and slavery once again, and it had failed. The great magicians who had shaped it had yet reached too far, and they, and the Mantis-kinden whose home had been their ritual ground, had been damned to a fate infinitely worse than death, eternal torture on the rack of thorns that was the blighted forest Darakyon, imprisonment in the Shadow Box, the twisted knot of spite that was all their ritual had achieved.

And that I held, and opened, and look what happened to me . . .

There were ritual chambers deep within the mountain but their walls, it seemed, were too confining for an enterprise on this scale. Instead Xaraea led the limping Achaeos upward, first through slanted corridors and halls that he remembered from his youth, then by ascending long flights of steps that had always been forbidden to him before. From the murky, incense-fragrant halls they led to she took him step-by-step up steeply spiral paths cut into the rock, cramped and tortuous routes that he had never known existed. The chill told him where they were going. The very top of the mountain had signified a place of childhood terror. It was where the Skryres communed direct with the spirits and the elements, wholly open to the lashing responses of either. It was *where they took you* if you failed the Skryres.

Well, they're taking me there now, he thought drily. There was light ahead, but it was a muted red. At first he thought it was fire glow but as he came out into the open air he saw that it was sunset. The entire Lowlands seemed to be in flames, as if the bloated crimson sun was searing the world to cinders.

"An omen, do you think?" There were only two figures waiting for them there. One was robed like a Skryre, but the voice told otherwise. The second was the Wasp girl, Raeka, which meant that the first must be her master.

"Tegrec," Achaeos rasped hoarsely, using his stick to lower himself to the ground. He felt as though even getting to the place of ritual might have killed him.

The Wasp magician cast his hood back. With it up, he had seemed forbidding and dangerous; now he looked only pale and worried. He cast a glance at Xaraea, but she was standing by the staircase, locked up with her own demons. Haltingly, Tegrec knelt down beside Achaeos.

"Second thoughts?" the Moth asked him.

"No," said Tegrec firmly. Raeka put a hand on his shoulder, and he reached back to grip it, a familiarity normally unforgivable under imperial law.

"We will be striking your own people," Achaeos reminded him.

"The technical term is 'smite,'" said Tegrec, mustering a smile from somewhere, "and I don't know if they ever *were* my people." He glanced back at the girl, and Achaeos noticed his hand tighten on hers. "You can't imagine . . . really, you *can't* imagine how it is to grow up so different from the others, and to have to hide it. If I'd been poor, I'd undoubtedly have died . . . only having servants, slaves, being of good family, that's all that saved me. Can you imagine living in a house where you sometimes can't even open the doors: you just fumble at the catches and the handles, and curse and weep, and you *just can't see* what it is that everyone else takes for granted. And it's more than that—you can't read their maps properly. You can't understand their accounts. I've faked a life for thirty years, and all that time I've been living off mere scraps: rags of knowledge, learning stolen from old ruins, from the Commonweal, from the Grasshopper-kinden and other Inapt slaves, and all gathered in secrecy because, of course, I could never let anyone know"—another backward glance—"except one. It started with the doors, you know. I bought her simply to have someone to open the doors for me. Everyone thought I was being very pretentious. I let them think that. A reputation for eccentricity was easier to live with."

Achaeos digested all of this, knowing that Tegrec was only divulging so much because he was nervous about what was yet to come. *We are both here solely because the Skryres wish to use us.*

The Wasp must have seen something in his expression because he nodded and continued, "We're both outcasts, really. The mad thing is, when this is done, and assuming any of us survive it, I'll stay here but they'll make you leave, won't they?"

"I have no wish to stay," Achaeos replied flatly. "I came because I needed their medicine. I stayed because they are my people and, despite it all, I'll fight for them. But when this is done, my home is elsewhere."

Tegrec stood up again, and Achaeos heard the shuffle of sandals on stone as other robed figures came up into the red-tinged air. He numbered a score of them at least, before he stopped counting. *They have called everyone they can*, he realized. All the most skilled ritualists of Tharn had been dragged up that same winding stair. There were at least a dozen Skryres, and there were other Moth-kinden who had never sought that position of power and responsibility: they were scholars, philosophers, skilled and private magicians. Here they all were, now, men and women all two decades older than Achaeos at least, and none looking confident or comfortable. In between them were others who had, like Tegrec, found a place here by virtue of their magic: there were Mantis-kinden and Spider-kinden side by side, a Grasshopper, two Commonweal Dragonflies, even a tiny, silver-haired old Fly-kinden woman who leant on a stick and looked as drained by the climb as Achaeos himself felt. Slowly, and without being directed, they formed themselves into two encircling rings, the Skryres inward, the rest standing behind them, closer to the edge of this little artificial plateau.

Xaraea then came and helped Achaeos to his feet, not out of compassion but from necessity. Hobbling, he took his place in the inner circle standing opposite from Tegrec. Meanwhile Xaraea and the Wasp girl Raeka retreated to the stairwell.

We are the eyes through which this ritual will perceive its prey, Achaeos knew. The work would be done, the power provided, by the others; he and Tegrec would merely focus it. Such rituals had often been done in the Days of Lore so many centuries before. But in living memory? No, and the power of the very last one performed within record had gone so disastrously wrong that, since then, nobody had even *attempted* what they were now about to do on the same scale. Of the meagre attempts that had been made, most had failed, some without issue and some with dire consequences. With magic so thin and so wan in the light of this new Apt world, nobody knew if what they were undertaking was even *possible* any more.

Che . . . He wished now that he had said more before she had gone off to Myna with the wretched traitor Thalric. Standing here on the mountaintop, with the sky on fire behind him, he felt so many regrets.

There was no preliminary signal. The ritual simply bloomed around them, burgeoning from the Skryres as they turned the force of their minds on the weave of the world and tried to scar their desires out upon it. Achaeos felt a ripple of shock run through the outer circle, the lesser magicians yoking themselves into that same great effort, so that the air around them grew hazy and shook with the power that they called up. He felt himself like a bow, taken up, strung and stretched, so that the arrow that they were jointly forming might be loosed. The strain, even right at the start, made him gasp. He became instantly, infinitely aware of the city of Tharn beneath him: of the Wasp-kinden intruders who did not belong, their soldiers and officers, the machines, their alien thoughts and minds.

The Skryres stretched his mind further, until he choked on the pain, and still they tensioned him further. He hoped Tegrec was lasting better than he did, for it seemed that any moment he might snap and fly to pieces. *Loose!* His mind cried. *For the sake of all, loose the shaft!* But they did not, only pulled and pulled, the arrow yet unformed. The Skryres and their followers were pouring everything they had—all their living craft and strength—into this one single shot.

And it was not enough.

The greatest magicians in the world, and it was not enough. The circle of Skryres and their acolytes swayed and chanted and *concentrated*, forcing their will upon the very weave of existence, and it was still not enough. The age of great magics was long past and they did not have the strength. The world was no longer so malleable to their minds.

Achaeos felt the air around him swim in and out of focus. His heart was like a hot stake being driven into his chest, flaring with pain at every beat, and the beats had become irregular, stuttering. He was held on his feet only by the collective will of those around him. Others had already fallen: the oldest of the Skryres was a crumpled heap across the circle; one of the Mantis-kinden had dropped to her knees.

It is not working. That much was obvious. Less obvious was whether Achaeos would survive this failure, let alone a success. Opposite him, across the circle, Tegrec's face glimmered under a sheen of sweat.

I can't . . . Achaeos could feel a tight coldness in his chest now, an unforgiving clenching that intensified with every breath.

Che, he thought.

There seemed to be a darkness blotting out the stars, but he knew this was in his vision only. The voice of one of the Skryres came to him, as if from far away.

"We do not have the power for this! We must stop before we lose what we have!"

Another voice cried, "Remember the Darakyon!"

"No!" It was the lead Skryre, the great force of whose mind was felt all about the circle. "We cannot give up now. We have this one chance only to drive the invader from our halls. Find more! Draw on every reserve you have! There can be no holding back. Drain your wells and give me *all*!"

What reserves? What wells? Achaeos thought numbly, but around the circle he sensed the grudging obedience of the others. Not all, maybe, but still there were many who reached and found in themselves some hoarded cache of strength to cast into the ritual. Some had artefacts from the Days of Lore to which a shred of glamour still clung. Others had places to which they had forged a link, receptacles in which they had stored their faith long years ago. Some had siblings they could draw upon, or else family, students and servants. Achaeos saw the Wasp Tegrec reach back, and the hand of his slave girl was in his own without hesitation. He saw Raeka pale as she gave of herself to him, the strength and will leaching out of her.

I cannot, Achaeos thought, but on the heels of that came, *I cannot stand, cannot last, unless I do.*

He had called to her once before, before ever she had given herself to him. How much stronger now was the bond between them.

Che! he cried, simultaneously in his mind and across the miles that lay between them. *Che! Hear me! Please help me, Che!*

The Wasps had now mounted two catapults on the palace roof, but the Mynan resistance had merely found mustering points that lay outside their angle of fire. It had been a costly lesson.

They had no time: that was what everyone knew and nobody said. The Wasps still held the palace despite a day of savage fighting. They had barricaded the doors over and over, and the resistance had stormed them with firebombs and crossbows, swords and claw hammers, and torn the barricades down or burnt them up. The prized furniture of the palace, which Ulther had spent years collecting, was mostly smashed and charred now, and yet the Wasps held out. They met the Mynans at every door, with sword and spear and sting, and they did not give an inch of ground.

Kymene knew that she was running out of chances now. Fly-kinden scouts were reporting hourly on the relief force on its way from Szar. If she had possession of the palace, then they might be able to hold off the reinforcements. Otherwise, as soon as they engaged the new force, the Wasps barricaded in the palace would sally out and take them from the rear.

"We just have to keep hammering at them all night," Chyses advised her. She knew that already, though it did not seem acceptable, in this day and age, to have no options but sheer bloody-mindedness.

"What about the new explosives?" she asked.

"Still being brewed," Chyses replied, and his tone made it clear that he knew they would be ready too late. "We've got another batch of the firebombs, though."

Kymene scowled. Those were unreliable weapons, just bottles of anything flammable with rags as their fuses. They had caused carnage amongst the Wasps, but had taken their share of the Mynan attackers too. If the flames really caught in the palace doorway, they could lose hours of progress in which all the Wasps needed to do was retreat up to the balconies above and watch an impassable blaze raging away below.

If we had our own flying troops . . . but all she had were a motley rabble of Fly-kinden who would scout for her, but not fight.

"We're losing too many fighters," she observed. Chyses merely nodded. He was someone who believed in the inevitability of casualties, an ingredient that made eventual victory all the sweeter. Kymene, however, could only think of her people and the price she was setting on their promised freedom.

"Issue the firebombs," she instructed him. "Pass the word along. Twenty minutes and we're going in again."

Che watched and said nothing. She was now wearing a chain mail hauberk of Mynan make, and so far she had stood anxiously at the edge of groups, even on the barricades that the Mynans had erected facing the palace, but had seldom been called upon to fight. She had simply watched the ghastly business unfold: the Mynans' repeated, bloody charges at the palace; the Wasps' equally costly defence. She had seen Kymene try everything, had even made her own suggestions. At her behest, they had made up a small catapult to pelt the palace door with grenades, but then they had run out of grenades and explosives, and the homemade fire-bombs were sufficiently volatile that not even Chyses would suggest delivering them by engine.

This is where it ends, is it? But that seemed ridiculous. After all, Thalric had been right about the Mynan situation, so everything should be working as planned. Instead the Wasps stayed stubbornly in place despite the losses that the resistance had inflicted on them. They knew that all they had to do was sit tight and wait.

Che.

She flinched. The sound of his voice was as though his mouth was at her ear, yet at the same time it was faint, far away.

"Achaeos?"

Help me, Che.

She looked over at Kymene, saw that nobody was paying her any heed. A shiver went through her. "Achaeos?" She could not simply form the name in her mind. She had to say it aloud. "Tell me you're all right."

I need you, Che. There was a terrible *wrongness* to his voice, and she thought instantly of his wounds and how frail he had looked when she left him.

Che, I need your strength. I'm sorry . . . please . . .

She did not even ask what for. She did not need to know. Her reaction was as unquestioning as a child's.

Take it, she said, and this time there was no need to voice the words aloud.

Beetle-kinden were not a magical people, nor were they great warriors, neither fleet nor graceful. Beetles, however, were enduring: their dogged pragmatism had made them a power in this world because they worked and worked tirelessly. They owned reserves of strength that other kinden could never guess at.

Achaeos suddenly felt the tenuous connection he had built toward Che start to wax and surge—and he touched her spirit, the core of her. It shook him to discover that within the one short and amiable Beetle girl there was such a wealth of power. Without hesitation it was offered to him, began flowing into him, and thus passing through his conduit into the ritual. Along with it he felt, like an aftertaste, her feelings and the love she held for him.

There was agony writ large on many faces around the circle, so when the tears started up in Achaeos' blank eyes, nobody noted or cared. Between them all the air shook and trembled, not through the force of their will, but with their sheer frustration. All throughout Tharn apprentices and servants gave of themselves, ancient archives of power were looted, gems went dark, books burnt and staves cracked. The Wasps were suspicious now: even they could tell that something was happening. Already they were seeking for their governor, not guessing that he was part of the conspiracy against them. Soon there would be soldiers storming ever upward, drawn by a taste in the air that would become stronger and stronger.

But not strong enough. Even with all this, with not a man or woman among them holding back, the ritual was failing.

It is too late, Achaeos thought. *Perhaps a hundred years ago, this could have been accomplished, perhaps even fifty, but we are too late.* Magic had died, year on year, giving place and ground before the monsters of artifice and engineering, fading from the minds of the Lowlands until only those like the Skryres of Tharn even believed in it still. And belief was all, in the final analysis.

We are too late. A little longer and those who scoffed at magic's existence would be proved right. Even with Che's borrowed strength, Achaeos could not force the ritual to happen. The tightness in his chest was only increasing, and there were constant stabs of pain inside his head as though men were fighting a war within his skull. All around him the other ritualists had started swaying, faces gaunt with exhaustion.

He took the power that Che had lent him, took it with his mind, with both hands, and in a last desperate cry he hurled his voice out away from Tharn, across the Lowlands, and cried, *Help us!*

It was intended to be his final act before acknowledging defeat, before letting the pain that was clawing at him drag him down at last.

But it was not.

We will help you, little novice.

The words were the dry rattle of old leaves across stone—and he had heard them before.

"No!" he started, speaking aloud, not that any of the others truly heard. Something chuckled in his mind.

We will help you. We are bound, you to us, and us to you. The Shadow Box is open, and for a moment we may stretch our limbs. He saw the limbs in his mind, and they were spined, thorned, many-jointed, not remotely human.

"I do not . . ." He did not want their help but he had opened the door to them, and in they came. He felt their approach as though he watched a storm scud over the sky toward him, coming all the way from the dark, rotten vaults of the Darakyon to Tharn. It was power that had lain in wait for a fool like him for five centuries, from the very cusp of the time that magic had begun to die.

Pure, ancient power. Evil power. Power of terrible, twisted might. It came to the mountaintop at Tharn like a crippled giant, tortured and raging, and it fell on them like a hammer.

Achaeos screamed. He was not the only one. At least one of the others fell within the instant, face gone dead white, pale eyes filled with blood. Achaeos tried to let go but he was held up like a marionette dangling from the Darakyon's broken fingers. He burnt. The vitriol of their power seared through him, and now he could not even scream.

The ritual exploded. There was a thunderclap of utter silence, a second's stunned pause, and they all felt the tide of their blighted magic force itself down into the mountain.

Within Tharn all the lamps, all the torches or lanterns, went out at once.

The screams came soon after, the screams of fighting men in utter terror, engulfed by a wave of invisible force they could not fight. It opened their minds. It found where their fears came from, and it released them, each man becoming the victim of his own beasts. The Wasp-kinden, and many of their Moth subjects also, went mad.

Some fell on one another, hands crackling with the loosing of their stings, mouths foaming, tearing with nails and teeth. Some just died, seizing up and stopping like broken machines. Most fled, crashing into walls and doorways, and into each other: fighting through the pitchy tunnels and hallways, trying to find the open sky. Those that found it cast themselves out, and some of them flew and others fell . . .

And Achaeos, with the whole might of this horror pouring through him, now unstoppable, felt something catch inside him. Such a small thing, but his next breath seemed intolerably hard to draw, and his wound was abruptly open again and bleeding, and something lanced through his mind, a pain so acute that it came almost as a relief, blotting everything else out.

And a falling away. And a darkness that even Moth eyes could not penetrate.

Che had been screaming for some time now, contracted into a ball, knees up to her chin. She could not hear Kymene or the Mynans demanding to know what was wrong with her, talking about Wasp secret weapons. She could only hear the spiteful, hate-filled voices of the Darakyon as they exalted in their first act of revenge for five hundred years.

She felt it through Achaeos. He was in her mind and so were they. She could not hear Kymene or the others. She would not unbend as their chirurgeons tried to wrestle her upright. She just screamed and screamed.

And stopped.

They dropped her, then, but she was already stumbling to gain her feet. Without warning, her sword was in her hand.

Her mouth was open, but no words came, only a small, hurt noise as she felt Achaeos suddenly *not there*.

"Che . . . what . . . ?" Kymene had her blade drawn too, as all of the Mynans surrounding her did. The air around Che seemed to boil and shimmer with darkness.

"Gone," Che finally got out. She was shaking uncontrollably. Where a moment before she had been so full, now there was a void inside her that had to be fed.

"Che . . ." Kymene started again, but a wail was building up inside the Beetle girl, a dreadful drawn-out keening sound of loss, loss and rage.

She was possessed. The fire of the Darakyon was still all about her. The world suddenly felt too small to her, too small to be penned in where she was. Achaeos was *gone*, taking some vital part of herself with him. She had felt him fall away from her into the cold hands of the dead Mantis people, and she could not bear that. She could not live with it.

Her wail became a scream, and before they could stop her she was over the barricade, charging the Wasps at the palace gates with her sword held high.

History would not remember her for it. History would remember Kymene instead, for, as Che made her charge, the Mynan leader followed after her from pure instinct. She had only been aware of a comrade in trouble, had been surely reaching for Che's shoulder to drag her back, but the Beetle girl had a surprising turn of speed.

And after Kymene came the Mynans. Chyses barked out his orders, seeing the rallying point for their whole revolution about to throw herself on to the lances of the Wasps . . . and suddenly there was a whole rush of Mynan warriors behind Kymene, and the Wasps braced their spears and thrust their hands forward to loose their stings. Few of them chose the Beetle girl in the fore as their target, yet enough of them to kill Che five times over.

And then, before they could loose, the tide hit them. Not the tide of the enemy that was just rushing within their range, but the fear. All about the Beetle-kinden girl at the point of the Mynan charge, the air was abruptly seething, writhing. She was surrounded by a host of half-seen figures: Mantis-kinden with claws and spears, fearful winged insects with killing arms, a leaning, arching train of thorns that tore up the ground toward them. The echo of the Darakyon had come to Myna, but the echo was quite enough.

To the Mynans it seemed that the Wasps at the palace gate simply broke. Some fled inside, some hurled themselves into the air. None of them held long enough for Che and Kymene to reach them. A moment later and the Mynans were into the palace, where the real fighting began.

TWENTY-SEVEN

T he sky was streaked with the smoke from failing orthopters.

The Solarnese had no control over the fighting. The Wasps were using their greater mobility to split the locals up, dropping squads of the airborne down between them, holding strategic alleys and avenues so as to divide the city into manageable sections. Jemeyn's people, some two hundred men and women of the Path of Jade, were now cut off from the rest of the fighting, and there were seventy or eighty of the enemy blocking their way, holed up in a narrow street with a few ensconced in the buildings either side for flanking shots. Time was running short. If another forty appeared behind them things would get particularly nasty.

"We have to take them!" Nero declared. Jemeyn shook his head, with teeth bared. He had a curving Solarnese sword clutched defiantly in one hand but his nerve was going. Nero could see it visibly fraying.

"We have to go!" Nero insisted. Jemeyn licked his lips. His fighters kept shouting insults and challenges at the Wasps, but they were keeping well out of sting range. Some of them had crossbows, but the Solarnese fashion was for little pocket-sized things that had no reach to speak of.

The Solarnese fight for style, Nero reflected, *while the Wasps fight for substance. This isn't going to go well.*

"Listen to me," he began, but he already had gone through all the reason and logic of it. The fact of it was simply that Jemeyn could not bring himself to grasp the nettle, and that was that.

"Behind us!" someone cried, and Nero swore, kicking up into the air to see better. Instead of another detachment of the black and yellow, what he saw gladdened his heart.

It was Odyssa the Spider-kinden, and not alone. Lumbering behind her were at least three score of her mercenaries: huge, broad-shouldered men with massive claws and jutting jaws, all Scorpion-kinden warriors from the Dryclaw desert, those inveterate slavers, raiders and sellswords. Nero was gladder than he could believe possible, just to see them.

He saw the same uplift of spirits surge through the Solarnese, too. These Scorpions, however dubious their reputation, looked the business.

"We need to punch our way through!" Nero proclaimed. "To get to where the real fighting's at." Odyssa merely nodded and he saw, all Spider masks and airs aside, that she looked pale and frightened. He guessed that she had never been in a real battle before.

The Wasps had closed ranks on seeing the mercenaries appear. They had raised a fence of spears, and they had their stings and their blades ready behind them. The Scorpions, however, had massive cleaving swords, five or six feet long, just made for the job of hacking a hole through a line of men who carried no shields. Others had heavy crossbows or throwing axes, most had at least a leather cuirass and kilt, but some were bare chested and their leader wore a breastplate over a long chain hauberk.

"Gonna hurt, this," the chief Scorpion remarked.

"And?" Nero demanded, as a flying machine hit the ground a street away. Whether it was Solarnese or imperial he never knew, but he did not flinch.

"So let's get to it," said the Scorpion, and he raised his great sword over his head one-handed and bellowed a roar that could have been heard out across the Exalsee, and which shook the Wasps as they consolidated their stand. Then the Scorpions were charging, and taking the Solarnese with them, in a sudden, rushing mob descending on the soldiers. Nero took up his sword, a short blade stolen from the enemy that was like a broadsword to him, and he lifted it high and joined the charge, his wings a blur, scooting over the ground in the very front rank.

He witnessed the sting blast that felled Jemeyn, the man pitching back to trip the two following behind him, but of the shot that then struck Nero himself he saw nothing at all.

Axrad was very nearly too quick for her, his striped orthopter darting out from beneath the barrels of her rotaries and dancing along the length of the *Starnest*. Taki's heart was heavy as stone. She had known Scobraan a long time and, although they had not always had kind words for each other, they had never been enemies. The *Esca Volenti* dived after Axrad, jinking with him, her aim creeping inexorably on to him.

Elsewhere, across the sky over Solarno, there were tens of private duels. Niamedh's beautiful, sleek *Executrix* drove into a Wasp fixed-wing and forced it down into one of the carrier blimps, propellers shredding the cumbersome dirigible's airbag. Drevane Sae's jewelled dragonfly stooped on the streets of Solarno, the city of his lifelong enemies, his arrows picking off Wasp officers who were trying to organize the defence on the ground. The ugly, blunt-nosed *Bleakness*, constant scourge of the Exalsee, fired its broadside banks of shrapnel casters at anything that came close, even as the *Bleakness* itself closed toward the great over-hanging canopy of the *Starnest*.

Axrad's flier was abruptly beyond the great dirigible's frame, and it dropped out of sight instantly. Taki cursed, pulled up and high, knowing that, in his position, she would have then looped round the airship's hull in order to meet her enemy. She was right, and he came back into view even as she was poised at the point of her dive, his fleet, agile ship leaping into sight for an ambush that she had not been fool enough to fall for. Instead he rose now to meet her, and she fell upon him, and their weapons began to blaze at the same time.

Two bolts clipped her hull, then a third smashed the window of her cockpit and clipped her shoulder, enough to make her tug on the stick without intention. She dragged her goggles down over her face against the blasting air, while Axrad's undamaged vessel passed over her so close that their beating wingtips touched.

In the instant she was spiralling away, fighting to get back on the level, and she knew that he must be wrestling for just the same goal, and then the *Esca* was hers again and she swung back toward Axrad, toward the *Starnest*, seeing him find his place and commence a mirror-image move.

He had killed Scobraan, and who knew how many others, but he was a pilot to reckon with and she could not take that from him.

Elsewhere, the Creev's *Nameless Warrior* danced with three Wasp orthopters. The half-breed slave, the finest pilot of Chasme, had a ballista bolt jammed through his leg, pinning him to his weakening hull, though he barely felt it. He had no Art-flight anyway, and if his ship died, so would he. His rotaries, four of them, spat out their bolts, and span together about one axis to make a storm of shot, smashing one Wasp flier entirely, shredding its wings to ribbons, leaving a punctured carcase of its hull. He was faltering, though, his body and ship both wearing thin. He would die above his enemies' city unmourned and unseen by any save for the Wasp that would bring him down—but not yet. He had some killing left to do before the end.

Axrad was now flying straight, and Taki knew that he would soon end it one way or the other. The *Esca* was shaking in unfamiliar ways: the poor ship had taken her share of beatings in this fight.

She pulled the trigger even as Axrad did, and she saw furrows raking into his hull before her rotary jammed altogether, and his shots slammed into the *Esca*'s undercarriage.

Oh.

She must dive aside now, but when she did he would find his place behind her, and then she would be lost. Another shot lanced past her, through the broken cockpit, heading for the engine casing.

She counted. Three bolts passed her by and one tore straight through the flesh of her arm. She screamed.

Taki pulled the release, and the broken frame of the cockpit fell away, and she kicked up, despite the pain, letting her wings flower.

Axrad pulled up at the very last moment, pulled up late because he had been so determined to bring her down that he had not realized he had already succeeded.

She was nearly caught between the two craft. Only a Fly-kinden's swift reflexes saved her as the empty, abused *Esca Volenti* drove straight into Axrad's flier, their wings snarling instantly, the *Esca's* nose snapping on Axrad's underside and then breaking through.

She did not notice if he was able to fly clear, as the two dying ships spun madly down toward the earth.

She had a dagger, and the *Starnest*, which blotted out her sky, was very large, but even so it was all right because someone else had a larger blade than that.

She should have known that Hawkmoth, the old pirate, had preyed on airships before. Who knew how many he had assailed in the sky, and sent plummeting down to the Exalsee, where his shipbound confederates would be waiting? Over the *Starnest's* taut canvas the *Bleakness* dipped low, a black and evil-looking flying machine, armoured and squat, with all the natural grace of a scarab in flight. From beneath it had unsheathed two curving blades, each the length of a man. There was no subtlety in it. The pirate simply threw his machine against the airbag and unseamed it, from stern to fore, with twin gashes seventy feet from end to end.

At first it seemed that even this had not affected this pride of the Wasp air-force, but then the difference told, the lighter gas venting out from the violated compartments, until the colossal bulk of the *Starnest* was dipping, sagging, and then falling down upon the city it had been sent to conquer.

〈〉 〈〉 〈〉

He would not come to bed. Stenwold, instead, sat at his desk with reports and maps and tried to make sense of it.

"You must sleep, surely," Arianna urged him. She was standing at the door to his study, wrapped in a robe of his that was vastly too large for her. "Stenwold, they will want you on the walls again tomorrow."

"And I shall go," he said. She noticed his hands were shaking. "Look at all this they have given me. The curse of this city is paper! We have a war on, and every man feels he must put it down on paper for me to read!"

"Then don't read them," she said. "They'll tell you nothing you don't already know."

"But there might be *something*," he said. "How could I go to the wall tomorrow knowing that I might have missed the one thing, the flaw, the gap . . ." His fists clenched.

She approached him, put her hands on his shoulders. "Stenwold, please, come to bed."

His whole frame was shaking. "What am I going to do?" he demanded.

"Sten . . . We fought the Vekken, didn't we?"

"The Empire aren't the Vekken. Their general even told me as much, but I didn't listen. The Vekken never hit us this hard so soon. The Vekken had not so many men who could just leap over our walls. I have lost . . ." He choked. "I have lost one man in three of my own command *already*, after just two days' full fighting. We cannot hold them."

"But—"

He blundered up out of his chair with a cry of rage and anguish, turning the entire desk over, scattering papers across the room. His face was distraught. She recoiled from him and he smashed a fist into a wall.

"In the Amphiophos they are already talking about surrender," he said, staring at the plaster where he had just cracked it. "They are already saying that we only managed to hold off the Vekken until Teornis came to save us. They say that, and it is true. But who will save us this time, Arianna? We have spread this war across all the enemy. We . . . *I* made sure that the Wasps would fight on all fronts: here, Sarn, the Commonweal, Solarno, the Spiderlands. Now we pay the cost! Who do we call on when our own walls shake? There is nobody!"

He had resumed a mask of calm, but she saw him shaking still behind it.

"There must be a way," he whispered. "Somewhere, there must be a way . . . but we are losing our air defences. We are a kinden never meant to fly, and our Mantids, our Dragonflies, our flying machines—the Wasps are destroying them. It is Tark all over again. Unless we surrender soon they will burn my city, Arianna. Collegium represents five hundred years of learning, of progress, and they will burn it."

She came to him, putting her arms around him. "You'll think of something."

He shuddered. "I have no more thoughts. My mind is hollow. Who can I turn to? Who do I have left? I sent Balkus to Sarn; Tisamon is fled, and Tynisa after him; Che is in *Tharn*, they tell me! Even Thalric, damn him, is gone! Any one of them might have the secret that would save us, *but they're not here*! Look at me, Arianna. I am a spymaster without agents! Was there ever such a wretched thing as that?"

She drew back from him. "Sten, you have to sleep," she said again. "You'll be good for nothing tomorrow." If there was a curious flatness to her voice he did not notice it. Inside her, his words had struck something cold. *Can Collegium be doomed, really?* She pictured the Wasps triumphant in these familiar streets, a victory that she herself had once worked so hard to bring about.

Stenwold righted his desk with a grunt and stared about at his scattered papers. "I can't sleep," he said wretchedly. "I have work . . ."

She looked at him: the fat and frantic Beetle now abandoned by everyone. Has it come to this? Had he been nothing but the sum of his friends?

She retreated downstairs, feeling shaken. She had assumed, as did all Collegium, that they would grind the Empire down at their gates. But the Empire had no use for gates. The Beetles were better prepared than the Tarkesh had been but the Imperial Army had not stood still either.

She began to consider that remaining here inside the walls of Collegium might not be the wisest thing to do. She began to think of what options she had left open for herself.

An hour later she returned upstairs to Stenwold, bringing him a mug of herb tea, which he drank gratefully, once again fully absorbed in his papers. It was bare minutes later that he fell asleep.

General Tynan yawned and stretched, subduing his temper. It had flared automatically when he was woken not much past midnight by one of his aides, but he had faith in their good sense, knowing they would not risk his anger on anything trivial.

His body servants dressed him in a loose robe and sandals, with a swordbelt girded over it. "This had better be good," he warned them. "Who's outside?"

"Major Savrat, sir."

Tynan's eyes narrowed. Savrat was Rekef Outlander, he had been given to understand. This unwelcome intrusion meant that either the Rekef would now give him some long-buried instructions, or that some intelligence had come to the Rekef that they wanted to share. If it was the latter, he certainly wanted to know about it. He had scouts spread out over several square miles north of Collegium in anticipation of a Sarnesh relief force. News from General Malkan and the Seventh was overdue.

Savrat was ushered into his tent and Tynan stared at him balefully. There was always the chance this man was Rekef Inlander keeping an eye on Tynan himself.

"What is it?" he demanded shortly. "I've a war to run."

"Then I may be able to win it more swiftly for you," Savrat told him with a smug little smile. "We have a visitor from the city."

Tynan scowled at him. "It's late. No guessing games."

Savrat ducked out of the tent briefly, and when he returned it was with a young Spider-kinden girl in dark, close-bound clothing.

"What's this?" Tynan asked, and then directly to her face, "Who are you supposed to be, that I should care?"

"Arianna of the Rekef Outlander, General. Stationed in Collegium."

He took a moment to digest that, and then glanced at Savrat. "That you've brought her to me at all shows you think she's genuine."

"She knows the code signs, General. They're old signs, but she was put in place before the Vekken tried to crack this city, so that makes sense."

"Why now?" Tynan asked Arianna.

"I haven't been able to get out unseen until now, General. There are currently fewer Collegiate soldiers on the walls, after the last two days."

"I suppose that's true," Tynan allowed. Savrat was looking intolerably pleased with himself, at this unearned victory of the Rekef. Tynan switched his scowl from him to the Spider girl. "You can give me a report on the city's defences, how they're holding up?" he asked. It was clearly going to be a long night, and a sleepless one. He went over to his camp bed and sat down on it, rubbing his face.

"I can, sir."

This could all wait until morning, was the thought crossing his tired mind. If the girl had any real secrets, though, he would want to put them into action as soon as the dawn came. The night was getting longer and later the more he considered it.

"Savrat, go make yourself useful," he snapped. "Fix us some mulled wine at least." The insulted look on the Rekef man's face, as he departed, was worth the early waking.

"So speak," Tynan said to Arianna. "Tell me how they're taking my visit, on the other side of the walls."

"Well, General," she started, "firstly the losses to Collegium's fighting men have been considerable. The Beetle-kinden are not a naturally martial race and, even though they have plenty of other kinden employed in their ranks as well, the fighting strength of Collegium is nowhere near that of a comparable Ant-kinden city-state or garrisoned Wasp town. When you do force the walls, or exact a surrender out of their ruling council, there will be little resistance. They may even soon grow to accept imperial rule quite peaceably."

"Good, good." He looked her up and down, wondering how a Spider-kinden had ended up in this position, so far away from her home. "If they'd choose to surrender tomorrow it would be gladly accepted by me. I have no wish to destroy anything the Empire can use. Of course, the soldiers will want their share of blood for the comrades they've lost, but after that . . ."

Savrat came in just then, looking surly, with drinks. Arianna accepted one gladly, and Tynan sipped his thoughtfully. Savrat took the opportunity to stand next to the Spider girl, with a proprietorial air. No doubt he would be expecting a commendation for this.

"Who were you working under, at Collegium?" Tynan asked. An odd memory had come to him. Was there not some Wasp officer who had been disgraced there? What was his name?

"Lieutenant Graf, sir," Arianna replied promptly, and Tynan relaxed. Whatever name he was thinking of, that was not it.

He yawned and stretched mightily, trying to rid himself of the last vestiges of sleep. "Well, tell me what cracks we can put the pry bar into, Arianna," he continued. "And then let us get this siege over with as swiftly as possible." He upended his goblet of wine, draining it with relish.

Something cold touched him on the side of the neck even as he swallowed. It was recognizable enough that he kept the goblet held up, quite still, until she removed it from his hand.

Major Savrat was slumped on the spot where he had been standing. She had driven her blade into his throat with a brutal efficiency. Now that same blade was at Tynan's own neck, still gory with the major's blood. He looked into her eyes, expecting to see the certainty of his death there.

He saw almost blank fear instead: she was terrified. In a way that scared him more than seeing eyes of a cold killer. If an assassin had not killed him yet, there was still hope, but this nervous girl might stab at any moment out of sheer fright.

He began to move his hands very slowly upward, but she jabbed him, drawing blood.

"Keep your palms out and away from me," she stammered. "I've worked with Wasps, General."

The knife she had was very keen. He felt a trail of warm blood from the tiny puncture on his neck.

"So what now?" he asked, slowly and carefully.

"I really am Rekef," she got out. "Or at least I was. Only I left them. I betrayed them."

"That explains a great deal," Tynan said, trying to sound amiable and failing. "Major Savrat deserves his fate for his poor intelligence."

"I don't imagine Major Thalric bothered filing a report about me before his own superiors tried to kill him," Arianna explained. He could see in her eyes the madly whirling thought: *What do I do now?* "Do you want to know why I have not simply killed you?"

"The question has crossed my mind," Tynan replied. "I should have seen this coming. For Spider-kinden this tactic is standard, to try for the enemy leader—cut off the army's head."

"But it works," she said. They had both remained almost motionless for a very long time, and one or other of them would not be able to keep it up much longer. The slightest move would destroy her advantage, and he would then be able to kill her with his sting.

"It doesn't work. The Commonwealers found that out years ago. An imperial army has a chain of command. If you kill me, I have capable colonels, they have experienced majors. Though I say it myself, a dead general causes minimal disruption in a well-run army."

The knife twitched again and cut another little mark beside the first, moved by nothing more than her nerves.

He hissed involuntarily. *How fast can I grab for the blade? How good are her reflexes?*

"This seems an odd display of bravado," he got out. *Should I hope that a servant or one of Savrat's people may come in? But they would be too surprised to act straight off, and if she kept her head she could still kill me in an instant.*

"Stenwold wouldn't want me to kill you," she remarked pensively.

"The Beetle general."

"Stenwold Maker," she replied softly. "He is a fat, bald, clumsy old man. Also, he is mine."

The third cut on his neck was due to his own surprised reaction. He was becoming impatient, his Wasp temper rising, in a situation where impatience could prove fatal. "So, what?" he demanded.

She doesn't know.

But she was already saying, "I had wanted . . . wanted to try to talk to you, to convince you . . ."

He opened his mouth to say something, and just then a lieutenant of the watch put his head into the tent, mouth open to speak.

Arianna stabbed, even as Tynan tried to hurl himself off the bed.

I *can wait no longer.*

Tynisa had been in the imperial city now for days enough to know that no magical voice would solve this one for her. She had distributed her affections among the groping hands of a half dozen well-placed Wasps, each believing her a slave, or a whore, or a Rekef agent, depending on what role would best unlock their confidences. She could easily have brought Stenwold back a hundred of the Empire's most guarded secrets.

But it was not enough to get her what she wanted, because she had run into an unexpected barrier. The Empire survived off its slaves, the living produce of its foreign conquests. Everywhere throughout the Empire all the menial work was performed by them. There was only one place where that was not the case: the imperial palace in Capitas, where Tisamon was currently being held.

She could not get inside. None of her besotted Wasps could get her in, for those very few slaves of other kinden that lived within the palace were there for specific reasons. There was no room for random and unaccompanied foreigners in this very heart of the Empire. So, unless she put herself forward as a pit fighter, and thus sold herself into real chains, she could not hope to enter the palace with the Empire's consent.

She had considered the situation very thoroughly, and she had no option but to assume that Tisamon wanted to be freed. Therefore if Tisamon desired to be free, yet was not free, it could only be because the pit fighters' cells held him so tightly he could not escape. In those circumstances she would become as much of a prisoner as he was.

So she would therefore rely on old-fashioned methods: the resources of her mother's and father's kin.

Tonight she intended assaulting the Emperor's residence to get her father back.

Reaching the palace through the dark streets was challenge enough, for Capitas was an ordered city and only Wasps were allowed about after nightfall. It was a well-lit city, too, with gas lamps flaring at each street corner, so that the Emperor could look down after sunset and see himself at the heart of an almost geometric constellation.

She stalked the palace from the shadows, a tiny hunter approaching her monumental prey unseen. The nightly patrols and watchmen, with their pikes and lanterns, did not see her. She drew upon the Art inherent in her blood until she was right beside the palace walls.

There was too much light here, but she had no time to catch her breath. The main door was impossible, but the Wasps erected their public buildings so that they rose in tiers, each succeeding step of the ziggurat narrower than the last. Somewhere up there, there must be an unguarded way in. She had to believe that.

What would Tisamon do in the same circumstances? And the answer was simple. He would just go, without all this deliberation. He would *act*.

She went skimming up the wall and on to the next tier in moments, her Art keeping her hands and feet close to the immaculately dressed stone, up the wall and over it, and down half that distance to the ground on the other side. It was a garden enclosed in a walled courtyard, she found: a low assemblage of shrubs and ferns that must be monstrously difficult to keep properly watered. There were doors at the far end of it and she skulked toward them.

Locked, of course, so she must still keep going upward. Someone was bound to have left a balcony door open, a window unshuttered. She staved off the thought that the airborne Wasps would not necessarily lessen their security at a higher altitude, and that Tisamon's cell would be deep below ground, and therefore that she was getting ever further away from him.

Tisamon would keep going, and so shall I.

She ascended two more tiers, staying well clear of the slit windows that might betray her presence. Each time, she found doors that were firmly sealed, or open doorways giving on to brightly lit rooms where Wasps were working: servants or clerks or scribes. Nowhere inside them was there a gap dark enough for her to slink in unseen.

She went up once more, covering each vertical as quickly as possible for fear that some late messenger might spot her clinging there. A glance backward showed her the Emperor's own view: the pinprick lights of his city spread like candles below her.

Anyone might have delusions of grandeur, seeing that.

She clambered up on to a low-walled balcony, feeling exhausted by the ascent, for constant use of her Art was draining her. Tynisa had never climbed so far and so fast. She crouched for a moment, crouched very low within the shadow of the wall, to catch her breath.

This must be some Wasp lord's private view, she decided, allotted to some favourite of the Imperial Court. There was a carved stone table where perhaps the lord took his meals, and beyond it . . .

Beyond it was the open door. Not all the way open, but some careless servant had left it an inch ajar. Not locked, not barred, but ready for her—as though it had been left so at her order.

Quiet as quiet, she slipped into the darkened room beyond. She found herself alone there, in some antechamber hung with drapes. She crept on, one hand close to her rapier's hilt.

"Your boldness astounds me," said a dry voice, "but I presume that would be the Mantis blood."

She could see no source for the voice, but her blade was in her hand instantly, impotently.

"Once you have been marked by my kinden," continued the thin voice, "we can always sense you."

"Show yourself," she hissed.

She was abruptly no longer alone. There was a dark-robed shape in the room's corner that she had somehow missed. She rounded on it with her blade drawn back to strike, but then darkness rose about her on every side, clawing at her and dragging her down. She felt the rapier fall helplessly from her grip, and then she too was falling, dropping further and futher and away.

Tynisa awoke.

There was a pain in her head, but not suggesting she had been struck, unless it was possible to sustain a blow from within the skull.

She opened her eyes. She saw only black and yellow.

She cursed, kicking herself to her feet from the cold stone floor, but there were chains clasped about her ankles and she stumbled back against the wall of . . . of a cell. She was in a cell with a single barred window high up, one so small that a Fly-kinden child would have difficulty squeezing through it even without the bars.

"Well now," said a dry voice.

There were two Wasp-kinden guards in full armour, motionless and faceless behind the full helms of the Slave Corps. Between them stood a slight, robed figure, face hidden within a cowl. Pale, long-nailed hands were folded demurely before it.

Tynisa said nothing. Even to ask, *Who are you?* or *What happened to me?* would be to show weakness. She forced herself to remain calm. Her mind held no memory at all of what had befallen her.

"We meet formally at last," said the robed figure. "I have previously had only my subordinates' reports about you, and they have not done you justice. Tynisa Maker, I suppose they call you amongst the Beetle-kinden, but it's clear to me that the name is only borrowed."

"You have me at quite a disadvantage," she replied, finally, and her voice was at least steady. She had no idea who this thin creature was, but there was no reason she could not win it over.

The fragile-looking man approached her, and she could now make out some of his pale face beneath the cowl. "You have shown yourself remarkably gifted in reaching Capitas still a free woman," he said. "Aside from a little push, initially, I have not needed to assist you in your journey at all."

She felt something uneasy twist inside her. "A . . . push?"

"Oh now, who do you think brought you here? Who gave you the idea? None but my servant, working according to my plan. Still, you have proved remarkably able. After this is done, perhaps I can find a use for you, if you survive."

"And for what possible purpose could you want me here?" she asked, but her voice was less steady now that he was so close. There was something about him that frightened her, for no reason she could have named.

"Insurance," he explained simply. "You see, your father is due to die for me tomorrow, and I thought that he might need motivating."

She went for him then, clawing for his face, but the chains that restrained her brought her up short. As he caught one of her wrists in his thin-looking hand, she found his grip was far stronger than it had any right to be.

"As it happens, our dear Tisamon seems more than happy to cast his life away. He considers it his destiny, and perhaps it is." The half-seen lips, bluish in that white face, twitched. "It is such a shame that my people never discovered the Mantis-kinden in the way our enemies did. They were the Moths' private army of fanatics for centuries: superstitious, malleable, easily led for all their pride. And you, my dear Tynisa, have inherited all that from your poor doomed father. I barely had to extend myself to bring you here. You practically locked your own shackles."

"You're going to kill Tisamon."

"No, no, he can see to that himself, being the expert after all. It seems likely though, that after all your travels you may not be needed after all." His eyes were red, she noticed. She could see them bloody and glistening under the shadow of his hood. He smiled at her, avuncular. "But still, why leave even that to chance? I shall keep you close to me, tomorrow, the slave of a slave, and if his heart turns before he steps on to the sand, then his daughter's blood shall provide sufficient leverage to change his mind." He smiled. "It seems you will get to watch him die, after all."

They set him against scorpions.

It was the anniversary of the coronation of his Imperial Majesty Alvdan the Second. There were public games being held throughout the Empire and the populace was encouraged to celebrate. On the whole the people did so willingly.

There would be a half dozen separate arenas shedding blood across the city of

Capitas alone but the Emperor would be present at this one only, the grandest and the largest. It was a great open space of sand surrounded by high barriers, with tiers of seats beyond, entirely roofed over with silk rendered luminous by the sun. Ult and his fellows, the trainers and jailers, had devised an ever-mounting spectacle of contests: men against beasts, men against machines but, more than any other matching, men set against men. Slaves had killed each other with awkward desperation to the crowd's amusement. Experienced pit fighters had slaughtered deserters. Rebels and criminals had died at the hands of imperial soldiers. There were those who had never held a blade before being cast out on to the sand, but also there were veterans of a score of fights, their brief moments of celebrity written in the scars on their bodies.

And then there was Tisamon. Few had ever seen a Mantis-kinden fight, for they did not submit themselves to capture and slavery often. Above all, none had seen a Mantis Weaponsmaster.

They had given him first the animal: a great pale-shelled scorpion, old and cunning. It had lain with its belly close to the sand and waited for him to come to it. He had stalked it, wary of those heavy claws held so tight to its body, but it had struck with its sting only, the claws providing shields to ward him off. The crowd had known it well, and called it "Opalesce" and expected it to win. They had called out its name frenziedly until the moment when Tisamon had vaulted over those protective claws to land on its back and, catching the lethal sting in one hand, had driven his claw down between its eyes.

He was back now, having rested for the space of five contests, and a murmur went through the crowd when they saw him. He heard his own name on their lips.

Ult sat close to the gladiators' gate, and Tisamon caught his eye briefly. The old Wasp merely nodded, a neutral gesture, but Tisamon saw doubt in his face. This was to be the promised unarmed match and Ult was not entirely sure that Tisamon was up to it.

Tisamon's opponent was already waiting: Scorpion-kinden instead of scorpion animal. He was built on a massive scale, twice as broad across the shoulder as Tisamon himself, barrel-chested and with arms almost contorted with muscle. His hands formed claws, thumb and forefinger grown into long blades of bone. He was stripped to the waist and the physiology thus revealed looked something beyond human.

Tisamon shrugged off his slave's tunic, looking like a child or a toy before the Scorpion, but his own blades flexed in readiness from his forearms. He dropped into his fighting stance, perfectly balanced and waiting.

The Scorpion moved faster than someone of his bulk had any right to, a sudden scuttle across the sand, claws driving for Tisamon's face, trying to run him back against the wall. Tisamon swayed to one side, feeling the man's finger-blade cut the air just an inch from his eye, while thrusting a leg out to trip the man in his charge. The Scorpion stumbled, but held his feet, delivering a murderously swift backhand blow as he passed. Tisamon disengaged, stepping out of range and back into his stance, watching to see how the other man had taken it.

There was no anger in the Scorpion's eyes: his savagery was entirely divorced from his emotions. Tisamon noted this, and reassessed his opponent.

He spotted the slight flexing of muscles before the Scorpion's next charge, and so was better ready for it. He moved in to meet the man, and hammer blows from the Scorpion, which would have broken his arm if he blocked them, were turned away by precise circular gestures of Tisamon's hands, until he stood calmly in the eye of the storm. The Scorpion had reach, though, and he kept Tisamon at the end of it, slightly too far to strike back. He kept methodically assaulting the Mantis' defences, looking for any weakness, seeking a way in.

Tisamon stepped out of reach three times without having struck a blow in return, and there was still no sign of fatigue or frustration at all in his opponent, just a dreadful patience. Tisamon watched carefully and waited.

The crowd was getting restless, shouting for this fight to be finished one way or another. Tisamon did not care: they could go hang themselves for all it meant to him. The Scorpion was a professional, though. The crowd's approval was his reward. It eventually made him take a chance.

Tisamon saw the feint coming, at the last moment realized it was the off-hand that would be the danger. The claws of the Scorpion's right clipped his shoulder in a little dart of pain, but then Tisamon was inside the man's reach, past the upward-driving left, and he brought his own spines down sharply on either side of the man's neck. He drew blood, but not enough, for the man's hide was Art-strong, durable as leather. Tisamon kicked upward, getting a foot on the man's thigh, then another on his shoulder, vaulting over him and turning to face him. The Scorpion backed off three steps, blood trickling its way down his chest.

There was a tremble in his eyes that had not been there before. He had scars, but they were old scars, or small scars, evidence that nobody had recently come so close. The crowd held its breath.

Tisamon attacked, moving from still to swift without a warning, but the Scorpion was still almost ready for him, blocking three blows before the fourth speared past his guard to cut a gash across his chest—not his throat as Tisamon had intended. The big man tried to carry the fight back at him, stabbing at Tisamon's stomach, but the Mantis twisted sideways about the strike, lashed his spines across the other man's face in passing and then dropped to one knee behind him. With clinical precision he sliced across the back of the man's legs, stepping out of the way as his opponent fell.

The crowd had gone silent as Tisamon stood beside his victim, hearing the man's breath hissing, raw, amid his pain. He knew the custom now, as Ult had explained it to him. It would be for the Emperor alone to decide.

Tisamon looked up at the Emperor for the first time since the man's hurried visit to the cells, and his eyes began seeking for a way in.

Below the first row of the crowd there was a ring of soldiers atop the high wall of the pit, men in full armour with spears. They would be the first barrier to overcome. The Emperor, of course, had his own private room facing the arena, a long enclosure constructed out of fabric that hid him from the crowd on both sides, so that only those sitting across from him could see him clearly, and then only from well outside of sting range. More soldiers were standing on guard directly before the Emperor and on either side of his box.

Alvdan the Second sat staring down at the victor and, when their eyes met, Tisamon thought he saw the man flinch. He noticed an older man, balding and thickset, seated almost beside the Emperor, and behind him . . .

For a moment Tisamon just stared, feeling something kick inside him. There was a darkness behind the Emperor that might be a robed man, a pale smear that must be a face half hidden beneath a cowl, and to one side a younger Wasp woman whose face resembled the Emperor's own, but on the other side of the cowled figure was . . .

Atryssa.

Atryssa, his long-dead lover, looked down on him, and she nodded. He saw it distinctly. She nodded her approval, her permission.

The Emperor drew a dagger and held it high, and Tisamon, obedient to the signal, drove his spines down into the Scorpion-kinden's throat, finishing him. The Mantis barely realized what he had done, though. He felt as though a monstrous weight had been suddenly lifted from him.

She approves. She forgives. He almost stumbled as he left the arena.

He never considered that she might be his daughter, not his lover. He was too far lost in the maze of his own honour for that thought. Instead he took her silent camaraderie for absolution, and he used it to cut free twenty years of guilt.

I am ready now, he decided.

TWENTY-NINE

There were four guards leading Kaszaat, clustered to either side and behind her as though uncertain what to do with her. She was not quite a prisoner, therefore, but far less than free. It was the Auxillian rank, of course, Totho realized. Kaszaat was a sergeant, after all, and it threw them a little to have been obliged to arrest her.

Totho saw Big Greyv shift, leaning on the haft of his axe, though still lurking in the shadow of the engine. It was astonishing, he considered remotely, how very quiet the Mole Cricket could be, how easily overlooked.

"Speak," Drephos commanded. Totho saw his superior purse his lips, but there was no surprise on his face, only a faint disappointment.

"We caught her at one of the machines," called up a soldier.

"She is an artificer, so how unexpected was that?" Drephos asked. He did not raise his voice, but his tone was sharp enough to carry. The wind promised for the morning had yet to rise, and the air was very still.

"One of *our* artificers reckoned she was breaking it," the soldier explained. The slight hint of stress showed what he thought of Drephos' ragged crew. "Sabotage, he said. Said we should bring her to you or, if you wouldn't deal with it, he'd take it up with the governor. After all, she's one of them."

"I had always thought," Drephos said, probably too softly now for the soldiers to hear, "that she was one of mine." For a moment he paused, staring down, disparate hands resting on the railing. Kaszaat glared up at him defiantly, looking so much slighter than the guards behind her. Totho felt something twist inside him.

"Sergeant-Auxillian Kaszaat, step forward," Drephos ordered. She did so instinctively.

"I placed faith in you," Drephos told her. "I had not thought I had done so badly by you as to merit this." His voice was carrying clearly again, finding her ears without effort. "I gave you station and position, drew you from the ranks of the slaves to be one of my chosen. How, therefore, has it come to this?" Hearing him and his genuinely aggrieved tone, Totho believed that the man truly did not understand—the master of machines was stuck with a problem that his own invincible logic could not solve.

Kaszaat was shaking her head slowly, and reflected in her eyes was the unnatural monster she was looking at, who could not himself see what was so plain to everyone else there.

The guards understand more than he does, Totho thought, as Kaszaat cried out, "Drephos, they're my *kin!*" Her admission changed the attitude of the guards, and Totho saw their hands flex, and one man shift his grip on the snapbow he was carrying. He met Kaszaat's eyes just briefly, and the loathing in them made him flinch. She had found him here with the enemy, and she could not know that he had come simply for the same purpose. *The same purpose—but I have failed. Even before she came Drephos had talked me out of it.*

"But, Kaszaat," Drephos continued, and he was still so dreadfully hurt, so absurdly hurt by her turning from him, "how can you choose an accident of birth over our *work?*" So spoke Drephos the half-breed, even as Totho was a half-breed: both men without kin and without homes.

And Kaszaat let out a shriek of pure anger, bursting forward suddenly, flinging her hand up toward Drephos as though in salute. Totho was shouting her name even as she did so, seeing the darkness shift as Big Greyv abruptly stirred into motion. She had caught them all by surprise, standing there guarded and unarmed but, like a good magician, there had been something up her sleeve.

It was a slender silver rod and less than a foot long, the simplest iteration of the snapbow she could construct. It was in her hand instantly, and the trigger pressed, and Totho saw something flash past his face—no precise shape, just the impression of movement. Drephos rocked back, and Totho saw the quilled end of the dart buried at the point where his shoulder met his chest.

Kaszaat was still moving forward, though he would never discover what she intended next. The first sting blast struck her a glancing blow to her side, though the snapbow bolt passed by her, the guards caught unprepared by her sudden move. It was Big Greyv's great axe, cleaving out of the darkness in a colossal double-handed swing, that buried itself in her chest, crushed her body entirely with the force of it, flinging her back into the guards and scattering them.

Totho felt the impact like a physical shock to his own body and his own snapbow, his glorious repeating snapbow, was now levelled in his hands and, without a moment's hesitation, he pulled on the trigger, feeling the weapon rattle, its mechanism still slightly rough and needing adjustment.

Three shots tore through Big Greyv, ripping into the massive Mole Cricket's frame and driving the huge man to his knees. The rest sprayed the guards even as they were gaping at Kaszaat's body, the weapon leaping wildly in his hands, but the bolts punching straight through armour and flesh without distinction. Only the last man to fall had some idea of what was happening, and he was able to look up and see his killer before the bolt found him.

And there will be more guards, Totho thought desperately, automatically fitting a new magazine just as he had when he tested the weapon. Even as he thought it, he heard running footsteps from the tower's other side. Two sentries who had heard the shouting were coming up, not seeing any bodies yet, hearing no massed attack and so suspecting little. They did not even hear the snapbow crack before Totho had shot both of them dead.

More, surely? But no more came. The sentries from the other side of the line must have been the same men who came with Kaszaat. The Bee-kinden rebels of Szar were well dug in, and nobody was expecting an attack.

A hand closed on the barrel of his snapbow and crushed the metal like foil, twisting it closed and useless. Totho jerked back and found himself at the rail with Drephos standing before him, the ruined weapon dangling from his metal hand. The master artificer looked at it sadly, recognizing the waste. He turned the same expression on Totho.

Totho went for him, fumbling for a knife at his belt. Drephos' artificial arm, the bolt still jutting from its shoulder, was quicker. It took his wrist in a vise grip that shot pain through Totho, forcing him back against the rail.

"Why?" Drephos asked him, but Totho had no answers for him. From the moment of Kaszaat's arrival here tonight he had felt that his choices had been stripped from him, and the path he might otherwise have taken was closed.

His left hand found the hammer in his tool belt and, despite the grinding pain in his other wrist, he pulled it out and struck. It was a small hammer, but he knew what he was doing now: striking not as a warrior but as an artificer. He hammered Drephos' arm three times, three precise strokes, denting in the elbow and the shoulder and locking them in place. Drephos' mottled face went pale at the last blow, and Totho knew that he had impacted something, some pin or plate, deep enough to reach the real man.

He deliberately struck again at the same place, and Drephos hissed through bared teeth, sweat suddenly standing out on his forehead as the metal of his surrogate body cut deep into the flesh he had been born with. He fell to his knees, dragging Totho down by his rigid arm, and Totho saw the tears of pain in his eyes. His living hand clawed weakly at the ruined shoulder. He did not cry out. Either his pride or the pain was too great for that.

Working carefully, left-handed, Totho removed the man's thumb. Once he had prised the covering plate off, it was surprisingly easy, but of course Drephos would have had to maintain it single-handed and so it had been designed for that facility. That done, Totho could remove his bruised wrist from the other's locked grasp.

Looking down at the carnage he had wrought, his first thought was to go below to join Kaszaat, but there would be no last-second reconciliation there, no last fond words or exchange of vows. Big Greyv's single blow had killed her as thoroughly as a catapult stone.

Drephos let out a long, ragged breath, and Totho turned back to him. The master artificer gripped a pair of pliers awkwardly in one hand, with which he was trying to release something in his trapped shoulder. His fingers shook and his face was clenched into agonized concentration. When he saw Totho watching him, he stopped, the pliers scraping on metal. His eyes were bright through his agonized mask.

"So what now?" he asked. "Do I scream for the guards? And what do *you* do now, Totho?" His voice was so quiet and clipped with pain that Totho had to hunch forward to hear him.

Totho looked beyond him past the gleaming metal of the engine toward the rebels' lines. The city was waiting in the still air, waiting for what morning would bring. He knelt by Drephos, wondering how easy it would be to free the damaged arm, or whether Drephos could even survive the loss of this mechanical part of himself.

"You've not so long left," Drephos said, his voice trembling despite all his self-possession. "Better make your decision soon."

"I have decided," Totho announced, standing up again. "And in a way, I think you would approve."

Toward morning, the Bee-kinden soldiers that had apprehended him brought him before their leader.

"What's this?" Maczech demanded, sparing him only a brief glance. If she was now queen of the people of Szar, very little of her status showed. She wore a studded leather cuirass over worn, dusty garments, and she stood hunched over a table, poring over a map of the city with three of her officers. Totho could see the positions of the Wasps and the locals marked across it as solid or dotted lines.

Time to redraw the map, he reflected.

"He was approaching the barricades," Totho's captor reported. "He stopped immediately when ordered. He also came unarmed."

She glanced at him again. She was young and, of course, reminded him of Kaszaat, just by her very race, the shape of her face and nut-brown skin. He had expected another Kymene, all fire and fierce leadership, but Maczech lacked that woman's unbreachable resolve, and he could read in her face an agony of fear that she would lead her people astray. She had come to her throne suddenly, and been made her people's war leader in the same moment, and she was afraid.

She looked as though she had not slept in some time, and for a moment they just stared at one another dully.

"A half-breed," she noted. "What else are you?" Before he could reply, she had looked him up and down. "Auxillian artificer," she identified. "But I don't believe in defectors—not this close to a battle."

The slip was evident there, of course, although nobody else seemed to have noticed. *Plenty of defectors before a battle*, Totho thought, *but not from the side that's most likely to win.*

"What do you want?" she continued. "You've a message? We will not accept terms that leave our city in chains." Her voice trembled slightly, but none of the surrounding Bee-kinden seemed to notice. She had their absolute faith, and it was torturing her.

Totho felt a lump in his throat at that. *She knows very well that they cannot hold against the Wasps, not forever.* The time would come, in the normal course of this fight, when they would accept whatever terms were offered them. Totho guessed that Maczech herself would be dead by that point.

"Your city is free," he said quietly.

"And will remain so as long as we draw breath," she declared, turning away.

"Your city is free," he repeated.

Man by man, a silence fell on the Szaren's little command room. Maczech and her officers turned their heads, one by one, until they were all staring at him.

"Explain yourself, half-breed," she said.

He felt himself start to shake, ever so slightly, at the thought of having to put it into words. "The Wasps are defeated. The Szaren garrison, I mean. Not the Empire, just those here."

Someone snorted in amusement, but Maczech's face remained stern. "Some Rekef trick," she said slowly, "though I cannot see what it is supposed to achieve. Just waste our precious time, perhaps."

"Send a flier," Totho said. "Send a flier over the governor's palace. *High* over, and he must not land."

"A trap," one of the officers decided.

"For one scout?" Maczech narrowed her eyes, trying to see past Totho's face to the thoughts contained behind it. "Send one of the Fly-kinden. They see best in the dark."

"But—"

"Please," she said, a calm word, without force, that silenced the man and sent him running to fetch a messenger.

"I think you are mad," she told Totho. "Either a deceiver, or mad."

He nodded tiredly. "You may be right." Abruptly his legs buckled and he fell to his knees. Something inside him was building, a pressure that he could not release. He shuddered, feeling the bile rise within him.

"Is he ill?" someone asked, and someone else called out for a doctor.

"There was a woman with us named Kaszaat," Totho said. "She was of your people. But she died." His words were almost too quiet for them to hear. "That is why I have done what I did." It was not true, of course, or not wholly true. Some of the reason that he had done it would make sense only to Drephos.

"Get him some water, at least," Maczech ordered, and a moment later Totho found himself holding a clay cup. He sipped and it tasted stale, chemical. He shuddered again. Meanwhile, around him, aside from the two Bee-kinden guards watching him with axes in their hands, the war council proceeded. He put his face in his hands, waiting.

Eventually the scout came back. Totho's only fear had been that curiosity would tempt the Fly in to land, but she had kept to her orders, a middle-aged woman who barely reached past Maczech's waist. On her return she looked unsteady, unsure of herself.

"Report," Maczech instructed her, but the Fly had to swallow twice before she could say anything.

"I saw . . . there are some Wasp soldiers leaving the city. I counted perhaps a few hundred, mostly in small groups." She glanced at Totho, and her eyes looked haunted.

Maczech was frowning. "What is this?" she asked.

The Fly held up a hand. "Nothing else," she said, and then forced the words out of herself. "There was nothing else moving behind the Wasp lines."

"Well, they are asleep?" started one of the officers, but the Fly broke in immediately.

"I saw bodies. Bodies of sentries, of men stationed beside the artillery. Nothing else. There was a kind of . . . haze over the palace . . . a yellow haze."

"What is this?" Maczech demanded again, but this time addressing Totho. The guards hauled him to his feet, and she saw something in his face that took her a step back. "What have you done?" she whispered.

"All gone," Totho replied. He thought of the effort, to haul those heavy kegs into the governor's palace, until he had three of them stacked in an upper storeroom, six in another on the ground floor, four in the barracks itself. One of the guards had even offered to help him, but he had refused. It was trained artificer work, he had explained.

I had to do it with my own hands. That way I can blame nobody else, not Kaszaat and certainly not Drephos.

He felt a hand grip his chin, drag his face around until he was looking into Maczech's eyes.

"What has happened?" she asked him. "Tell me clearly. Please."

"All the Wasps are gone," he said simply. "The whole garrison is dead. Except a few who must have been too far away from it." Her eyes still held him and he continued. "It was their own weapon, that they were going to use against you." So simple it had been, with those kegs, to rig explosive charges with a clockwork timer, and then creep out of the garrison again. Only small charges, ones you'd barely hear.

"That's impossible," one of the Bees said. "That means thousands of soldiers."

"Yes," said Totho, feeling the shakes return. "And auxillians, and servants and slaves, and beasts. But they're all dead now. The city's yours." He choked on the next thought before he could add, "Except for the palace and garrison quarters. I wouldn't go there for at least a month. Maybe two months, just to be sure. And maybe you should draw your people away from your barricades, just in case. Put a few streets' clear space between you and . . . it. It's too heavy to drift far in the wind, but even so . . ."

They were all staring at him now and he saw that they were beginning to believe him. With believing came not triumph but a kind of stunned horror.

"We never wanted this," Maczech said hollowly, shaking her head. "We wanted our freedom back. Was that so wrong? We wanted to drive them away, so that we could live in our city in peace. How has this happened? What have you done?"

The Bee-kinden were shuffling away from him, as though what he had become might be contagious somehow. They looked on him and saw an atrocity, a destroyer beyond their capacity to comprehend. An entire army dead in one night, with not a blow struck, not a battle cry—just a small detonation and a slight yellowing of the air. Their expressions suggested that he, Totho of Collegium, had become an abomination.

He could not help but agree with them.

◊ ◊ ◊

Major Krellac considered his options, none of which appealed to him.

He was a dutiful officer, who had never been considered anything other than dependable by his superiors. That was why they had given him the Myna relief force, where his orders would be straightforward, the tactical position simple. Colonel Gan had despatched him from Szar with strict instructions.

The situation had changed, however. He was conscious now of being a man confronted with history, a man whose name, for better or worse, would be remembered. *For worse* seemed undeniably more likely, whatever course he chose.

On the one hand he had his orders: they were to enter the city of Myna, relieve the besieged garrison and put down the rebellion. Implied in that was his triumphant return to Szar, where Colonel Gan and the rest of the higher command would be celebrating their own swiftly anticipated victory over the local insurgents. There was no ambiguity in Krellac's situation insofar as his orders went.

His scouts had just come back from Myna reporting that there was no garrison left to relieve. Krellac's forces had been joined by almost half a thousand Wasp soldiers lucky enough to escape the city, and many of them were too badly shaken to even make proper report on the disposition of the enemy. Instead of catching the resistance in a pincer, he was presented with a battered but unified city. Colonel Gan had given him a siege train so, if necessary, he could pound down the city gates and fight the Mynans street to street, but that was not what his orders had detailed and he was unhappy about it.

It was while he was digesting this unwelcome development that the messengers from Szar reached him. "Messengers" was actually too grand a term for what they were, but he refused to think of them as refugees.

The Szaren garrison was gone.

"Gone?" he had asked, and the survivors had said, "Yes, gone." And the more they divulged, the more Major Krellak had felt a creeping chill rise within him, because the Szaren garrison had not been defeated in battle, had not fallen to some sudden surprise attack of the Bee-kinden: it had just . . . died. There had been a kind of fog, and men had dropped dead even as they began to notice it. The men who had found their way to Krellac had been those on sentry duty or patrol, minding the new artillery or keeping watch on the rebels: the men furthest from the governor's palace and the garrison. Nobody else had escaped. *Nobody*.

Compared to that, the other news seemed nothing. Fly-kinden messengers had arrived at Myna, some mistakenly dropping into the city, but others realizing their mistake and diverting to find the nearest Wasp camp, which meant Krellac. They came from the provinces northwest of Myna: provinces that had become part of the Empire only after the Twelve-Year War against the Commonweal. They were sent to warn all standing forces that there was some manner of Dragonfly-kinden force massing beyond the borders, therefore after all this time it seemed that the Commonwealers were going to reopen the old wounds. Of course the Empire had a strong force stationed there, if for no other reason than because taking over further principalities of the Commonweal was constantly in the minds of some generals. But how would they fare now, with Myna and Szar in the hands of enemies, and their lines of supply severed?

Everyone was now waiting for him to come to a decision. Some of his officers had advocated pressing on to Myna; others said that he should return to Szar as quickly as possible. Some even said he should press onward to Maynes, closer to the Commonweal, to combine forces with the garrison there. The decision was Krellac's alone.

But he found he could not make it. He was a man who obeyed orders, and orders had suddenly abandoned him. He sent messengers to Capitas imploring instructions, and had his men set up camp, and then did nothing.

THIRTY

Uctebri shifted in his seat, momentarily discomforted.

Tisamon would do. He had proved to himself long before that Tisamon would be the perfect tool. Now he wondered whether the man might be *too* good, too fit for the purpose. That had not occurred to him before. He had seen the way that Tisamon had looked at Alvdan, and he was not surprised. What had shaken him was the way that Alvdan had stared back.

He knows, Uctebri thought, followed by, *He can't know* and then again, despite all logic, *He knows.* Not about the plot, of course. Not about Seda or Uctebri's own perfidy, but about Tisamon. Alvdan knew that Tisamon intended to kill him.

It was impossible, of course. The best of duellists, the most determined of killers, could not achieve it. Yet Uctebri had seen Alvdan flinch when the Mantis' gaze was turned upon him.

"Your Imperial Majesty," he murmured, leaning forward.

Alvdan did not return his gaze, but said, "That man, we do not like him."

General Maxin gave a short laugh from the other side of him. "Then you are in an ideal position, Majesty, since you can watch him die."

"We have ordered it," Alvdan agreed. "If he does not die fighting, we shall have him executed."

Uctebri saw Maxin's brow wrinkle at the bad form of that, but he shrugged and nodded.

"As your Majesty decrees."

Alvdan's mouth twitched. "Uctebri," he snapped, "slave."

"I am here, Majesty."

"It will be tonight as you have promised. I will accept no more delays."

So that is it, Uctebri realized, and berated himself for not understanding sooner. The promise of death in Tisamon's eyes was a final reminder of mortality. Alvdan had given himself over now to the dream of sorcerous eternal life that Uctebri had held out before him. The ritual that Uctebri had promised him was the removal of all worries about an heir and the succession. Uctebri had indeed assured the Emperor that it would be realized tonight, on the anniversary of his ascension to the throne. He had even prepared a room for the promised moment, with eldritch markings on the floor, with candles and bells and crystals, and an altar, of course, for the sacrifice. All of it dressing, all invention, for the ritual would take place sooner than Alvdan had guessed, and to a very different end.

Both Ucterbi's pale hands were clutched about the Shadow Box, resting in his lap.

The Mosquito-kinden glanced to his right. Chained to the floor and crouching like a pet was the Mantis' half-breed daughter, just in case Tisamon should, at the last moment, need some additional persuasion.

He looked toward Seda, seated between himself and the Emperor, seeing her fidget distractedly. Her time, which would be his own time, had almost come. It now needed only the blood of an Emperor, and Uctebri knew exactly where to acquire that. With such blood on his hands, and therefore on hers, she would be his to control, and the great might of the Wasp Empire would be at his fingertips.

He was still undecided as to which way to turn it. The Moth-kinden were due an extinction, since they had done their best to extinguish Uctebri's people so long ago, but Uctebri rather thought that his first act as the power behind the throne would be to teach the naysayers of his own breed a lesson. He would root them out of their holes, drag them into the light and before the throne. He would then show them his creation, his puppet, the witch-queen Seda, and perhaps he would have some of them exsanguinated as in the old days. Yes, the Empire was ripe for the reintroduction of a few customs from the Days of Lore, and all the easier since these Wasps were such a guilelessly cruel and energetic breed.

Seated beside him, Seda glanced around again. She looked ill at ease and nervous, but inside she was noting the faces around her that she knew.

They are all in place, those of them I can see. She would be either victorious or dead by dawn, she knew well. Either way, she could no longer live under the shadow of her brother's spite, or of Maxin's knife. Always plots within plots within plots.

Crouching behind Uctebri, Tynisa had eyes only for Tisamon. Her hands were shackled, her feet chained to the floor. A cold and terrible feeling overwhelmed her. *I do not want to watch this.*

But I must. Because someone must, and that should be someone who knew him, and who cared. Whatever was about to happen, there must be a witness.

When he stepped out before them, the crowd fell very nearly silent, as though seven hundred Wasp-kinden were collectively holding their breaths. It was not just for him, of course, for Felise had stepped out to face him across the arena at the very same time. She had been fighting her practice matches too. They had watched her, just as they had watched him, and it had not taken much imagination to realize that now at this climax of the games they would come together.

They had taken away her iridescent armour that was glittering proof against sting shot. She wore only a band of cloth across her breasts, a leather binding about her shoulders and back, and otherwise the same loose, short britches that Tisamon did. The Wasps liked to see their blood on display, their wounds clearly visible. Her pose was defiant, as though she had never been captured, and Tisamon realized suddenly that she had not, just as he had not.

We are neither of us prisoners, not standing here with our blades drawn. These are the parts of us that mere bars cannot hold.

His mind felt clear now. It was twenty years since it had been so clear. What a mad time for him to suddenly become sane! What a moment for him to understand, in front of all these witnesses, that he loved Felise like nothing on earth.

He looked Felise straight in the eyes. The shock of such visual contact made him misstep as he walked toward her. Her return stare lanced into his mind with the fierce intensity of her passion.

Not hate, love. *She has every reason to hate me.* Standing before the host of his enemies, preparing himself for his last fight, Tisamon considered, *I am a lucky man and I am thankful.*

She carried her sword, of course: that long-hafted Dragonfly blade that moved like light and shadow in her hands. He himself had his clawed gauntlet, his constant companion that was like part of his body. This would be a match such as had never been seen before by imperial eyes.

The bindings about her shoulders were not armour, nor merely decorative. The Wasps had given some careful thought to how to banish a slave's Art wings without stopping her moving freely. They wanted her to fight, but not to fly.

He held her eyes. He did not even need to mouth anything, or look anywhere else but there. She *understood*, and she let him know what she could give him. They faced each other across the sand in the stance of rival combatants but they were of one mind. He could feel his own mind letting go, piece by piece, stripping itself down to this one honed purpose. The Wasp crowd was now so quiet that it was as if they were merely part of the plan. The hush was almost conspiratorial.

He had drawn his blade back, his off-hand extended forward to parry, his weight resting on the back foot. Felise's sword rose vertical before her, leaning slightly forward. His view of her face was now bisected by the blade.

He felt as though they were dancers, awaiting the music.

As she moved, sword blurring, he swayed aside, first left, then right, and the blade came down toward his face, and he brushed it aside with the palm of his free hand. Meanwhile his claw came in. He gave her no time, slashing at her head, at her side. She spun out of the way. Abruptly there was distance between them again. They circled, and the excitement of the crowd grew feverish. Such a flurry of blows, each one intended to be fatal, and not a drop of blood. They were both so swift, so sure, that the watchers were left disentangling each pass, marvelling that one or both had not yet been struck dead.

He lunged at her, and felt a joy that he could use every ounce of his skill against her, his blade dancing and flashing about her guard, skittering from the straight steel of her own weapon, snapping out again into sudden thrusts at her eyes, her stomach, her throat. There was no need for him to hold back: she was good enough to hold him off, and when she came back at him it was for real. She was trying to kill him. They were striving, with every drop of blood, to kill each other, secure in the knowledge that it could not be done.

Are we immortal? Yes, for this dance of moments they were immortal.

He cut close. She jerked her head aside and the blade nicked her cheek. Her sword clipped his shoulder. She was smiling, and he realized that so was he, both conscious of the sudden whisper of shock around the pit, at the first sight of blood. They broke apart again.

Her blood, some several drops of it, was on his claw. He touched his lips to the metal, tasting it. The crowd loved that. They relished the bestial barbarism of the foreigner. Only Felise recognized the kiss.

She understood entirely.

She went for him, and her sword cut wide arcs to either side of her opponent. He lashed for her chest and she deflected the blow with a swift circular motion, turning it instantly into a riposte that was likely to split his head open. He dropped to one knee, crooking his claw inward and driving it for her ribs, but she stepped in close so that it was his spined forearm instead that cut her. She reversed her blade to drive it point-down into him, and he threw himself forward, catching her about the waist with his free arm, registering the shock of feeling her skin against his, the warmth and the strength of it. Her blade, thus jolted, cut a shallow line across his shoulder blade and he carried her forward, his claw whipping across her shoulders, left and right.

He released her, backing off for the next charge. He could hardly contain himself. *So alive!* She had by now dropped into a defensive stance in readiness for him. He tensed himself to spring.

For a brief, lost moment he wondered if there could have been more than this for the pair of them. That seemed unlikely. *We were doomed from the start.* Tragedy without regret: it was a very Mantis-kinden concept. *Perhaps I am a good Mantis after all.*

It was only after he had started running toward her that she shrugged her shoulders and the leather bindings parted where he himself had cut them, and her wings flashed into life.

His blade was still drawn back as they met. He took her sword from her, and her hands grasped him under the arms, and she kicked off.

Not far, because she could not have borne him far. All he needed, though, was six or eight feet added on to his jump and, before the astonishment of seven hundred Wasps, he found footing on the top of the barrier and killed three soldiers as he landed. Felise had retrieved her sword from him by then, and they began to fight for real.

The soldiers stationed along the perimeter bunched forward around them, because Felise had taken them straight to the imperial box and she and Tisamon were now less than five yards from the Emperor and pressing forward. There was a confusion of armoured men trying to block their way amid a clutter of spear shafts. Spears might be ideal for keeping people confined in the pit but they needed space to be brought to bear. The wretched guards could not step back, for every foot conceded was a foot closer to their lord. Their spear shafts merely tangled, so they dropped them. Their stings flashed past or between the two fighting slaves, burning only empty air or each other. In such close confines the short blades of Felise's sword and Tisamon's claw performed a rigorous test of the guards' armour and their training, and found them wanting, every weak point penetrated, every seam opened up. In the first few stunned seconds, the nearest Wasp soldiers seemed to unfold outward from the mêlée like the petals of a flower.

The soldiers lined up before the imperial seats were now running forward, drawing their short swords, shouting for their companions to get out of the way. The soldiers stationed behind Uctebri and the princess were rushing to join them. Even the Emperor's scribe had his penknife in his hand, ready to make a stand against this sudden incursion.

Tynisa stared helplessly, feeling the weight of the chains about her. She stared at her father in his moment of terrible glory. All around, the crowd were shouting, screaming, even cheering, a riot in the making, but her own world seemed to have gone silent. She saw only those two battling figures, continually eclipsed by the Wasp soldiers and then suddenly in sight again. She saw that Felise now had a bloody gash across her ribs, and the weal left by a sting's near miss along her back. A soldier took his broken spear and managed to jam the point of it into Tisamon's leg before the Mantis killed him. The wound did not seem to slow Tisamon at all. Tynisa felt tears coursing down her face. *He cannot do it. There are too many of them.*

She looked over at the hateful pale man beside her and understood that it was not his plan that Tisamon should succeed. Tisamon had already accomplished what he had been intended to do, and Uctebri the Sarcad was taking advantage of it.

He is perfect. Uctebri thrilled at seeing the Mantis weave through the storm of stings and spears and swords, with his jointed claw constantly in motion, cleaving again and again and casting the refuse aside. Beside him the Dragonfly woman was just as swift. He saw her sword dart and dive, her movements small and controlled and utterly savage, lopping at wrists and necks, goring unprotected throats and bellies. Then it got caught in the body of one of her victims and she abandoned it instantly, the claws of her thumbs folding out. Her presence was unexpected, and for a moment he even wondered, *Can they . . . ?*

But they could not. More soldiers were arriving all the time, pushing their way around the edge of the arena or coasting across it, and if it had been possible for Alvdan to die at the hands of a pit fighter then he would be dead already. Uctebri realized that he had been caught in the trap he had set for everyone else, staring in horror and fascination at the frenzied knot of bloodshed. He had work to do, and Tisamon and Felise, through their final flurry of skill, had gifted him with exactly what he needed. Nobody was watching him, or even the Emperor. As was proper for a pit fight, they had eyes only for the killing.

He glanced about, seeing that all the guards that had so recently surrounded him were now committed to the fight. With amusement he found that General Maxin, instead of rushing to his lord's aid, had backed as far as he could go from the fray, eyes fixed on the bloody stalemate that was now seething at the edge of the pit. No danger there.

Now. His hands tightened on the Shadow Box, that had been so hard to come by. He needed power for this, strength beyond his own, strength from a time when men like him were truly strong.

Laetrimae, come forth, he commanded. *Come forth to serve me.*

She boiled into the air, a writhing smudge of thorns and briars within which hung her human form, pierced and crucified. The eyes she turned on him were a faceted glitter shining with her dispassionate loathing.

"Kill him," Uctebri commanded, not needing to say who. "Give me his strength."

The strength of an Emperor, he sought. Alvdan might underneath it all be simply a mortal man, a ruler merely by accident of birth, but such symbols carried power within magic. The strength of an Emperor could bind an empire; the strength of a brother could bind a sister.

Laetrimae lurched forward, flickering in the dim air, but Alvdan saw none of it. His hands were locked on to the arms of his throne, as he pressed back into the seat. He stared at Tisamon and, from the midst of the throng, from the eye of that blade storm, Tisamon stared back at him.

Uctebri saw Laetrimae raise her own mantis claw, composed of steel and chitined flesh. He gripped the Box so tight he felt his nails grind against it.

Tynisa threw herself forward, crying out, but was heard by nobody, not even Tisamon. They were flagging now, those two fighters. The weight of the Wasps was crushing them. Felise had a bloody wound at the side of her head that had closed one eye. Her hands were steeped in gore up to the elbows, her thumbs constantly stabbing and cutting. Tisamon took a sword thrust in the side, and Tynisa saw the shock of it wash over his face without leaving a mark. He was shouting now, but no clear words emerged, just a scream that sounded almost triumphant. The Wasps were steadily burying them.

Tynisa cried out again, feeling the physical shock as one desperate Wasp rammed a spear home into Felise's back. The Dragonfly woman arched backward, but without the reach to find her tormentor. A sting shot seared past her, to punch a soldier on the far side of the fight off the wall and hurl him into the pit. Felise drove her thumbs into a soldier's eyes.

Tynisa kept straining forward, reaching with manacled hands as though she could somehow stop what was happening and wrench it all to a halt. She watched Felise double over a sword suddenly forced under her ribs. The faces of the Wasps were terrible to behold: exhibiting not hate or rage but sheer heroic courage in giving their lives to keep these monsters away from their Emperor.

Felise was by now on her knees and Tisamon fell alongside her, another sweep of his claw killing the closest assailant cleanly and driving the others back momentarily. He had his other arm about the Dragonfly, though his off-hand was a ruin. She was leaning into him limply, and Tynisa knew that she was dead.

A Wasp lunged forward with a spear and Tisamon rose up to meet it, taking the point past his left shoulder and snapping out his claw to pierce the wielder's neck.

He was laughing, she saw. He was weeping.

Alvdan contorted in his seat as Laetrimae drove her claw right through the wooden back of it and continued on, until the smudge of its grey tip had torn out of his chest. Uctebri saw the Emperor's mouth gape in silent horror, so wide that it seemed his jaw would snap. Then he was lost amid a tide of writhing thorns and insect limbs. Uctebri saw the Mantis woman's face dip down to feast, beautiful even when disfigured by scalpel-sharp mandibles.

He took out his knife and held it poised above the box. It was not a special knife, possessing no golden hilt, unadorned by jewels or silver inscriptions on the blade, but he had no need of a magical knife, he knew, for the holder of the Shadow Box was magic in his very being.

Give him to me, he commanded, and the blood began to well—not across the unmarked yet spasming body of Alvdan, but along the length of Uctebri's dagger. At first a drip, then a running red trickle, and then it had become a stream coursing down the blade and spattering the box, saturating Uctebri's robes beneath. For his kinden, the blood was all things.

He brought the impossibly flowing blade up to his mouth, let his tongue taste an Emperor's blood. Then he held it out to Seda. His red eyes transfixed her.

"Taste it," he said.

She stared at him, almost grinning, but shook her head. "No."

"Immortality," he hissed. "You cannot tell me you don't believe in magic."

"Oh, I believe," she told him. "I believe in what you could do to me."

"Taste it, you little fool!" he spat at her, the blood from the knife flowing down his arm, pattering on to the floor. Seda's face twisted with an emotion even all her years of dissembling could not conceal and with a scream she struck the weapon from his hand.

"You fool, you are bound to this! You have *nothing* but this!" hissed Uctebri, but Seda was no longer even looking at him. She was abruptly retreating, staring past him.

He looked around instinctively. He could not, in that moment, help himself.

Out of the tangle of fighting Wasp soldiers a single figure had fought clear. It was drenched head to foot in blood, with one hand gone, a spear's broken shaft jutting from its leg. Even as it burst forth, a soldier drove a sword into the apparition's back and lost his grip on the slick hilt. The bloody, mangled thing was then free to hurl itself up the tiered seats, keening a battle cry.

Your prey is already dead, Uctebri thought, seeing the drained corpse that had been Alvdan the Second, Emperor of all the Wasps. It was still his thought as Tisamon reached him with that fearsome claw drawn back.

For a split second Uctebri fought to assemble his magic to overwhelm the susceptible mind of the Mantis who had been his tool for so long. Tisamon's mind was all pain and fury and ravaged love, so slippery with blood that the Mosquito struggled for purchase on it. For a second he had the man again in his power, but then something lanced through Uctebri's leg, tearing his robe, laying his flesh open with dreadful pain from the calf downward to pin his foot to the ground. He experienced a second's horrified realization that the blade that now shed his precious blood was the dagger that Seda had knocked from his grasp—and that its new wielder was Tynisa.

Her hands gripping about the dagger hilt, Tynisa watched a Wasp soldier, his own face slashed open by Tisamon's claw, slam his blade up to the hilt in Tisamon's back, alongside the sword already lodged there, and Tisamon shuddered, crying out something, a word or a name. It could have been *Felise*.

The claw descended and Uctebri screamed, holding out the only thing he had left to defend himself.

Tisamon drove his blade into the Shadow Box, still howling that formless name, so that its wooden sides, with all their distorted carvings, flew apart like kindling, and for a moment there was a boiling, evaporating *rip* in Uctebri's hands, but shrivelling and dying even as Tynisa watched it.

Uctebri heard the triumphant cry in his head, the voice of his slave Laetrimae, and of all of her kin, of the entire doomed place of the Darakyon, as the anchor that held them to the world was suddenly gone, the snarl in the world's weave unravelling.

Tisamon's claw buried itself deep in the Mosquito's narrow chest, and the Sarcad's own blood washed across the floor, to become lost in the stolen glory of the Emperor's.

THIRTY-ONE

She had seen the *Bleakness* go down.

Even as the corpse of the *Starnest* was settling on Solarno, the Wasp fliers had been attacking. They had been mad, then, almost jostling each other out of the air for a piece of him. Hawkmoth's ugly, armoured vessel had turned back over the city but they had been putting bolts into him already, and Taki could do nothing. She had hung in the air, naked, unshelled, a poor Fly-kinden girl with nothing but a knife, watching the end of the most notorious pirate of the age.

In a flurry of yellow and black orthopters he had gone, the *Bleakness* thundering out over the Exalsee as if Hawkmoth was seeking to return to one of his island hideouts. The shrapnel throwers had shredded the air to either side of him, and at least two of the Wasp machines had been knocked out of the sky, spinning over and over on suddenly ragged wings before tumbling away. But there were a half dozen others still strafing him, passing back and forth and pounding the *Bleakness* with everything they had.

She had watched the *Bleakness* begin its long dive toward the cold waters of the Exalsee, with the Wasps chasing it still.

And now she sat on the ground in the silence that followed, and wept.

It was not truly silence, since so much of the city had burnt, and some was burning still. There were a few knots of Wasps still holding out, in this quarter or that. To her it seemed a silence though, being without the sound of engines and the rush of the wind.

They had won, apparently.

Scobraan was dead, she knew. She had felt it in the way the handling of the *Mayfly Prolonged* had suddenly changed, known that within that metal and wood casing he was dead, his hands slack on the controls. The Creev was dead, and Hawkmoth too, he who had borne the Solarnese no love but had come to help them fight the greater enemy. Te Frenna, who had been more of a dandy than a duellist, was dead. With them had fallen dozens of others: Solarnese pilots, pirates of Chasme and the Exalsee, dragonfly-knights from Princep Exilla, and hundreds of citizens of Solarno who had turned out on to the streets to fight the Wasps.

Nero was dead, too. He would paint no more. Cesta, bloody-handed, a name feared and hated and courted, Cesta also was dead. She could not imagine a world without his loathsome shadow.

She did not weep for them, though she had cause. Her loss cut keener than even her own brother's death had cut. Her *Esca Volenti* was gone, smashed on the streets of Solarno along with Axrad's flier, and probably Axrad himself. There would be other orthopters, she knew, but never one like that, so perfect, so loyal. In the midst of so much death she wept, like a child for a lost mother, over a machine.

A footstep nearby made her look up, red eyed. Niamedh crouched beside her, put a hand on her shoulder. Her *Executrix* had come unscathed through the fire, one of very few. Niamedh understood, though. Behind her stood the Dragonfly lord, Drevane Sae, leaning heavily on a staff with his leg splinted. His painted face was drawn and his expression grim. His mount, carefully nurtured from the egg as they all were, had been shot from beneath him. He also understood her grief.

There would be work to be done, and soon. Those citizens who were not mourning, or rescuing their possessions, or putting out fires, were already looking northward. There was an Empire out there that they had barely guessed at, and the same thought occurred to all of them: *What if it comes back?*

It would definitely come back if it could. Unless Che and her friends could strike enough of a blow, then this triumph would be nothing. The victory that had cast the invader out of Solarno was just a stone bouncing off armour plate to the Empire. It would not leave any dent in history, unless so many stones were thrown at once that even the Empire would have to pause, step back, raise a shield.

Taki found that she did not even care. The way she felt at the moment, Solarno was hardly her home. So much that she genuinely cared for here had been cut from it.

"They've cleared out the last of the Wasps," Niamedh informed her. "They surrendered, I think. They're going to be sent north with some suitably defiant message."

"Suitable?" *How about "Please don't kill us?"* But Taki did not voice it. "So what now?"

"Ceremonies," the other pilot said drily. "You know how we Solarnese are about such things. They'll want to give you something in reward, probably. I thought I'd let you know in case you wanted to dodge it."

"Let them give me a new machine," said Taki hollowly. "Then let them let me go." Right now she wanted none of it. She was sick of it all.

◊ ◊ ◊

The princess stood up. The crowd seated about the arena was in seven stages of panic and confusion. They did not know what was going on. Perhaps she was the only one who did.

Seda looked upon the body of her brother and, for the first time in her life, she felt sorry for him. He sat rigid in his chair, but twisted sideways, his skin bleached and on his face an expression of the most abysmal horror.

She turned to one side, and her eyes met those of General Maxin. The chief of the Rekef was shaking. As he tore his gaze from the drained features of his Emperor, he looked back at her.

He could never know the sheer depth of the plot, but he understood. He saw it was her doing, somehow.

"Take her!" he bellowed, above the shouts and wails and fighting of the crowd. It was the voice of a man whose agents are never far away. "Kill the little bitch! Now!" His own sword was in his hand but he did not dare approach her.

The Rekef agents came instantly from the crowd, though she could not have spotted them before they made their presence clear.

"She's murdered the Emperor!" Maxin yelled. "Put her to the sword!"

One of them said something to him, which she was sure was, "We're sorry, General." They took his sword and held his arms, wrestling him to his knees. Maxin's face was instantly all incandescent incomprehension, and he began bawling and yelling at them as though they had simply made some ridiculous mistake.

There was then a figure coming up beside Seda, and she recognized General Brugan. He looked shaken by what he had witnessed but he had done his work well these last tendays, by replacing or subverting the men that Maxin had put in position. Maxin had been so fixed on his more outspoken adversary, Reiner, that he had never perceived the threat.

She nodded briefly, having no sense of drama when it came to these things.

Brugan drew his dagger and stomped over toward Maxin in a businesslike way.

Maxin was the lord of the Rekef, of course. He had ten times as many agents as Brugan, all across the Empire. He had the power, and had possessed the Emperor's favour. Right here, though, in this limited slice of that vast Empire, the men were Brugan's and Brugan held the knife.

Have I now avenged my siblings? Seda decided that she was too honest with herself to believe that.

"People of the Empire!" Brugan was shouting. "People of the Empire!" but the crowd was still too wild to hear him. He made a curt, angry signal, and there was a sudden explosion. One of his people, standing by one of the entrances, had shot off a nailbow or a piercer, or something with a firepowder charge. The ripples spread through the crowd, until they were quiet enough to hear the general shout.

"Your Emperor is dead!" Brugan bellowed at the top of his lungs. "He was slain by his outlander slave, and through the treachery of his closest advisor! I am General Brugan of the Rekef, and I have now slain the traitor."

There was no applause for him. The murmuring of the crowd was frightened, at the brink of violence. They wanted to see what would happen next.

"I therefore declare the Princess Seda, last of great Alvdan's bloodline, to be the new Empress!" Brugan boomed.

"No!" someone shouted, and then others were calling out, "A woman?" in sheer outrage. Seda stood before them, knowing that if the scales tipped against her they would tear her apart. Within the chorus of defiance she heard other voices, though, shouting her name—insisting that she was the only choice. Gjegevey and her other ministers had done their work well, spreading the poison of her popularity. These here, attending the Emperor's private games, these were the great and the good of the Empire, the rich, the powerful, senior officers and scions of good families. These were the ones who must be won over to her side.

"Listen to me!" Brugan was demanding. "Who else is there? The imperial line must be kept pure!"

They were wavering, however, and she knew that there were many who would not willingly accept her as she was. She had plans for that, if only she could survive these next few minutes. She would take a partner into her bed. She would give them a figurehead of a man to respect, while she consolidated her grip on her brother's empire.

She listened to the riotous arguing of the crowd, while she waited for the balance to tip.

◁ ◁ ◁

The next morning, before the walls of Collegium a Wasp messenger arrived, with Stenwold's name on his lips. He was escorted to the War Master's door, and there he and his Collegiate guards were made to wait some time before Stenwold presented himself. When he did so, the Beetle looked half dead: hollow eyed and grey faced, dishevelled and shaken.

"What has happened?" he demanded, emerging out on the street.

"I bear a message from General Tynan," the Wasp announced, staring at Stenwold with utter disdain. "He suggests that you, and you especially, General Maker, come to the east wall to observe something this morning. He will even delay his assault for that purpose."

Stenwold knew, at that moment. For the last hour he had been sending messengers out across all Collegium in the hope that they would find Arianna, so abruptly vanished. The Wasp emissary did not need to explain any further. Stenwold pushed past him and hurried to the walls.

He ignored the greetings of his officers and charged the steps like a siege engine, knocking down anyone who got in his way. He did not stop until he stood atop the battlements, looking down on the Imperial Second Army.

And seeing what he did, he uttered a hoarse cry of grief and horror.

"War Master, what is it?" asked one of the defenders nearby, a man less familiar with Wasp-kinden customs. "It's just two crossed spears they've put up. What does it mean?"

Stenwold took a deep breath, clenching his hands tight on the stone. This was how the Wasps disposed of their most despised prisoners: the slow death they gave to their traitors, their failed officers, their recaptured slaves. He went to his elbows on the crenulations, clasping his face in his hands.

When he looked up, the Wasp messenger was waiting, with a thin smile on his lips. "Shall I tell General Tynan you shall speak with him?" the man asked.

Stenwold only nodded.

But even winged messengers took time to do their work, and he had a quarter of an hour in which to consider precisely what he should say.

I have only the one thing to offer.

Then the messenger returned, saying that General Tynan would be only too happy to talk.

The walk from the gates of Collegium seemed the longest of Stenwold's life. He had done his absolute best to turn back his escort, but three dozen Beetle-kinden insisted on accompanying him and ignored every plea that they return behind the safety of the walls. The Wasps awaited their approach perfectly peaceably, ready for the morning's assault but holding their hand. General Tynan was clearly anticipating his surrender and was prepared to sacrifice half a day's blood-letting to obtain it.

Stenwold stopped at the crossed pikes. When they eventually brought her out, the spears would be thrust through Arianna's body and she would be left to hang there, dying slowly and in agony. He understood that this Wasp custom went back to days when they were still uneducated tribesmen. The passage of time had made them more sophisticated, but no less cruel.

"Wait here for me," he instructed his escort. It was not the first such order but, so close to the might of the Imperial Army, they finally took him at his word and stayed behind. It would still not save them if the Wasps decided that they should be cut down. Feeling ill and frightened, Stenwold passed the crossed pikes, passed the front ranks of the waiting Wasp army. Drawn up like this, their ranks seemed to go on forever. He saw the heavy infantry, the massed light airborne, the sentinels and artificers. He saw the Auxillians: Mole Crickets, Skaters, Ants, Grasshoppers. He saw the war engines primed to launch shot at his city, or grind forward toward its walls. It seemed that there was not enough expanse of world to contain all the might of the Second Army, and he walked and walked further until one of the general's aides collected him and brought him to Tynan's tent.

There were a dozen soldiers within, or perhaps they were officers, for Stenwold just saw armoured Wasps. General Tynan himself was seated behind a folding table, with a swathe of bandages about his neck and jaw. He looked pale and stern and unsympathetic. Shackled at his side by chains drawing her to her knees was Arianna.

Stenwold could not help himself. He ran for her. He heard the clatter of drawn swords, and a single sting shot crackled over his shoulder as he crouched down beside her. He heard Tynan ordering them all to hold, banging on the table to emphasize his point. He heard all this and did not care, enfolding the trembling prisoner in his arms.

Oh my poor dear Arianna. He thought suddenly of Sperra, tortured by the Sarnesh. The Wasps had spared his Spider-kinden the questioning at least, and perhaps he could spare her the pikes. She was weeping uncontrollably, and he knew she must be cursing him for having put himself into the enemy's hands, but he did not care.

"General Maker," Tynan began in a wounded, raw voice, "your assassin was not successful."

Stenwold glared up at him. "She is not my assassin. She is mine, though."

"So I understand." The general's face creased with pain, and he bared his teeth in annoyance. "She has spoken of you, and of your wretched city there, while my surgeons were bandaging the wound she dealt me. She has even tried to poison me with your doctrine."

Stenwold looked from him to Arianna. *A child of Collegium after all.* "What do you want, General?"

"You know what I want."

"I cannot give you the city. I have no authority to do so, nor will I betray Collegium." Seeing Tynan nod resignedly he hurried on, "But I will take her place on the pikes, where all the city can see. Surely that will mean more to you?"

Arianna cried out, tried to push him away from her, fighting desperately against the chains. He held her in, begging her to be quiet. Through it all, General Tynan stared stonily at him, saving his breath. When at last there was quiet, he merely said, "What's to stop me putting up another pair of pikes?"

Stenwold stared him in the eye. "Nothing, General. Nothing whatsoever. What else do I have that I can give you, though? Not my city. Only me."

Tynan stood up, wincing from his injuries. A Fly messenger had come to the tent's flap, aviator's goggles pushed up his forehead, and was signalling to the general urgently. "If this is your city sallying out, you shall both regret it," the general croaked, and pushed himself over to hear the message.

"Oh, Sten, why did you come?" Arianna demanded quietly.

"And why did you go?" he countered, raising the ghost of a smile.

"I had to do something."

"And I see just how close you got."

"He's going to kill us both."

"That seems likely." He held her tighter as General Tynan reentered the tent. His expression was strange, twisted by more than the pain of his wound. Without even looking at Stenwold he beckoned the other Wasps toward him, giving them hurried orders and watching most of them depart. Only then did he glance back at his prisoners.

Stenwold met his scrutiny, seeing a world of thought move behind it: this was the man who had crushed the Felyal and was well on his way to bringing Collegium to its knees. He was no fool.

"The pikes, sir. It has to be now," urged one of the other Wasps. "We still have the time."

Tynan just stared at Stenwold and Arianna, on and on, while his officers grew impatient.

"Unchain her," he rasped at last, and one of them pushed Stenwold roughly away and released Arianna's bonds. Standing, shaking still, she clung to the Beetle.

"You will return to your city," Tynan said, "and you will instruct your army to stay within its walls. If the least Fly-kinden emerges from Collegium in our sight, we will destroy it."

Stenwold frowned. "I don't . . ." he started but he was drowned out by the protests of Tynan's own officers, demanding immediate death for both the prisoners. Tynan simply glared them into silence, and even struck one across the face when he would not be quiet.

"Outside," he ordered, and led the way into the morning light. Stenwold emerged after him to see the Imperial Second Army stood down and already about the business of striking their tents with hurried efficiency.

"What in the wastes is going on?" Stenwold demanded.

"If I did the decent thing and had you and your Spider whore properly excruciated, what would it profit me, save to make me worse enemies that I have not the time to crush?" Tynan rasped. "Perhaps I could even take the city this day, but I can no longer spare the men to hold it. When we meet again, General Maker, you remember what I could have done." He blinked, staring at the white walls of Collegium, seeing where his army had blackened and scarred them. "Now get your men behind your city gates and take your woman with you."

Looking out from the wall now, it seemed impossible to believe that there had been a Wasp army camped here such a short time ago. Stenwold had to admit that the enemy were neat in their leaving.

It was only days later that they had heard the news from the Empire: the bloody event that had savaged the imperial capital a tenday before Tynan arrived at the gates. The news which had summoned General Tynan, and every other senior Wasp officer, back home.

He leant his elbows on the wall. "I have seen so many sieges and battles," he said, "and I'm not sorry to have this one cut short."

"Nor I," said the Spider-kinden man beside him.

"But you're Lord-Martial," Stenwold pointed out. "Surely war is what you do?"

Teornis chuckled. "Purely a ceremonial title, *War* Master. One I'm happy to be stripped of. I'm merely a man. They'll put me back in my place when I go home."

"No hero's welcome?"

"You don't know my people very well," the Spider pointed out. "I have defeated an army and won a war, and brought my people new allies, and if I'm very, very lucky they'll post me somewhere so far away that nobody can even remember what that place is called. I took risks with my family's wealth and station, Stenwold, and with the very sovereignty of the Spiderlands. Even though the Wasps have withdrawn from Seldis, my family won't easily forget. No, I'll be taking my time in going home to face the music."

❖ ❖ ❖

The Collegium airfield was still quite bare. Between the Vekken siege and the war with the Empire, the air trade had yet to regain its hold on the city. There was a chill wind gusting off the sea, and Stenwold wished that he had thought to bring a cloak. *Getting old*, he thought. Arianna would claim differently, and he would know she was lying and love her for it. She, at least, was one of the people determined to profit from the end of the war. It was a Spider-kinden's natural instinct he supposed. She was somewhere in the city even now, probably trying to talk people into appointing her a member of the Assembly.

The broad-shouldered Sarnesh man was waiting for his response. "Come on, Master Maker, what do you think?" At least he was not still saying *War Master*. The title otherwise showed alarming longevity.

"I don't know if I can imagine it," Stenwold said. "A new city in the Lowlands."

"I don't need to imagine it," said the big Ant. "I've seen it already being laid out. All of Salma's people that survived, and a whole load more from the Foreigners' Quarter in Sarn. They're all out digging the foundations right now. They want a free city. A city without a kinden." Balkus shook his head in wonder. "I've never heard of anything like it, but it's happening. He made the Sarnesh promise, you see, and he made sure everyone else knew it." His hands squeezed the shoulders of the frail little Fly-kinden woman with her head nestling against his stomach.

"Who's running it?" Stenwold asked.

"Oh, you'd certainly approve. They got a kind of a council of people chosen by all the other people, like you got here. Some old boy, Sfayot, he's Speaker there—or at least, they call him the steward or some such. *Her* steward. You know, that colourful girl."

Stenwold nodded. He had never really met Grief in Chains, the woman who had become Salma's lover. "How is she taking it?"

"She doesn't see anyone," Balkus replied sombrely. "Anyone except her advisors, I mean. They love her even more than the Sarnesh loved their queen. They say they're doing it all for her—and for him. He was a good man."

"Yes, yes he was."

"They're calling the new place Princep Salmae."

Stenwold had to take a moment to fight down the lump in his throat. "I'm surprised you didn't stay there. It sounds quite remarkable."

"Oh, I'm going back," Balkus said, with absolute conviction. "I just came to pick up Sperra, then we're both heading back. After the fight with the Wasps, I reckon I can live that close to Sarn again without them wanting my head, or me wanting to go back, but I'll never be properly Sarnesh, and . . ." *And Sperra would never go to Sarn again.* He did not need to say it. "Only I thought, before I went there, I might go with Parops to see them retake Tark from the Wasps. They reckon now, with things being like they are in the Empire, that as soon as the Tarkesh get word that an army's on the way to relieve them, they'll rise up and throw the Wasps out. They know nobody'll be coming to set fire to their city again any time soon." He grinned suddenly. "Some of them are saying Parops'll be king, but that's rubbish. The man's a commander, no more, no less."

The airship that Stenwold had been watching for some time was now slowly descending onto the airfield. It could have been one of two, and he saw that it was the *Buoyant Maiden*, property of the ever-reliable Jons Allanbridge. The man was here on his last errand for Stenwold before he went off, he claimed, to seek his fortune in the Commonweal. Stenwold started forward, even as the airfield crew caught the ship's lines to secure her down.

Jons himself was shinning down from the deck, but the one person Stenwold really wanted to see just stepped straight from the rails, her wings catching her awkwardly and carrying her down to the ground.

He wanted to speak, but he had no words.

Her face said it all in that moment, as he ran toward her. Cheerwell Maker, in the uniform of a Mynan fighter, her sword slung at her side so naturally that he hardly noticed it. Her face was not that of a triumphant warrior but the face of a widow.

She had known, in that instant at Myna, what had happened. Stenwold would later hear how she had forced Allanbridge to take the *Maiden* to Tharn, how a

Moth woman had flown out to them and curtly told her no more than she had already known: Achaeos the seer, pawn of the Darakyon, was dead. She had begged, she had pleaded with them until they had drawn back their bowstrings and threatened to shoot her, and Allanbridge had been forced to manhandle her back aboard the *Maiden*. They had not even let her see his body.

For a moment Che seemed so changed, so stern, that Stenwold ground to a halt, just staring at her. And then she saw him, and she was suddenly his niece again, throwing herself into his arms.

"Uncle Sten!"

You're safe. Hammer and tongs, but you're safe. He just held her close for as long as she would let him.

Taki arrived the next day, coasting in over the sea on a fixed-wing that she had flown on a single-legged journey from Porta Mavralis. At the airfield, nobody knew who she was, and they assumed she had come from Egel or Merro, until they had the chance to examine her flier. After that, the mechanics and artificers had a great many questions to ask her. Eventually, by repeating the name enough, she got them to go find Cheerwell Maker.

"They made me an ambassador," she explained, as Che studied her, shocked by the changes she found in the woman. The lively spark had gone, replaced by a listlessness. "It was the price of the machine. I'm now ambassador to all the Lowlands, because I was the one person that cared a curse about the place."

"What will you do?" Che asked her. She had done her best to make herself Stenwold's right hand, since her return. Her mind was thus kept busy, because it was the only way through the pain.

Taki shrugged. "All I want to do is fly my *Esca* . . ."

She had told Che all about the retaking of Solarno, and Che had felt a hollow pang when she heard that she would never see Nero again. Another name to add to the list of the fallen and the missing. It was clear where Taki's heart had gone, though.

Che had already spoken at length with one of the airfield artificers and with one of Stenwold's colleagues at the College. She pursed her lips. "I have an idea, while you're here."

Taki cocked an eyebrow at her.

"After the war with the Wasps, everyone is thinking about the future, and it's clear to everyone that flying machines are part of that. A big part, too. The Wasps took Tark by air. We defended ourselves by air. There are artificers all over the Lowlands just waking up to the fact."

Taki nodded, showing finally at least a mote of interest.

"Well then, you Solarnese have been fighting in the air in a way we never did. Maybe it's because of your Dragonfly neighbours. Here in the Lowlands we've been dragging our feet, because fighting on the ground was always enough for the Ant-kinden. So you're ahead of us, with your designs. Even that fixed-wing you brought here has people excited, and I know that it isn't . . ."

Taki nodded. "What are you trying to say, Che?"

"What we've got here is a city full of very clever artificers," Che continued. "Any one of them would be more than happy to work with you—to design a new flier for you. That way you'd save them ten years of trial and error. We're not a naturally airborne race, we Beetles. We badly need what you can teach us." An idea struck Che suddenly. "And you know what else we need? Pilots. There are people all over the Lowlands who'd come here just to learn."

The Fly-kinden was looking slightly alarmed by now. "Teaching? I don't think I . . ."

"Who better?" Che insisted. "At least consider it. Uncle Sten could get you a place at the College. They'd create a whole new post for you, I'd bet on it. So at least think about it."

The other woman's look was still cautious, but at least something had surfaced that hinted at the same Taki she had known in Solarno.

"One other thing," Che said slowly. "If you're now ambassador to the Lowlands, I think I already have an official appointment for you."

"Oh?"

"We're expecting a . . . special guest shortly. His airship's on its way, due to be here any day now. If you're here on behalf of Solarno, you should definitely be there to meet him."

The airship manoeuvred ponderously above the Collegium airfield. Looking up at it, Taki had to fight the urge to run for her flier, to take to the air and fight. Some quirk of supply had produced the exact same blimp carrier that she remembered so vividly, even down to the four stripe-painted orthopters that roosted beneath its pontoons. She supposed that an important Wasp envoy would inevitably travel well protected, but still . . .

There were only a few of them waiting there on the field itself, comprising Stenwold's personal retinue. The great and the good of Collegium, and of Sarn and Seldis and the Ancient League, had taken their stand closer to the walls of the city, with guards of honour and flags and musicians. For now it was just Stenwold and those few who had walked his road with him, or done his work: namely Arianna, Che, Balkus and Sperra, Parops of Tark, Taki.

Veterans, Che thought. *Survivors*. There were too many faces that should have still been there. She knew the same thought must be in everyone's mind.

The Wasp airship finally lowered itself to where the ground crew could secure it. The hatch above was already opening as they rushed to wheel the steps over.

From this distance, the man who appeared could be any other Wasp-kinden, with his gold-edged black robes left open over his banded armour.

About half a dozen of them came out, trying to maintain proper military order whilst coming down the steep steps. In the end their leader lost patience and just opened his wings to touch down the faster, so the descent of the others, too heavily armoured to follow suit, became an undignified scramble to catch up with him.

Stenwold stepped forward, aware he had wanted it this way, this moment at least, before the ponderous bulk of the Collegium bureaucracy could heave itself into motion.

"Welcome to Collegium," he said. "Is it . . . Regent, I should call you, or General?"

"Formally it's Regent-General," the Wasp replied, "but you can call me Thalric, since I know that titles coming from your mouth wouldn't mean much anyway." He turned to one of his followers. "Major Aagen, have the men stand down and our passenger sent for." Thalric looked older, Stenwold observed, and he wondered whether it was his visitor's incarceration by his own people or his being the consort of an Empress that did it.

"Aagen will be our imperial ambassador to Collegium, at least as long as we need one," Thalric explained. "I named him so for two reasons. He understands machines, so maybe he'll understand you Beetle-kinden as well, and also he's an honest man. I'm experimenting with good faith. I don't know whether I'll take to it, but we'll see."

"So you think there's room for good faith?"

Thalric shrugged. "Probably not." He looked back up at his airship as Aagen returned with . . .

Stenwold felt his heart skip, just as he heard Che exclaim in surprise and delight. He glanced at Thalric, seeing the same hard-to-read expression the man had worn whilst a prisoner at Collegium.

Stenwold rushed forward just as the woman reached the ground, throwing his arms around her. "We thought you were dead," he said hoarsely. "We'd heard nothing. We thought you were dead, Tynisa! Where have you been?"

She was now shaking in his arms, her face buried in his shoulder, and he realized she was weeping, desperately trying to speak. He held her at arm's length but she would still not meet his eyes, and eventually he made out her words.

"I'm so sorry, Stenwold. I couldn't save him."

She had something in her hands, two metal tokens, and it was a moment before he recognized the sword-and-circle badges. One was her own, the other . . . The other was the badge that Tisamon had not felt himself fit to wear when he left Collegium. The message was clear.

Stenwold felt as though he had been holding his breath for tendays, in anticipation of this moment. Things left unknown but long suspected had fallen into place, ends tied up. *So, he is dead*, and it occurred to Stenwold that, of the little band of fools who had set out to fight the Empire all those years ago, he himself was the only survivor. Marius and Atryssa were long gone, Nero and Tisamon so recently, and only he had lived to see their work even half done.

"Thank you," he said to Thalric. Behind him, Che and Tynisa were embracing, not-quite-sisters reunited.

Thalric shrugged. "It will never be believed of me, but, left to my own devices I'm an honourable man."

"How are things in the Empire—what's left of it at least?" Stenwold turned to guide Thalric toward all the waiting delegates and Assemblers.

"We progress," Thalric told him. "Seda and her advisors have already managed to convince almost half the Empire that an empress can rule just as well as an emperor. The central cities remain loyal. The South Empire has disintegrated entirely, a mass of generals and governors and colonels who each of them want to rule the world. We're taking it back piece by piece. I don't know what you've heard about the West Empire . . ."

"I've heard enough to know it's not the West Empire."

Thalric smiled at that. "We have given a lot of employment to the map makers recently, haven't we? No, Myna and Szar and Maynes have made this Three-City Alliance nonsense."

"And Helleron has redeclared its independence, I hear—whilst retaining close ties to the Empire, of course," Stenwold recalled cynically.

"Whatever pays the most," Thalric agreed. "When we start looking west again, none of that will make any difference."

"You think it will come to that?" Stenwold asked unhappily.

Thalric stopped abruptly. "I will have to become the diplomat in just a moment, and tell pleasant lies to people. Stenwold, you know there will be war again, between the Empire and the Lowlands. We will all put our names to the truce today, the Treaty of Gold, and everyone will rejoice, but every man who signs it will know that they are writing in water, and that the ripples will be gone soon enough. The truce is convenience, until one of us is ready for war again, and we both know it. I'd like to hope that it doesn't come in either of our lifetimes."

Stenwold looked at him and nodded briefly. "I believe you in that. Have I misjudged you?"

Thalric shook his head. "Not that I noticed."

Stenwold moved on, then, to join with the other great men of his people, leaving Thalric and his retinue waiting for their formal introduction. Whoever had decreed that the peace should be signed outside the walls of Collegium had not reckoned for the wind today, and vitally important documents were being hurriedly weighted down with stones.

"Thalric?" Che approached him almost tentatively. He had been many things to her, after all, comrade and captor and fellow prisoner, undoubted enemy, even doubtful friend.

"Cheerwell Maker." He gave an odd smile, as he looked on her, and she suddenly wondered if he were thinking *What if . . .* while contemplating a world without the Wasp Empress or the war.

"I owe you a great deal," she said. "But that's all right, because you owe me as well, from before. I've done the tallying, and I think I'm in debt to you still, overall. At the end, you did a lot. For Myna."

She saw him go to make a flippant comment, to shrug it all off, but something dried up the words in his mouth, and instead he just gazed at her sadly. He had told her once how he had a wife back in the Empire, and now imperial writ had decreed a new one for him, and anyway she had felt throughout that the pairings of the Wasp-kinden were merely intended for progeny and convenience. Yet there was regret in that glance of his, a fond regret from a man too pragmatic to act on it.

She hugged him briefly, feeling his armour cold against her, and then let go. "Thank you," she said, and then they were walking onward—with treaties waiting to be signed, history to be made.

◊ ◊ ◊

The workshop's owner ducked back into the room, under the sloping ceiling. A garret room and, after the machines had been moved in, precious little space to move about.

"This is all I can spare you," he explained to the solemn young man who followed him. "You make good, then maybe you'll get something better. You waste my time, you'll regret it, understand?" His expression was all suspicion and dislike, but it was free of prejudice—because he was a half-breed, just like Totho was.

Chasme was a city of half-breeds. Since arriving the day before, Totho had never seen so many. One out of any two of this ramshackle place's occupants was of mixed blood: Ant and Bee, Spider and Dragonfly, Solarnese Soldier Beetle and Fly-kinden, or a bastard mingling of any combination. A man like Totho attracted no stares.

Oh, he had noticed that many of them were slaves, and many others menials or factory workers. It was not a universal rule, though. Chasme was fluid, not fixed like in the Empire or the Lowlands.

The garret workshop was better than he had hoped. Chasme was a little jewel of civilization on a barbarous shore, powered by the need of Princep Exilla to match the aerial and naval might of Solarno. It was therefore a fortuitous, sheltered little backwater for an artificer to work in.

"I'd better see something from you before the end of the month," the owner warned him. "Or you're on the street."

"I'll show you now," Totho said. "As a down payment. Just bring me a target mannequin or whatever else you use here."

The man studied him, narrow eyed. He himself was of such a mixed ancestry that there was no deciphering it. A flick of his wrist sent one of his slaves off, to return an awkward minute later with a stuffed leather torso on a stand, a mess of patches and rips.

Totho gave a nod for the slave to position it, and he unslung his latest prototype, pumping up the pressure as he did so with ratcheting winches of the handle. It was his showpiece: too delicate for war work but it made a pretty display.

"I give you the future," he announced, and emptied the snapbow at the dummy, shearing off everything above the navel, even the post that supported it.

The workshop owner said nothing for a long time, to his credit. Totho could almost see money being counted in the man's eyes. Small concerns, petty profits, but they would outgrow this place soon enough. There would shortly be a revolution here in Chasme. Progress, which had stumbled at the end of the Wasps' war, would begin its march once more.

"I'll leave you to your work," said the owner, almost reverently, before turning to go. He stepped aside quickly as Totho's companion came in, hooded and robed.

"This will do, for a start," Totho said. "And they've manpower and materials enough for us here in Chasme. I thought we'd complete the arm first, and then . . ."

Drephos tugged his hood down, one-handed. "And then the future," he suggested. "And then the world."

◁▷ ◁▷ ◁▷

It became aware of itself between the trees, awakening to agonized existence shot through with thorns and briars.

Where—?

Around it, the forest was twisted and dark, each tree knotted and diseased and forever dying, never quite dead. It knew this place, immediately, instinctively. There was no mistaking it.

The Darakyon.

Yet this was not the true Darakyon, that brooding forest east of Helleron that, for centuries, had turned back or consumed any travellers foolish enough to breach its borders. The true Darakyon lay untenanted now, its ghosts faded from between its tortured boles, the sun breaking in through its matted canopy. The five-hundred-year-old work of the magicians who had blighted it with their hubris had been undone.

So there was only one place that this could be, it knew. It had been touching the Darakyon. It had been part of a great ritual. It was inside the Shadow Box.

Awareness was coming back, and bringing the echo of memories. It—no, *he*—looked about himself. There was a mist at the edge of the trees now, and it was growing closer. Where it touched, the briars shrank back, the trees themselves faded and were gone.

The Shadow Box had been destroyed. The snarl that it made in the fabric of the world was being unpicked. The world was being dismantled around him, and soon it, and he, would be gone.

For a long moment, watching the greyness creep closer, he could not think why this should be a bad thing. He had not gained such joy out of life, most especially out of the ending of it, that he should wish to protest his extinction. Tree by tree, the heart of the Darakyon was undone, and he, the last inheritor of its power, watched dispassionately.

He had lived a strange and violent life, at odds with his own people, with ambitions utterly alien to the rest of his kind. Would it be so wrong to simply let go now?

Then he remembered some more, shards of his life falling upon him like blades, and he knew he could not go.

No.

No, not like this. He would not give up the world for this grey death-in-death. *I have work to do.*

He stood, unfolding himself, drawing the stuff of his body from the thorns and the knotted wood and the evaporating darkness.

I have not finished.

It was clear in his mind now. He had something left undone, and there was nobody else who would do it. He bared his teeth at the encroaching nothingness.

There must be a way out. The disintegrating world around him told him that there was no such way, but in life he had never much listened to the rules of others. He dashed from tree to tree, faster and faster, a narrowing spiral as the end came for him. *I will not give up. I will not surrender. I haven't finished. It isn't over.*

And then, at the very last, with the world no more than an arm's length on either side, he found it.

The ritual, the Darakyon, all those ancient magics torn open and unleashed upon the cold world of the Apt, they were not gone. They lived on in him, for all that he was dead, and . . .

There was another. He felt the distant call of kindred power to power. Out in the world of the living there was another, if he could only find the way.

He stretched out for that faintest of threads, the ebbing reverberation of the Darakyon's power in the world.

After that was silence: the Shadow Box destroyed, the Darakyon empty, all its tormented prisoners released.

But he was gone before the mist came, pulling himself hand over hand into the world of the living.

I haven't finished.

He had work to do.

ADRIAN TCHAIKOVSKY was born in Woodhall Spa, Lincolnshire, before heading off to Reading to study psychology and zoology. For reasons unclear even to himself, he subsequently ended up practicing law and has worked as a legal executive in both Reading and Leeds, where he now lives. Married, he is a keen live role-player and occasional amateur actor, has trained in stage fighting, and keeps no exotic or dangerous pets of any kind, possibly excepting his son.